THE SEEKING SERIES

JOSIE RIVIERA

This book is dedicated to all my wonderful readers who have supported me every inch of the way.
THANK YOU!

INTRODUCTION

Dear Friends,

A heartwarming story is the hallmark of a romantic read. Savor the magic of the Romany Gypsies with this collection of Regency Christian romances.

Find out why readers are falling in love with The Seeking Series & staying up all night reading! Cozy up with your favorite beverage, and lose yourself in the joyful seasons of romance.

Seeking Fortune

A Golden Pen Winner, Seeking Fortune received over 6000 nominations on Kindle scout.

There are lies more believable than truth.

Losing his wife and daughter to influenza shook James Colchester's faith in God. As another epidemic threatens, he's torn between what's best for his fragile son: fleeing to his Welsh homeland, or staying put. In a moment of weakness, the black-haired, green-eyed Gypsy's delicate touch on his palm quells his fear...and her beauty ignites a warmth he hasn't felt in years.

Desperate to return to her people, Valentina goes against every lesson her mother taught her to soothe the Englishman into a false sense of security. But as James's quiet faith sparks a hunger to know it for herself, she realizes she's made an unforgivable mistake. One that could rob James of his most precious gift—and destroy their chance for lifelong love.

Seeking Charity

Does he love the girl she was...or the woman she has become?

When Charity ran away with the Romany Gypsies, she left everything behind. Her name. A way of life constrained by English rules. The punishments her cruel father meted out in the name of God. And the young man who made it all bearable.

Certain things she can't hide, even in wild, remote Wales. A secret longing for the ease of English life. The wisps of faith that still linger. And her reaction to a handsome face she thought she'd never see again.

Daniel Hayward would recognize that voice anywhere. That unruly, copper-colored hair. Those piercing blue eyes. But what is Charity Weston doing wearing Gypsy garb in Wales...when she died years ago?

For a moment, the grief that never quite left him is transformed into joy. But the walls between them now are built from bricks of culture clashes, bitter memories, and fear. To find his way, Daniel will have to trust as never before that God will guide their hearts home at last.

Seeking Patience

Do people prove their worth by strength, or by character?

Half-Romany, half-English lord, he lives a perilous Gypsy life ... until a sweet English rose saves his life, and perhaps his soul. Widowed by a cruel husband, she's given up all hope of love. Brought together in peril, they dare to reach for a brighter future together.

Luca Boldor, Romany leader, lives a nomad's life in Regency England with his Gypsy caravan. Believing his noble father abandoned him at birth, he refuses to acknowledge his English blood, or live a settled life. But when a vicious attack by a rival leaves him bleeding on an English lady's doorstep, he has no choice but to accept her help. Her gentle faith stirs his heart in a way he has long denied.

Lady Patience Blakwell, widowed countess, lives

in near poverty. Her husband's heir uses threats to keep her from demanding her rightful inheritance. With a few faithful servants, she exists quietly in the country, only her faith keeping her strong ... until the day a bold, handsome Gypsy collapses in her hall. He's unlike any man she's ever known, and she'll confront any subterfuge to keep him safe.

But when a secret from Lady Patience's past emerges, Luca must face his own past, or lose her and all hope of love. Will this strong man humble himself to open his heart for his lady?

There are lies more believable than the truth.

Seeking Fortune

USA TODAY
BESTSELLING AUTHOR

JOSIE
RIVIERA

This book is dedicated to all my wonderful readers who have supported me every inch of the way.
THANK YOU!

PRAISE AND AWARDS

USA TODAY bestselling author

#1 First Place Golden Pen Award

CHAPTER ONE

Si khohaimo may patshivalo sar o tshatshim.
There are lies more believable than the truth.
Old Romany saying

ngland 1811

"*B*ury me standing, for I have been on my knees all my life."

Valentina Rupa bowed her head to hear her beloved mother's last words, to see the twitch of her eyes beneath her eyelids, the rise and fall of her chest beneath the thin blankets.

Her mother's breath faded, already settling into the bleak night, already gone.

Unearthly quiet filled their makeshift canopy. The dwindling light from the nearby campfires of their Romany tribe seeped through the canvas.

"*Daj.* Mother ... don't stop speaking." Tears blinded Valentina's eyes, defeated her voice. She focused on her mother's lips, willing her to speak once more. What good did it do to be a *drabardi*, a powerful fortune-teller and healer, if she couldn't save her own mother?

Valentina's younger sister, Yolanda, stood beside her. Yolanda coughed violently, then wheezed.

"Please, Daj, it's not your time." Yolanda's hoarse voice faded to a whisper. "Her lips, she's breathing ..."

"Nay, it's the north wind." Valentina peered at the oak tree branches bending against a biting gust, threatening to collapse their crude canopy. Wagon wheels creaked, groaning into the dirt, familiar sounds, yet so distant. Their mother had lived her entire life in the caravan, traveling from village to village. There was no other way for her. Only the way of the Romany.

The air hung thick and heavy, weighty against Valentina's damp cheeks. She didn't care, didn't bother to wipe them. She hated the weakness of crying. Crying meant loss and loneliness and defeat.

She glanced at Yolanda, noting her ashen face,

the stoop of her slight shoulders. "Try to rest for a while."

"I'm not tired." Yolanda rubbed her temples. "Now that both Mother and Father are dead, we're orphans."

"I'll not abandon you." Valentina choked back her fears and crushing uncertainties. She was the older sister. She always took care of Yolanda.

With shaking fingers, she tucked the threadbare blankets around their mother's feeble body, smoothed the wrinkled fabric, and folded the ends back. Neatly, the way her mother liked it done. Tucked, smoothed, folded. Tucked, smoothed, folded.

"Daj, you starved yourself so we could eat. We'd have found the food we needed somehow." Her hands glided purposefully. "Why do the English treat the Rom as if we're animals?"

"Because this is the land of the English," Yolanda said. "They make their own rules."

Long shivers rippled through Valentina's body, a cadence of trepidation and doubt. In a single, deliberate breath, she blew them out.

The friends who'd discreetly stayed out of the way melted in now, coming from their wagons to gather around the deathbed. The sad cries of the caravan penetrated the dusk. Purple-lipped, the elderly, ragged men and women huddled together, stamping their feet to keep away the chill.

With the sleeve of her frayed cotton gown, Valentina wiped her eyes. Her hands were still wet from retrieving water from the river. She'd used the water to bathe her mother, an ironic Romany custom relying on her mother's willingness to go to her death.

Yolanda helped Valentina gather their mother's personal belongings and carried them to the camp-fire. The flames rose against the night sky and consumed the remnants of their mother's life—a well-worn apron, a silky fringed sash. Their people burned most possessions of the dead, believing the possessions were unclean and defiled the living.

Valentina skimmed her index finger across her mother's double-edged dagger and accidentally drew blood. Grimacing, she licked her finger. She didn't have the heart to destroy the weapon, so she thrust the dagger into its sheath and tied it on a cord along her gown's seam.

Then she slid her palm across the last treasure, her mother's yellow scarf, her *diklo*. Bringing it to her face, Valentina closed her eyes and inhaled. The scent of oak and jasmine, exotic and mysterious, flooded through her. She remembered her mother jauntily tying the diklo around her greying hair each morning.

Valentina knew she was supposed to take one small token before burial, instead she took two. She'd never been one to obey rules. She folded the yellow scarf into a perfect triangle and tied it loosely around her throat. It didn't match her faded scarlet gown, and that didn't matter.

Nothing mattered now except her sister.

Yolanda's pretty, round face contorted in grief as she placed small multicolored stones around their mother's body. Valentina inserted pearls in her mother's nose, a Romany custom to keep out all wickedness. Her hands wavered, and she avoided touching the body for fear of contamination.

Inhaling the fragrance of a drop of frankincense, she smoothed the spicy golden oil along her arms to protect herself against evil spirits. A shadow of skepticism crossed her soul, and her hands stopped. Maybe spirits didn't exist at all. They certainly demanded endless rituals, and in return granted ... nothing. Glancing around at the eerie silhouettes dancing in the firelight, she dabbed a few more drops of oil on her wrists, just in case.

The men of their tribe had moved to sit in the grassy clearing on the forest's edge, the scent of sweet blackberry brandy filling the brisk October air. They'd stolen it from an unsuspecting Englishman in town. Several grizzled dogs lay listless at their feet.

Luca, the caravan's young leader, was the only man who stood. His baggy green pants were fitted at the ankle and billowed in the wind. He mourned Valentina and Yolanda's mother in a plaintive cadence and guided the elders in solemn chants. Although all the other young men had gone off in search of food and never returned, Luca hadn't deserted the tribe.

"I'll get more hot water, Yolanda, before we prepare for Daj's burial." Valentina retrieved her wool cloak and then hoisted a pot of water off of a smoky campfire. With her free hand, she brushed a strand of hair behind her ear, longing for a warm bath. However, custom prevented her from washing until after her mother's burial.

She made her way past the lamenters to the small tent the women shared. An afternoon rain had washed soggy leaves over the ground. One of the dogs lifted its head and sniffed, the thick fur around its neck bristling. A sudden crackle—somewhere a tree branch snapped.

Her senses sharpened. The last few nights she'd dozed while nursing her mother and had dreamed about a man. A rich man. A powerful man.

Scanning the dense woods, she sensed someone was watching. She had the gift of second sight, her mother had said, but Valentina shook the thought away. Besides, her tribe was far too secluded to be found.

∼

*Y*olanda labored through the night with a deep, raspy cough, while Valentina brewed a mixture of vegetable matter and barley water and fed it to her sister. Still, the cough persisted.

By morning, Yolanda's breathing came rapidly; her skin was pale. Curing Yolanda's chronic cough had been beyond their mother's skill, and Valentina's, also. With each day, Yolanda's condition had steadily worsened. Perhaps she had an infection.

Luca entered the tent. His brows furrowed as he studied Yolanda's sweaty face. "There's a gentleman who owns an estate in Ipswich, and a physician might live nearby," he said.

Valentina caught Luca's worried look and stood, deliberating.

"Perhaps the physician can prescribe a tonic medicine." She squeezed Yolanda's chilly hands reassuringly. "If we leave now, we'll be back at the camp before nightfall. Daj's burial isn't until tomorrow. Are you well enough for the walk to Ipswich, Yolanda?"

"Aye, of course." If Yolanda wanted to portray strength, the effect was spoiled by the look of hesitation in her deep-brown eyes. And then by a violent cough.

The midday sun loomed by the time Luca led Valentina and Yolanda to the outskirts of a grand country estate with a vast two-story home made of stone and the surrounding land dotted with tenant farmer cottages. Through the tall boxwood hedges that screened them from view, Valentina spotted a thin boy skipping stones on the banks of a slow-flowing stream.

The refreshing autumn breeze had renewed her spirits. Although still saddened by her mother's death, she was certain her sister would soon receive the care she needed to recover.

Luca stepped over a fallen stump and remarked how the color was returning to Yolanda's pale cheeks. "The walk has done us all good."

Valentina smiled, appreciating his attempt to encourage them.

"After your mother's burial," he continued, "we'll head south toward the coast."

"Before the winter, hopefully," Valentina answered, guiding Yolanda past a low wooden fence. From the corner of her eye, she thought she glimpsed movement at the edge of the field they were skirting. For a moment, she froze.

"Luca—" Her voice rose in alarm as she saw two men running toward them.

"What are you Gypsies doing here?" one of the men shouted. His hair was silver-white, and as he neared, she could see numerous lines creased his forehead.

Valentina's hands flew to her chest. "We're—"

Yolanda's lips quivered as she pressed her elbows to her sides. "Please. We're not doing anything wrong." She coughed so hard her face flushed crimson.

"Are you trying to steal from us? You'll answer to Mr. Colchester." The silver-haired man fixed his gaze on the other man. "Aye, Roland?"

Roland, a rough-looking man with huge shoulders, nodded. "Aye, Geoffrey. Gypsies aren't wanted here."

Prickles made their way up the back of Valentina's neck.

There was no time to explain. She whirled and grabbed her sister's hand. Frantically, she scanned the field. *Where was Luca?*

Trembling, shaking, gasping, she tugged Yolanda back toward the forest. The undergrowth whipped at her ankles. Her lungs burned.

"We should've stayed at the camp. I don't need a physician." Yolanda's cough was incessant as she tried to keep up. "If they catch us ..." She slipped and fell, bracing herself on both arms as she hit the ground. Her head went down, and she cried out in pain.

"Valentina!" Yolanda glanced at her arm, twisted at an odd angle, and blanched. "It hurts. The pain is throbbing. I can't run!"

Absorbed in her sister, Valentina allowed herself one gasping breath and risked a look over her shoulder. The two men—Geoffrey and Roland— were dashing straight toward them.

Valentina slid her arm around Yolanda's shoulders, assisting her sister first to a kneeling position, then gently to her feet.

Yolanda pursed her lips, her eyes darkened with pain. "My arm feels hot."

As she murmured assurances to Yolanda, the trees rustled and Valentina peered upward. Luca had launched himself into the heavy branches of a tall, mossy pine. The limbs cracked under his weight as he braced his bare feet on branches on either side of the trunk, balancing with ease. Raw-boned and dark, he coiled and yanked a carving knife from his boot as the two men reached the women.

Valentina tried not to glance at him, fearful the men would see Luca and ruin his ambush. Before the men could speak, Luca vaulted to the ground and locked his muscled arm around Roland's throat.

"Romany men don't share, and no one takes our drabardi anywhere." His blade glinted in a shaft of sunlight.

Roland struck a heavy jab to Luca's chest and threw Luca onto the ground. His head bounced hard, his eyes closed. Then Roland turned to Yolanda, now sobbing from pain.

"I'll take the hurt lass to the house," Roland said to the other man. Without waiting for a word from either woman, he scooped Yolanda up and lumbered toward the estate.

Valentina took judicious note of Luca. He was breathing steadily, and his eyelids flickered.

Geoffrey extended his hand. "Come with us. Your sister is hurt and needs help."

She ignored his hand. "Is there a physician on the estate?"

"Nay, although he lives close by. He can tend to her arm come the morrow. I fear it might be fractured."

Come the morrow. Valentina scraped a hand through her heavy, tangled hair. They had planned to return to camp by nightfall.

Briefly, she squeezed her eyes shut. Her mother's body required a proper burial ritual. However, her sister's injury required a physician to attend to her.

Valentina glanced over her shoulder at Luca. His quick, reassuring nod settled her conflicting considerations. In a wordless exchange, he assured her he'd attend to her mother's burial.

Pushing up the sleeves of her scarlet gown, she straightened her shoulders, and her five-foot stature seemed to lengthen. She matched Geoffrey's swift strides, concentrating on Yolanda and the grand house that awaited them.

Daj would want her to focus on Yolanda's care, she assured herself. Come the morrow, they'd return to their caravan.

CHAPTER TWO

Devlesa araklam tum.
It is with God that we found you.
Old Romany saying

James Colchester rubbed his eyes, struggling with the fatigue of numerous sleepless nights. As a commissioned officer, he'd fought another senseless battle in King George's name. Time he would've preferred to spend near his son. Once the battle in Spain had ended for the time being, he'd quickly returned home.

His son's excited squeals of laughter as he'd run into James' arms had been his reward for his efforts. Warmth moved his heart, lifted his spirit. Now, with the boy finally asleep on his lap, he forced his shoulders to relax, and he lifted a prayer.

"Thank you, Lord, for watching over my son and keeping him safe."

James shifted in the straight-backed chair. It pressed unyieldingly against his sore muscles and was barely able to contain his long form and his little son's too. Despite his prosperity, he favored simplicity. His bedchamber contained little more than an unadorned fireplace, a clean bed, a wooden table beneath a woven tablecloth. He shook back an errant strand of hair, grown long from neglect. He'd haphazardly tied it back with a leather thong.

Geoffrey, James' steward, stepped into the room.

"Trouble, I hear?" James reached for his goblet of port wine set on the carved rosewood side table beside him. "A Gypsy woman on the estate?"

"Two Gypsy women, sir. They're sisters. And one Gypsy man, who would've been more than happy to slit Roland's throat. Roland and I saw them near the estate this afternoon, a few hours before you returned. Roland was feeding the wild animals near his cottage while I was attending to one of the tenants. Anyway, when we confronted the Gypsies because we assumed they were stealing, they tried to run off. The younger sister injured her arm."

"And the Gypsy man?"

"He was no threat." Geoffrey shook his head,

adding a dismissive hand gesture. "Aside from the one woman's injury, the both of them looked like they hadn't had a decent meal in weeks. That's why I brought them here."

"Tell Wiborow to have guest bedchambers prepared for them both, as well as a warm meal. I'll call for the physician come the morrow."

"I assumed you would and have already made provisions for the women when we arrived a few hours ago. The injured sister is resting. The other sister is waiting in the parlor. I wasn't certain if you wanted to speak with her before you retired." Geoffrey squinted at the sleeping child in James' lap. "Forgive me for not asking about your son sooner. How is he?" He sighed. "Poor boy."

"My son was born deaf. Rest assured, he isn't poor."

"Aye. I only meant—" Apparently thinking better about continuing, Geoffrey took a long breath and threaded a wrinkled hand through his sparse hair. He perused the sideboard before selecting a ripe pear. "May I sit?"

"Of course."

Geoffrey's heavy profile cast a stooped shadow along the candle-lit room. He angled his chair near the fireplace, grabbed a glass of ale from the sideboard and took a lengthy swill. He'd been James' loyal steward since James had inherited his parents' estate six years earlier.

"I overheard several servants speculating in the hallway," James said, "and they mentioned one of the Gypsy women is a fortune-teller."

Geoffrey leaned forward in his chair. "Aye. Some of the servants have gone to their camp to have their fortunes told by the older sister, I believe."

"Perhaps she is the woman who once read my late wife's fortune. 'Twould be a coincidence, aye?" James stroked the stubble on his chin, and adjusting his sleeping son on his lap, stretched his legs toward the warm fire. He was still chilled from the battle. Anxiety threaded his words, despite his attempt to disguise it.

Geoffrey stared at his tankard and didn't meet James' gaze. "After your wife's death, the entire manor fears another outbreak of influenza."

"May I remind you, Geoffrey, that living here in the country, we're much removed from this latest epidemic."

"I trust you'll make the right decision, Mr. Colchester, and settle our departure. Wales is your birthplace and you must be anxious to return." Geoffrey finished his ale. "My advice is to remove Jeremy from the memories of his sister and mother."

"Please don't mention my beautiful daughter and my late wife in the same breath." Absently, James stroked Jeremy's pale cheek with his thumb. "'Tis not easy to travel with a son who hasn't been healthy. He might not be able to withstand such an arduous journey."

"Still, we should depart before winter."

James took a long breath. "Where did you say you found the Gypsies?" The chair prodded and poked into his back, refusing to bend. He shifted. Changing position didn't help. Nothing helped.

"At the edge of the property near the boxwood hedges. Roland spotted them, and I overheard the man say something about breaking camp and heading south toward the coast."

The coast. The sea. Beatrix. James closed his eyes against the sharp ache that clenched his stomach whenever he thought of his cherished daughter. He could still hear her sweet babbling voice echoing through the hallways.

He sank back in his chair, attempting to find the balance missing in his life, anything to ease the gnawing, ceaseless despair. What parents could ever recover from the death of their beloved child?

He should've heeded the fortune-teller's warning those few short years ago instead of disregarding it. He should've heeded it. He leaned against the stiff wooden back of his chair and briefly closed his eyes. If he had heeded the fortune-teller's words, Beatrix might still be alive.

Nay. The Bible warned about fortune-tellers.

He swallowed, tasting an agonizing thought. Really? Why? And where was God, then, because God hadn't listened to James' prayers in a long, long time.

He stood, lifting Jeremy. The boy wrapped his small arms around James' neck. His chest swelled at the love he felt for his son, constant and fierce.

"I may request a reading from this fortune-teller," he said quietly.

Geoffrey lowered his thick white brows and shook his head in an emphatic 'nay'. "Mr. Colchester, we are Christians. 'Do not turn to mediums or necromancers; do not seek them out, and so make yourselves unclean by them: I am the Lord your God.'"

James nodded. "Leviticus 19:31. I'm well aware of that specific Bible verse, Geoffrey." Cradling his son, James strode into the oil-lit hallway. He found Jeremy's nurse in the kitchen. "Elspeth, 'tis hours past Jeremy's bedtime." He placed the child into her outstretched arms.

Jeremy opened his greyish-blue eyes and stared up at his father. Tears pooled in the dark circles beneath his eyes. As James gazed at the innocent boy's innocent expression, a stab of pain pierced his insides. Jeremy's sweet face mirrored his twin sister, Beatrix. The same bubbly smile that touched people's hearts, the same joyfulness, the same hair color, as blonde as their late mother's.

"You'll be safe, son, I promise," James murmured.

"He's fine, Mr. Colchester." Elspeth's polite smile

didn't go any farther than her mouth. The servants had been on edge for months, ever since James' wife had died.

Elspeth rocked Jeremy's slight body back and forth. "When your son realized you were gone, he dreamt those terrible nightmares again."

James smoothed the fine hair from his son's forehead. A deep gentleness surged, mingling with desperation. "Let's pray Jeremy's dreams will soon return to happier times." With a brief nod, James quickly left, striding across the pale blue carpet, heading for the parlor and the fortune-teller.

~

*V*alentina kept her gaze on the eight-foot longcase clock positioned on a side wall in the parlor. The hour was nearing nine.

Despite the fire burning in the parlor's fireplace, she rubbed her arms, chasing away the chill, her rings sparkling in the candlelight. She yanked her multilayered gown around her feet as she sat stiffly on a settee with scrolled ends and lion-carved legs. Her once vibrant clothes were now muted, matching her unwashed body and soiled appearance.

The door opened and she straightened, studying the tall, good-looking man who'd stepped into the room. His features were chiseled, his build muscular, and he strode across the carpeted floor with quiet authority. Beneath dark arched brows, his piercing grey eyes observed her with frank interest.

Her chin went up as she returned his gaze. "Bury me standing. *Prohasar man opre pirend.*" She repeated her mother's words in her native Romany tongue.

"I don't understand." He stopped abruptly and folded strong arms over his high-collared waistcoat. His face was hidden in the shadows, although the aristocratic lines were apparent. He was lean with broad shoulders, and she had to admit he was very handsome. And he was observing her with unconcealed interest.

"I speak the language of the Romany. My language." She wiped her palms along her gown, taken aback at the sweat on them despite the chill in the air.

"I'm James. James Colchester."

She blinked, startled that he'd used his given name.

Her dream came back in a rush. A rich man. A powerful man. He'd whispered to her when her sleep deepened and disappeared before she could reach him.

He stepped forward, his compelling gaze fixed on her face. "And you are?"

"Valentina Rupa." She stood, grimacing at the shooting cramp in her legs. She'd barely moved the previous day, kneeling at her mother's deathbed, and that had been followed by today's long walk and then by sitting for hours in this cold room. She trusted they wouldn't buckle and betray her weakness.

He must have seen her wobble, for he reached out and grasped her elbow. "I have been told that my men mistakenly assumed you were all trying to steal something—although I'm not certain what. In the confusion, you and your sister fled, resulting in your sister's arm being injured. Correct?"

She shook off his hand and didn't answer.

Annoyance flickered across his face. "Correct?"

"Aye. We came here seeking a physician for my sister's cough, and now she has two reasons to see one."

"I'm sorry she was hurt. We'll know more come the morrow after the physician examines her."

Valentina gave a cool nod framed in steel. "Where *is* Yolanda?"

"She is resting comfortably in one of the upstairs bedchambers."

"She is safe?"

"Safe? Aye, of course." His smoky gaze surveyed her. "And I believe you're the fortune-teller from the fair in Ipswich some years back."

"How would you remember me?"

"I remember your eyes. They glow like polished emeralds."

"I don't remember you." She surveyed his wealth

of black hair, his self-commanding presence. "All gadje look alike to me."

Moonlight winked through the panes of the leaded windows giving an eerie golden glow to the room. "I want to see my sister."

"Let her rest."

Would he hurt Yolanda? Nay. His eyes were warm, his manner gentle. Still, she didn't know anything about him, except that he was a gadje.

Her gaze darted to the doorway. Perhaps she should find Yolanda and leave.

As soon as the thought formed, she headed for the door. James caught her from behind, one arm wrapping around her waist. The warm fabric of his muslin shirt slid against her bare arms. "Please. You have nothing to fear."

"You certainly are right." Shrugging off his hold, she swiveled to face him. "Because we've committed no crime."

His lips twitched, so subtle she might've imagined it.

She went on. "'Tis necessary that Yolanda and I finish the burial rituals for our mother." A tear slipped down her cheek and she attempted to discreetly wipe it away. "I must be assured we leave at first light."

"I'm sorry about your mother's death. 'Tis up to the physician, not me." James hesitated, then added. "Besides speaking to you, there was another reason I wanted to see you tonight before you were shown to your own bedchamber."

"Because your needs are more important than ours?

He frowned. "Of course not."

Men like him were only interested in themselves. Perhaps he had no intention of calling a physician. Perhaps ...The word *bedchamber* rang in her ears, and panicking, she ripped her mother's double-edged dagger from its sheath and raised the weapon.

With the swiftness of a trained soldier, he grabbed her wrist. "Give the dagger to me, Valentina."

CHAPTER THREE

Te na khutshos perdal tsho ushali.
Try not to jump over your own shadow.
Old Romany saying

*V*alentina's hands wouldn't stop shaking. She'd never used a dagger before. Sweat broke out on her skin, dampening her gown.

James grabbed her other wrist and pulled her toward him. His hard thighs brushed against hers. "Valentina, drop the blade."

She breathed quick, thin gasps of air and met his furious stare. With a low groan, she released the dagger. It clattered to the floor and spun out of reach.

"I haven't hurt you or your sister, nor do I intend to, so there's nothing to fear. I'm a man of my word." He picked up the dagger and set it atop the wooden mantel. Then he lit a candle in an iron spiked candle holder and placed it beside the dagger.

"Please come here." He gestured toward a narrow ornate table in the corner of the room.

With a hard swallow, she eyed the dagger just out of reach. Then, with a lift of her head, she purposely walked ahead of him. She insulted him by doing so, although he wasn't aware of it. In the Romany culture, a woman never walked in front of a man.

He pulled out a heavy mahogany chair beside the table and beckoned her to sit. "I'd like you to read my fortune."

Her hands dropped to her sides. For a moment, she was at a loss for words. "You gadje think the Rom ways are mere superstitions."

"Aye, and my Christian beliefs also forbid fortune-telling."

"So why ask me?"

"At the fair, you demonstrated an astonishing ability to foresee the future." He avoided her gaze, his deep voice a monotone. Dragging up a second chair, he sat across from her.

"So that's why I've been waiting in your parlor for hours?"

"I apologize. I've recently returned home from a

meaningless, violent war." He shook his head, then reached out his hands to her.

Valentina had gotten used to the gadjes' unfamiliar smells and filthy palms. She breathed the nearness of this man—a manly scent of earth and leather. His palms were clean.

"And if I refuse to read your fortune?" She focused on the cut-glass chandelier hanging from the ceiling to distance herself from his stare.

His fingers stroked hers. "I'm hoping you won't."

Valentina jerked her hands away. Smoothing her heavy dark hair, she was surprised she was suddenly self-conscious of her soiled appearance.

Her thoughts scrambled to understand his request. Perhaps she'd misunderstood him.

Perhaps she hadn't.

She shivered.

He stood and slipped off his waistcoat, an intricate black design woven into rich wool. So beautiful, the garment could fetch enough money in the marketplace to feed her tribe for months.

He draped the soft fabric around her shoulders. "You must be cold."

She glided the waistcoat between her fingers and opened her mouth to protest.

His mouth quirked and he shook his head, effectively silencing her. He rolled up the stark white sleeves of his shirt, revealing the solid strength of his arms. His gaze was steadfast and single-minded.

In frustration, she sighed. "Let me see your hands."

He set both his hands on the table and she bent her head to examine them.

"Does it matter which hand you read first?" he asked.

His nearness created a disconcerting tingle in her chest. The heat emanated from his body and melted on her skin.

"Give me the hand you write with."

Even if she were in the proper frame of mind to read his palm, 'twould be done under her terms and conditions. She preferred to do readings in her own setting—among her kinsmen or at a makeshift table set alongside a dirt road. Either way, she ought to be in control, not him. He gave her no choice about the setting for his reading, but there were other ways she could maintain control.

He turned his right palm up. Out of sheer habit, she lifted his hand and traced his lifeline, the most important crease on the palm. As she guided her thumb against the firm line, an unexpected flow of heat passed between them.

She dropped his hand. His fingers fell against her leg and scorched through the fabric of her skirt. She grabbed the table to steady her nerves.

His dark eyebrows rose. "Try again?"

She picked up his hand. Complex and extensive

lines shown on his palm, representing a wealthy and successful life. Very likely, considering his elaborate home.

Examining his long fingers first, she then traced the outer edge of his palm. "These tiny lines are your worries."

He lowered his head, examined his palm and frowned. "There are many."

A star shape embedded across his travel line indicated a crisis. Still to come? She hadn't seen a star on anyone's palm in years. She bent her head. Aye. Deeply embedded in his right palm. Danger. Sadness.

The head line began above the life line and spanned horizontally. Both lines were joined, signifying a strong sense of mind ruling over body. But the angle of luck, the space between the life line and head line, was small. The smaller the space, the smaller the luck. She glanced at his unreadable face and swallowed.

His voice, surprisingly heavy, interrupted her thoughts. "I'm pondering a move to Wales."

"Why?"

"To escape the influenza epidemic."

"Then go."

"'Tis not that easy with an entire household." He avoided her gaze and contemplated the elaborate longcase clock against the side wall, its weight-driven pendulum swinging back and forth. "Someone very dear to me is frail, and 'twould be difficult for him to travel long distances. Because of the danger of contracting influenza, we'd need to avoid main roads and larger villages, thus doubling the length of our journey."

"And you want to know what I think?"

Aye." He looked back at her. "Is it safe to remain in England until the spring? Or should we risk the journey?"

The urgency in his voice worried her.

He didn't believe in fortune-telling, yet he seemed to need assurance his household would be safe. Instinct told her to be careful. He was landed gentry; he was dangerous.

Should she reply impersonally?

She grazed her fingers over his calloused hands. Webs of jagged scars traced up his arms, reddened against his dark skin. Most likely, he'd fought in frequent battles. England was forever either signing a peace treaty or at war.

The length of his forefinger reached the bottom nail of the middle finger. This meant confidence and ambition.

His eyebrows furrowed. "Explain as you read."

Her gaze moved to his palms. She ran her finger along his heart line. His heart, intense and deep, swaddled her like a blanket.

"You're not explaining," he said.

"I'll speak when there's something to say." With a light touch, she drew a path down his palms. Several smaller lines showed death. She tried to keep her face calm, her manner subdued. Might this loss be from his past, or his future?

His travel line was more intriguing. A vivid square appeared, a sign telling her 'twas safe for him to travel. The danger reflected in the smaller lines meant any peril might occur in England.

She kept her gaze lowered. If he knew 'twas safe to travel, might he—despite his assurances—insist on taking her and Yolanda with him, perhaps to entertain him with more fortune-telling along the way. Then months would pass before she and Yolanda returned to their mother's gravesite and the caravan.

Valentina flattened two fingers against each eye and forced them closed. Charged silence filled the air.

Once, she'd told Yolanda she judged a person's character and secret desires by the lines she read on their palms.

Daj had taught Valentina the code of honor the Rom lived by—reveal what was probable

and say nothing more. Of course, Valentina embellished her readings to please the customer and make more money. So as not to distress them, she might omit a disturbing truth. That was all.

A wealthy man sat across from her. He was not a customer, though, and she would make no money. But he was a man with power over her.

The memory of his nonchalant words crowded her indecision. *"I'm unaware of your Gypsy ways and I'm sorry about your mother's death."*

Hollow condolences. Did he truly care about her mother or Yolanda's injury?

"Si khohaimo may patshivalo sar o tshatshim," she half-whispered.

"Speak in English," he said.

There are lies more believable than the truth.

Her mother's tender guidance intruded on her instinct to tell less than the truth. *Respect your gifts. Use them wisely.*

Valentina opened her eyes and focused on the magnificent painting of a horse hanging on the opposite wall. "Then all I can tell you from the lines I see on your palm is that I'm uncertain."

"Nothing else?" he prompted.

She fingered his waistcoat draped around her. A bitter taste lingered in her throat as she shook her head. By not explaining everything she'd seen, she was betraying the ancient gift passed down to her for safekeeping by her beloved mother and generations of Romany women before her. But this was the best way she knew to protect her and her sister.

"Thank you, Valentina." The warmth of his smile

was reflected in his tone. His white teeth contrasted with his wind-burned skin. Minute lines crinkled around his mouth and the small freckle above his lips. As the firelight flickered across his face, she noticed the shadow of a dark stubble outlining his firm chin. "Thank you," he repeated.

She heard the desperation in his voice now, and sudden tears welled. He looked exhausted.

He needed time to regain his stamina, to rest after a difficult battle. There was no need to alarm him, no need for him to trek halfway across the country.

Besides, there hadn't been an outbreak of influenza in months.

~

*J*ames exhaled, quiet and slow. His hands trembled, ever so faintly, with his relief. He feared his son would be unable to fight influenza if it struck. However, they need not endure the difficult journey to Wales.

He closed his eyes and whispered a grateful prayer to God, along with a request to forgive him as the beginning of the Bible verse, Isaiah 8:19, nudged at him. "And when they say to you, 'Inquire of the mediums and the necromancers who chirp and mutter,' should not a people inquire of their God."

This was different, he told himself. With painful accuracy, Valentina had foretold Beatrix's death.

Still fresh in his memory, the early spring morning had been clear and cold. Despite his objections, his late wife Alyce had insisted on having her palm read by a young Gypsy woman at a nearby traveling fair. The reading had disturbed her—their daughter was in grave danger. He'd dismissed Alyce's concerns with a skeptical laugh, but then he'd locked gazes with the green-eyed Gypsy. He'd always remember her, those green eyes and those words that had predicted his daughter's death. Could fate have brought her to him a second time?

Valentina had given a quiet nod to confirm her prediction. Then she'd concentrated on her next customer's outstretched palm.

James rubbed his hands against his thighs to stop the familiar despondency wracking through him. Such strange Gypsy words Valentina had uttered, an enigma with her superstitions.

Aye, many people believed Gypsies were unscrupulous. Nonetheless, he'd gathered from the crowd milling around her that this woman held a reputation for being forthright.

The smoldering fireplace cast the room in subdued shadows and veiled silhouettes, while Valentina continued to bite her full bottom lip. Her cheeks were flushed, the color rising with each word she'd spoken. Her nerves showed. 'Twas doubtful she'd read a man's palm in his own home before.

Despite her ragged appearance, her exotic features and spirit fascinated him. Coal-black hair tangled around her face, disheveled and caked with mud. Loose tendrils softened the strained expression on her heart-shaped face.

He stood. "Valentina, would you care to bathe?"

Her small chin lifted. "I can't." Her proud Gypsy nose gave her an air of integrity.

"So 'tis true? Gypsies don't bathe?"

She stood, shoving back her chair and plunking her hands on her hips, accentuating her small waist. With a flourish, she shook off his waistcoat and flung it to the floor. Her stormy gaze flared with outrage. Thick black lashes cast a sooty outline under her wide-set eyes and olive skin.

"You believe my people don't wash?"

He was wise enough not to answer that. "The servants will heat water and bring a tub to your chamber."

"They may heat the water, but I will not bathe. And I've no interest in seeing my chamber. I prefer to sleep outdoors." She took a step, apparently attempting to brush past him, but then her eyes closed and she slumped.

James caught her in his arms as she fell. She might not be as tough as she appeared.

He held her, enjoying the fullness of her warm body, knowing he should let her go.

He drew his lips together and inhaled. Even in her filthy state, her skin smelled subtly of forbidden spices. Attraction heated through him, toward her, a Gypsy woman, a woman who showed no fear. His grip tightened under her arms in an attempt to keep her upright. She'd had an exhausting night, on top of the recent death of her mother.

As abruptly as she'd fainted, her eyes flew open. She tore from his grasp. "Don't think you can touch me whenever you please, because I won't allow it."

He held up his hands, not knowing where to put them. He liked to keep his hands folded behind him. However, she made him feel like he should be clasping them together, begging for a morsel of understanding.

"Presently, you're not in your caravan. Here we are considerably civilized and we bathe often." He softened his tone and dropped his hands to his sides.

Her small tongue moistened her lips. "'Tis the Romany custom to wait until after our mother's burial to bathe."

"Surely, you would agree you need a bath. Let me show you to your chamber."

Stains of scarlet spotted her high cheekbones at his suggestion.

An unexpected burst of wind blew open the door, extinguishing the candle in the iron spiked candle holder and darkening the room. The burning scent of wax shriveled the air.

Valentina frowned, looking as apprehensive about the unexpected draft as he. As the last curl of smoke disappeared, she seemed uncertain. But then her glare, set to challenge, regarded him with re-bellion.

"I will go to this chamber, but I will not bathe."

CHAPTER FOUR

Te bisterdon tumare anava.
May your names be forgotten.
Romany saying

"Your bath will be brought up to you, although you should be made to fetch it yourself." The scathing pronouncement from the housekeeper, Wiborow, came down the stairs and collided with Valentina's scowl.

Valentina focused her attention on the pinpoint flame of the beeswax candle Wiborow carried. The candle shed little light as Valentina climbed the staircase behind the servant. When they reached a landing, Wiborow opened a door leading into a spacious chamber.

"Mr. Colchester requests you sleep here for the night."

Valentina blinked at the richness of the canopied bed in the center of the luxurious room. Lustrous draperies in powder-blue silk were tied with heavy gold rope, exposing matching sheets. Snowy white pillows crowned the headboard underneath a silver-white canopy. A dancing fire flared in the grate of the carved stone fireplace.

Awe veered to anger. Anger swelled to outrage. No doubt, Mr. Colchester wanted to remind her of his affluent lifestyle compared to the squalor of her ragged caravan. The realization kicked at her like a starved dog groveling for a bone. Her chest constricted with hurt, with loss.

"'Requests?'" she repeated with sarcasm.

"Your sister is asleep." Wiborow's stance indicated she'd physically force Valentina to stay in this room. Her thin eyebrows drew together in a scowl. "Someone of your station should be more appreciative of Mr. Colchester's kindness."

Someone of her *lowly* station? Valentina clamped her mouth shut, biting back her retort.

Wiborow marched to an ancient trunk tucked in the corner of the chamber. "You should have everything you need for your bath." She rummaged through the trunk, spilling the scent of rarely used linens into the room, and pulled out a fine cotton nightdress and dressing gown.

Valentina flicked a glance toward the rattling coming from the hallway. A freckle-faced servant with a mass of red hair tumbling down her shoulders carried two lit candles through the open doorway. A half-dozen flustered housemaids followed, hoisting a large tub and buckets of steaming water. They poured the water into the tub, then pulled a screen around it to close off the drafts.

Wiborow glowered at the red-headed servant. "Clare, set the candles on the mantel. Be careful. You are so clumsy of late, you're constantly bruising yourself."

Valentina guessed Clare's age to be close to her own and offered a tentative smile. In response, Clare clasped her freckled hands in prayer, her fingers pointed upward.

Valentina recognized the mistrustful sneers, the furtive squints, the raised brows. She'd seen it on most English faces whenever her caravan settled at the outskirts of a new town. The despised gadje had formed their opinions before the Rom even arrived, although they were eager to have their fortunes told. And she was eager to take their shillings in return.

Disdainfully, Wiborow sniffed. "I'll fetch clean clothes and discard your wretched gown."

"My clothes are also at fault?" Valentina considered her once colorful scarlet gown, now mud-spat-tered and torn. With the determination of a proud woman, she forbade herself to cry as the servants departed.

The house quieted a few minutes later.

She stepped to the half-open window and peered down. A night breeze lowered the clouds, sending a faint wind across her face that made her tremble. Mr. Colchester would be pleased if she bathed, believing she'd abided by his request.

"*Te merel amaro kuro o lasho,*" she began, intending to curse his horse. Then she closed the window and rested her head in her hands. No use in cursing an innocent horse.

Pivoting, she eyed the clear water of the tub and tucked her hair behind her ears. The scent of the clean water and soap tempted.

Valentina untied her mother's diklo, allowing the bright scarf to unravel and float to the floor. She secured it into a knot under the carved foot post of the bed, then stripped off her filthy clothes and immersed herself in soapy water up to her chin. Surely, the Romany spirits would understand that she had to bathe at some point.

Warm water lapped her skin, and the fragrance of pine and mint wafted from the rosemary soap. She erased the torment of the night by scrubbing her hair until her scalp was sore, then settled back into the soapy water. Her overwrought nerves calmed. She closed her eyes and dozed.

Two bold knocks awakened her. A pucker-faced Wiborow tromped into the chamber carrying a bundle of clean clothes and crisp linens. Clare accompanied her, toting a tray, and thin odors of cooked cabbage and carrots streamed through the chamber.

Valentina glimpsed Mr. Colchester leaning in the doorway. He still wore his white muslin shirt, black pants, and suspenders. He folded his solid arms across his chest, a bemused expression on his face, before averting his gaze from hers.

Valentina's heart thudded in degradation as she covered herself with her arms, thankful for the screen that shielded most of her. "Get out of my chamber." In furious rebellion, she tipped up her chin and glared.

"I believe the chamber is mine," he countered.

She took a deep breath and dunked beneath the bath water. When she emerged, gasping for breath, he and his servants were gone, and the chamber door had been closed.

~

Thirty minutes later, James knocked on Valentina's door.

He waited.

"Surely you can't be speechless," he said after a

full minute of silence. "Are you finished with your bath?"

"Aye."

"May I come in?"

"Aye."

He opened the door and stepped inside. Fully dressed in the clean clothes set out for her, Valentina sat on the edge of the bed.

"I didn't wash to please you," she said.

"Somehow this edifying bit of information doesn't surprise me."

Was she aware of how provocative she looked, the seductive allure of her plain gown? Her emerald eyes slanted at the corners and gave the appearance of a tigress's eyes—points of yellow flickering in the center of a green pool.

He moved forward, his footsteps muted by the thick royal-blue carpet. All that separated them was three paces and his sharp breathing.

Standing, she eased back toward the wall, but she slipped, her bare feet apparently still wet from the bath. He caught her, a pleasant pastime he seemed to excel in lately.

She struggled upright. "Don't touch me."

"Once again, I'm attempting to save you from dropping to the floor." Despite his authoritative tone, he raised his hands and retreated. Somehow, she managed to make him feel like a criminal in his own home.

"Yolanda is sleeping?" Those warning sparks again in those huge emerald eyes.

"Aye. A servant checked on her a while ago."

He couldn't help focusing on Valentina's lips, moist and inviting in the shimmering candlelight. Her glowing skin and lyrical voice reminded him more of a wayward angel than an angry Gypsy.

She backed up, twisted and frowned at the wall behind her, and then turned back around to face him. "What time are we leaving come the morrow?"

There it was, that innocent question reeking of a demand.

"We've discussed this, remember? As soon as the physician examines your sister's arm."

He could've given a number of clearer responses, although he couldn't think of what they would be, so he added, "A fortnight ago, there were reports of highwaymen along the roads. The danger is too great for women traveling alone, which is why I'll ride back to your camp with you."

For a moment, he thought she might cry. Why? He was only trying to help.

He extended one hand. "I'm truly sorry about your mother's death."

Quiet vulnerability wrapped around her small form, along with a tinge of sadness. "Your sympathies ring hollow. If Yolanda and I don't return to our tribe come the morrow, the Rom spirits will bring disaster."

"Tell your impatient spirits you can't risk your or your sister's life for them, and you'll return to your caravan soon."

"You're arrogant to imagine you have the right to plan my life."

"I'm not planning your life. I'm simply planning your safe return to camp." He should grab her by her shapely shoulders and shake away the droplets of water still clinging to her neck from her bath. But the corners of her lovely mouth had turned down, and he couldn't lift his hands.

He regarded her empty tray of food neatly set by the door. "If your sister requires a lengthier recuperation, you're both welcome to stay in my home for as long as you'd like."

Somehow, the idea of her living in his house lifted his mood. He had the distinct feeling she thought just the opposite.

She blasted him with a mutinous expression. "Whether we stay a week or a day, you won't be bedding me."

For a split second, his breath was suspended. Smiling stiffly, he scratched the coarse stubble of his whiskered chin. "I'm a Christian man who follows the Lord's teachings, which doesn't include bedding a woman I've known for less than one day." He compressed his lips and studied her. Her slim body had filled out since he'd last seen her years before. He hadn't expected the breathtaking woman who stood before him, so close that the warmth of her body touched his skin.

Nay. Involvement with a woman wasn't his forte. His failed marriage was proof of that.

He gave himself a firm mental shake and pushed desire far from his thoughts. Valentina had come to him for help because of her injured sister. In a moment of impulse, he'd asked her for a palm reading.

His conscience whispered a reminder. He had no reason to encourage her and her sister to remain any longer than was necessary for Yolanda's recovery.

But his conscience always had been a nuisance.

Still, he enjoyed Valentina's jaunty rejoinders, and the softness that came over her fiery expression when she spoke of her mother and sister.

Averting his gaze from her face, he stared into the fading embers of the fire. As he turned back to her, an unexpected spark cast her features in a bright cinnamon hue. Her demeanor had changed, neither demanding nor challenging.

"We won't be needing anyone to ride with us to our caravan, and we're certainly not afraid of highwaymen."

He inhaled the scent of black pepper and exotic spices, and his leather boots propelled him forward, one step, two. Her lips reminded him of the full coral lips he'd once admired in a fine painting, too beautiful to be real.

"I've always wondered—where do your people wander?" he asked.

"Wherever there is food and relative safety from the English."

Despite himself, he grinned. She spoke with all the haughtiness of a newly crowned monarch.

"Valentina, the English are not the ogres you believe."

"If you lived in my caravan, you would think otherwise."

Her fringe of black eyelashes fluttered like an agitated bird. Truly she was an exotic, enchanting, exquisite creature.

He moved another step closer. The idea of kissing her had nothing to do with reason.

Women. Dependency. Relying on someone else for happiness.

Nay. Never.

This could be different. He'd never felt so attracted to a woman.

He closed the distance between them and tenderly pushed a wayward tendril from her cheek. "Valentina, I—"

"I told you not to touch me." She jerked away from his hand and drew a lengthy, suffocated breath. "Now get out."

She was right.

"I apologize. I overstepped my boundary."

In his own house.

She scoffed.

"What I meant was ..."

Perhaps he could speak as a reasonable man if he were speaking to a reasonable woman.

She lifted her face toward the ceiling as if she'd already dismissed him. Him, the man who was attempting to care for her and her sister so they wouldn't starve.

Moonlight streamed through the window, outlining Valentina's perfect form, her crossed arms, her high chin.

Reining in his annoyance, he strode out of the chamber and slammed the door.

～

The fire in the grate had burned low and gave little heat. Chilled to her toes, Valentina wrapped her nightdress closer around her. She lit two candles, placed them on either side of the mantel, and then settled into bed. With a lengthy sigh, she rolled to her side.

She wouldn't allow any man to get too close. She'd learned *that* hard lesson years before.

Troka, an ungainly man with yellowing teeth and perverted urges, had stunted her yearnings before her breasts had ever bloomed. Even now, she remembered the stench of his sticky bear-claw hands closing over her mouth. His groping fingers had probed her young body, her flat chest and slim hips. His threats of hurting her family if she didn't submit had killed the last of her screams.

Much later, Luca had found her, disoriented and rambling, wallowing in the sludge of tears and dishonor. He'd spoken in a deceptively calm tone, brought her back to the caravan and had kept her secret all these years. They had forged a silent agreement. When her explanations to her family of where she'd been had sounded guilty, Luca had merely nodded. A good friend, her protector, adding credibility to her feeble story.

Every man, barring Luca, was the same. They wanted things done their way, on their terms.

And she'd vowed, as a rock had settled where her heart had once been, that what she'd endured one muddy night years before would never happen again.

CHAPTER FIVE

I chatski tsinuda de tehara, vai de haino, khal tut.
The true nettle stings from the beginning.
Old Romany saying

*T*he following morning, Valentina pulled herself awake from a restless sleep.

She changed into a soft olive-green percale gown from the trunk and tied her mother's yellow diklo around her throat. She cleaned her teeth, combed her fingers through her clean hair and scurried into the long hall and down the wide staircase.

Following her nose and ears, she found her way to the smoky, bustling kitchen.

Without meeting Valentina's gaze, Clare handed

her a slice of warm buttered bread topped with spicy apple preserves.

Valentina set the bread on the table. "Has anyone seen my sister? Is she awake"

"She's being looked after." Affected by a slight lisp, Clare whistled over the words.

Valentina followed Clare through the pantry and outside into the herb garden. "'Tis morning and Yolanda and I are supposed to leave."

Wiborow appeared at the doorway and screwed her lips into a knowing smile. "You'll see your sister in a short while, at the midday meal. You should know that the only reason he's tolerating you Gypsies is because of Beatrix."

"Who's Beatrix?"

No reply from either servant as they headed back into the kitchen, leaving Valentina in the herb garden.

Expelling an exasperated breath, Valentina grabbed a handful of parsley. A whiff of freshly tilled dirt met with her nose. Bright autumn days colored in golden leaves normally gave her strength. Not today. Today her throat ached with loss, with loneliness for her sister's absence, for their mother's death.

She chewed on the parsley stem and eyed the wide variety of herbs— tarragon and wild mustard, stinging nettle and foxglove—used to enhance all manner of food, as well as remedies for ailments.

Deciding to avoid the kitchen, she walked around the house and reentered through the marbled front foyer.

A housemaid, cold malice imprinted on her ruddy face, pushed up the sleeves of her gown as Valentina walked past. "Gypsies are dark because they never wash," she declared to no one in particular.

Already, the English's ignorance was showing, and Valentina hadn't walked five steps.

She raised her head, and her gaze collided with Mr. Colchester's. He wore a coal-black waistcoat over a white linen shirt, the sleeves emphasizing his solid arms. A faint light shone in the grey depths of his eyes. "Good morning, Valentina. The midday meal will be served soon."

"Aye, so I've been told." He either hadn't heard his maid's comment, or he'd chosen to ignore it. "By the way, your herbs are sorely uncared for."

"Are you interested in tending to my herbs?"

His quiet inquiry checked her in midstep. "Perhaps in a thousand years."

He scanned her face and her gown, taking his time. "I prefer the Gypsy clothes you wore yesterday," he said with a relaxed smile. "They suited you better."

She knew his teasing voice was meant to charm. And it did. She stiffened her resistance.

"This gown is from your house," she answered, "not mine."

"I didn't realize you had a house."

"A home doesn't need to stay in one place. It should move with you."

He peered around at the chairs covered in cream silk brocade, the expensive paintings in elaborate gold frames, the terraced courtyard beyond the bow windows. "I cannot imagine taking all my belongings wherever I go."

"Because you have everything a man could ever want in a lifetime."

His gaze held hers. "Not everything."

Her mind groped madly for another subject. She took a deep breath, but only inhaled his scent of leather and horses and worn saddles. "I assume you intend to keep your promise, Mr. Colchester."

"Which promise?"

Her gaze wandered to the prominent freckle above his lip. Spurred by impatience for noticing, she shrugged in mock explanation. "To allow my sister and me to leave, assuming the physician agrees."

"You've always been 'allowed' to leave. Somehow, I don't believe anyone could keep you anywhere for long without your consent, anyway. And your sister should be downstairs shortly. Perhaps we should wait for her in here."

He escorted her into the dining room, where servants were carrying in food. He spoke to some of them, who paused in their duties to answer, and he listened attentively while they spoke. Yet Valentina was still the recipient of suspicious looks, and the servants' malice increased her anxiety about seeing her sister again and then finally leaving.

"I haven't seen Yolanda since last evening," she said when Mr. Colchester turned back to her. We've never been apart this long." She scanned the hallway, wondering how many more minutes it would be before she saw her sister again.

She glanced back at Mr. Colchester, trying to be upset at him, although when she searched her thoughts, there was nothing to be upset at him for. He wasn't guilty of anything except genuine kindness.

He escorted her to a chair that was to the right of the head of the table. "One of the reasons I wanted you both to dine with me is to silence any wagging tongues, to dispel any tales that you're a witch disguised as a Gypsy."

She studied the mahogany table, sunken with food and drink, and chewed her bottom lip. "Thank you. You've been most generous. Although you're still a gadje."

"Somehow, I'm guessing you're not complimenting me."

"You're a stranger to the Romany because you are an English—"

"Valentina, I didn't recognize you! You're wearing such a rich-looking gown!" Yolanda's melodious voice sang from the hallway.

Valentina whirled. There Yolanda stood in the doorway, precious and pale, her ebony hair falling in a cluster of waves around her face. Her injured arm was wrapped in a sling.

"You look beautiful." Valentina raced to Yolanda and embraced her. "Are you all right?"

"Aye, except my arm hurts. A physician was supposed to be called in, although 'twas determined to summon a bone setter instead. My forearm was set without too much pain, although it still throbs."

Valentina raised her brows. "And your cough?"

"Definitely better."

"Now all you require is time and rest and food in order to heal," Mr. Colchester said.

"I slept in a wonderful bedchamber last evening." Yolanda gestured to a basket of fresh, yeasty rolls on the sideboard. "The food is in such abundance here, and I bathed. The water was actually warm and smelled of lavender. Do you think the spirits will be furious about my bath?"

"I hope not," Valentina murmured.

"Mr. Colchester is so generous."

Sighing, Valentina quickly steered Yolanda away from Mr. Colchester's wide smile and to a corner of the splendorous blue and gold dining room, grateful for the noisy clatter of the silverware as the maids began serving. "However," she whispered, "he has a misguided fear for our safety."

"I've spent my first night in luxury. And the bone setter said I wasn't strong enough to travel for a few days because of the fracture."

Worry filled Valentina at her sister's words. The scent of cooked game and salted vegetables, which had been enticing, now overwhelmed her. She was jostled from behind as a servant stepped past her, carrying a platter of baked ham.

"There are robbers among us who'll steal the clothes off yer back," he muttered.

Valentina scowled at the thick-jowled servant, his ruddy cheeks, the unflinching distrust in his watery blue eyes.

Yolanda squeezed Valentina's hand before she could speak. "Don't let ill-informed people upset you."

Before the servant could scurry away, Mr. Colchester joined them. His sharp glare, packed with a frown, froze the servant in place. "Valentina and Yolanda, I apologize for his ignorance," he said clearly.

His concern touched Valentina. However, these people lived and worked in his home. Shouldn't they know better?

"Englishmen can never understand a Rom's suffering," she replied.

"I am from Wales."

"Still, you wouldn't understand." She blinked back unexpected tears. To cry in front of a gadje shamed her.

"Help me understand." His words, tender as a breeze in the stifling dining room, held an empathy she hadn't expected.

For an answer, she took her sister's uninjured arm and returned to the table.

Once Mr. Colchester had seated them, Valentina on his right and Yolanda on his left, he sat and lifted his wineglass. "I'm pleased you're reunited with your sister. Even though I'm a gadje—which surely means I'm honest and agreeable."

Valentina ignored his attempt to lighten her mood, preferring to examine the gleaming silver spoon beside her plate.

"Perhaps an apology is in order for your attack on my good character?" he added.

She glimpsed his chiding smile, although she felt like she was drowning in shame. Hadn't he realized she'd been crying?

She pushed back her chair and stood. "And perhaps dining with you wasn't such a good idea."

He stood as well. "Please stay. You haven't tried the venison, nor the potatoes." He placed one hand lightly on her shoulders.

Before she was able to pull away, a little boy entered the dining room and marched determinedly to Mr. Colchester. He tugged on the man's waistcoat with one hand and held a squirming flat-nosed puppy with the other. Although the boy didn't speak, he made his intentions known. He pointed toward a window, back to himself, then out the window again. He had the innocent face of a cherub and an oddly familiar grin. Valentina had the urge to scoop him up in her arms.

Mr. Colchester released her and crouched to eye level with the boy. "Jeremy, 'tis too cold for you to play outdoors."

The boy's face puckered, and he aimed his gaze insistently toward the doorway and the foyer beyond.

Mr. Colchester tenderly touched the boy's cheeks, then tousled his hair. "Perhaps for a short while you can play outside. Elspeth will fetch your cloak and boots." He signaled to a woman who stood in the doorway, and lowered his tone as he directed, "Be certain Jeremy stays near the older boys and supervise him at all times."

The boy clapped his hands and set the puppy on the floor. The puppy bounded away, Jeremy on its heels.

"Who is that little boy?" Valentina asked. "One of the tenant farmer's children?"

Mr. Colchester granted her a broad smile. "Jeremy is my son."

She grabbed the back of her chair in astonishment.

Of course. The boy was a miniature version of his father—the same silvery eyes, the same smile, the same slim build. Except the boy's grey eyes were specked with blue, as blue as a robin's egg. And his skin was pallid, the dark lines hinting at a recent illness.

"I didn't realize you were married," she said, surprised she could speak.

"My late wife, Alyce, died several months ago."

Valentina heard his voice as if he were speaking through a thick fog.

"She contracted influenza," he was saying. "The finest doctors couldn't save her."

His wife had died, and her death explained the tiny lines creasing his palms, indicating sadness. Memory of the previous night's fortune-telling left a bitter taste in Valentina's throat. "How old is your son?"

"Six. He had a twin sister. My daughter Beatrix."

Had.

"You should know that the only reason he's tolerating you Gypsies is because of Beatrix," Wiborow had said.

Valentina's breath caught. "Is Beatrix here?" She scanned the room, absurdly expecting to spot a little girl about Jeremy's age.

"She died."

If Valentina hadn't been watching Mr. Colchester so closely, she would have missed the wave of grief sweeping over his face.

She swallowed. Her vision blurred. "How?"

"She went wandering." Briefly, he closed his eyes. "Jesus said, 'Let the little children come to me and do not hinder them, for to such belongs the kingdom of heaven.'" He opened his eyes and met her questioning stare.

"And your son is—"

"Deaf."

No wonder the boy hadn't spoken.

"He cannot hear your laughter," she said softly, half to herself. "Nor a bird chirping, nor his puppy barking."

Mr. Colchester's gaze flashed a warning. *No pity.*

No one could fault him for his protectiveness. He was a widower, trying to do his best to raise a child on his own. And he was proving to be a far more complex man than she'd originally assumed.

She surveyed the dining table, laden with more food than her tribe could eat in a week. Chunky loaves of brown bread, sharp and pungent wedges of cheese, ripe apples and pears. An overabundance of plenty while her mother had starved herself to death to preserve their family and tribe's meager amount of food.

Her gaze skated back to Mr. Colchester. His nods to the maids were courteous, his laughter to an earlier joke genuine. Yet he'd lost his daughter. And his wife.

A man who feared influenza. A man who loved his son.

Hardships on his palm. She'd dismissed them, although the lines had demanded attention. That she could do that fortune-telling again ...

"Our king balances his peace treaties with a war now and then." From the kitchen, Geoffrey's gravelly proclamation rose above the servants' voices.

"I wondered if my knees were still attached to my legs after crouching in the dirt all those miserable soaking nights," Roland's voice added.

"The king has brought prosperity to England and —" Geoffrey gasped. The sound of a shattering wine glass sounded from the kitchen.

"Geoffrey's choking on a slice of pear!" a servant shouted.

James jumped to his feet and reached Geoffrey first. He delivered several back blows between Geoffrey's shoulder blades.

Both Valentina and Yolanda shot up. Despite Mr. Colchester's efforts, Geoffrey was unconscious.

"I'll get some herbs from the garden," Valentina said.

From the kitchen, Mr. Colchester met her gaze. "Go."

Yolanda grasped Valentina's gown and slowed their flight as they raced through the kitchen and into the herb garden.

"There are stinging nettle plants growing here."

Valentina bent among the spindly plants and dug through tarragon and wild mustard.

Wiborow marched into the garden and elbowed Yolanda out of the way. Her tiny eyes narrowed, her withered face appraised. "Do you enjoy gardening?"

Valentina met Wiborow's gaze. "Aye. I'm a Rom."

"And my sister is a natural healer," Yolanda added.

Valentina yanked the spiky nettles from the ground, pricking her finger on the needles. She raced back to the house and steeped the stinging needles in tepid water, creating a sour brew. Steadying herself, she carried her potion into the kitchen. Yolanda and Wiborow followed.

Valentina settled beside Geoffrey and Mr. Colchester. Geoffrey was groggy but breathing normally. Carefully, she placed the potion to his dry lips.

Roland hovered over her. "If you harm Geoffrey with that witch's potion, you Gypsy—"

Valentina jumped at his shouting, spilling the brew over her fingers.

Mr. Colchester silenced Roland with a slight raise of his hand, but a shadow of apprehension creased his brows. Beads of sweat formed above his tightened lips.

"Don't be alarmed," she said to reassure him. "This brew will calm Geoffrey."

He nodded his assent for her to continue.

Geoffrey's weathered skin had taken on an ash-colored hue. She allowed him seconds between each sip to catch his breath, closing her eyes and chanting in Romany. "*May angle sar te merel kadi yag.* Before this fire burns out," she translated, "please spare this man from any pain today."

"I like the English words better." With a slight smile, Geoffrey opened his eyes, crinkling the creases above his white brows. "Now allow me to walk out of this room upright as a man."

"I'll assist him." Deftly, Mr. Colchester brought Geoffrey to his feet, and Roland helped him out of the room.

"What happened?" one of the assembled servants whispered to another.

"The deer meat is rancid," the other servant answered.

"The meat is perfectly fine, you dolt," said the third. "Geoffrey's an old man and his body is weak. But if you were paying attention, you'd know he choked on a pear."

Mr. Colchester turned, seeming to concentrate on every speculative word. When his gaze reached Valentina, his expression was grateful. "Thank you, my Gypsy *cariad,* for helping me tend to my dearest friend."

"I'm happy to do anything I can. Geoffrey is a gracious and considerate man."

"Aye."

The room quieted.

Mr. Colchester turned to the gathered. "Let us pray for my steward's full return to good health. With God's grace, he'll recover admirably."

He spoke to them all, although his admiring gaze remained on Valentina. His silver eyes, mesmeric and burning, drew her to him.

CHAPTER SIX

Saka perkero charo dikhel.
Everybody sees only his dish.
Old Romany saying

Two hours had passed since the midday meal.

Everywhere she went, Valentina heard the servants in the house murmur that she was a sorceress. After all, she'd helped Geoffrey using herbs and Gypsy chants.

And didn't they understand? If she were a sorceress, she and Yolanda wouldn't have been forced to steal and beg all those years to stay alive.

When she stepped into the kitchen, hoping for a

cup of tea, overweight cooks peered up from their kitchen tasks and smiled, all of them red-faced from the heat of the ovens. A friendly nod from Clare proved both welcoming and troubling. Formerly snobbish servants started rushing into the kitchen, vying with each other for her attention as they went into excruciating details about their dizziness and aching bones, asking for some remedy, some relief. The same servants who'd avoided her since she'd arrived.

For the next half hour, she patiently explained how to brew medicinal teas using dandelion root, flaxseed, water and honey for dizziness and digestion. For pain relief, she recommended a mixture of lemon balm, coriander, nutmeg, and vodka.

She kept up her descriptions of the simple ingredients required for the cures until all the servants' questions had been answered. Speaking with them she felt emboldened, no longer angry at them for being English, and subsequently, inexplicably guilty for thinking otherwise.

They went back to their tasks and only Clare remained. "Thank you for helping us," she blurted.

Valentina eyed the young girl's curly carrot-red hair and fair complexion. Clare looked so unlike the robust, olive-skinned Romany women Valentina had grown up with. Despite being a servant, Clare reminded Valentina of a pampered flower.

So why *was* she helping the English? Valentina

asked herself. She certainly shouldn't trust them because she'd only known their cruelty, one of the causes of her tribe's deprivation.

She shook her head, chiding herself for her prejudice. If she expected to drive a change in their views toward the Rom, shouldn't she be the first to steer the change in the right direction, becoming more tolerant of their culture? Didn't they have their own explanations for their viewpoints? Weren't there other options besides hatred toward other people because of differing beliefs?

But if the English got too close, they might force her to care about them, their lives, their heartaches, their illnesses, a small voice pointed out.

And so what? Was that so wrong, to take down these boundaries?

With Clare beside her, she walked to the wide entry doors leading to the front lawn. As she'd spoken with the servants, her gaze had milled the hallway, searching for a glimpse of Mr. Colchester's reassuring smile.

Valentina fastened a borrowed wool pelisse over her gown, tucked her yellow diklo beneath the collar, and secured a bonnet over her unruly hair.

Seeing Wiborow bearing down toward them, Clare jumped and started away. Valentina stopped her with a quick question. "Clare, do you know where Mr. Colchester is?"

"He looked in on Geoffrey earlier and is most likely at church now. He attends service daily."

Stepping outside, Valentina peered at a sizable gold cross dwarfing the steeple of a distant parish church. The front lawn greeted her with the scent of oak trees and acorns and a crisp midafternoon sun. Fragrances of tart olive soap and burning wax filled the air. She embraced the day and took a heartening breath.

Glancing to a nearby outbuilding, she saw Yolanda engaged in watching a woman weave sheep's wool at a loom. Standing near her was a heavy-set blond man who, judging by his attire and well-muscled arms, was a blacksmith.

A smile touched Valentina's lips. As a Romany should, Yolanda had fit easily into her new setting.

Jeremy's giggles drew her attention. He was chasing his golden-brown puppy around the grass in a carefree circle. The puppy concentrated on chasing its short tail, a comical twitch of intent on its squared-off jaw. Jeremy stopped and bent his head between his knees, then collapsed on the ground. His little face flushed with exhaustion, his slim body heaved with the exertion of catching his breath.

Valentina hesitated. They met each other's stares, hers watchful, his gleeful. He extended her a hearty wave. The sweet gesture warmed her insides, and she grinned and waved back before walking over to her sister.

"How is your arm?" she asked when she reached Yolanda.

The blacksmith nodded to them both and walked away.

"Better," Yolanda said, and then frowned. "Valentina, I'm sorry I'm delaying our departure. Daj is waiting to be buried."

"I'm certain Luca is taking care of everything. He'll bury Daj with the dignity she deserved."

"But Luca was injured—"

"Knowing Luca, he wasn't hurt for long. Besides, you need time to relax and eat proper food. Soon you'll be recovered from your cough and your arm will be strong again."

"I like it here and Mr. Colchester said we could stay as long as we want." Yolanda clasped her hands loosely and gazed at the ground. "I miss Daj, I mourn her, but she'd want us to stay, wouldn't she?"

"Aye. Knowing our caring mother, she certainly would. And far better you convalesce here, where you can heal properly and be well-fed."

Yolanda swallowed a relieved ripple of giggling. "I'm so happy you agree."

With a buoyancy she hadn't felt in weeks, Valentina hugged her sister and then set off to explore the estate. As she wended through gardens and lawns and beyond, to where acres of harvested fields stretched as far as she could see, tenant farmers treated her to admiring stares. Others peeked from behind the safety of doors open just a crack. A few men with leathery faces greeted her by name and dipped their hats respectfully. Besieged by her confused emotions, she murmured inquiries about their health.

For one of the men's hand inflammation, she recommended a poultice of bark powder and warm water, advising him to wrap his hand in a linen bandage for a couple of days. To aid in helping another man's wife to sleep better, she suggested lemon balm water mixed with a teaspoon of honey.

Leaving the farmland behind, she pulled her pelisse more tightly around her shoulders and made her way to the edge of the woods. Stone walls bordered a path that grew narrower with every step. Her sturdy leather boots pinched her feet as she navigated up a sloping pasture. Normally, she ran barefoot, but Mr. Colchester had had the boots delivered to her chamber that morning.

However, he wasn't here. She tugged off the offending boots and threw them into a sparse field. She'd find them later and sell them. They'd fetch a good price in the marketplace.

Cool, black soil wedged between her toes. She found another meager footpath concealed by slippery leaves and avoided a shy cow with moist brown eyes in a bordering pasture.

All this land. If only she had no boundaries and could truly go wherever she pleased. Oftentimes, a Romany's life was restricted to camping on the outskirts of villages.

"Enjoying the view?" Mr. Colchester's soft inquiry came from behind her. She hadn't heard him approach, although when she spun to face him, he was so close she felt the heat emanating from his skin.

She stared at his white shirt showing beneath his black waistcoat and cloak. Always the well-dressed, urbane and thoroughly handsome gentleman.

"Must you constantly emerge when I least expect?" she chided.

"I'm not one of your spirits, appearing and reappearing on a convenient whim."

She glanced at the weather-beaten rocks lining the top of the hillside. The wind picked up, and the branches of the pine trees swayed restlessly. With a slight shiver, she pressed her elbows to her sides.

Amusement shone in his gaze, then speculation. "Surely a brave woman like you can't be afraid of heights?"

"I'm not afraid of anything."

"Not even me?"

She shook an invisible piece of soil from her pelisse. "Especially not you."

"In any event, you're safe and under my protection." He watched her. Shielding. Safeguarding.

Warding off imagined and unimagined harm. Harboring a warmth for her under a veiled expression she recognized as desire.

Instinctively, the armor around her heart rose. "Has church let out already? I assumed English vicars droned on for hours."

"I prayed quickly and added an extra 'Glory to God' for you. Would you like to join me at service come the morrow? I'll introduce you to Richard, the vicar."

"Many Romany tribes attend church. Not mine. We chant to the spirits."

"Does it help? All that chanting?"

The painful slice in her chest reminded her that the spirits hadn't helped her mother to survive. "Sometimes, when I was a child, chanting gave me peace," she said softly.

"You might find such power in prayer you'll want to accompany me one day."

She sidestepped him. "How did you find where I was?"

He glanced over his shoulder. "You left a pair of boots in the last field."

"I don't need boots." She wiggled her toes in the crisp grass and returned his smile. "And I don't want them."

His chuckle was so boyishly appealing, she could hardly believe he was the same man who ran this vast estate with such obvious, if relaxed, authority.

"I understand a number of servants and villagers spoke to you about cures for their illnesses," he said.

"I explained several simple herbal cures. However, my knowledge is limited, even as a drabardi, so please don't ask me too many questions."

"I know a drabardi is a highly respected healer in your culture. And although I'm sorry about your sister's injury, I'm assuming you'll be staying on until she recuperates?"

She agreed, but added, "I won't be a pigeon held captive in your fancy cage forever."

"On the contrary, you're an exotic bird and a most welcome guest who can come and go as she pleases."

She retreated and leaned back against the trunk of a blackthorn tree. 'Twas too fine a day to quarrel. Scanning the distant view, she spotted a river meandering through the outlying forest, rising and spilling into the tended fields. A sprinkle of sheep and cattle dotted the pastures.

"Your estate resembles a make-believe kingdom. 'Tis a mystical *paramitsha*." Assessing his casual stance, she wondered at his skill in appearing always relaxed, no matter the surroundings. A realization struck her with a tinge of regret. He was everything she'd always dreamed a man should be.

"Wales is my favorite home," he said. "Rough, untamed—so different from England."

Like you. He didn't voice it, although the words hung silently in the air around them.

"As you can see," he went on, "my home here was built on a cliff. 'Twas where Beatrix died." He drew a sharp breath and turned away, touching the corners of his eyes. "The memories of Beatrix are so poignant." He faced her again. "Just promise you'll never venture near the edge."

"I promise." A high cloud obscured the sun, and a breeze ruffled the hem of her gown. The softness in his voice contrasted with the hard lines of his face, and his quiet words made her pulse stall, thus slowing her speech. She gravitated closer to him. Sympathy poured from her spirit, drawn by his sorrow and the sweet little girl who had captured his love.

"Our home quieted without both children." His infinite silver eyes filled with grief. And a silent flicker of vulnerability that touched her heart.

He'd exhibited a tenderness toward Jeremy that few men showed toward their children. Her stomach knotted and she inhaled, unable to fill her lungs completely with pure air. She'd never marry, never bear children, because no decent man would want her. She was considered *marime* to the Rom, soiled because of the rape. A wave of shame swelled through her.

The branches of the blackthorn tree rustled, and two blackbirds sang from their elevated perch.

She whipped around and stepped blindly away from him.

His hand caught her arm. "You'll be staying for a while longer, then?"

"Aye."

"Good." He pulled her a fraction nearer, until her nose almost touched his chest. He lifted her chin and studied her face for several long seconds. "Your heart is beating like a startled bird. I'm simply a man who wants to protect you."

She focused on a yellow leaf wafting to the ground before glancing uncertainly at him. "Then may I ask you a question?"

"Of course."

"Beatrix died at a young age?"

"Aye." He stared at a point somewhere beyond her. "'Twas an accident that should never have happened."

"I'm so sorry."

His expression filled with overwhelming grief. "My late wife had left Beatrix alone. We were forewarned our daughter might be in grave danger, but we disregarded it. Beatrix never recovered from the fall, and our home became empty without both children running about."

"Your wife ... The death must have been agonizing for her to accept."

"Perhaps." A muscle worked in his jaw. "We had Jeremy, of course."

"Your son is adorable."

"He's very special. He requires a considerable amount of care because of his deafness."

Unexpected tears flooded her eyes. "My tribe adores children, as do all Romany. My kinsmen are kindhearted."

He touched her cheek, catching a teardrop with his forefinger. "Do Gypsies marry before having children?"

She jerked back and plunked her hands on her hips. One minute he was wiping her tears, the next he was asking if the Rom bedded each other before marriage! "My culture isn't immoral. All Romany are expected to marry."

His quiet reply stopped her from continuing. "Lately, all my thoughts are about you and your fascinating culture. I meant no disrespect. Please, am I forgiven, Valentina?"

"Aye." She accepted his guarded apology and couldn't help a grin. "Have you ever eaten roasted hedgehog, by the way?"

"Not unless the animal disguised itself as a cooked peacock."

"'Tis a favorite dish at our Romany weddings."

"Perhaps you can prepare one for me." His whole manner changed to brushed velvet, languid and smooth.

"I'm not known for my cooking skills, only my abilities with herbs."

Several seconds ticked by.

"How old *are* Gypsy women when they marry?" he asked at last.

She flicked an unmanageable wave from her forehead. "Many are betrothed at fourteen."

"And you are older than this?"

"I am one and twenty."

His expression sharpened on her. "Are there many suitors waiting for you at your caravan, Valentina?"

She looked up at the branches above her before gesturing to the two blackbirds preparing to take flight. "I've had little time for courtship. We begged for food, for clothes, whatever we needed." She cleared her throat and grimaced. "And we steal."

He grabbed her trembling hands. "Your secret is safe with me. I'll always protect you."

She met his gaze. "I need no protection from a gadje."

"A gadje who is intrigued by your traditions. Please continue."

She drew a quiet breath and pulled from his grasp. "Romany marry only Romany, or our entire line is polluted."

A disquieting image of a baby flickered through her mind. A baby she'd never seen, with light olive skin and gleaming grey eyes. A baby girl, she knew instinctively. She held still in expectation of a closer look, but the baby vanished from her thoughts.

"There are people in my household who would disagree and think quite the contrary," he said, "believing my blood would add merit to the Gypsy line."

"Your *proper* blood? To be fair, I've seen worse-looking proper gentlemen than you." She shuddered. "Far worse."

He threw back his head and laughed. "And I've seen far worse looking English and Welsh women. We now share a common bond, as do you and your indigent Gypsy suitors."

"Fancy words, Mr. Colchester."

They shared a smile.

He turned her face up, forcing her to focus on his lips, so close that their breaths merged. "Valentina, around you I'm a driven man, a bee drawn to a perfect flower. You can add me to your list of suitors."

"Mr. Colchester, surely you're—"

"Please call me James."

"Or shall I call you a rogue, because you believe you can seduce me with shallow verses?"

"You should insert one of your Gypsy swear words between breaths. 'Twill add credibility to your insults."

His confident gaze held her spellbound, and she could feel the warmth tinting her cheeks.

Forcing herself to look down, she smoothed her gown. "You believe you rule everything and everyone around you."

"On the contrary, I try to live by the wise words in Luke 6:31: 'Treat others the same you want them to treat you.'" Again, he lifted his hand and touched her cheek. His rough, firm hand. "I didn't mean to upset you. Talking about my daughter, my son, led me to thinking about children and family."

She attempted a smile. "Please don't apologize."

His gaze, ever perceptive, probed hers. His hand burned like molten steel against her skin, and she was utterly at a loss to speak, to move, to think, because she was melting.

He bent his head and his lips lightly grazed hers. His eyes turned a slate-grey as he watched her, reminding her of a shadowy dusk and secret, shared evenings. Silver needles and silken threads kept her body from moving.

"We should leave before it gets any later." With a sigh, he took a step back and extended his hand. "Let's walk back together. I'll show you some of the outlying farms."

She accepted his hand, and he laced his fingers through hers. Together, they began their descent down the hill. As he guided her in the direction of the main house, he explained the workings of the land, which was divided into forests, pastures, and cultivated fields. After a few minutes, he gathered her hand and placed it in the crook of his arm.

They strolled beside the river, and she studied

him from the corner of her eye. Impressively fine-looking and commanding, he owned more acreage than she thought any man, any one person, could ever own. Seeing how comfortably he strode through his idyllic setting reminded her she didn't belong here. Whom did she think she could fool?

He paused to discuss some matter with a tenant farmer, and as he laughed she went over her earlier decision. She and Yolanda would stay. Yolanda needed to build herself up after the past few months, when she had gotten so sick and the entire tribe had verged on starvation. Moreover, as the day waned, she knew Luca and the elders were attending to her mother's burial.

Strengthened by her decision, she smiled at Mr. Colchester as he returned to her side. He seemed taken aback, then quickly returned the smile. Their excursion led them to the stone church. As Valentina studied the ivy-covered stonework, she wondered what her life would be like with a man like him. The deflating breath she took quickly returned her to reality.

As she turned to regard the swelling hills they'd just left, their peaks stretching to the canvas of a darkening sky, a small figure walking across one of the tenant farmer's acreage stood out.

Yolanda.

Valentina's forehead puckered with wariness. Her sister wandered alone.

Although her injured arm was still suspended in a sling, she swung her other arm freely, obviously in good spirits. Now where could she be off to?

"Do you not like what you're seeing?" Mr. Colchester asked, interrupting her thoughts. "Are you in need of my prayers now that we've arrived at the parish church? Perhaps the vicar will join us."

"The vicar is most likely inside praying for *you,* because you didn't pray long enough today. If I ever need prayer, I'll call upon Maximilian."

He quirked a dark eyebrow. "Considering the pious pope has been dead for some time, you might need a vicar, instead. I'll leave a Bible in your chamber this evening. Can you read?"

"Of course I can read. Do you think I'm illiterate? Your ideas about the Rom are sadly lacking in substance." She bit her lower lip. "Bury me standing, for I have been on my knees all my life," she said quietly.

He leaned against the wall of the church and regarded her with compassion. "'Tis a sad saying."

The gentleness in his deep voice pulled the air from her lungs. "'Tis the life of the Romany."

"I cannot ever imagine you on your knees, Valentina."

"There are hardships you cannot imagine, Mr. Colchester."

Starvation, desperation, ever-present grief as members of the tribe died, or simply left for a better life. She knew she'd told him too much, knew there was so much more she wanted to tell him.

His gaze reached hers—sobering, offering a quiet understanding.

She heard a sudden intake of breath, not knowing if the sound was his or hers.

"Call me James," he reminded her softly.

James. She mouthed the name silently, allowing the *J* to waft on her tongue. Calling him by his name felt familiar and easy.

Temptation prodded, but reality doused her with a reminder of her place in society. A Romany beggar. She blinked and turned to admire James' grand house. The reflected sunlight off the glass-paned windows blinked back at her.

≈

*R*ecalling with effort where they were and that plenty of servants and tenants were around, watching them, James stepped away from the church and offered his arm again to Valentina. High time they returned to the house.

Her words had peeled off layers of buried feelings despite his decision never to care again about any woman. His disastrous marriage had cured him of love—the endless heartache, the affection that hadn't been returned, and betrayal.

The plain bonnet Valentina wore accented her

oval face—and her bewitching eyes and enticing smile. Tears fluttered on her thick black lashes. She refused his arm, instead wrapping her wool pelisse closer around her body and walking on to the main house.

The day had begun bright and sunny. Now the air was bitter, the oak trees bowing to the insistent north wind, the sun beginning its descent.

Romany have no homeland. We are nomads.

He shivered. The icy chill of the wind went right through his bones.

CHAPTER SEVEN

Na daran, Romal, wi same sam Rom Tshatsh.
Do not fear, you Gypsy men, for we are Gypsies too.
Old Romany saying

*S*everal days after her outing with James,
Valentina retreated to her chamber for the
afternoon. As she gazed about the room, it never
ceased to amaze her, the riches James was accustomed to: the exquisite silk wall coverings and
drapes, the elegant mahogany furniture, the sophisticated books and expensive artwork. She wandered
to her bedside table and picked up the Bible he'd left
for her. She'd begun reading the Psalms each day,
which James had recommended.

"'Tis a collection of poems from the Old Testament," he'd explained. "Some call Psalms expressions of the heart."

She particularly loved Psalm 8:1: "O Lord, our God, how excellent is thy name in all the earth! who has set thy glory above the heavens."

The previous afternoon, when she'd strolled with James in the rose garden, she'd discussed that particular psalm with him.

The brilliant blue sky had been spotted by puffy white clouds, and they'd walked to the gazebo nearby, sitting across from each other on wrought iron chairs, sharing a pot of tea. Though the cool breeze of late October carried the lingering scent of roses, Valentina had been glad for her short, fitted jacket.

A quarter of an hour went by swiftly while they'd exchanged contemplations about the Bible. James had enlightened her about several facts, explaining the sacred book had been written over a fifteen-hundred-year span by many authors. Pausing, he'd asked her what she thought was the main theme of the Bible.

"God? Salvation? Heaven?" Thoughtfully, she stirred her tea. "What do you believe?"

He gave her a meaningful look. "I believe the theme is hope and salvation, and the promise of the Kingdom of God."

"Sometimes I feel as though the words in the

Bible were written directly for me, acknowledging the troubles I face," she said. "Although, how would God know the hardships of the Romany, or understand the terrible things we do in order to survive?"

James took her hands in his, nodding with his usual astuteness. "If your mind is troubled, the Psalms will give you comfort, as well as practical advice. God assures us we were created to live forever with Him. Every day is a struggle. Just try to live in the peace God promised."

She sighed and scuffed at a stone with her lace-up boot. "My reality hasn't been peaceful, and I've never thought of myself as a good, righteous person. I've been pushed into a difficult life—pressured to do things I knew were wrong."

"Perhaps because of the way you've lived, your expectations are unrealistic. Be kind to yourself. You're a brave woman. As well as kind and compassionate and honorable."

She averted her gaze, her mind replaying the pickpocketing, the robbing, the begging, the busking. She certainly didn't feel honorable.

He gazed down at her, and then he kissed her, long and tenderly. So, this was what it felt like, she thought, to be kissed with such affection by a kind and gentle man. With him, she felt respected and protected.

When he lifted his head, he murmured, "While you were being pushed into dishonor, God was pulling you in another, more honorable direction. His sacred hand has always been on your shoulder, guiding every aspect of your life."

Remembering that conversation—and the kiss— Valentina stood by the window in her bedchamber clutching her Bible and admiring the now-familiar view of James' estate—the sprawling, flowering vines glancing around a stone wall, the sun-dappled gazebo where they had enjoyed that afternoon tea, and thatched cottages outlining the fields.

The late October day was glorious—which was how she thought of the hours spent with James every day. Their time together had an otherworldly quality, tarnished only by the frequent reminder that one day soon, she'd be leaving and returning to her life as a Rom.

She stretched out her hand to trace the cool glass of the window.

Where was the elusive peace God promised? She'd never experienced it. Conflicts and reprimands dwelled within her heart, disturbing any serenity she sought. To add to her disagreeable opinions of herself was one plaguing thought—she'd omitted telling James everything she'd seen when reading his palm. Aye, she'd once regarded reading palms as a game, yet he had had the right to hear the truth.

A light rap on her door brought her thoughts back to the present. Reluctantly, she placed the Bible on her night table and hurried to the door.

"I need your help." Clare's smile was angelic as she stepped inside Valentina's chamber. "My aunt Dionise is in a bad humor. She complains her bones ache in the cold weather, and I'm concerned."

After a few moments of deliberation, Valentina replied, "I use all types of plants for treatment, mostly found in the forest. The Romany call your aunt's condition *prikasza*." She pulled on a woolen cloak. "Illness isn't natural, and 'tis the reason why your aunt is irritable."

"I've lived on Mr. Colchester's estate since I was a child and know the grounds like the hairs on my legs," Clare said. "I've finished my chores for now, so I'll help you find whatever plant you need."

For more than an hour, the women scoured the woods adjoining the main house and gathered rotting chestnut leaves. Back in the kitchen before the preparations began for the evening meal, Valentina boiled her tonic in a heavy kettle on the wood stove, which Clare had taught her how to use. She closed her eyes to visualize the recovery and speed the healing. She ladled some of the tonic into a bottle for Clare and handed it to her. "Your aunt must drink this tonight."

As she spoke, Roland lumbered into the hallway. He paused at the kitchen doorway and sniffed. "What am I smelling?"

"Boiled chestnut leaves," Clare teased. "'Tis one of Valentina's Gypsy remedies."

"I wouldn't tolerate a Gypsy woman's tainted brew." His enormous hand grabbed Clare's wrist. "Besides, I want to be fit for tonight. Meet me at my cottage."

Clare lightly swatted his hand. "You're hurting me."

He shrugged. "Sometimes I don't realize my strength."

Valentina kept her voice matter-of-fact. "Most men never do."

He grabbed an apple out of the fruit bowl on the table and bit into its green flesh. "Men are free to take whatever pleases us." Gathering a handful of apples, he deliberately dropped several, sending Clare on a scurry through the kitchen to retrieve them.

Valentina bent to recover an apple that rolled under the table. When she lifted her head, she gaped. Hatred had found a comfortable place on Roland's unsmiling face.

"I've worked for Mr. Colchester's family my entire life," he said. "And if there's one type of woman he loathes, 'tis a deceitful one. You don't git any further than Wednesday if you think I don't see your intentions. You want to steal everything he owns. When he realizes this, you'll no longer be welcome."

A swell of sadness sent a rush of heat to Valentina's face. The combination of Roland's bad breath and apple made her eyes smart. "Mr. Colchester stated that

Yolanda and I are welcome here." Her voice stayed steady as the sweep of Clare's skirt came into view.

Roland dazzled Clare with a smile. "I'll find you later."

Clare fixed a shiny-eyed gaze at his hulking back as he left the kitchen. Her hands gripped the bowl of apples before she set it on the table. "I wish he'd take more notice of me."

Valentina pinched herself to keep from shaking sense into Clare. "He's noticed you."

Because he apparently lusted after every female within one hundred miles.

Clare massaged her wrist. "At present, he's besotted with Lowdie, the new servant from Wales."

Valentina studied Clare curiously, since Clare did care for the brute. What kind of woman wanted a callous man?

"Can you help me with your Gypsy magic?" Clare asked. "I want to win him back before I lose him completely."

The delightful idea of bringing Roland to heel prompted Valentina's smile. "I know the perfect charm and 'twill bewitch him."

The spell might force Roland to care about Clare and not hurt her, soundly worth the effort. Valentina squeezed Clare's hand, concerned for the young servant who expected so little of herself.

"Do you know where he sleeps?" Valentina asked.

Clare blushed and nodded. "He's Mr. Colchester's gamekeeper, and he sleeps in the gamekeeper's cottage."

"When he's asleep, snip a lock of his hair. Carry the lock at all times, and you alone shall hold his heart."

"He thinks I'm another stone on the wall. I want him to love me."

"After this spell, he'll be entranced with you. 'Tis a Romany hair charm and extremely effective."

Clare smiled, and Valentina lowered her gaze to mask her own mischievous grin. Definitely, the charm reaped benefits for all.

∼

*A*t the end of the evening, Valentina sank onto her bed. The household had quieted at last. She picked up the Bible and pondered Psalm, 31, which was quickly becoming her favorite psalm. She read aloud verse 24: "Be of good courage and He shall strengthen your heart, all ye that hope for the Lord."

Could this passage give her the hope she'd been searching for? Should she take responsibility for her future, look within herself and to the God James spoke about?

She prayed quietly, and in the space of a few minutes, she felt calmer. She put her hands behind her head and fell asleep.

Hours later, a low growl prodded her awake.

"Valentina?"

She rubbed the blurriness from her eyes and peered into the night shadows. The figure of a man hovered above her, and she could clearly see the out-line of a strong nose and high forehead, and the glint of one gold earring in his ear. Even in the dark, his fiery dark eyes glittered.

Valentina threw off her blankets. "Luca? How did you find me?" He leaned down, and she gave him a welcoming hug. Smoky scents of firewood and raw brandy greeted her, so recognizable she sobbed out loud.

"I've watched the estate for days," he said.

"I'm so thankful you're well. Daj is buried?"

"Aye. Your mother's funeral was honorable. You and your sister would have been proud."

She choked back tears she knew he'd loathe. Still, one slipped down her cheek and she wiped her face against the coarse wool of his cloak. "At first, I feared you were hurt when we were taken."

He gripped her hands and settled them on her lap, then stood and shook back his silky black hair. "My head ached for two days, but I'm fine now." Grabbing a candle from her bedside table, he strode to the fireplace and used the ashes flickering in the grate to light the candle.

"How did you get past all the servants?"

"I scaled the wall." He placed the candle on the mantel. "Get your wrap. We're leaving." His eyes shone with a wild, bright fire. The candlelight revealed the harsh creases near his mouth and the line of his unyielding jaw.

Fully alert, she sat upright. "You want me to leave with you? Now?"

"Aye. The caravan is preparing to depart. We'll travel south where it's warmer."

"I can't go anywhere without Yolanda."

He nodded. "We can return for her come the morrow and then catch up to the caravan." He pulled her from the bed and guided her to the open window. She shivered in the cold as he pulled a thick coil of rope from his cloak.

Valentina reeled. "Nay. Absolutely not."

Luca gripped her forearms and searched her face. "When have you ever been afraid? Trust me."

She drew a breath. "There are safer ways to leave than flinging ourselves out the window. All I have to do is tell James—"

"James?" Luca dropped his hand and paced. Small steps. Incessant. Irritated. After a few moments, his cool smile returned, a brilliant camouflage he employed whenever he grew annoyed. "Come."

Accustomed to his thinly disguised commands, she nodded reluctantly. He'd never directed his anger at her. Nonetheless, she'd seen the result of his wrath when someone opposed him. He'd brutally beaten many an opponent.

He looped the rope around her waist. "Kick your legs when you swing too close to the wall and hang onto the rope as I lower you."

She picked up her wrap, set it back down. "This isn't a childhood prank we can laugh about afterward. Be sensible for once."

"I'm the leader of our tribe. 'Tis your duty to obey my decisions or the spirits will be enraged."

"Or *you* will be enraged."

His face reddened. His shoulder muscles tightened.

She inhaled a jagged breath. Deliberately, she stared at his forearms, tough and lean beneath his ragged shirt. "You go. Yolanda's arm was injured and she's still recuperating. We'll catch up with you as soon as she's able to travel."

The smile he offered was cheerless, and without speaking he wound the rope around the oak bedpost and secured a knot.

She trembled as she stood beside him, following his fingers as he fixed the knots securely. She had learned to rely on him, although a disturbing tempo, beating disaster, drummed along her spine.

Thinking at first she'd imagined the indistinct shrieks from the hallway, Valentina swung around as her chamber door swung open.

Wiborow blasted in like an enraged hobgoblin. "I knew I heard a man's voice." She gaped at Luca. "Who—"

Valentina quickly stepped in front of Luca. "He's a friend."

Her hair disheveled and nightclothes askew, the housekeeper's eyes rounded to twin full moons. She spun and bolted from the chamber, her piercing scream sounding an alarm. "Gypsy bandits. They're attacking! Come to Valentina's chamber quickly!"

Luca grabbed the rope. "We must try now."

"Nay." Valentina gripped his arms. "Listen to me. I'm not going."

She felt, rather than saw, his wave of impatience. All his reactions poured from his skin—a fierce, primitive emanation of power in a sleek, panther-like body. She wanted to protest, although her mouth was too dry.

Footsteps pounded down the corridor.

"Valentina, what are you doing?" James' voice ripped through her chamber.

She whirled. "How dare you charge in here?"

"In my own house?" He untied the rope from the bedpost and flung it to the floor, then stared past her at Luca.

This couldn't be happening. Luca was here, in her chamber, and it looked like she was leaving with him. James would never forgive her.

James' fists closed at his sides. "Were you *both* trying to get yourselves killed?"

Luca pushed up the sleeves of his shirt. "I don't take orders from a worthless gadje."

Valentina's body grew clammy with sweat, her gown sticking to her legs.

James' gaze was riveted on Luca and a sharp dawning of understanding lit his eyes. "You must be Valentina's Gypsy suitor." He motioned to a white-faced Wiborow and a scowling Roland to stay in the doorway.

Luca's nostrils flared. "Why are you keeping my Romany women?"

"*Your* women?"

Valentina drew in a ragged breath. "Mr. Colchester, please, don't."

James didn't turn. His muscles hardened beneath his rumpled shirt.

"Don't defend me." Luca directed a hard stare at her before glaring at James. "I can take care of myself."

"Luca, you need to go. You're outnumbered." Valentina moved closer to the two men. They glowered at each other with controlled, frightening rage. Her chest tightened in dread.

"Fight me, Mr. Fancy Gentleman." Luca enhanced his threat with a short, cynical laugh.

Valentina could predict Luca's actions as surely as she had five fingers on each hand. He wouldn't fight if he thought he couldn't win. He'd taunt, assess, and bide his time until he had the advantage. Nevertheless, he'd never win against James, because the tenant farmers and servants were everywhere, and Luca wasn't invincible.

She spoke through a throat that refused to allow a full breath. "Mr. Colchester, I'll never forgive you if you hurt my friend." The air closed, the defeat heavy. "Please ... James."

Invisible tension rippled the muscles in James' back. He never moved, never turned.

"How often, Valentina, have you asked me for a favor using my given name?"

She jammed her fists against her thighs. "I'm asking now."

James raised his arms and stepped back, the abrupt crack of the floorboard jarring the silence. "Roland, haul our vagrant clear of the grounds."

"Mr. Colchester—"

"Do as I ask, Roland." James' voice lowered to a murmur as he turned toward Valentina. "And tell this man not to come here again."

"Luca." She drew a long, quavering breath. "Go quietly. Yolanda and I are all right."

Skewered by the men's glares, she gave a disparaging laugh. In her heart she knew she served one role. She was a possession to both these controlling males. Nothing more.

Roland stepped forward and jerked Luca's arms

behind him. "Your Gypsy face isn't wanted here. Don't you remember that lesson from last time?"

Luca nodded reassurance to Valentina as he strode from her chamber. "I'll alert the others. We're traveling to the coast, near Brighton." His gaze was cold, his voice ominously soft.

She didn't reply. There were no "others" to alert. Their tribesmen were elderly, frail, and powerless.

After the door shut behind Luca, James twisted to face her. Anger flickered in the depths of his grey eyes. "I thought you and your sister were happy here."

"We are. I had no idea Luca would show up in my bedchamber." She scowled at him with what she hoped was a perfect balance of fury and defiance. "If you're waiting for me to apologize, you'll be waiting until the spirits sprout wings."

"If you attempt another foolhardy idea that might get you killed, you'll wish *you* had wings." He strode three paces forward. "I was alarmed. I reacted too quickly."

"You mean overreacted."

"All I could picture was the rope around your waist, and you attempting to climb down from the window." He whispered a word he'd used before—cariad—although she didn't understand what it meant.

"I'm not that foolhardy anymore."

"If you fell ..." He rubbed his thumb across her

lips, not making the slightest attempt to veil the flame in his eyes. He kissed her eyes and nose before finding her mouth, slowing and deepening his kisses.

Her rigid muscles relaxed. She couldn't pull away. She *had* to pull away.

Shamelessly her body didn't listen and ignited. His tongue outlined the corners and creases of her lips before moving slowly into her mouth. A sweet, searing, mindlessness flooded her veins as her tongue responded to his plunging and probing. When he lifted his head, she gasped, weak and confused, surprised to feel his heart thrashing as wildly as hers.

After he'd left her chamber a few minutes afterward and she'd found her balance again, she stared at the door. She could still feel his tender embraces, and the taste of his hard, firm lips moving against hers.

CHAPTER EIGHT

Feri ando payi sitsholpe te nayuas.
It was in the water that one learned to swim.
Romany saying

*V*alentina relived the scene with Luca countless times, denying her rush of relief when his reckless plan had been thwarted. Why had she questioned him? He was a part of her tribe, her past, her heritage.

With each passing day, she couldn't shake the awareness that she and Yolanda were growing more and more content. However, was it so wrong to enjoy a soft, cushioned bed and well-cooked food? And aye, she'd begun to look forward to her daily outings with a tall grey-eyed gentleman who warmed her entire body with his slow, devastating smile and recklessly good looks.

Every morning, she sought Yolanda's company for support and comfort. Yolanda was as loyal to Valentina as nobles had been to King Henry.

Two days after Luca had visited Valentina's bedchamber, she and Yolanda sat in the middle of Yolanda's bed, underneath a bright lavender canopy. The bed was piled high with plump apple-green pillows. Although not as grand as Valentina's chamber, Yolanda's chamber boasted well-appointed cherry furnishings and a stone fireplace.

Valentina rested against several of the pillows. "We'll leave when you're completely healed, Yolanda. Perhaps before Christmas."

Yolanda stared out the window before flicking an unfocused look in Valentina's direction. "Luca gave Daj an honorable burial. There's no urgency to leave anymore."

As hard as Valentina blinked, she realized her complaisant sister had uttered the last words she'd ever expected. "How else will we ever see our tribe again?"

"You go if you miss them so much." Dressed only in her linen chemise, Yolanda rose to stand near the window. As she pushed the bottom pane open a crack, a whiff of crisp autumn air cooled the chamber. "I want to stay as long as Mr. Colchester will have us."

Valentina fumbled between bewilderment and resentment. "Have you forgotten? Under the pretense of all this finery we are Romany beggars."

Yolanda twirled the ends of her wavy brown hair. "I like being taken care of. I like eating white bread instead of brown. I'm tired of freezing and going hungry and endlessly wandering."

"Since when?"

A smile broke over Yolanda's face. "Since I began seeing a wonderful man."

Valentina snatched a pillow and playfully tossed it at her sister. "You've always stated there was no one suitable for you in all of England."

"Several fine-looking, gracious men live on this estate."

"And who is this one particular fine-looking, gracious man?"

"His name is Reginald. He's one of Mr. Colchester's blacksmiths."

"I know who he is." Valentina chewed her bottom lip until it burned. "He's a large brute of a man who ought to keep his affections to himself. There's no sense in becoming attached to someone you'll soon be bidding farewell."

"Reginald is very interested in our customs. He asks all sorts of questions."

"He uses our customs as an excuse to get close to

you." Valentina tucked her legs beneath her and tapped her fingers together. "Remember, he's a gadje."

Yolanda couldn't have looked more defiant than if she were playing the role of a two-year-old child who wouldn't eat her supper. "You're not my mother or my father, and you cannot force me to agree with you."

Yolanda was a follower. What had happened to her sister? The answer came from every corner of the chamber—where they sat, where they ate, where they slept. They'd lived in James' beautiful home and grown accustomed to finery they hadn't even imagined.

"Seeing Reginald isn't a good idea. 'Tis my responsibility to steer you away from people who will cause you heartbreak."

"Reginald makes me happy."

A short-lived happiness if influenza ever threatened James' household.

Valentina scraped back her hair. Now where had that thought come from, and with it, the churn of anxiety in her stomach?

Abruptly, she stood and padded to the window. "There's something I must tell you," she whispered in a strained voice.

Yolanda's doe-like eyes took on more fear than they could hold. "You haven't used that serious of a tone since Father died. What is it?"

Valentina exhaled a lungful of agitation and eyed Yolanda's soft white chemise, the fine pin tucks accenting her sister's tiny waist, dark hair pulled back in a ponytail and caught in an embellished velvet bow. Her delicate sister deserved happiness, not anguish. Besides, Valentina no longer believed in Rom spirits, superstitions, and fortune-telling.

"'Tis nothing." She blew out a breath and gave Yolanda's slim hands an encouraging squeeze. "Reginald must be very important to you."

"Aye. He is." The cheery fire in the fireplace made Yolanda's complexion glow radiantly.

As the days passed and November neared, Valentina monitored Yolanda closely.

What would she do if anything happened to her sister? She was so young, so inexperienced. Valentina feared her sister wouldn't be able to stop Reginald, such a burly man, if his passion became too ... passionate.

Whenever Reginald and Yolanda were together, Valentina waited for a sign that her sister needed protection. She'd be there. She'd be ready to aid Yolanda in any way she could.

But Yolanda's smiles came more easily. Her steps were lighthearted, her laughter downright exuberant. And the sign never came.

CHAPTER NINE

Bi kashtesko merel i yag.
Without wood the fire would die.
Old Romany saying

On a soggy day in early November, Valentina spent the afternoon tilling soil in the herb garden. Several of the herbs had died as winter approached, although the whiff of a forgotten mustard seed carried on the light breeze.

"I'd wondered where you'd wandered today," a resonant, familiar voice teased.

She dropped the shovel and sent overgrown weeds tumbling.

"Spying on me, as usual?" He sat astride his

horse, and her gaze wandered admiringly up the polished black boots covering his well-muscled legs. His thick wool waistcoat scarcely concealed the hardness of his body, nor the male strength brewing just beneath his polished exterior. Although she'd given herself innumerable lectures not to be affected by him, her disloyal heart sang each day as they walked the grounds of his estate or enjoyed afternoon tea or supper with Yolanda. She knew the servants and tenants objected to her being with him, knew that society expected her and James to be chaperoned, although everyone kept their displeasure to themselves.

"I'm attending to some unpleasant tasks today," he said. "I've feuded with my neighbor, Mr. Wellsey, for years. I'm hoping to put an end to our disagreement once and for all."

"In the garden?" she goaded, hoping for a rise. He'd purposely sought her. The thought tickled her with an unexpected smile.

"I'll be riding over to his estate."

She tightened the yellow diklo around her throat. "Will you return by this evening?"

"Aye." His eyes darkened. "Will you miss me?"

"Perhaps."

Their laughs came as one. He looked disgracefully handsome sitting atop his horse, the superb animal pawed fitfully at the ground. The white markings on its smoky-black coat were well defined, and the one on its head resembled a star. Similar to the star she'd seen on James' hand when she'd read his palm.

Her chin quivered.

"Anything wrong?" He leaned down and nudged a stray wisp of hair from her face. The light touch of his hand curved to her cheekbone.

Her breath caught. "Nay."

He laughed, the hearty, good-natured laugh now so familiar to her. "Surely you'd never lie to me?" He dismounted and coiled the horse's reins around an oak tree, then strode to her. He lowered his head, his lips stopping an inch of hers. "Don't run off with your Gypsy suitor while I'm gone."

She saw the craving in his eyes. Now she couldn't breathe at all. "I have no Romany suitor, nor any suitor."

"You have no suitor *yet*."

"I want no suitor *ever*."

"A distressing thought for any male within fifty paces of you." He swept weightless strokes up her back, a subtle gesture of possessiveness that opened a door to emotions that she intended to keep closed.

Before her mind became a blank, she asked, "Do you know what I wish for?"

"A suitor? Shall I list the reasons why I am best?"

"Absolutely not."

"I insist." His mouth inched closer. "We can begin with your assessment of my kissing."

Inwardly, a gala of feelings erupted. Her mind screamed caution, her mouth screamed hunger.

"'Tis the first step in your assessment," he continued. "Say *very well* and kiss me back. Fortunately, 'tis a skill which takes considerable practice."

Enticingly forbidden, she gloried in the pleasure of his firm mouth on hers, and her arms wrapped around his nape. He cuddled her, the insistent pump of his heart solid and reassuring, his fingers stroking teasing pathways along the inside of her arms. "Shall we continue with another rehearsal or a full recital?" he murmured.

In a haze, she almost nodded before her foggy brain skidded to a halt and reason reared. "You're outrageous," she said shakily.

"I'm simply drawn."

"To herbs?"

His knuckles brushed her cheekbones. "To one particular Gypsy woman who's beautiful and intoxicating."

Keep him at a distance. She resisted the tremor that shook her resolution and groped for a subject to break the attraction spinning between them. One issue James never wanted to discuss was his son's deafness.

She fell back a step. "May I tell you a story?"

A look of forced patience spanned his face. "Now?"

"Aye." She hesitated and bit her bottom lip.

"Many years ago, a little deaf girl lived in a neighboring tribe."

"Really?" he drawled. "And?"

"We treated her the same as all the other children, although we always made sure she was looking at us when we spoke." The moment of quiet affection they'd shared dissolved, and she rushed her words. "However, when the girl grew into her teens, we all noticed there were many random things she hadn't understood, things we took for granted along the way."

"Communication takes constant effort." James offered a cool nod. "Elspeth, Jeremy's nurse, spends half her time trying to get his attention."

"Other than deafness, all children are the same. The only difference is language."

Warily, he contemplated her. "I give Jeremy the same love as I gave Beatrix.

"Aye, because you're his father." Valentina laid a hand on his sleeve. "May I make a suggestion?"

She felt his arm tighten, although he shrugged uninterestedly. "Of course."

"Allow Jeremy more freedom. Presently, his puppy is his only companion. He's a little boy who wants to play with other children."

"He's deaf. He's not like other children." James' features became unreadable. "I appreciate your suggestion. However, as you've said, I'm his father. I know what's best for him."

She let out an exasperated huff. "You don't always know what's best."

From the corner of her eye, she noticed Yolanda cross the lawn and head toward the river. Yolanda shaded her eyes as she looked in their direction, and then shied away.

James gestured toward Yolanda. "You might consider thanking me like your sister does instead of passing on your opinions concerning my son."

"How can I thank you when you're a gadje?" Valentina's face heated, her breath sputtered. "Luca and I were starving when we left camp to find a physician for her. No one cared."

Wearily, James sighed. "You insist on punishing me for your difficult past instead of focusing on the present. Is there no place in your heart for gratitude?" He turned abruptly and strode toward his horse.

She waited. He might turn one last time. He always did, usually accompanied by a teasing smile.

Instead, he uncoiled the reins and mounted the stallion. Without a word, he jabbed his heels into the horse's flanks and broke away.

Disappointment deflated her chest as her anger subsided. He hadn't exhibited any joy when she'd voluntarily touched his sleeve, hadn't supported her suggestion by lightly squeezing her fingers.

In utter exasperation, she swung toward the

main house, believing she imagined Yolanda's cries for help.

Nay, it couldn't be.

There. Again. The echo of a muted scream, coming from the river.

Valentina stopped. The air was motionless.

Another cry. Yolanda.

She clutched her gown and ran toward the river, tripping over the broad roots of an oak tree, passing by an old stone wall. She gulped back a horrified scream as she reached the bank. Yolanda was flailing, up to her neck in water.

Not daring to look away, Valentina snapped off a brittle tree branch and darted toward the water. She stretched the branch as far over the water as she dared without plunging in.

"Yolanda, reach for this!"

Yolanda struggled to grab the branch. Her head tilted back, her nose hardly visible above the water. Then she disappeared beneath the current as she was swept downstream.

Fright swept Valentina's whole being. Yolanda couldn't swim and neither could Valentina.

Terror had to be swallowed.

She lifted the hem of her gown and rushed into the river. Icy water blackened her world. The swift undercurrent whipped her heavy gown around her ankles.

"Valentina!" James's shouts penetrated the weighty depths.

Desperately, she kicked and broke through the water's surface.

James. Their gazes met. He stood on the river-bank, pulling off his coat, preparing to jump in the river. The cold water sprayed and splattered. Crests of water, smelling of fish, roiled to her chin.

A moment later, his strong arms were around her. He lifted her from the river and onto the muddy bank.

For several seconds, her voice wouldn't emit a sound. Sobs blocked coherency. "Yolanda ... drowning ... Must save—"

"Yolanda? In the water?" His tone held firm. "Stay here."

Nodding her head up and down like a marionette yanked by an invisible string, Valentina pinched her lips together to stop her teeth from chattering. Her soaked gown clung to every crevice of her body, sending an army of bone-chilling shivers down her spine.

James dove beneath the surface, up for air, then back underneath. Swallowing a sob, Valentina clung to a single hope. James would never let Yolanda drown.

Still sitting on the ground, she stared at the sun-light glinting off the water's surface. The water stirred. Quieted. No churn. No ripple.

Her chest heaving as she tried to draw air into her lungs, she wiped her cracked lips with her sleeve, hunching with her nose to the ground. A lone green sprig grew near her feet. She snapped it by the root and sniffed a tinge of spicy basil. Unspoiled and alive, the smell of hope. Basil was the most dependable of herbs, flavorful and sweet, her mother had said.

Still holding the herb, she came to her feet. She studied each swell of water, assessing the golden-brown sheen coating the surface.

"Yolanda! James!" Her mind screamed louder than her voice.

Too many seconds had passed. The water calmed, the surface a white froth of foam.

She closed her eyes, fell to her knees, and prayed. One night after the evening meal, James had read from the book of Matthew, 21:22, and she'd memorized the passage because it spoke so true: "And whatever you ask in prayer, you will receive, if you have faith."

"Please God," she whispered, "hear my prayer." She kept her eyes closed, kept whispering the same prayer. "Be my guide. I don't want to feel lost and alone anymore. Meet me here in my darkest sadness."

Opening her eyes and scanning the river, she saw James first. He swam toward the riverbank towing her sister's limp body.

Valentina doubled over to put distance between herself and her impending grief. Then she ran to them both, clutching Yolanda so tightly she knew she'd leave finger imprints on Yolanda's skin.

"Is she dead, James? Nay, please nay," she sobbed.

"Trust me." Laying Yolanda on her back, he compressed his hands on her ribcage and bore down. Water spurted from Yolanda's mouth.

Valentina sank to the ground, welcoming each gasp, each cough, each sputter, because it meant her sister would survive.

"Why would Yolanda venture so close to the river when she couldn't swim?" she murmured through relieved tears.

"I'll ask you the same question." James raised Valentina's chin and wiped her damp cheeks. Distress sparked his eyes before they narrowed. "Can *you* swim?"

Valentina sniffed. The foul smell of the river clung to the insides of her nose and throat. Coarse silt stuck to the roof of her mouth, and she had no choice but to swallow.

"Can you swim?" he asked again.

She couldn't carry the burden of almost losing her sister, so she leaned against his chest.

"If I weren't afraid of water, I would have learned how to swim."

"You cannot swim," James repeated, searching Valentina's wide emerald eyes. Sheer trepidation shone back at him. "And yet you decided to dive into a raging river to save your sister."

He examined Yolanda, relieved at the color returning to her face. Keeping her within his sight, he shifted to Valentina.

She was watching her sister as well, but her expression was distant. "I didn't think. I wanted to—"

"Save her? You cannot swim. Of all the insane acts of ..." *Courage* came to his lips.

He enveloped her in his arms, her wetness molding to his drenched shirt. With her hair smeared around her lovely face and her eyes bright with fear, she resembled a frightened fawn. Only the overpowering impulse to protect her kept him upright.

He clasped her nearer, swaying from side to side, absorbing her. "You exquisite, foolish woman."

She muttered a peculiar foreign word, followed by the force of sobs quaking against his chest. He couldn't release her. He gathered her so close she became a part of him.

He bent his face nearer her lips. "Why are you cursing me?"

"I'm not." Her voice broke. "Although I should."

He wiped the stream of tears off her cheeks. Sopping wet and trembling, she was the most divine creature he'd ever seen. He cupped her face with his hands. "Because I saved you?"

Brokenly, she cried, "Because lately you seem cross with me."

He was cross? Odd, he didn't remember. Of course, that swaggering Gypsy man appearing in her chamber a few weeks earlier hadn't helped his thinking of late.

He closed his arms around her, breathed in her achingly fiery scent, and felt her hammering heart.

She huddled her trembling body close for another few moments, accepting his warmness, but then she broke free to tend to her sister. Yolanda was shivering badly and just as frightened as Valentina. As he picked up his discarded waistcoat and laid it over the girl, he knew he would protect Valentina with his life.

He lifted his head at muffled hollering in the distance.

"Our help is rallying," he told them. "When we return to the house, Yolanda, you should be checked thoroughly. Hopefully, your fracture hasn't worsened. I'll call on the bone-setter to be certain."

She whispered her thanks as he picked her up and carried her to his horse. He settled her in the saddle and then veered back toward Valentina, helping her onto the horse as well, in front of Yolanda.

"Thank you, James." Respect illuminated Valentina's gaze. Her words were pure, filling his heart.

"'Tis not difficult to thank me. You don't have to *ask* for my help, you merely have to *scream*."

A weak smile curved her lips. She wrung out her hair with quivery fingers. "Why did you return?"

"I heard your shouts. Thank God I found you."

Briefly, she closed her eyes. "I loathe feeling helpless."

"You're safe now."

"I prayed. I hoped that God was listening, that I was in His presence. I thought that couldn't happen unless I was in church, but I felt He was here."

"You don't need to be in church to be in the presence of God."

They continued on in silence, until her delicate brows pulled together and she glanced down at him. "Now you'll be late for your meeting with Mr. Wellsey."

"Another time, perhaps." James sifted through his thoughts, trying to recall why he wanted to meet with Wellsey. Nothing of importance came to mind. Nothing was important except Valentina's safety and the safety of those he loved.

Loved.

He shook his head. The thought just came. Had it been sitting there, idly, all this time, waiting for the right moment to admit how much he cared for her?

Impossible. They'd only known each other a short time.

Love was a mindless, romantic concept that had no place in his life.

"I never learned how to swim, but I couldn't allow Yolanda to drown," Valentina was saying. "I'm sorry I placed you in so much danger."

Touched by her fearlessness in the face of danger, he raised his hand. "Please don't apologize."

His fear for both women's safety evaporated as he reflected on the past few minutes. Valentina was soaked and exhausted. Yet she'd sought the security of his embrace when she'd been most frightened.

"You are an exceptionally brave woman," he said.

Her uneven laugh floated through the fields. She flecked a dismissive wave toward herself. Twisting, she inspected every nick and bruise on Yolanda's arms before meeting his gaze. "You saved us both. Thank you, James."

He might have lost her.

A shudder rattled his gut. "You would have done the same for me."

"Who wouldn't risk their life to help someone?"

Staring ahead, he couldn't control the tremor in his voice. "Apparently not you, cariad," was all he could manage. "Apparently not you."

CHAPTER TEN

Te xav to biav?
May I eat at your wedding?
Old Romany saying

Two weeks later, after Jeremy had finished his studies with his tutor, Valentina gaped at his smiling face across the black and white checkerboard. "You trounced me again. How did you succeed in winning this time?"

After a fortnight of playing checkers with the quiet boy, Valentina welcomed his enthusiastic giggle. She came around to him, lifted his arms and twirled him round and round and round. Perfectly terraced lawns sped by in a blur. Their whirling world came to a tumbling halt when they both rolled to the ground.

"I ... am ... a ... win-ner." Jeremy laughed, his cheeks alive with color.

She pulled him upright, unable to contain her joy at hearing him speak. He chuckled at her tickles and comical gestures as she admitted defeat.

His tiny hands hugged her neck, his fingertips barely touching. "*Mam?*"

The Welsh word for mother.

With a pang and a nod, she embraced him. "I'll do my best to be your mam for the time I'm here." She stretched her legs out on the lawn, cuddling him on her lap and scanning the expansive lawn.

James and several other men had ridden off at daybreak in a flurry of horses' hooves and high spirits, intent on hunting red deer and wild fowl. The sudden swoop of a falcon signaled the men's return. In tandem, Jeremy and Valentina lifted their gazes to the graceful bird soaring and diving with the wind. Kenelm, a falconer, strode from the barn and followed the bird's flight with his gaze. The falcon flew to rest on his gloved hand.

Jeremy wiggled out of Valentina's arms to greet the bird. He raced across the lawn, his rapidly growing puppy following his lead. Valentina imagined Jeremy's twin sister, Beatrix, running across the lawn beside him. The thought made her throat knot with grief and her grin die away. James had endured so much sadness.

Yolanda, a warm shawl wrapped around her shoulders, stood in the doorway of one of the out-buildings. She spoke with an elderly woman who sat inside at a spinning wheel, spinning raw wool into cloth, holding the yarn away from the wheel on her loom to add a crink.

Valentina smiled with amused consideration. Why her sister was interested in such a tedious task as weaving, she'd never understand. But then Yolanda's interest shifted as a heavily built man tromped over to her.

Reginald. He wiped the blackened hairs on his arm with a piece of cloth from the loom. Whatever he said made her laugh, and she gave her shiny hair a shake as they glided toward the pear orchard arm in arm.

These were the times that Valentina's hope strengthened, when the day bloomed optimistic and full of promise. And, of course, there were her daily hours spent with James.

The previous day, he'd guided her to a clearing that boasted a spectacular view of his home. Carved chimneys braced either end of the daunting manor house, the splendorous pitch of the high roof soaring toward feathery white clouds. The numerous farmers working the farmland completed the halcyon picture. The English countryside was so beautiful, she'd murmured, although a rush of homesickness had evoked sadness. If only her tribe could find this sort of peace and not continually struggle to survive.

"What can God possibly do in my life?" she said to James, turning away from the view. The life she did not deserve. "He'll never forgive all my sins."

"Have you repented?"

"Aye."

"Then do your best not to sin again."

She bit her lips to stave off the grief. "I'm a Rom, and I've done terrible things in more nameless towns than I can remember."

"The future is more important than your former ways, Valentina." Lightly, James kissed her temple. "Don't judge what God's going to do in your lifetime by what happened in the past. Your life is bigger than just a nameless town. The rest of your story is still unwritten and, best of all, God knows your ending."

She nodded, experiencing a sense of peace. Spending time with James, listening to him, she'd begun to see herself in a new light—not as she used to, ashamed for doing whatever it took to feed her family. Now, she'd begun to believe God had placed her on this landed gentry's estate for a reason, and she was right where she belonged—with James, a truly good man, a man of God.

And she was beginning to feel deep affection for James. He felt it too. His attentive gaze, his judicious expression, spoke louder than words. Whenever their conversations became too pensive, he'd tease her until she responded with a quip. He'd laugh with her, his handsome features enlivened by his good humor. She wanted to deny the attraction, knew 'twas impossible for them to be together.

A thunderbolt of activity broke her thoughts as James rode his horse out of the woods at a breakneck gallop. Immediately, her pulse began to thrum. He appeared so in control of his swift, powerful horse.

He brought his horse to a halt near the rail by the stable and dismounted. The horse balked and shied clear of the falcon. "'Tis merely a bird, Albern." James stroked the horse's sweaty mane, calling his horse by name.

Jeremy ran back to Valentina. Hand in hand, she and Jeremy wandered closer to the stable.

The falcon is tame, Valentina told herself, keeping a distrustful gaze on the black falcon and its magnificent wingspan. "The Rom are fearful of owls." She caught Jeremy's attention, dropped her hand and pointed to her lips. "Falcons, hawks, and owls are all predators." Bracelets jingling, she added a flap of her hands to imitate flying.

"Pre ... da-tor?"

"A predator is—" she emulated a man on horse-back—"a hunter."

Jeremy nodded that he understood and gave her and James a quick hug before skipping away in the falconer's footsteps.

Glad the falcon was gone, Valentina turned to James, only to find him regarding her with some amusement. He must have noticed her wariness around the bird.

"The Rom are fearful of owls," she muttered.

"Now why would Gypsies be afraid of a harmless owl?" he asked.

Valentina sucked in a swift breath as he stepped closer. Beneath his hunting jacket, his white shirt was open at the collar. His weather-darkened face showed a slight shadow of a beard, and his hair was damp from the hard ride of the hunt.

The bright noonday sun enhanced the lines of amusement playing around his mouth, and his eyes glinted with a mischievous sparkle. In a desperate attempt to ignore his charismatic grin, she focused on his skittish horse. "Your horse and I share the same feelings about birds of prey. We realize these birds are untrustworthy."

James handed a stable boy his horse's reins, then caught her hand and urged her to walk with

him. "Why are you fearful of an innocent bird and little else?"

"A falcon is a predator. So are owls. To the Rom, an owl's cry is very bad luck."

"Really?" Leisurely, he picked a dry leaf off her hair. His long fingers backcombed several strands, beginning at her scalp and ending with each loose wave tumbling down her back.

Her cheeks heated, her heart skipped, her arms riddled with pinpricks. "Surely there isn't a whole tree in my hair?"

His smile broadened. "An owl is a useful bird."

"The owl's hoot is a foreboding omen, an inevitable sign of trouble and sadness. Their cute, heart-shaped faces are a trick to fool the person who doesn't know any better."

"Aye, looks can be deceptive."

"If you believe an owl is harmless, you're shockingly blind."

"I assure you, I'm not blind." His gaze roamed over her face. "Shall I tell you about the woman standing before me?"

A delicious shiver coursed in her belly.

"I see a mysterious woman—"

"As usual, Mr. Colchester, you're not listening." *Move,* she commanded her rooted-to-the-ground feet.

"James, remember?" He slid his hands up her arms, his roughened fingers prickling her sensitive skin even through the sleeves of her coat.

She rolled her tight shoulders and pretended not to be affected by his burning, weightless strokes.

"Have you chosen to forget where we are—in full view of your son and falconer and grooms?" She cast a pointed gaze in Jeremy's direction. Beside the barn, the boy huddled in concentration near the falcon and Kenelm.

James raised his hands in an innocent gesture before placing them back on her shoulders. "My son isn't interested in us. A bird is indeed more fascinating."

"I can assure you that everyone who works for you is very interested."

"They're too busy to be concerned with me."

In fact, several servants had paused in midtask to watch them. Not stopping to explain, Valentina twisted away from him and dashed toward the stables.

James caught up with her as she entered an empty stall. With a kick, he closed the heavy door behind them. She waited, her back to him, keeping her gaze on thick bales of fragrant hay alongside the walls.

His arms circled her waist, his breath rousing her neck to gooseflesh. Her face brushed against his wide shoulder as she turned. Dreamy intimacy was all she knew, coupled with the heady awareness he wanted to kiss her.

"I thought of you today." The quiet tenderness in his tone stopped her breathing for a moment.

"You thought about me while you were hunting?"

His grey eyes changed to the color of raindrops on a drizzly day. "Aye. Whenever we're apart, I think about you."

When he spoke in silvery, discreet tones, Valentina forgot where she was, who she was. And when he added his languid, reassuring smile, her reasons to stay away from him dissolved. She examined the natural strength in his face, the set of his stubborn chin, and the temperamental freckle above his lips.

He brushed his mouth over hers, coaxing her lips to part. She closed her eyes and savored the sensation. The erratic beating of his heart coupled with her own.

She stirred.

His arms wrapped protectively around her and rested his jaw on her temple. "Don't move," he murmured. "I like having you near me."

The sharp scent of leather and horses filled her nostrils. Streams of sunlight shone through a crack in the stable's outer wall, exposing floating dust laced with straw.

In an impulsive gesture, Valentina smoothed his hair in place, sliding the glossy texture between her fingers. She wiped the sweat off his moist forehead, his dark brows. She rubbed the back of his neck where the hair was crisp, full. and black.

It would be so easy to fall in love with him.

~

*J*ames knew every last person on his estate was by now aware that he and Valentina were alone in the stable, but he didn't care. She fit so nicely along his body that he loathed moving, delighted she was letting him hold her for so long. "I don't see nearly enough of you," he said. "You're either weeding your herb garden, making who knows what kind of healing tonic in the kitchen, or caring for my son."

With his finger, he outlined the fullness of her lower lip.

Before Yolanda's near drowning, Valentina had been the delightful core of his shameless imagination. Lately, she brought out an affection in him he didn't recognize and couldn't analyze. His exquisite, willful Gypsy woman.

The past few mornings, he'd pondered and prayed, and he'd reached a decision. He'd grown tired of living alone and of rearing his son without a mother. A good, caring, selfless mother. Valentina displayed every one of these traits.

He'd made up his mind days ago. Nay. He'd made up his mind weeks ago, before the scare at the river.

He'd continuously encouraged Valentina to remain with him on his estate, unable to understand his consuming interest in her, his need to protect her. Certainly, her sister's injury had restricted her travel. However, the women could have returned to their caravan at any point. And they hadn't.

His fingers traveled up her temples. "You're attentive to Jeremy's needs—much more so than my late wife."

"I've heard that Alyce was beautiful."

"Her interests centered only on herself. Not her daughter. Not her son." James searched Valentina's flushed face and attempted to read her thoughts. Perhaps if she had her own family to love and nurture ...

He smiled. Certainly, his days would never be dull. Nor his nights.

He examined the small marking behind her ear. "Have you always had this birthmark? 'Tis in the shape of a horseshoe."

She forced away his hand. "I cover the birthmark with my hair. My mother said a horse kicked my father when she was pregnant with me and it left this mark. 'Tis disagreeable."

"There's nothing disagreeable about a spot that resembles a horseshoe."

Her grin was immense. Her light laughter took him back to happier days. She'd lived a humble life and bore her suffering with grace.

"Romany women believe in the stigmata," she said. The smile fled from her face. "However, the Rom asserted that the mark proved I was a *shuvani,* one of the wise ones."

His mind calculated his options. They could continue to live in England, as discreetly as he could manage. When the threat of influenza subsided, they'd move to his remote estate in Wales.

He used the birthmark as an excuse to kiss her there. "Does this 'stigmata' mean you're a witch?"

"'Tis said all Romany women are witches, which gives us the freedom to mold ourselves into any setting. A mocking gift to the Rom, to fit in everywhere and be wanted nowhere."

"You can be anything?"

"I can *be* anything." Her gaze sparked caution. "Not *do* anything."

His heart surged at the delightful idea of spending the rest of his life with her.

He raised her hands to his lips and kissed the inside of each palm. "Valentina, will you be my wife?"

～

*V*alentina jerked back. The hay on the stable floor spun. She bent her head to conceal her confusion. No man had ever asked her to marry him, certainly not a gadje. She couldn't believe she'd heard him correctly, for the question had no home in her consciousness. James had no reason to want her—perhaps only as a servant. Yet he was offering her his name.

How could she ever dream of staying with this man when her sins against God ran as bottomless as the river? She wasn't enough, with all her failures, her scarcity of purpose other than survival.

James had often advised her to rely on God's grace and forgiveness.

Wasn't God's grace enough?

Aye, it should be. She could accept James' offer and abandon the idea of returning to her tribe.

Inwardly she shook her head. *Nay. She wasn't worthy of a man like him—landed gentry, a virtuous, respectable man.*

She gazed at the rough-hewn wall behind him. Her blurred vision changed the wooden boards to a sheet of washed-out brown.

James was watching her. "Surely you, of all people, can't be tongue-tied."

She averted her gaze. She didn't fear telling him about the rape. She feared his reaction. His admiration and respect for her would be gone. His eyes wouldn't glitter with amusement when they sparred.

And then, there was the half-truth she'd told him when reading his palm.

She swallowed a worn-out gulp. "First, I must speak to you about something."

Why had she assumed, with complete and utter

foolishness, that she wouldn't have to explain her recklessness? Now she'd pay for it tenfold by losing his trust.

His hands held hers, gentle yet firm, heating her fingers. "You'll enjoy everything my wealth can provide, although we'll need to be discreet and cannot wed until we reach Wales."

She contemplated the conviction in his clear grey eyes.

Tell him. Her lungs weighed heavy, her breath came rocky. Heavy guilt at deceiving him berated her.

His lips touched hers. "I haven't asked you to witness my execution. I've asked you to marry me."

"A Gypsy wed to a Welsh gentleman," she hedged. "'Tis unthinkable."

He grinned. "Eventually, your tribe will come to accept me."

He'd sidestepped any declaration of love. Men in his position weren't concerned by such an impractical notion, although a small part of her had hoped he truly cared.

"And my son adores you." His hands slid up her arms and caught her shoulders. He was all male. His skin smelled of horse and sweat, and his lips were so enticing. As if hypnotized, she locked her fingers around his nape and gave in to the attraction.

He seemed to sense the moment she surrendered. With an effort that seemed to drain the power from his body, he stopped the kiss and leaned against the stable wall. His uneven breath told her that he, too, struggled for control.

"Your people will never respect me as your wife," she said.

He arched a brow and waited a beat. "We'll travel to Wales when the weather warms."

"I'm a Rom. I belong with my tribe and cannot leave England."

"Not anymore. Now you belong at my side."

At his side. As his wife.

She swallowed hard and locked her gaze on a chipmunk crawling through the dry straw at her feet. If she stared into James' eyes she would say aye, aye, aye, and press her face against his heart, pleading forgiveness for deceiving him with a half-truth.

Although she wouldn't do that, because she was a coward. She'd always been a coward.

She drew a heavy sigh. "I must return to my caravan where I'm best suited. My people are nomads and I'm one of them."

"You'll have a new life with me." For a second, susceptibility rang through his tone before the expression on his face veiled any further emotion.

A tremor quivered her lips where his fingers still rested. Ironically, she gripped his upper arms to stay afloat, the man who made her feel adrift in the middle of a murky river.

"You don't need to give me your answer yet," he said softly, despite the resolute, unreadable glint in his eyes.

Perhaps, just perhaps, she shouldn't start with herself when she gave a response. Perhaps she should start with God, and then the man she was falling in love with.

CHAPTER ELEVEN

Kon del tut o nai shai dela tut wi o vast.
He who willingly gives you a finger will also give you
the whole hand.
Old Romany saying

A film of smoke had been in the air for days.
Valentina leaned against the trunk of a wild cherry tree, the gummy tree wounds sticking to her back. She watched as the farm animals were butchered, one by one. Dried and salted meat would be ready to eat throughout the dreary winter months ahead. The tenants called November *blood month* for good reason. The smell of blood permeated the tiniest pores of her skin.

Groups of servants salted ducks by the smoke-house, reminding Valentina of the elderly women in her tribe. Romany women toiled day and night, similar to these women, fiercely clinging to their traditions and beliefs.

Valentina's thoughts drifted to James. Until the spring thaw, she would stay at his home. Traveling in wintry conditions was too difficult, and it might take her weeks to catch up with the tribe. Yolanda could decide at that time whether or not she would accompany her.

She shook her head. In truth, she knew much of her decision wasn't based on the difficulty of traveling, but on not wanting to leave James.

Only yesterday, during one of their daily walks, she'd given him advice on a decision concerning one of his tenants. Despite those walks, she'd recently felt his aloofness. He held her at a distance, his polite smile a wall she didn't have the courage to broach. Always, he was the elegant gentry, superbly dressed in grey tailored trousers and matching waistcoat, the master of all he appraised.

Sometimes, she thought she'd imagined that day in the stable. He'd never wanted her as his wife. Why would he? Then, she'd catch him watching her, his face displaying an affection that took her breath away. And she knew he'd meant every word and was waiting for her reply.

~

A month passed. Except for Yolanda, the spacious upstairs hallway was deserted on an unusually warm and sunny December afternoon. The servants were all busy with their chores.

Wrapped in a gown of fine royal-blue wool, a smiling Yolanda made her way to the stairway landing humming a Christmas carol, "The Holly and the Ivy." She looped her linen undersleeves to create ruffles at her wrists. Her arm sling had come off a few days earlier.

"Will you help me decorate the hallway with Christmas decorations?" Absently, she handed Valentina a bough of fragrant holly.

"Aye." Valentina smiled as she accepted the bough. "As long as you answer a question which has plagued me for weeks. Why did you venture so near the river the day you nearly drowned?"

Yolanda lost her smile and stopped singing. "I tripped. 'Twas slippery because of the rains, and I wasn't thinking."

"You weren't thinking," Valentina repeated, "because you were daydreaming. Most likely about Reginald."

"Aye, I think about him all the time. Are you still planning to return to the caravan in the spring? If so, you must realize 'twill be without me."

Yolanda said the words so nonchalantly, Valentina dropped her bough. These past few weeks, her sister had grown into a young woman with a mind as willful and exasperating as a newborn colt.

She wove a bough through the banister. "I see how attentive Reginald is toward you. Nonetheless, your involvement with him shouldn't continue."

"You spend hours with Mr. Colchester and I don't insist otherwise." The delicate lilt of Yolanda's challenge was encased in a tidy point. "Rumors about you two fly faster than falcons. He cares a great deal about you, and I doubt you notice anyone else is about when he's near."

Valentina expelled a breath and regarded her sister solemnly. *Now or never,* she encouraged herself. Taking a few seconds for composure, she set the holly branches aside and pulled Yolanda to sit with her on the carpeted landing. "I have two secrets to confide, both of which you must promise never to breathe a word to anyone."

Yolanda leaned forward. "You have my word." Her cheeks shone tanned and dusty in the patch-work sunlight filtering through the stained-glass window directly above them.

Valentina opened her mouth twice before she waded into the uncomfortable silence.

"Mr. Colchester has asked me to marry him," she finally said, surreptitiously watching her sister. She tried to fix a calm expression on her face, although the warmth moving up her cheeks was fast giving her away.

Happiness shone in Yolanda's velvet-brown gaze. "Valentina, that's wonderful."

"I'd never consent."

"Whyever not? Daj would approve because Mr. Colchester is a respectable and decent man. He can protect and properly care for you."

"Are you forgetting he's a gadje?"

Besides, Valentina silently rationalized, what was the point of caring for him if she was leaving in a few months? Wasn't that what the Rom did? They never stayed anywhere for long.

Yolanda arranged the holly branches in a neat pile and stood. With that determined march to her steps Valentina knew so well, Yolanda tromped to the stairs.

"Yolanda, where are you going?"

"I'll not listen to your excuses." She shook her head, wisely, as if she were an elder dispensing wisdom, then stepped back to Valentina. "He isn't the type of man to accept nay for an answer, though 'tis little wonder you're cautious. 'Tis said his circle of friends reaches to London."

Valentina visualized James looking impressively handsome in formal black evening dress, comfortable and smiling among the most elite members of

London high society. No doubt the gentlemen invited his friendship, and the women longed to be held in his arms.

In a mist of glossy brown hair, Yolanda knelt beside Valentina. "You've turned pale. Why?"

"A man like him ... he'd never want me as his wife after ... If he knew—"

"You spoke of two secrets and marrying him is one. What is the other secret?"

Valentina sank her face in her hands. "Sometimes, I pretend it never happened. If I don't think about it, perhaps it will go away."

"Nothing goes away. Worries only fester unless you unburden yourself." Yolanda gave Valentina's fingers a short, emboldening squeeze. "Talk to me. Please."

"I don't know where to begin."

Conceivably, if her sister heard the wretched truth, she'd understand, and Valentina badly wanted to confess to someone. Exhaling, she tried to piece the explanation together. "The first night we arrived, I read his palm and—"

"And most likely you embellished your reading, the way you always do."

"Thank you for putting it so kindly." Valentina's eyes watered. She clasped her hands together on her lap. "You remember how frightened we were. All I had in my mind was finding you, returning to Daj and our tribe. So, when he requested I read his palm, I told him a half-truth."

"What did you say?" Yolanda's voice held a slight tremor. Slowly, she stood, pulling Valentina up along with her.

Valentina reached out to touch her sister, then drew back and hung her arms at her sides.

"He wanted a reply to his question about traveling to Wales to escape the influenza epidemic." Harder and harder to keep down, the familiar taste of remorse rose in Valentina's throat. She swallowed and focused on the gleaming wooden staircase. "I thought 'twas a silly game, he couldn't possibly believe anything I had to say. I was so angry ... so, I assured him he'd be safe in England."

"Isn't he a Christian?"

"Aye. Although he'd just returned from battle, and he's always so concerned about Jeremy."

"Perhaps he was seeking reassurance because there's so much hysteria whenever influenza is mentioned. He may have been desperate."

"A man like him would never feel desperate. He has a strong faith in God."

"Perhaps his faith faltered. Perhaps he felt overwhelmed because of his past sorrow and losing Beatrix. Everyone chatters about how hard he grieved when she died."

Valentina lowered her voice. "When I read his palm, I saw small lines of danger and a square on his travel line. Nonetheless, I told him *not* to travel to Wales."

"Why did you tell him that?"

"He seemed to want to hear something that would make him feel confident in his decision to stay here."

"Well, there's a simple solution. Tell him exactly what you've told me. We both know fortune-telling isn't true."

"I can't. Too many weeks have passed and I wouldn't know how to begin." Breathing frayed, anxiety raw, Valentina refused to sob. Crying, as she'd learned, solved nothing. Only determination and resolve brought about any results.

Outwardly, she held her stomach.

Inwardly, she screamed one silent question. *What should I do?*

Although she already knew and her sister was right. She would confess her half-truth to James. She was brave, she was fearless. Hadn't he told her those were the qualities he admired most about her? He didn't want her meek and timid, fearful of his anger.

Through James' faith, she was becoming a faithful follower of God. "'Whoever conceals their sins does not prosper, but the one who confesses and renounces them finds mercy,'" she whispered, adding, "Proverbs 28:13."

"I don't understand the Bible," Yolanda said.

"I'm beginning to understand it."

Valentina stood, solidly, at the ready.

She was through with false superstitions. Aye, she'd studied the Bible on so many evenings, alone in her chamber. That was the easy part. Now 'twas time to apply the Bible's teachings.

CHAPTER TWELVE

I phuv kheldias.
The earth danced.
Old Romany saying

*E*yebrows arched like two broken arrows, Wiborow marched into Valentina's chamber the following afternoon.

"Choose a gown to wear for the Christmas Eve banquet this evening," she said. "Mr. Colchester ordered these gowns from Ireland for you and your sister." Two servants hoisted a trunk into Valentina's chamber, and then Wiborow led them back into the corridor.

"Ireland!" Yolanda's infectious enthusiasm spilled into the room, while Valentina scurried to open the trunk and sort through one extravagant gown after another. Amidst a kaleidoscope of taffeta and silk, Valentina fingered the fabric of each gown, the exquisite Irish lace. They were beautiful, the craftsmanship of the highest quality.

An hour later, prompted by Yolanda, Valentina chose the simplest gown of pale lavender with a square-cut bodice. She folded the others away, reflecting on how many starving Romany children could be fed with the cost of even just one gown.

She flattened the chosen gown over her curves, the silk fabric draping fetchingly over her full bust and rounded hips. Over the gown, she laced a see-through tunic in a vivid shade of lush green.

"Do lavender and green match?" Yolanda teased.

"Only at Christmas. I'll wear Mother's diklo to complement the colors."

Yolanda chuckled. "Yellow?"

As she stood, Valentina flashed a bright grin at her reflection. Inhaling deeply, she turned to the night table and reached for her hairbrush, sweeping it through her shiny black hair until her hair crackled. She fastened a pearl clip at the crown and let the unruly curls twist in ringlets down her back.

"We're Romany women," she said, satisfied with her appearance. "The starker the clash, the better."

Yolanda chose a pearl-dove empire-waisted gown lined in rich black velvet. She wrapped a glistening golden net around her hair to match the trim on her gown. Assisting Valentina with folding away the furs and lace strewn on the floor, Yolanda beamed. "We're wearing gowns made for royalty, in a gentleman's home, on the most festive night of the year!"

"Our tribe wouldn't recognize us."

"'Tis generous of Mr. Colchester to invite even his servants to the Christmas banquet."

"Aye." In some quiet place in her heart, Valentina reflected on the knowledge that this was James. This was his nature. He was strong and dependable and true to his word. Despite his position, he treated his servants and tenant farmers with respect. He showered Jeremy with care, and always made time for his son. And he was respected by all who knew him.

Of course, he was so handsome, with thick arched brows and dark lashes framing his grey eyes, his angular jaw and tousled raven-black hair. Although, 'twas what was within—his noble spirit and kind ways—that really mattered.

And tonight, she decided, after the Christmas banquet, she would tell him about her deceit and ask his forgiveness. She'd planned to speak about the fortune-telling incident after her conversation with Yolanda, but the right opportunity never presented itself.

No more excuses. Tonight was the night.

A few minutes later, the women stepped into the elegant ballroom and were greeted by a blast of heat from the blazing Yule log.

Scores of candles illuminated gleaming copper urns filled with greenery and splashes of red ribbons. A feast, resplendent with roasted peacocks, pheasants, swans, and partridges, more meats than Valentina had eaten in her lifetime, lined the side tables. Yolanda accepted a cup of wine from the ever-present Reginald.

Despite the fluttery feeling in her stomach, Valentina quickened her pace across the cream-colored carpet. Never had she worn a gown as grand or attended an affair as brilliant. She lifted her head and breathed in, her gold hoop earrings brushing against her shoulders. Hesitant, she searched the crowd for James.

He caught her gaze and rose to his feet. With courteous nods to the men surrounding him, he strode to her. His possessive gaze captured hers, pinching her breath and gripping her heart.

"You look beautiful tonight, cariad."

"Thank you." She bit back her exclamation of admiration. James wore a variegated purple velvet waistcoat, edged in gold, offset by wine-colored breeches and low black boots.

The evening promised exhilaration, a night over-

flowing with magic. An enormous gemstone chandelier hung from the ceiling in the grandiose room,
and the display of the ladies' vibrant gowns was reflected in the mirrored walls. The hum of laughter
buzzed to a fever pitch, and expectancy hummed
through Valentina's veins.

James tucked her fingers in the crook of his arm
and guided her past a dozen carolers singing
"Greensleeves," holding the final note for several
beats. He waited for the exuberant applause to subside, leading Valentina to the far end of the room
and curving one arm around her waist.

"Can you dance?"

"About as well as I can swim. And you cannot
dance with me." She shook out the skirt of her
lavender gown and stared past the wave of colorless
faces. Well-balanced on a raised platform, the carolers opened their mouths into perfect Os, the horn
player positioned the mouthpiece to his lips, and the
music commenced with a lilting chord.

"You are the most exquisite woman in this ballroom tonight, and I can dance with whomever I
choose." Genuine pride flashed in his eyes.

"You can't dance with a Gypsy woman. People
will talk."

"Other people are not my concern." He
swooshed her through the first few bars of an elegant dance, then effortlessly eased her onto a small
outdoor alcove.

Although James had ignored his guests as they danced, Valentina had noted the contemptuous English faces. Distinguished nobles raised their eyebrows slyly, hiding their distaste beneath lively conversation and tinkling laughter.

The ballroom had shrunk, and Valentina was grateful for the cold air that greeted them on the alcove. Memories of her Romany life, so humiliating when compared to James' elegant life, came back in a rush. Mere inches separated her from James, but those inches contained two lives of enormous dissimilarities.

With a toss of her chin, she loosened the diklo, for it cut off her breath.

"Am I exquisite because I'm dressed in your fancy English clothes, Mr. Colchester?"

"My name is James." For a moment, his gaze narrowed. Bending his head nearer, he brushed his lips across her ear. "You are exquisite in anything you wear, although I like your Gypsy clothes best." His breath ravaged her sensitive earlobe and heat warbled down her neck.

The musicians played louder, the singers bursting to a climax, and James whirled her around the tiny space of the alcove. His well-muscled body glided with surprising grace as they danced, and his fingers tapped the rhythm of the lighthearted tune on her forearm.

She tried to follow his lead, although the alcove

spun. "Please, you're dancing too fast." She laughed with pleasure and held his shoulders to keep her balance.

"Am I?"

The teasing affection on his face made her smile. "You must be the envy of every landed gentry because of your dance expertise and nimble tongue."

"Dancing is one of my hidden talents. Will you dance in my arms until sunrise now that you've discovered my secret?"

"Will I need to dance every dance?"

"I have other talents that I'll share with you when we grow tired of dancing." He challenged her with a gaze as intent as his voice. Bending his head, he smiled down at her as if she were very, very precious.

She met his gaze. "Thank you for a wonderful evening," she said quietly.

Two striking women in billowing floral percale and jeweled accent brooches swayed by the open doorway. They greeted James with deferential nods. Their behavior toward Valentina was prudently disguised behind false smiles, although gossip and malice couldn't be far behind.

Slowly, Valentina's self-assurance faded. Against her will, hot tears burned the back of her eyes. People's opinions shouldn't matter, but this night was magical. Everything mattered.

"I'll never be accepted into your world, Mr. Colchester," she murmured.

"Aye, you will. I give you my word." His slow, re-assuring grin rendered her helpless. He gazed at her in a way he never had before—as if he would never let anyone hurt her.

A tingle warmed her body. The closest she'd ever come to happiness beckoned. This persuasive gentleman with his impeccable speech and refined manners wanted her as his wife, not as a lowly servant.

The instrumentalists added a drummer and bell player to their ensemble and slowed the tempo. Valentina gave a resigned sigh at the intricacy of the dance steps as James continually guided her.

"For a man of your height, you dance superbly and never miss a beat," she said.

"Take two steps to the right, not left, and follow my lead."

"All this effort to dance in a circle and begin again in the same place. My tribe dances to gay violins and broken tambourines. This type of dance is restricting."

He tightened his arms around her and drew her closer. "And you're a woman who doesn't like to be restricted."

Jeremy scampered past the door to the alcove. He spotted them and offered a quick wave in her direction.

Valentina touched James's sleeve. "Your son doesn't want to be restricted, either."

"So you've said."

Despite James' attempts to guide her, Valentina shuffled to the left. "Sorry, I think I stepped on your foot."

He grimaced before the sides of his mouth tugged up. "Not a problem, I have two."

"I hope I don't take him away from his studies."

"My foot? 'Tis quite intelligent and dances this particular dance quite well."

She covered her mouth to stifle her laughter, then placed her hands back on his shoulders. "Not your foot. Your son."

"Aye, of course." His low chuckle vibrated through her fingers. "And, nay, you don't take him away from his studies. He receives excellent instruction from his tutor every morning, so he can spend his free time with you. He'll begin formal schooling in a couple years, where he'll study Latin and mathematics."

"And then he'll be able to spend more time with other children."

"Perhaps."

She dragged her gaze from his and stared at the display of sugar confections the servants were arranging on a sideboard. The carolers burst into a rendition of the "Boar's Head Carol", and James led

Valentina back into the ballroom. Then he hummed, loudly.

During the carol's refrain, he dispatched a servant standing close by. Placing one goblet of wine in Valentina's hand and taking another for himself, James resumed his humming, effectively discouraging any further conversation. By the fourth verse, his melody bore little resemblance to the original Christmas carol. Undeterred, he tapped his foot in time to the pounding drumbeat. On the other end of the room, Yolanda danced with Reginald, learning each new dance with self-confidence. Her dark hair bobbed through the crowd, and Reginald assisted when she missed a cue. After the dance, they wandered to the tables to enjoy the feast—sumptuous supper meats, roasted thighs of turkey and raisin-filled festive breads.

Valentina shook her head. "I've never known a man so stubbornly opposed to ideas that weren't his own."

"Perhaps the lovely woman I am with is more stubborn."

"Now you can hear again?"

"If the musicians added a fiddle and triple harp, I'd sing all night, reliving my younger days in Wales." Youthful charm lit his expression over the rim of his goblet. "Truly, I like to sing, almost as much as I like to dance."

"Remind me to give you singing lessons," she teased.

"Remind me to give you dancing lessons."

The carolers began singing "Away in a Manger", and James and Valentina joined in. His rich baritone melded with her soaring soprano. Spicy sweet heat lulled her senses, her limbs warmed by the wine. She wanted to shout to the world how splendid she felt standing beside this tall, competent, refined gentleman.

When the song ended, his tone dropped to a whisper. "Valentina, there's a matter we must discuss. And you need to heed my words carefully, because your response means a great deal to me."

"There's something I need to tell you too." She meant to take a sip of her wine but was suddenly too nervous to drink it.

"May I speak first?" he asked.

"I hope you're not displeased by my singing."

"You sing like an angel. A Gypsy angel." He shook back his slightly unruly hair. His skin was tanned from all the time he spent outdoors with his son and the farmers. "We need to discuss a simple matter regarding my name. Please, please, always call me James."

"I will try."

"And I will continue to remind you, cariad." His eyes deepened to the charcoal grey color that always sent her senses into a tailspin.

She curled her fingers around her goblet and breathed in the heady scent of sweet wine. "I'm relieved the dance is over ... *James.*"

"Good. I will reward your efforts by spending my days teaching you how to—"

"Dance," she finished.

His expression held a note of suggestive promises. "Once we are wed, I will fill your nights with dances and dreams." He held up a forefinger before she could protest. "Because if my memory serves me well, there is an offer I've made in a stable that awaits your reply."

Her brows drew together as she focused on his striking face. If only her hands would stop trembling. Her instinctive response was to ask him to hold her, so that she would be aware only of his strong muscled body protecting her while she shouted the answer he wanted.

Aye. Aye. Aye.

Aye, she would marry him.

Aye, she would cherish his son.

Aye, she would love him.

Her intrusive conscience snickered a rebuttal. *Not until you tell him the truth about the palm reading.*

"James, I—"

"Give me a moment."

She watched as he crossed the ballroom to refill their wine glasses.

Among his friends, James presented the perfect

portrait of an urbane gentleman. This refined, unde-
niably attractive man had teased her about his foot
and hummed an entire Christmas carol to her a
short time ago. Wrapped in her musings, she misin-
terpreted the significance of Geoffrey standing beside a messenger boy by the doorway to the
ballroom.

James unrolled the sealed paper the boy handed
him, and his expression changed in a series too rapid
to note, settling on acceptance.

"'Tis a dispatch for me to depart for war under
Viscount Wellington," he announced, turning to his
silent and stunned guests and servants. "The Portuguese are planning a siege against the French in
Ciudad Rodrigo, Spain, and require British support."

"Tonight?" Geoffrey asked.

The messenger boy nodded.

Tonight?

Panic exploded, quashing Valentina's security.
Her heart raced to keep up with her feet.

She hastened into the lively kitchen and leaned
against the sink basin. The partridge roasting on a
spit in the open fire made her heave. She bunched
her hands together to fight off the nausea.

She was still there when Isabel, the head cook,
raised her floury face and nodded in her direction as
James strode through the kitchen. He'd already
changed into his riding clothes—black breeches and

a slate-colored hooded cloak—and emanated controlled authority and an aura of command.

The warm rush of pleasure surging through
Valentina had nothing to do with the heat of the
kitchen. He'd come to seek her. Her handsome, sophisticated gentleman.

To appear as if she hadn't noticed his arrival, she
turned and started to clean the dirty mushrooms in
the sink. His booted footsteps tap-tapped, tap-
tapped, across the kitchen floor, and he stopped directly behind her. "I didn't realize mere mushrooms
held such appeal." He leaned forward to drum his
fingers along the edge of the sink.

She kept her hands in the dirty water.

"Turn around. I must depart."

His breath teased the back of her neck. Sweat
trickled down her armpits. She glanced behind,
taking in his broad chest, his muscular shoulders, his
ever-present composure.

She jerked her hands from the water and wiped
the grainy soil on her lavish gown. With an attempt
at a smile, she swung around to face him.

"Promise you'll miss me when I'm away."

She hesitated and swung her hair away from her
face. Her stomach was sinking. Her throat was
swelling, the taste sickly sweet. "James, I ..."

His features darkened. Slowly, he ran his palms
over her arms. "Aye?"

Her insides were shattering. "Another war awaits. Please be safe."

"We'll celebrate the holiday when I return."

"James, I am ..."

I am frightened for your welfare. Never in all her careful planning had she imagined *he* would leave his home before *she* did.

He nudged her into the dimly lit hallway. "You'll miss me more than I imagined. That brings me great pleasure." Boldly intimidating, his fingers outlined her lips in a deliberate, circular motion.

She tried for a flippant response, although when she went to speak, her voice failed altogether.

She cleared her throat. "I'm sorry you're forced to leave on Christmas Eve."

His nod was agonizingly tender and heartening. "I know these wars well enough, and I'll not be away longer than thirty days. Promise me you won't do anything foolish in the meantime. No jumping in rivers or leaping out windows."

She offered him a faint smile.

"Promise me." He cupped her chin, lifted her face and kissed her forehead.

Her throat tightened. "I promise." Her feelings were so conflicted, she truly considered

begging him to stay and bawling her fears into the smooth folds of his waistcoat.

"'Tis settled, then. Will you extend a proper farewell to seal our agreement?" He stroked her back, calming her uncertainties. A fire kindled, spreading through her limbs, a curlicue flame.

Ineffective Romany endearments came to her lips, one resounding above the others.

Ves'tacha. Beloved.

She lifted her head to receive his kiss. His moist, solid mouth demanded a response. She relinquished control, because he would be leaving, because she had no control when he was near anyway. She stood on tiptoes and wrapped her arms around his neck.

"Tad." A familiar little voice carried through the hallway. James' lips trailed over Valentina's forehead, and she whirled as Jeremy came into view. She attempted to wiggle from James's grasp, but his grip stayed locked on her forearms.

Jeremy ran to his father and grabbed his leg.

James looked down at his son. "I must travel to London and will return soon." He released Valentina, crouched beside Jeremy, and hugged him. "Until then, I leave you with someone I trust."

"Then you will go on your way in safety, and your foot will not stumble," she murmured.

He gazed up at her. "Proverbs 3:23?"

"Aye." She stared at them both, one hand arrested on her lips, the other bunched at her side.

James stood. "You'll care for my son while I'm away?"

Jeremy beamed up at her with a whimsical smile and held out his arms. "Mam?"

Valentina blinked, recovering from James' surprising announcement. She would've taken care of Jeremy regardless. With one arm, she lifted Jeremy's slight body and steadied him on her hip.

"He can teach me how to play checkers better, although most likely, he'll still win."

James grinned and slipped on his tan riding gloves. A moment later, he was gone.

And her confession would have to wait.

CHAPTER THIRTEEN

Ma-sh-llah!
As God wills!
Old Romany saying

A fortnight after James' departure, Roland sauntered into the kitchen while Valentina was preparing a poultice for a cook who'd burned her arm. He stretched his thickset arms over his head, exposing his fleshy, hairy stomach. "The weather is brilliant and I'm in the mood for a good, rousing fight."

Recalling the mass of rumbling clouds she'd seen earlier, Valentina wondered what brilliant weather he was referring to. The sun hadn't shone for days, and a stark wind blew tree limbs to the ground in defeat.

Clare sliced a loaf of finely ground white bread and handed him a thick slice. "Tobias and Geoffrey are overwhelmed with their responsibilities. Mr. Colchester has been gone for over two weeks."

With a barmy smile and a wink, Roland kissed Clare's cheek, as if they were privy to a secret.

Valentina ducked her head to hide her smile and reached for her cup of morning tea. The house droned with anticipation of an impending wedding between Clare and Roland. No purple bruises had appeared on Clare's arms of late, and the old ones were fading. Hopefully, Valentina thought, the beatings had ceased.

At midday, though, Roland trudged back into the kitchen and complained of a severe headache, quaking so violently the words came in spurts. He refused the food Clare set before him.

Clare threw off her linen apron and guided him to the servants' quarters in the attic, and then ran to fetch Valentina, who was reading in her chamber. As they covered Roland with heavy quilts, he started coughing.

Nay. The breath in Valentina's chest fluttered, as if a host of bats awoke in a cave with nowhere to fly. She felt Roland's forehead. Too warm.

"He never gets sick," Clare said. "What could possibly be the matter?"

Doubt swamped Valentina's body, and she wiped the sweat from the back of her neck. "He may be unwell," she said tentatively.

Of course, he couldn't be. And even if he was unwell, certainly 'twas not influenza.

She offered to stay with Clare and sit with him, and by midafternoon his thirst was unquenchable. His reddened gaze darted restlessly. "I need to sleep ..."

From her perch on a high stool by his side, Clare flung off his quilts and cooled his feverish skin with wet linens. "No sleeping. I'll sing to keep you awake."

Day turned to night. Roland's condition worsened. In between charming English songs and cheerless ballads, he sputtered a last, erratic gasp and died.

Valentina's feet turned to lead, and she imagined the planks holding the floor together would cave from the weight of the burden she carried.

Clare wailed to the agitated servants hovering near. "Wake him. Please."

"He's departed to meet his maker," Wiborow said, her voice stale and strained.

Her face expressionless, Lowdie wrung her apron. "Clare, Roland favored you over all the other women." Her Welsh brogue sounded soft and utterly unconvincing.

"He died so quickly. What ailed him?" another servant asked, her question ringing as a clarion.

Valentina squeezed her eyes shut, frantically attempting to calm her worst fears.

Isabel, the head cook, swayed back and forth, her glassy blue eyes confused and afraid. "It could be influenza."

The innocent conjecture created an immediate hush to a room that had previously shrieked anxiety.

Panic-stricken faces turned toward Clare, Roland, and then Valentina.

Sweat beaded on her forehead. "Don't be alarmed." Her voice fractured. "I will—"

What would she do, exactly?

She jostled past the servants and staggered down the stairwell and toward her chamber.

Her heart thrashed so violently, she couldn't catch her breath.

'*I leave you with someone I trust.*' James' words to his son resounded in her ears.

He depended on her to protect Jeremy. She groped along the wall to her chamber and slid to the floor just inside the doorway. And then she prayed until the indigo evening crept to midnight. When Valentina glanced out her bedchamber window, a surly mist had settled over the rooftops of the tenants' homes, and winds ghosted across the lawn.

～

*B*efore dawn, Yolanda burst into Valentina's chamber. "Roland died?"

"Aye." Valentina jerked upright on her bed. "I've been praying."

High color stained Yolanda's cheeks. She studied Valentina as if she were a strange being whom she no longer recognized. "When Mr. Colchester returns, tell him everything. You should've told him before he went off to battle."

"I intended to, although he left before I had the chance." Valentina flung off the bedcovers, stood and breathed deeply. Walking over to her sister, she smoothed a wisp of hair escaping one of Yolanda's plaits. The tang of fiery black pepper and garlic no longer clung to Yolanda's hair. Lately, Yolanda smelled of lavender and fine wine, the scents of an English woman living in a gentleman's home.

Yolanda jerked from her touch. She grabbed a bright-pink pillow, squeezing until it lost its shape. "You may not believe you have a gift, but I do and I'm frightened."

Suddenly aware she hadn't seen Yolanda at all the previous evening, Valentina asked, "Where were you last night when Roland died? Were you with Reginald?"

"Aye." Yolanda straightened to her full length of five feet. "And I love him."

∽

The January days passed in eternal droplets, splatters with no beginning nor end. Night after night, Valentina rocked Jeremy to sleep. She sang Romany lullabies from her childhood, each song a reminder of a long-ago life.

"Your father will come home soon," she assured the boy each night he snuggled his head in the crook of her arm. She enunciated clearly, encouraging him to focus on her lips so that he might understand her words. And then she prayed with him. James had said he wanted Jeremy to understand God was close and always available.

She'd begin their prayers by thanking God, then pointing out things in Jeremy's chamber that Jeremy was thankful for. She'd end with, "Heavenly Father, we come to you needing your healing hand. Guide us toward health and wisdom. In your name we pray. Amen." With a warm hug and kiss, she'd tuck Jeremy into bed and wait until he was asleep.

∽

On the Monday of the third week since James' departure, Valentina spent the afternoon digging through the garden, the herbs brief and coated with snow. The sun was setting when the hushed sound of men's voices came toward her. Tobias, a footman of medium build with brown hair and light-framed spectacles, strode toward her with Geoffrey. She regarded Tobias as friendly, dependable, and honest.

"Geoffrey is taking a small group of men and riding toward London, then on to Spain," Tobias told her. "We're summoning Mr. Colchester back to Ipswich."

"Thank you, God." Valentina breathed her first relieved breath in weeks.

When the house quieted that night, she retreated to her chamber and sat on the bed. Her thoughts were of James, always of James. She could still see the pride in his gaze when he'd danced with her at the Christmas banquet, his playful smile, his genuinely thoughtful way of listening to her when she spoke. He could have chosen any woman as his wife. Yet, he had chosen her.

Clutching her diklo as a drowning person gropes a lifeline, she whispered the words she would say when next they met. "James, I made a mistake, and I need to be honest about something I did that was very, very wrong. I'm sorry and take full responsibility for my rashness. Please forgive me."

She followed the imagined scene to its inevitable conclusion.

At first, he might be at a loss for words. He'd look down, or away, or he might study her, his gaze unfocused. Eventually, despite her explanations, his posture would stiffen and he'd refuse to respond. And then he would dismiss her from his life.

She leaned back against the headboard and squeezed her eyes shut. Why could she not face the life she would be forced to lead without him?

She tried to sit upright and carry her guilt, her regret, her sorrow, but she couldn't. The pain was too heavy. Her chin quivered, her head sank onto her chest. And then she cried. Violent sobs wracking her insides, so fierce she feared her heart would splinter.

CHAPTER FOURTEEN

Mandat tsera tai kater o Del mai but te avenge tumenga.
From me a little money, but may God give you
plenty.
Romany saying

*A*cutely aware he was little more than an obedient soldier in another ceaseless war, James fought bravely throughout the long, dark nights. The siege on Ciudad Rodrigo was over, the fortress' walls were blasted by heavy artillery, and the fortress was successfully stormed. He boarded a British Squadron gunboat from Spain to England, then retrieved his horse. On his ride back to Ipswich, he stopped at a nobleman's townhouse, Lord

Stephen Standish, in London. He was immediately offered a bed, clean clothes, and the invitation to stay as long as he liked. There was a party that evening at another nobleman's house up the road, and James spent the time socializing with the dazzling and pompous upper class. He'd forgotten how boring they were, prattling about the petty dalliances of the rich and privileged.

Brazen, lavishly dressed ladies approached him to express their condolences over his late wife's death. They all looked alike with dainty hands and fair complexions. They all dressed alike in their absurdly elaborate gowns. They all talked alike in persnickety, ladylike lilts.

No one had honeyed skin. No one had sparkling emerald eyes, nor tantalizing retorts to his teasing questions. Because no other woman was Valentina.

Leaving the party, James paced the corridors, decked with evergreens. He stared out the mullioned windows at the banks of the River Thames, blanketed in a cold, wintry fog. Heavy clouds rolled overhead, successfully blocking out the moon.

He tossed back his wine and glanced impatiently at his watch. He'd leave tomorrow afternoon, a day earlier than he'd planned. Wryly, he rebuked himself for acting like an infatuated schoolboy, driven by an unreasonable keenness to see Valentina again.

What a stubborn woman she was, refusing to give him an answer to his marriage proposal. By now, she'd probably listed several more reasons why she couldn't marry him. His gorgeous, spirited Gypsy woman.

He knew, by the way she responded to his kisses and caresses, that she desired him.

And he desired her.

When he returned, his only desire was that she would love him as much as he loved her.

Love? He frowned into his empty goblet. Then, with a lengthy, sardonic sigh, he acknowledged the truth. He was in love with Valentina.

~

The following day, James politely admired the family portraits hanging on his host's walls. Preparations were well underway for the evening dances and masqued entertainment. The ballroom would quickly fill for a second party, reminding James of his own Christmas Eve banquet, dancing with an audacious and laughing Valentina.

He stood in the drawing room, avoiding the crush in the ballroom, when Lord Dermot, a dignified, older man, caught his gaze. The viscount had been a longtime acquaintance of James' family.

"So good to greet you again, Colchester," Lord Dermot said with amiable geniality.

Not happy to be taken away from his reflections of Valentina, James sipped his heavily spiced wine, hoping to quench his thirst for her. He swished the wine in his mouth, swallowed and grimaced. He'd never liked the taste of nutmeg and cloves. He liked his wine dark and bitter.

"And you, Dermot." He set the silver goblet on a nearby tray, grabbed a slice of syrupy apple, and dismissed an overbearing server hovering near his elbow.

Lady Dermot minced toward them, taking pretentious steps past the wide expanse of eight bay windows that overlooked the street. When she arrived, her ample chest heaved from the exertion of her short promenade. "So sorry, Mr. Colchester, to hear about your late wife's untimely death. A terrible disease, this influenza. Once it gets hold, it seldom will let go."

James raised her gloved hand and kissed it. "'Tis a pleasurable greeting, Lady Dermot, that I, too, extend."

"How is your son? Still deaf as a post, I presume. He must miss his twin sister terribly."

Lady Dermot's genteel accent seemed too cultured to be asking such unintelligent questions. And her eloquently arched eyebrows were raised a tad too high.

A persistent, irritating cadence drummed in James' temple, and he gave a not-so-subtle shake of his head. "Thankfully, he's in good health. Still, I

must take offense. My son may be deaf, but his affliction doesn't restrict him."

He wouldn't be lured into discussing Jeremy nor
eyeballed by Lady Dermot's pitying stares, and he
wouldn't tarnish his precious daughter's memory by
speaking her name aloud.

"Because your children were twins, they were
surely quite close," Lady Dermot said.

James replied with a cool semblance of politeness. "My son thrives in the country. The forests are
fresh and clean, not tainted by the filth of the
London streets."

Lady Dermot fanned her rapidly reddening face.
"Good heavens, our city is clean."

"You reside far from civilization, Colchester." Lord
Dermot clapped James on the back. "London offers the
finest food, wine, and women. You cannot mourn your
wife's death forever, although I can understand—"

"I assure you, Dermot, I do not mourn my late
wife." James half-smiled as Lord Dermot's condolences died on his lips.

"Our city physicians are most skilled and may be
able to treat your son's deafness," Lady Dermot inserted in a helpful tone.

Nobility and wealth, James decided, was not a
true indicator of class.

"I do not believe my son needs a physician. However, I will consider your advice." James pretended

to give the matter some thought by tapping two fingers on his chin and looking pensive.

He nodded absently to stray servants as they strolled past him carrying silver trays laden with neglected food. He glanced at the half-eaten hard-boiled eggs and discarded pomegranate seeds. His gaze fixed on the elaborate marble staircase, envisioning Valentina descending the stairs in her colorful Gypsy clothes as a regal princess, looking heartbreakingly gorgeous.

Why was she so wary of becoming his wife? She was proud, yet so fearful of wagging tongues.

He wanted to begin a new life with her in Wales, on his secluded Welsh estate—far from the prying eyes of the English aristocracy. He wanted her to be a mother to Jeremy.

Not in a month, or a year, or however long it might take her to come to a decision.

He wanted her now, because he was tired of waiting.

In his heart, affection and tenderness erupted, the feelings so strong that they staggered him. He cleared the odd lump in his throat. She was smart, selfless, brave, and bold, and he couldn't wait a moment longer to return to her.

He regarded the last trace of wine from his goblet and set it on a nearby tray.

"In a hurry, Colchester?" Lord Dermot inquired.

James forced a polite grin. "I've been gone from Ipswich far too long."

He turned and strode through the hallway, passing several pairs of hastily raised oval spectacles. He ignored the greetings as he passed. He was too busy trying to calculate how many hours it would take to reach his estate if he rode all night.

CHAPTER FIFTEEN

Gadje Gadjensa, Rom Romensa.
Gadje with Gadje, Rom with Rom.
Old Romany saying

*L*ord Standish had encouraged James to ride escorted, but James declined and rode on alone. He didn't want anyone with him, questioning the stop he intended to make, and he didn't want to be slowed by another rider. Besides, Albern, his horse, provided perfect company. He understood James' commands and didn't speak.

As he rode, his thoughts returned again and again to Valentina.

Sensual and breathtaking, she was a natural

beauty. She had the curves of Venus and the mischievous grin of a cherub, although it was her inborn charm and grace he most admired. Her witty intelligence and impertinent humor were so much like his. When she sparred with him and met his banter with a sharp quip, he laughed out loud. And it felt good to laugh again.

What made her deny the attraction that he knew she felt for him? Each time he held her in his arms, her body would quiver as she unconsciously molded herself to him. What stopped her from accepting his offer besides her inflexibility to accept him—her preconceived notion that just because he was a gadje, he wouldn't respect the Romany culture? As a member of English society, he was certainly class conscious, although his Christian beliefs negated prejudice. The Bible passage from Galatians went through his thoughts: "There is neither Jew nor Greek, there is neither slave nor free, there is no male or female, for you are all one in Christ Jesus."

Riding northeast toward Ipswich, James made his way through an intricate maze surrounding a nobleman's house on the outskirts of London. Bathed in an icy landscape, a fountain in the central courtyard sat silent. Precise configurations of plants, flowers, and shrubs sat dormant under a thin coating of snow. Several gardeners gathered fallen twigs, apparently taking no notice of him.

Before he'd left for battle, there was much he'd wanted to settle with Valentina—including

their move to Wales in the spring. He'd willingly accept the inevitable shock from his peerage because of his marriage to a Gypsy woman. Nonetheless, he had to think of his own happiness, and the well-being of his son.

He grinned at the image of her submissively complying when he demanded an answer to his proposal from her. Perhaps, he'd need to persuade her so she wouldn't refuse. First, he'd kiss her until her breathing centered only on him. Then he'd bury his face in the intoxicating fragrance of her silken hair. And then she would say ... aye.

By nightfall, he watched for the Gypsy encampment he'd spotted when he'd ridden weeks earlier, finally catching a glimpse of a campfire through a thick patch of forest. He crossed a stream, his horse's hooves muffled by the slush of melting snow.

When he reached the camp, he pulled back on his horse's reins and stared.

At the center of the camp, a group of Gypsy women danced on the frozen grass. With a devil-may-care attitude, they swayed their hips in time to rattling tambourines and their quickening tempo. James drew a lengthy, shaky breath as he imagined Valentina dancing like this for him—privately.

Four Gypsy men were seated around the campfire. They studied James with wary expressions and narrowed eyes. One woman tended to a rabbit roasting on a wooden spit. Her hand froze in midair while she subjected James to unblinking scrutiny.

"We're not causing any harm, sir," an elderly man with a grizzled white beard said.

All the men exchanged inscrutable glances. James understood that a gadje riding into a camp didn't bode favorably for a tribe of Gypsies.

One of the men stood. "Is anyone riding with you, sir?"

James had no intention of giving the men the impression he rode alone. He surveyed the destitute campsite, dismounted and tethered his horse's reins to a gnarled tree. "I'm here to ask some questions, not to cause unease. My men are not far behind me."

Keeping a prudent watch on the Gypsy men, James retrieved a coin from his cloak. He approached the campfire and handed the coin to the elder who'd spoken first. "I'm willing to pay for the answers I seek."

The man stuffed the coin into his torn shirtsleeve. "Happy to oblige, then. Drink first, questions later."

As if by an unspoken agreement, the tribe relaxed. Several men shared a jug of brandy and gestured for James to join them. He accepted their offer and took a swig, then lifted the jug in a gesture of friendship.

After the jug had been passed several times,

James sat back and regarded the group. These people were Valentina's people. Independent, humble and determined.

He kept the thoughts close and said, "A Gypsy woman of my acquaintance is to be married. Are there any special rituals for a betrothal?"

A dark-bearded man broke the stunned quiet. "Aye, although first the man must pay for the honor of marrying the bride. *Lowe k-o vast, bori k-o grast.*" He laughed and translated, "Money in hand, bride on horse."

"How much money?"

"As much as a man can afford. Isn't that always the way when courting a woman?" The bearded man howled with glee, slapping his knee at his own jest. "Some women are worth more than others," he continued. "The groom pays the bride's parents after he haggles for the best price. All parents want the most money they can get for their daughter, although the groom wants to offer the least. Otherwise, the marriage won't be profitable for him."

One younger woman, wearing a swirling orange and red embroidered blouse, and opulent headdress, shook her head in feigned disagreement and tossed her glossy ebony hair behind her shoulders. She bent and tasted a fatty broth cooking over an open fire, licking her fingers and sneaking quick glances at James. The aromas of fennel and spicy garlic, of sweet licorice and foreign spices, reminded him of

Valentina, and how much he wanted to get back to her.

Gazing at the campfire, he asked quietly, "Suppose this woman's parents are both dead?"

"The next male relative would speak for her," the elder replied. "If everyone agrees about the wedding, then we have a *pliashka,* a betrothal ceremony. First, the groom's father takes a bottle of brandy and wraps it in a handkerchief."

The man beckoned the young woman. "Miriah, give me your ribbon." He grabbed the moss-green satin ribbon the woman pulled from her hair. "To this, we attach gold coins and make a necklace." He turned to James with a smile that displayed two rows of decayed teeth. "Do you have any extra coins to spare, sir, so I may show you how to make a *pliashka?*"

"Aye." James dropped the gold coins he carried into the man's palms.

The man polished them between his aged fingers. "Miriah, get a needle and thread and attach these coins to the ribbon."

Without a word, Miriah took the coins and ribbon and disappeared into a tent. She came out in a reasonably short time and handed the elder the necklace as he was explaining other Romany wedding traditions to James, including the fact that although Romany men were allowed to marry outside their culture, Romany women were not.

"Because 'tis the women who keep the Rom culture alive for the next generation," the elder explained, shoving the jug aside and grabbing the necklace from Miriah. "The future bride wears this necklace, which symbolizes the bond of marriage."

"I'd like to give her this necklace for the betrothal," James said.

The elder's forearms ticked beneath his mismatched sleeves. He exchanged glances with the other Gypsy men still seated on the log. "Who is this woman, sir? Does she have merit?"

"Of course, and she's very beautiful." James glanced around. It dawned on him that the murmurings of the Gypsy men had risen.

"All Romany women are beautiful," the elder replied.

A pair of capricious feminine eyelashes fluttered. Miriah bent to brush away the mud sticking to the bottom of one bare foot and smiled at James in much the same way Valentina did when she worked in the herb garden.

"Beauty is least important," the elder was saying. "Romany men judge a woman by her health, her stamina."

"This particular woman fears nothing and is very strong."

"Be warned. The stronger the woman, the stronger her temper."

James answered with an appreciative chuckle. "Of that, I am fully aware."

"Men like a woman with a little fire, aye?"

James gave his riding cloak an emphatic shake and stood. "To whom do I pay the bride price?"

The burliest man in the group rose, and several women who had peered from their tents grabbed children by the shoulders and pulled them to the fringes of the camp.

James' heart pounded in double time. In his restless preoccupation to learn more about Valentina's heritage, he'd let down his guard. Glancing around, he fingered the sheath of the knife concealed in his cloak.

"This Romany woman who is to be married—is she someone we might know?" The elder held out his outstretched palm and indicated to each man to do the same.

"Nay." James kept his tone friendly as he assessed the men.

More men, emerging from their tents for the first time, sauntered toward the fire, encircling it. Not even on the battlefield had James witnessed such menacing hatred directed solely at him.

"Do you have a coffer full of gold to make a finer necklace?" the dark-bearded Gypsy asked. "Gold can aid us in hiding yer secret of this mysterious bride, *Mr. Gentleman.*" He grabbed a branch from the ground and snapped it at James. Mouth hard, glare deadly, he spat, "We recognize you high and mighty gadje anywhere."

James reached for his knife. *Nay.* He didn't want to fight these men.

"Don't do anything you'll regret," he warned.

"We're protecting our own against the likes of you." The largest man with thick sausage-like fingers struck James in the chest, knocking him to the ground.

Furious contempt at his foolishness pushed James to his feet. He thrust a rock-hard jab to the man's fleshy nose. The Gypsy rubbed his nose, now bent to the side, and his eyes widened at the blood between his fingers. He grabbed a heavy branch, heaved it over his head, and swung. James ducked and grabbed hold of the man's thighs, forcing them both backward.

A rickety tent collapsed beneath them, the wooden frame shattered. The man's eyes rolled up and he twitched as he fell unconscious.

James' stomach bottomed, his breathing a shouted curse as he fumbled for his knife. It eluded his grasp, and he willed himself up.

The other Gypsies closed their circle around him. Years on the battlefield kept him upright and alert. He launched forward and connected with a vicious pair of cannonball fists.

"Ain't used to fighting with your hands, *sir?*" a

man shouted. He yanked James' arm with such brutal strength, a shooting pain crippled his wrist.

His thin, chastising breath came with the same whispers. *Valentina. Valentina.*

Infatuation had distorted his reason.

One of the larger men kicked and kicked and kicked and kicked and kicked.

James' mouth choked with mud. Stop. He wasn't dead. Pray.

He prayed silently, on and on, holding onto a sense of control and peace.

~

*J*ames kept his eyes closed, aware of the angry pain mushrooming in his skull. Groggy images floated and blackened, and his mouth sucked in breath after squalid breath. He felt the weight of a heavy pendant around his neck. Whenever he tried to touch it, it swung out of reach.

Squeezing his eyes shut to control the pain, he staggered to his feet. Blood ran down his throat. Overhead, a murky stream of stars obscured the nightmarish twilight. He wobbled, fell back into the slushy snow, and vomited. Making his way to his horse, he tried to mount Albern, but the effort was too much. Wrapping his cloak around him, he collapsed into the snow.

He woke as dawn broke, and he could make out a group of men riding toward him. He expected the ghostly images to disappear, for they were familiar men.

Geoffrey reached him first and dismounted. "Mr. Colchester?" Peering up at his face, James noted that Geoffrey's gaze had dimmed to cautious shadows.

"Do I look as bad as all that?"

"Worse."

"Help me stand."

"Tell us who did this."

His men weren't moving. They remained on their horses like silent statues.

"What is it?" Apprehension sparked inside him like an untended fire, leaving him burned and weak. Grateful for Geoffrey's steadiness, James tried to hold his body erect. "Have you all lost your tongues?"

Geoffrey cleared his throat. "Tobias and I agreed that you needed to come back to the estate immediately." He lifted his palms, ever so slightly, attempting a shaken explanation.

"Is someone attacking us?" James struggled for a semblance of understanding. "If so, then why aren't you there protecting the estate?"

"'Tis not who, Mr. Colchester, but what." The elder man's fingers dug into James' arms. His gaze sobered. "You see, the wretched influenza ..."

James tried to swallow the dried lump in his

throat, rancid where the dirt stuck, tiny trickles of blood threatening to choke him. "Is anyone dead?"

"Roland."

James shook off Geoffrey's assistance, conscious of a roaring in his ears overtaking all rational reasoning. "Jeremy is safe?"

Geoffrey wet his lips. "Aye."

"And Valentina?"

"She is also safe," Geoffrey stared at James' throat, then at the ground. The expression on his leathery face changed from a guarded mask to one of disbelief, causing James to flounder for the pendant around his neck.

Several gold coins swung from a ribbon. He felt the coldness of the coins, the smooth satin of the ribbon.

Then his knees buckled.

CHAPTER SIXTEEN

Mashkar le gajende leski shib si le Romenski zor.
Surrounded by the gadje, the Rom's tongue is his
only defense.
Romany saying

*B*ooted footsteps and distraught whispers resonated throughout the front hallway as servants scurried and announced Mr. Colchester's homecoming.

Valentina sat on a high-backed chair in the nursery and rocked Jeremy, suppressing the urge to race down the stairs and greet James. Jeremy snuggled closer—an encouraging sign he might sleep through the night. She waited several extra minutes, then eased him onto his bed. Tucking him under his favorite blanket, she kissed him good night.

She tiptoed out of Jeremy's chamber, her gown brushing against the carpeted floor. The downstairs hall had hushed and she went directly to the privacy of her chamber. Too tired to take off her gown, she slipped into bed. Lying on her side, she propped two snowy-white pillows behind her, pulled her knees up to her chest, and stared at the low fire burning in the grate.

At daybreak, she would tell James about the fortune-telling and be done with it once and for all. Aye, she'd tell him at daybreak. Dead tired and grateful for her comfortable bed, she burrowed beneath her wool coverlet and closed her eyes. James had returned. All was well.

⌒

*S*omeone was watching her.

Valentina tried to peer beneath her heavy lids and force her mind to focus. The weight of a sleep-deprived haze dragged her back into unconsciousness.

She awoke a second time, dimly aware of a strong hand sliding along her cheeks, outlining her mouth. She rolled onto her side and inhaled a whiff of dirt and sweat and ... dried blood!

A scream surfaced in her throat and she clutched

the wool coverlet to her chest. Blinking in bleary bewilderment, she stared at a familiar, handsome face. In the flickering firelight, James' battered face peered down at her.

"James." She raised her hands to stroke his cheeks. "What happened?"

He shoved her hands away. "I haven't given you permission to touch me."

"Permission?" A twist of tension took root along her spine.

"Of course, you've never asked permission to do anything in your life." He seemed to be speaking to himself. "What could I possibly be thinking?"

"Are you foxed?"

"Not as much as I'd like." His tan breeches, linen shirt and waistcoat were ripped and grimy, damaged beyond repair. He gestured to his clothes, as if by way of an explanation. "I returned earlier this evening."

"I—I know."

"Yet you didn't come downstairs to greet me."

"I planned to seek you come the morrow."

"Were you waiting until then to inform me that influenza has already killed one of my men? Or that some of my tenants have run off in a panic?"

She fixed her stare on the silver-white canopy above her bed.

He gripped her hands. "How did Roland contract influenza?"

Her throat worked to find air. "Are you mad? Release me!"

"I must be mad to listen to a fortune-teller." Pointedly, he wrenched his hands from her and stepped back.

She bolted out of bed and darted for her chamber door, intending to place as much distance as possible between herself and this bruised stranger who'd taken James' place.

His swift strides echoed behind her, and she whirled to face him.

A storm brewed in the depths of his silver eyes. Then his features softened. "You're trembling."

"You're scaring me."

"I'm sorry." He wobbled back toward the bed and stepped on the untied laces of his boots. He tripped and landed on the bed with a groan.

"Have you been in a brawl?"

His sharp laugh ended with a grimace.

"Did you quarrel with ...Were your battles difficult?" She rationalized that he was undoubtedly exhausted, prompting his unreasonableness.

"If the battles were difficult, I assure you, I wouldn't be here."

"How were you hurt, then?"

"I received a message from your 'kindhearted' Gypsy kinsmen."

"What message? Why?"

"Because I rode into their camp with an inquiry."

"Why?" she persisted as she moved toward him, her questions coming so rapidly she scarcely shaped her words. "Did you attack them?"

"Do I look like I attacked them?"

"The Rom would never strike a gentleman unless provoked. We all know the punishment—a lifetime in an unforgiving English prison." Her chin lifted. "You must've threatened them."

"Am I such a threat to a tribe of Gypsies who far outnumbered one man?"

"My people are fair and caring and ..." Two dozen denials skirted through her mind. She fumbled for answers, anguish cramping a warning in the pit of her gut. "Dear heavens, they did this to you?" She lifted her fingers to stroke his face.

James flinched and jerked away.

Brushing back tears, she scrambled to the wash-basin to fetch a linen cloth. "What were you inquiring about?" Her real question, the one unspoken, ricocheted through the chamber: What were you inquiring about *in a Romany camp?*

She kept her back to him. Her conscience took the lead in blaming herself for the danger he'd faced.

He lifted a hand. "I don't need you to tend to my wounds, Valentina."

"I insist." She wrung cold water from the cloth and swallowed a frayed, futile sigh as she turned to him. "Can you please tell me what happened?"

"I rode out of London alone and into a Gypsy

encampment. You are asking a lot of questions tonight, and I have questions of my own."

He continued to perch on the edge of her bed, swinging one leg much too casually.

"James, I must tell you something," she blurted. She paused and swallowed. After taking this monumental step to finally initiate this conversation, she couldn't stop now. When she read palms, she was an expert at telling people what they wanted to hear. She was a master at outsmarting an unsuspecting farmer and stealing all his chickens. Why couldn't she speak up now when it mattered most?

Be brave and meet his gaze.

She dug her fingernails into the cloth. No words came, only a blur of tears.

You've rehearsed this a thousand times. Say "I loathed you when we first met. Now all I want to do is love and protect you." Speak. Say the words.

He expelled a ragged breath. To her shock, he began the conversation for her. "That first night, when I asked you to read my palm, I had reason to believe you were a fortune-teller of merit. In hindsight, I never should have disregarded my religious beliefs. Why did I want to take a shortcut and not believe God?"

Heat wicked up her face. Aye, she was good— very good, at reading fortunes. And it had all been a game to her to fool the gadje. However, what mattered now was honesty and integrity. Where once she had fiercely intended to hold onto her Romany way of living, now all she wanted to hold onto fiercely was him and a humbling God.

"The future is God's to know, not us." She glanced at James' hard jaw line and spoke rapidly. "God decides everything in His own time. So, if you wanted to see your future, you should have gone to your chapel and prayed directly to Him for guidance, not ask me."

"I did ask Him. He hasn't answered me since Beatrix died."

Neither resignation nor anger showed in his expression, only sorrow. And the sorrow broke her heart.

Filling her lungs with air, she squared her shoulders and stepped from the washbasin.

His eyes closed. The muscles in his arms knotted. "Don't," he ordered.

She gazed at his pale, tortured features and closed the distance between them. *Please let me touch you,* she silently pleaded. "Your wounds need to be washed," she said aloud, "and you know I don't obey orders well."

He didn't protest. She stripped off his slate-colored waistcoat, unlaced his muddy shirt and slid the shirt down his back. His wounds had been bound with strips of cloth, which she carefully removed. Trying not to put too much pressure on his gashes, she kept her motions careful and measured.

His breath was shallow and quick on her fingers; his heart thudded hard and fast.

Using light strokes, she wiped the moist cloth along his bearded neck.

He grimaced and stretched his legs out on the bed. His salty sweat pervaded her nostrils. She lowered her hands, slowly, to wash his chest.

He caught her wrists. "I went to my son's chamber tonight and watched him sleep. He's unharmed by all that's happened?"

"Aye."

James expelled an infinite breath. Deep lines etched around his mouth. "I try to protect him."

"He's had a difficult time without you. I've had ... a difficult time ... without you."

In her secret heart, Valentina had the irrational hope that James would whisper reassurance and encouragement, assuring her he'd had a difficult time the past few weeks without *her*.

Instead, he dropped her wrists, rubbed the bruises on his forearms and groaned. "Sometimes, I don't understand your culture. I want to understand. I try ..."

This proud man who'd bravely returned from battle—her kinsmen had hurt him so much.

Unable to keep the choked sobs from her voice, she asked, "May I tell you a story while I wash your wounds?"

Slowly, thoughtfully, he answered, "Aye."

Her throat ached, her vision blurred. Determined to continue, she drew a breath.

"Many years ago, Daj taught me a cure for influenza." A poignant kaleidoscope of images floated in Valentina's mind's eye—her little brother, her mother and her father.

"My late wife died from influenza," he stiffly informed her.

"I'm sorry."

Unemotionally, he observed her. She gazed at him in her darkened chamber, feeling a need for him so intense she could scarcely catch a breath. He was so superb, so handsome, that if he'd added a slight smile, she would have clung to him and pleaded for understanding because she'd wronged him.

Her hands were shaking as she tried to concentrate on washing his wounds.

"Daj tried to save my little brother, Stevo, from the disease. She attempted many Romany remedies, all without success."

A cool nod from James was all she needed to continue.

"One rainy afternoon when we'd camped near London, Daj brought me and my brother and my father to the edge of our camp. She chose a sapling and told my brother to shake it."

Valentina glimpsed James' flat gaze and tripped over her words. "My father ordered my mother to cease and argued that her cure was hopeless. I cried

and blocked my ears. A few hours later, Stevo died."
Valentina fingered the edges of her mother's diklo.
"I stood next in line as a drabardi, and my mother
said I needed to learn the ancient ways of the healer.
Instead of assisting, I ran and hid like a coward."

More memories, the ones she couldn't share.
Vulnerable, afraid, and alone, she'd been found by
Troka, and he'd raped her in a deserted London al-
leyway. Her body had gone cold, her limbs lifeless.
Profound sobs shattered inside her, a young girl
screaming mutely to an earless world, a woman
washing the wounds of the man she loved.

In the years following the rape, she'd buried her
wretchedness under a dazzling bravado. She summoned that bravado and met James' steady gaze.
"Luca found me the next morn."

"You weren't a coward. Your parents were
arguing."

She was so tormented by her remembrances, she
couldn't pinpoint when James' hand came to hold
hers, or when he'd begun gently, supportively en-
folding her fingers in his.

"And your mother's peculiar remedy?" he asked.

"It sounds superstitious ..." James sent her a
skeptical half-smile, and her sadness lightened. "Romany believe if you shake a tree, the fever will pass
from the person who's suffering to the tree, and the
sickness will be cured."

"Stevo died," James reminded softly.

She pulled her fingers from his and huddled her arms to her chest. "I blamed myself for not being brave enough to help my mother save him."

"None of it was your fault." James swung his legs around the bed and sat up. He braced his head in his hands, then studied her.

"Yesterday," she said, "when I dug some herbs from the garden, I recalled Stevo's death."

"'Tis a sad memory." Grunting with the effort, James came to his feet and walked toward the door. "Forgive me. I've had my fill of Gypsy superstitions for one evening."

She grabbed the bedpost for support. "Don't leave me."

He turned, one hand on the brass latch of her chamber door. Standing on the edge of her decision, she advanced a step.

He shook his head, although his gaze wouldn't let her go.

The dying embers of the fire licked red shadows onto the ceiling. She tried to pull air into her throat, enough for her constricted voice to speak. She waited for a minute, remembering the way he'd wrapped his arms around her in the stable and asked her to be his wife.

A muscle twitched in his jaw. His eyes flickered. Silver moonlight streamed through the window lighting his bruised and handsome face.

Two more paces. Tentatively, she massaged his shoulders.

He closed his eyes and leaned back against the door.

Straight and proud, she waited until his gaze met hers. "The night you left for battle, you told me to miss you."

His body stiffened. "And?"

"I missed you more than I ever dreamed."

Infinite seconds ticked by, while he looked away, an attempt to distance himself from her. When he gazed at her again, he said quietly, "I missed you too."

"Then will you please put your arms around me?"

His taut expression eased. He embraced her, and she wrapped her hands around him so tightly, her fingers bit into his back.

He devoured her with scorching kisses, a possessive act of ownership, staking his claim. He murmured her name into her mouth, her hair, her neck. She responded with all the passion in her heart. Eagerly, she kissed the bruises on his chest and inhaled all of him, his sweat, his wounds, and his maleness.

"My beautiful cariad, my sweetheart," he murmured. He whispered other words, Welsh words she didn't understand.

Tears ambushed her eyes. Her throat clogged.

He kissed the wetness from her lashes. "Amidst

the cries on the battlefield, only thoughts of you held me together. When I saw my comrades fall—"

Hot tears streamed like silent waterfalls down her cheeks. She rubbed her palm along the coarse hairs of his beard and whispered, "Please don't let me go."

His fingers kneaded the small of her back as he kissed her tenderly, lovingly.

"Do you realize how gorgeous you are?" he murmured.

She shook her head in denial as he reclaimed her lips.

"You're the most magnificent creature in the world." He kissed her birthmark, steadied her face in his large hands and grinned. "Remind me to get thrashed more often."

"Don't speak of such things."

A velvety chuckle resonated from his body. "You're allowing me to kiss you because of my charming appearance."

She covered her face with her hands. "You do look dreadful," she admitted, opening her fingers to view him. "However, 'tis your impeccable manners—beginning with the way you crept into my chamber and frightened me—that was the ultimate charm."

His delighted laughter filled the room. She laughed with him.

Standing by the door, talking to him in the shadows, his arms wrapped around her, gave her a joy she'd never known. How secure it felt, this unforeseen gratification of belonging.

He sprinkled kisses on her forehead. "I didn't expect to come home to this—influenza and panic. I apologize for my anger. My thoughts were unclear."

"Will you please explain what happened between you and the Rom?"

"Someday." He smiled down at her. "Come the morrow we leave for Wales."

"Wales? In the middle of winter?"

"Aye. 'Tis the reason I visited your chamber tonight, to inform you of my plans. I've instructed the servants to pack their baggage."

"A journey clear across England will be difficult in the coldest months."

Amusement flickered in his eyes. "We'll mark any young trees along the way in case we need to shake them." He jested before becoming serious again. "Jeremy is stronger and must be kept safe. My estate in Wales is even more remote than Ipswich, rugged and untamed. My hope is you'll grow fond of it and one day come to love the countryside as much as I do. In fact, Wales reminds me of you."

"I remind you of a country?"

"Wales is tempestuous, wild and unpredictable. *Cymru*, the land of the comrades." He smoothed her hair behind her ears and brushed two soft kisses on her birthmark. "And very, very precious to me."

She laughed at the comparisons, somehow appropriate. She drew a solitary breath and glided her fingers up the span of his powerful chest.

Tell him about your half-truth. He'll forgive you.

"James, there's something else I must—"

He strode to the mantel and lit a candle. Then he returned to her to hold her again, cradling her close to his heart.

Tell him.

He'd never regard her in the same way again.

Valentina inhaled a long breath, reluctant to release it.

She'd always been a coward.

"I shall regale you with battle tales as we travel," he was saying.

I won't be with you to hear your stories, nor see your beloved Wales. But I will hear your voice in my dreams and picture your rugged country in my mind. You'll be there, caring for your son, riding in the hillsides. Without me.

"I imagine your home is quite fancy," she said aloud.

"'Tis comfortable. Several neighbors are noblemen, although you wouldn't want to be a part of all that."

"Because I wouldn't fit in?"

Of course, she wouldn't. She was nothing more than an uncultured sham.

His fingers traced the curve of her lips. "You

wouldn't want to fit in, although your presence would add a sparkle to every home."

"'Tis wrong for me to imagine myself as a wife to a gentleman."

"Only wrong for you to think otherwise." He sprinkled kisses on her temples. "I've been wrong too, you know."

"Wrong about what?"

"Wrong about thinking you wouldn't accept my proposal of marriage." He gave her a smoky male smile, and his lips found hers. "I hope you plan to get used to this."

She gloried in his smile and stroked his handsome, bruised face.

Ves'tacha.

Beloved.

CHAPTER SEVENTEEN

Devlesa avilan.
It is God who brought you.
Old Romany saying

After James left her chamber, Valentina meandered in and out of wispy dreams. Hours passed, daylight neared. Propping a pillow behind her, she lit a candle on her night table.

He'd bathed her in complimentary words. He'd told her she was dear to him. He'd told her she was exquisite. But he'd never said he loved her.

She stared at the lone candle. Superstitions and Romany spirits weren't real, and no palm reading was needed to tell her future. Without James, it loomed empty and desolate. And that was real.

She rose, tied her mother's yellow diklo around her neck, then slipped a plain woolen gown over her head. She blew out the candle, then scurried from the chamber, cautious not to rouse the household.

The long hallway was illuminated by one flickering oil lamp, and she eased her way in near darkness to Jeremy's chamber. She unlatched his door and stepped inside. Noiselessly, she hovered by his bed. He resembled an innocent cherub, breathing quietly though his small, turned-up nose and pink lips. Faint, short hiccups punctuated his dreams. His favorite nubby blanket lay twisted at the foot of the bed.

She pulled the blanket snugly over his shoulders. "Your father will take good care of you. He loves you dearly." She wiped heavy tears from her lids. "I must leave, little man. A decent man deserves an honest woman as his wife."

One last farewell kiss, and Valentina headed to Yolanda's chamber. She rapped, then hit the latch.

"Yolanda, wake up," she whispered.

Yolanda sat up in bed and her eyes widened. "Valentina. What is the hour?"

Valentina lit a candle on the night table. "'Tis almost morning. I came to tell you I'm leaving."

"Before dawn? Why? Mr. Colchester is back. Did you quarrel—"

"Aye. Nay. Well, maybe at first."

"Was he angry when you confessed your reading?"

"I didn't tell him." She covered her mouth to catch a sob. James' scent lingered on her fingers.

Yolanda wrapped her arms around her legs and rested her chin on her knees. Her shiny dark hair tangled in waves down her back. "Why not? Were you too foolish or too proud?"

"A little of both. He's leaving for Wales today."

"I know. I've already packed." Yolanda nodded to a small knapsack by the door.

Valentina's heart sank. "I've decided to rejoin our tribe. You wouldn't want to come with me, would you?"

Yolanda swung her legs off the bed and smoothed her muslin nightdress. She grabbed her tunic and draped it over the nightdress, taking the time to tie each lace perfectly. When she looked at Valentina again, her eyes took on a rounded sadness. "Where do you suppose our tribe has gone?"

"Luca said somewhere warm, near the sea. Brighton, I believe."

Resignedly, Yolanda shook her head. "I can't leave Reginald."

Valentina watched her sister and let a silent beat pass. "I'll go alone, then."

The candlelight spilled across Yolanda's pensive features. For the third time in as many minutes, she sighed. "The nights are long and cold, and 'tis too dangerous to cross the footpaths on your own. I'll accompany you."

She stood and evened the rumpled sheets. "I will need a few minutes to explain to Reginald. He's an understanding man, although not *that* understanding."

Valentina flew to her sister and embraced her in a grateful hug. "Thank you, my darling sister, thank you."

"Don't cry. You're the brave one," Yolanda whispered. "We'll take the back stairwell. 'Twill be deserted at this hour."

Yolanda dressed, blew out the candle, and threw on a russet wool cloak. She assumed the lead and led Valentina down the back stairs and along a narrow passageway.

Valentina paused and scrutinized alternate doorways, trying to place where they were. She turned, about-face, and walked down a different passage.

"Valentina, you're going the wrong way!" Yolanda's tone echoed heavily in the darkened hallway.

"We must fetch Daj's dagger in case we're forced to defend ourselves while we're traveling, and I know exactly where 'twill be hidden."

James had relocated his sleeping quarters closer to hers a few nights after she'd arrived. His former chamber was in the north wing.

Yolanda lagging at her heels, Valentina creaked

opened the door to James' former bedchamber and her mouth dropped. His chamber was much different from what she'd imagined, especially compared to the grandiose chambers she and Yolanda enjoyed. Beyond the neatly made bed and mahogany bureau, the chamber was furnished with only a high table and chairs.

She braced her arms on the doorframe and tried to catch her breath. His presence filled the air, so compelling she felt like she could see him walking through the room. A pair of his worn black leather boots, shined to perfection, stood propped against the bureau.

Shaking aside his image, she hurried into the room and opened the bureau's top drawer. "The dagger must be here somewhere."

The double-edged dagger sat in the bottom drawer, meticulously waffled between two of James' linen shirts. She tied the dagger and its sheath to the inside of her cloak.

The sisters pulled the door closed, then quickened down another set of stairs and through the pantry. They sped past the herb garden and across the darkened cobblestone courtyard.

Yolanda raced to the stables. "Reginald will assist us. He sleeps with the horses." She hoisted open the stable door. "Although he despises them."

"A blacksmith who sleeps in a stable and despises horses?"

"A horse bit him when he was a boy. He's never been able to forgive the entire breed, yet the smell of hay and leather helps him sleep."

The women entered the stables and weaved around bales of hay. Despite the darkness, Yolanda found her way to the corner where Reginald slept. She nudged him awake.

He chafed his hands through his matted blond beard and heaved himself to his feet, grinning at the unexpected sight of Yolanda.

"We need your help," Yolanda began, but was interrupted by his kisses. When he lifted his head, the glower he shot toward Valentina was caustic. "I'm not sure if I should be thrilled to see Yolanda before dawn, or very, very worried."

"Mr. Colchester has returned and plans to depart for Wales today," Valentina began.

"Aye."

"And Valentina cannot travel to Wales with him," Yolanda said.

Reginald's heavy blond eyebrows gathered into one ominous line. "But you will come with me to Wales, Yolanda?"

"I won't abandon my sister."

"Are you both mad?" Reginald all but shouted. "Mr. Colchester would never approve. Tell Valentina you're staying here where you belong."

"She's right in front of you. You tell her. I must go where I'm needed, and for now, my place is with my sister." Yolanda caressed his face and nuzzled his bearded chin, her expression one of pure innocence. "Valentina and I must leave before daybreak and we require a good horse."

Reginald swore as a horse kicked from the next stall. "Absolutely not."

"I'll wait in the courtyard." Valentina paused and offered her sister a silent plea—*convince him*—before leaving the stables.

Outside, she alternated her pacing with staring at the wide stable door that muted the argument within. Finally, a hulking Reginald and a petite Yolanda emerged leading a shaggy, saddled chestnut mare.

Yolanda beamed up at Reginald, and then turned a heartening smile on Valentina.

Reginald's actions confirmed what Yolanda had said the first day she'd met him. He was a brave man with strong morals, and he was proving it by endangering his livelihood to assist them.

And he loved Yolanda.

When they reached the end of the path leading away from the stables, they reached an old stone wall near the river. The mare snorted and thumped Reginald with its front leg. Reginald dropped the reins, swore at the horse, and enveloped Yolanda in his arms.

"Is the mare always this temperamental, Reginald?" Valentina asked.

"Only around me."

Reginald and Yolanda conferred, and Yolanda answered his brusque questions with quiet reassurances. Clearly in no hurry to release her sister, he directed terse instructions to Valentina. "Guide the horse to swim across the river."

Valentina scanned the lightening horizon. "Beyond the cliff, the water runs shallower."

"No one ventures near the cliff since Beatrix's death. In winter, any attempt to scale it would be near suicide. I won't allow you to place Yolanda's life, or your own, in peril. Here, the river is crossable."

Yolanda inspected the water, slapping against the banks, a shimmer of golden black in the pale predawn light. Her pallid face was painted in terror. "I can't swim across that river. Valentina, you know I can't."

"You won't swim." Using the stone wall as a mounting block, Valentina put her foot in the stirrup and eased up and over the mare, settling in the saddle. "The horse will."

"When Mr. Colchester is settled in Wales, I'll come for you." Reginald lifted Yolanda's slim body and settled her on the mare behind Valentina. "Please be safe."

"We'll travel to London first," Valentina said. Uttering the name of the city she hadn't seen since the rape did nothing to settle her nerves. "A Romany caravan will be camped somewhere near the city's outskirts. From there, a *vurma* can direct us to our tribe."

Noting Reginald's puzzled squint, Valentina explained. "Romany have no addresses, so we rely on a vurma to help us find each other. A vurma is a Romany woman who knows where everyone is located when our caravans are traveling."

She clicked her heels into the mare's flanks. The mare obediently stepped into the river, and murky water rose to her knees. Reginald stood on the riverbank, his smile forced, the last of the moonlight revealing lines of worry on his hard-set face.

Valentina held her breath and grabbed the horse's mane. The water deepened.

Yolanda squeezed her arms around Valentina's ribs. "I'm so afraid."

"Bite your lips and close your eyes. The mare is strong and can swim." Valentina's long gown swished and sloshed and swilled. She blinked through splashes of water, her cheeks wet, her eyelashes spiked. Frost clung to the skeletal branches of blackthorn trees, giving the landscape an eerie, wintry glow.

Yolanda's body was shaking uncontrollably. "Soon the water will be over our heads."

Valentina squeezed Yolanda's hands reassuringly. "Dry land is near." She held the reins tighter and guided the mare out of the water. Only then could she exhale, sending noiseless white clouds of breath into the chilly air. "Yolanda, you can open your eyes now," she said affectionately.

Ever so slightly, Yolanda loosened her knotted fingers from Valentina's ribcage

Valentina glanced behind them. Reginald was merely a speck on the other side of the river.

Her throat tightened until she could hardly breathe. Even a distance away, James' majestic estate formed an imposing silhouette against the sky. The home of the only man she'd ever love.

Keeping the mare headed to the south and west, Valentina urged her through forests and frosty silver fields at a fast pace.

"Mr. Colchester will be very unhappy when he realizes you're gone," Yolanda predicted. "You should have told him you were leaving."

Of course, she should have, except she couldn't because she was weak.

She was hiding behind the fear of being judged by God and by James. She couldn't face his heart-broken gaze when she confessed her deceit. She had prayed, believing that God had placed her with James, exactly where she belonged. Perhaps He had. If so, she was the failure, because she couldn't believe in herself.

Wasn't her fear also keeping her from becoming whole? If she concentrated on herself and not God, she'd end up with scarceness.

Too exhausted to respond to Yolanda's prediction, she said, "Someday, he'll come to realize 'tis the right decision. He and his son will be safe, and he'll live his life in peace."

Call me James.

His voice was so clear, that although she knew 'twas impossible, she looked around for him anyway. He wasn't there. He wouldn't be, yet her foolish heart had hoped. She lowered her head, staring blindly at the ground speeding past, refusing to give in to the agony of her loss.

She fingered a strand of James' dark hair caught in the fabric of her cloak. It broke from her numbed fingers and blew away in the whoosh of an acrid wind.

The Rom believed discarded hair was a guarantee that two lovers would go their separate ways, her invasive conscience reminded.

Romany nonsense.

An owl hooted and swooped across a field, evidently intent on its prey.

Both sisters snapped their heads upward and then exchanged nervous glances. Both were hesitant to say the word aloud.

The owl's cry. *Bibaxt. Very bad luck.*

CHAPTER EIGHTEEN

What bak the divvus?
What luck today?
Kker rya.
I never have any luck.
Romany saying

*S*omeone was missing. In fact, two someones were missing. At least, that was what Geoffrey was droning as he shook James awake.

Groggy from a deep sleep, James rolled to his side and opened his eyes a crack. The pale light of dawn sifted through the thick blue draperies of his chamber. He'd rest a few more minutes, he muttered and shrugged off Geoffrey.

When next James woke, sunlight soaked his eyelids. He kept his eyes closed and imagined Valentina waking him, certainly a more delightful prospect than the insistent Geoffrey.

He'd trace the perfect curves of her face while reassuring any reservations she had about becoming his wife. They'd discuss wedding plans, for when they reached Wales they'd be married in a Christian church, far from the condemning eyes of London.

At her request, they'd also have a Gypsy wedding. If the tradition brought her happiness, he'd even jump over a broomstick for her, a Gypsy custom she'd undoubtedly tease him about for years. They would be blessed, enjoying a lifetime of joy and serving God. A lifetime of meaning and principles, pleasure and peace. She'd teach him to love and trust again. In return, he'd indulge her with the finest herbal garden in all of Wales. And cherish her.

"Mr. Colchester."

Resigning himself to Geoffrey's presence, James opened his eyes and glared at his steward. "I don't require a nursemaid. My injuries will heal, I assure you."

"I'm sure they will, sir. There's some news, and I'm uncertain how to tell you."

James' eyes flew open. He sat up, straight and rigid, startled to see the sun so high in the sky. They would not make an early start that day. Perhaps 'twould be best to leave for Wales come the morrow. "Tell me what?" he asked Geoffrey.

Geoffrey stepped back, no doubt from the blast of impatience from James' gaze. "Valentina and Yolanda are missing, sir. Although," he added a little too desperately, "I'm sure they haven't gone far."

Before the next second split, James was on his feet. He washed and dressed quickly, then hastened to the window. He didn't see Valentina scurrying about anywhere.

He swung from the window and strode to her chamber, surveying every corner of the room, half-expecting to see her. Perhaps she was assisting the servants in packing for the long journey ahead. Or, he visualized her in the kitchen, boiling dandelions in one of her mysterious brews, perhaps to soothe someone's sore throat. Or perhaps she was at one of the tenant farmer's cottages, tending to an ailing child.

Aye, all plausible explanations. Valentina always thought of others first.

He nodded complacently, his smile magnanimous, certain she would appear by noon.

He envisioned her curvaceous body, her generous smile and full lips. And perhaps again she could come close to him and whisper, *"Will you please put your arms around me?"*

*W*here could she be? Tight-lipped, James shaded his eyes from the midmorning sun brightening the fields. Already far behind schedule, his household readied to depart for Wales.

Hoisting Jeremy onto his shoulders, he searched every dreary nook of his home. He did not find her, and none of the servants, busy with packing and readying the house to be empty for an unknown length of time, had seen her.

In the kitchen, Isabel was ordering the maids about as they packed food for the journey. She suggested Valentina might be in the herb garden.

"Whenever I've seen her in the garden," Wiborow said waspishly from the kitchen doorway, "I've noted that Valentina had a fascination for foxglove."

"Is foxglove another potion?" he asked her, absently patting Jeremy's wiggling knees.

"Hardly, Mr. Colchester. Foxglove, added to food or drink, causes great harm."

James harbored no uncertainties about Wiborow. Her observation was meant to alarm him. Casually, he remarked, "Valentina finds plants that save people." With deliberate, unhurried movements, he lowered Jeremy from his shoulders and waited until his son had dashed off. Then he turned back to Wiborow.

"Now say what you mean," he ordered, "and be done with it."

"The afternoon Geoffrey choked on a pear, my suspicions about Valentina were confirmed. Beforehand, she'd dug through the herbal garden for several minutes."

"She spends many days outdoors in the garden because she's a healer."

With a thread of self-righteousness in her smug smile, Wiborow asked, "Is she a healer or a murderess?"

James pursed his lips. His tolerance lowered. His anger soared. "Your accusations are grave, unfounded and cruel."

"Gypsies cannot be trusted. The day of our midday meal, I suspect she attempted to poison Geoffrey."

"When? She's fond of Geoffrey and eased his discomfort that day by brewing a tonic." Trying to recall the events of that afternoon, James sifted through his thoughts. One of the servants had shouted from the kitchen that Geoffrey was choking on a pear, and the servant had been right. Someone else mentioned the deer meat being rancid—perhaps one of the cooks.

Wiborow crossed her arms. "Might Valentina harbor a reason to hurt you?"

"Nay," he snapped.

"I said my peace." Wiborow positioned her mouth into a somber, dull streak. "Be warned."

He studied her spiteful face and arsenic eyes. "Your observations are completely unfounded. Don't speak of this matter again."

Wiborow gave a curt bow, the stiff, mousy strands of her bun coming undone. A servant who understood no life other than serving the Colchester household, she marched away in a thinly veiled huff.

∾

*A*s the sun was setting, James strode outdoors to consult with Tobias about the readiness of the horses, wagons and carriages that would transport his household. A pinch of sunbeam danced off the river beyond, then disappeared behind encroaching grey clouds. The day had been cool and he spotted Jeremy sitting on a fallen tree trunk, spinning red and black checkers. He clapped eagerly each time the checkers collided.

James bent to smooth Jeremy's white frilled collar over his heavy cotton jacket.

The boy stared up at him. "Val-en-tina?"

"I don't know where she is, son." James cupped the boy's chin so Jeremy had a better view of his lips while he spoke. "However, I'll tell you a secret. She and her sister better have an excellent excuse for disappearing."

Once the afternoon waned and turned to evening, James' mood darkened. Like a lion confined to a cage, he paced his home with feverish impatience. Valentina wouldn't be able to travel far alone, he reasoned. Sooner or later, she'd reappear, most likely where he least expected her. Yet as the hours since her disappearance grew, so did his suspicions.

Maybe she and her sister didn't want to be found.

Nay. She'd never leave without telling him. Never. He commanded himself to take slow, deep breaths and banish that ridiculous thought from his mind. His chest grew empty even thinking such thoughts, much less speaking them aloud, because he loved her with an urgency he hardly fathomed. She must have developed feelings for him, too, in all the weeks of their shared quips and lively conversations.

Certainly, she had more fortitude than anyone he'd ever known. He recalled how she'd met his eyes unflinchingly the night before, as she'd walked across her chamber to him, like a trembling yet proud queen.

"Have you seen Valentina, Geoffrey?" he asked when he went into his study where his steward was sorting through estate paperwork.

"Not since the last time you asked," Geoffrey replied.

James gestured at the papers scattered on the desk. "Instead of dealing with such inconsequential ledgers, use your time wisely and find the two women. And find them quickly, because I'm going to talk some sense into Valentina when I see her."

"And Yolanda?"

"I don't think for a hare-brained minute Yolanda is to blame. She's afraid to put two sentences together if the words might lead to her being reprimanded." Worry growing inside him for the women, he stared at Geoffrey while his insides split and his heart weighted heavy. "Where can they be?"

"Perhaps the women are packing their belongings in their trunks—somewhere obscurely."

Both of the men knew the women had no belongings to pack, nor trunks to stow their lack of belongings in.

Geoffrey couldn't ignore years of ingrained respect and kept his features politely downcast. "I believe you ... ah ... visited Valentina's chamber last evening. Therefore, you were the last person with her."

"No secrets of my whereabouts?" James asked.

"Not a one."

Spinning on his heels, James strode from the room, calling for Tobias to organize a search party. As he and a dozen men met with torches by the stables, he disregarded the meaningful glances the men gave one other, the concern furrowing Geoffrey's white brows. When he stopped thinking about the sound reprimand he'd give Valentina when he found her, he worried some accident had befallen her. She might be hurt, alone, in a barren field, or submerged at the bottom of the swollen river.

Fear and alarm rocked him, and he mounted his horse and galloped with his men to the river's edge. He'd given her explicit orders to stay away from the river the day of Yolanda's near drowning. And Valentina had promised, murmuring aye between blue lips and chattering teeth.

His breath trapped in his throat. The familiar agony of losing someone he loved sapped his strength. He stared at the river, unmindful of the frozen drizzle sticking to his cloak and coating his cheeks with tiny icicles. He turned away and ordered Tobias to take half the men out to the pastures where the tenant farmers lived. He, Geoffrey, and the others set off toward the hills.

"How long do you plan to delay our departure? Geoffrey asked. "Influenza might reappear at any time."

"We will find them," James said, holding his torch high, probing the ground for clues and misguided footsteps.

Geoffrey nodded. "Even if Valentina has some sort of Gypsy magic, two women don't vanish. Unless they had help from their so-called spirits."

"She doesn't believe in Gypsy spirits anymore."

Even so, in her most vulnerable moments he'd detected a sense of urgency—a single-minded purpose to tell him something. In all their afternoons spent together, he'd never given her the chance, too intent on bending the conversation toward his own gains. That was a tormenting thought and he swallowed, tasting a firm upbraiding at himself.

James and Geoffrey returned to the courtyard where Tobias and his men waited. Tobias reported that there had been no sign of the women and asked when they would leave for Wales. "All of the supplies are loaded onto the wagons."

"We'll depart within a couple of days." James swung off his horse with such suddenness, Tobias jerked back.

~

*A*n hour later, James was trying to make sense of the ledgers that Geoffrey had left on his desk, when Tobias knocked on the door. Stepping inside, he cleared his throat and examined the wall behind James with rapt concentration.

"One of the mares is missing," he said.

James scratched his jaw. The bristling of a neglected beard crackled beneath his tense fingers.

"Surely, you have something better to do than report on a horse."

Displaying a brilliant imitation of a man who was about to say something he didn't believe in the slightest, Tobias said apologetically, "The mare may be grazing in an outer meadow. We checked everywhere, although you can never be sure—"

"A horse is missing," James repeated. "One horse, only one, decided to gallop away."

In the space of a hairsbreadth, the realization staggered him. He jerked back his chair and stormed past the open-mouthed man with lengthy, purposeful strides.

"Mr. Colchester, is it possible the Gypsy women rode that little mare right off the grounds of your estate?" Tobias called after him.

Of course they did, because any other possibility was a coincidence.

James's strides increased to a run as visions of Valentina clouded his eyesight.

Her beauty. Her laughter. Her deceit.

His mind screamed, refusing to believe. How could she leave him without a word?

Tobias ran after him, reaching him as he strode toward the stables. He bent his head to his knees, gasping. "Mr. Colchester, 'twould be remiss if I didn't mention—"

"Go on." Tobias' hesitancy strained James' overstretched nerves.

"Were you aware Yolanda and Reginald were seeing each other?"

James' sigh was loud and volatile. "I'm aware now, Tobias."

He headed toward the stables to confront a wayward blacksmith. Geoffrey, Tobias, and some of the other men formed an invisible column behind him.

Reginald was at his forge outside the stables, clanging his ironwork, preparing to shoe a horse. In stark contrast to the blasting heat of the open fire, the wind blew wintry flurries upward. So close to the fire, he wore only a shirt and breeches beneath his leather apron. His space blistered with the remnants of charred metal.

"Reginald," James began, pleased he was able to control his voice, "it has come to my attention that you and Yolanda have become close."

Reginald plunged a horseshoe into a bucket of water before looking up. "Aye, Mr. Colchester."

"When was the last time you saw her?"

Reginald wiped shaking, sooty palms on his blackened apron. By the blood-red firelight, sweat formed a riveting stream down his forehead. "I cannot place the exact hour, Mr. Colchester. I'm sorry."

"I find I cannot believe you." James stepped closer. "Where did the women go, Reginald?"

Reginald shook his head. "I have nothing to say."

And by not saying, James learned two facts. One, Reginald was far bolder than most of the men on James' estate, which didn't particularly interest him at the moment; and two, Reginald had assisted Valentina and Yolanda in their flight, which interested James a great deal.

"Your actions may condemn them to a frozen death," he said shortly.

Reginald's expression closed. He screwed his thick lips, raised his mutinous gaze to James and then turned back to his forge.

James stormed back to his house where he found Geoffrey waiting for him in his study. He accepted a glass of wine from James, then said, "It occurred to me that upon her arrival, Valentina mentioned returning to her mother's burial site. Perhaps 'tis the reason why the women ran off."

James grabbed the thin back of a wooden chair to steady his frustration. "You refer to occurrences happening months ago. Why would she leave now?"

Quick to acknowledge James' excellent choice of wines on the sideboard, Geoffrey seated himself by the fire and shrugged. "I wonder, though, that although Valentina was correct when she foretold Beatrix's death, her influenza prediction was off the mark."

Was it? The revelation hit James with such explosive force, he snapped the brittle back of the chair. Aimlessly, he stared at the piece of wood in his hand as if it were a curious oddity.

After a prolonged hesitation, Geoffrey set down his glass and said, "She deceived you."

"When she read my fortune?" James scowled. "Fortune-telling isn't real. Valentina knows this."

"That's not the point," Geoffrey persisted.

"'Twas real to her at the time, and she may have seen more than she was letting on. Let's not forget her Gypsy friend Luca made no secret about hating the English. In the end, Gypsies are wanderlust people who can't be trusted."

James shuddered violently. Denial clouded his thoughts. In the recesses of his mind, he wondered if he could stand upright.

What a besotted, ignorant fool he'd been. Vaguely, he wondered if he'd made any rational decisions since Beatrix had died. He'd been anchored in bitterness and fear. And then he'd attempted to cling to a hope, any hope, even a false hope.

He inclined his head toward the door, bidding a blunt goodnight to Geoffrey. After a moment, the steward nodded and quit the chamber.

In three paces, James strode to the window. He pushed his hands into his pockets and uttered, "My steps are ordered by the Lord." He repeated the verse from Psalms over and over in his mind, then groped inside his waistcoat for the moss-green ribbon necklace. He'd intended to give Valentina the necklace when he'd returned from London.

He grasped the delicate ribbon, swung the gold coins back and forth, and let it slip from his fingers. "Good-bye Valentina," he whispered.

He should have felt satisfaction when the coins hit the floor.

Instead, he felt empty.

CHAPTER NINETEEN

Jek dilo kerel but dile hai but dile keren dilimata.
One madman makes many madmen and many
madmen make madness.
Old Romany saying

"I'm tired." Yolanda slumped lower on the mare. "My fingers are numb and the wind is freezing my toes."

"'Tis better to ride a few more hours and take advantage of the daylight." Valentina turned to her sister, noting the long-suffering look on Yolanda's angelic face. Valentina managed a reassuring smile. "Did I ever tell you that Luca didn't even blink when we stole three chickens from a wealthy villager's farm? We ate well for days."

Yolanda tilted her chin down and scowled. "You've told me that story at least a half-dozen times. When we were children, I often wondered who was more daring, you or Luca."

"Luca," Valentina assured her.

Yolanda laughed. "He's like the wind—completely unpredictable."

"He cares for our elders and has never deserted the tribe."

"You always defend him, and I'm not interested in Luca." Yolanda sobered, adding, "I'm interested in Reginald and I hardly had a minute to bid him a proper farewell." With an audible humph, Yolanda pressed her head against Valentina's back.

"When I rejoin our tribe," Valentina said, "you'll see Reginald again."

"And I'll become a proud and fancy Englishman's wife."

"You act like Reginald is bestowing the crown jewels on your head because he wants to marry you. I had hoped we'd fit into the English world, although now I'm not so sure." All the swallowing in the world didn't relieve the unexpected lump of sadness in her throat. "We can't change who we are, nor the color of our skin. At the end of the day, we're still Romany—strong and proud."

"Little good it's done us," Yolanda contradicted. "We're poor and hungry and resort to thievery."

"You must be exhausted. 'Tis why you're speaking disrespectfully about our people." Valentina scanned the trees, searching for long-hanging, supple limbs. "We can stop here and build a *bender*, a tent, to shelter us for a few hours."

"We'll not need to build anything." Yolanda pointed ahead of them. "A very strange man is coming toward us from the bottom of the hill."

Valentina reined the mare in sharply. Her startled gaze fell on a short, egg-shaped man emerging from the woods. She held the mare's reins steady, knowing she and Yolanda would look guilty if they tried to bolt.

The man hiked nearer. "You wenches are trespassing on Mr. Wellsey's estate!"

Trespassing meant imprisonment.

Valentina stilled her twitching hands, praying her worries were premature.

The man drew closer, squinting at them as he touched his stringy red beard. "I don't recall any reports of Gypsies roaming these lands."

The mare leapt beneath Valentina, and her gaze flew nervously across the empty fields. "James confided that the Wellsey and Colchester families have feuded for years," she murmured to Yolanda.

"His feuds shouldn't matter," came Yolanda's sharp retort. "You left him, remember?"

Valentina flinched, her tormented heart protesting. She half-hoped Yolanda might soften her response, perhaps adding that James would never have wanted Valentina to leave, that he would be searching frantically for her even now.

Yolanda didn't speak anything of the sort. In fact, she didn't speak to Valentina at all. Instead, she said to the man, "Sir, we've been guests of Mr. Colchester."

Valentina glanced back at her sister with a warning scowl as she shook her head.

The red-bearded man fingered the mare's reins, and the horse gave a panicky lurch. "If you're telling the truth, then Mr. Wellsey will want to meet you and extend his pardon."

There was no time to think. Things were moving too swiftly, and images of what might happen rushed across Valentina's mind. She did not trust this man, nor did she trust that she and Yolanda would find a warm welcome at the Wellsey estate. Yanking the reins free from the man's loose grip, she wheeled the mare around in a tight circle and then urged it into a charging gallop.

The man expelled a violent oath and called for help.

The breeze tore at her long hair, tossing it riotously about. She threw a glance over her shoulder. The man ran after them uselessly, and no one else was about. He was no match for the mare. The women bolted along a stream, then tore over a low stone bridge. She focused on the mare, speaking encouragingly. As they neared a sharp bend, she sensed that the mare was tiring. As the mare rounded the next curve wide, Valentina saw the heavy limb jutting from an oak tree.

A swell of panic volleyed through her. She held her breath as time slowed.

"Yolanda! Lower your head!"

Valentina felt the blow to her head as both women were unseated from the horse. Then her world went black.

CHAPTER TWENTY

May kali muri gugli avela.
The darker the berry, the sweeter it is.
Old Romany saying

A peculiar shout. Rushed footsteps.
"Mr. Colchester!"

James awoke to a distressed shriek and rubbed his hand over his face.

Wiborow stood in the doorway of his study, staring at him, and yet not appearing to see him. She seemed to be attempting to speak, although she stuttered.

Between his worry about Valentina and her sister, and then needing to get up early to see many of his household servants off on their journey to Wales, he had barely slept the night before. When he'd retreated to his study after the last wagon had disappeared, he had fallen asleep at his desk. The strange shriek and Wiborow's appearance jerked him up from his chair. An idle fire burned low in the grate.

Trained for battle, he yanked his knife from his boot and raised the blade. Then he blinked and scanned the room. He saw no danger.

He focused on Wiborow's ashen face. Wiborow never cried, yet tears poured down her cheeks. He raced to her, grabbing and shaking her bony forearms.

Eyes wide, she sputtered between mispronounced words, nearly incoherent. "Jeremy! You're cursed, Mr. Colchester!" She looked around. "First Beatrix, now Jeremy—"

"Jeremy? Cursed?" James' breath pierced his lungs. He couldn't say any more.

He tore past her and leapt the stairs two at a time. *His legs. His legs were too slow. When had his balance become so pitiable?*

Seconds later, he stopped at the open door to Jeremy's chamber and froze. Jeremy thrashed on his small bed. Sweat matted his hair and trickled down his flushed cheeks.

His son. Sick. Here in England. Impossible.

James let out a cry that couldn't be contained and brought a shaky hand to his temple.

He plunged toward the bed.

Elspeth wiped a linen cloth over Jeremy's forehead. "He's not well, Mr. Colchester."

He waved her away and leaned against the bed frame. Continually, he shook his head. "I should have taken him to Wales weeks ago."

"Tad?" Jeremy stirred beneath a pile of blankets.

James's chest tightened. He couldn't breathe. Despair submerged him—the same heaviness he'd felt after Beatrix's death. He'd never have the strength to emerge a second time.

He sagged to the floor by his son's bed and clutched Jeremy's small fingers. "Stay awake, son. I'm here." *Calm, calm, calm, for Jeremy's sake.*

The boy gave a ragged huff, his eyes fluttered, opened, closed. "Sleep ... y."

"Nay! Don't go to sleep!" Powerless, he clasped his son's hands tighter, and prayed. "Dear Lord, I put all my faith in you."

Through the morning and into the afternoon, he recited verses from the Bible—from Proverbs and Psalms—and words from hymns. When Richard, the vicar, stepped into the chamber, he blessed Jeremy and sat on the floor next to James.

"We can do nothing for him, Mr. Colchester. Influenza, as we've experienced, must run its course." Richard kept his gaze downcast, his drooping shoulders giving little hope. "We must seek God for our answers. Everything is in His time."

James nodded, wordless. Jeremy lay fitfully on his bed, moaning, his face flushed with fever.

Clare hesitantly entered the chamber, keeping her head down. "Mr. Colchester, might we attempt Valentina's cure? She spoke to me about shaking a sapling—"

"Nay." Looking past Clare, he noted Tobias and Geoffrey, and wondered how long they'd been there.

"Pardon us, Mr. Colchester." Tobias made an exaggerated show of fumbling for something in his waistcoat. "One of the tenant farmers said they've located Valentina and Yolanda."

"Alive?"

"Aye, and ..."

James exhaled slowly. "And?"

"And not far from here. Apparently, they were crossing Mr. Wellsey's estate when they had an accident. Valentina suffered a blow to her head, but no broken bones far as anyone can tell. Did you want me to bring her back here?"

James sank his head onto his chest, shaking it back and forth. Nay. Nay, nay.

His shriveled heart refused to beat. His mouth felt so dry.

The women had been only a few miles away? He'd imagined they were halfway across England by now, while he'd wasted all of a precious day and night searching for her. A day and night when they could have been far from here, traveling to Wales, away from the influenza.

"I'll accompany you."

"Mr. Colchester," Clare said, "Valentina cared for my aunt Dionise, so perhaps—"

He raised a hand. "Please, no talk of supposed Gypsy cures." He rubbed his fingers against his son's damp cheek and kissed Jeremy's burning forehead. "I won't be long, son," he whispered. "I'll return within the hour."

"What exactly do you intend to do, once she's back here?" Geoffrey asked.

"I'm not a fool, Geoffrey. However, if she's hurt, I'll not abandon her."

Several minutes later, James and several men drove their horses into a full gallop amidst a shower of mud and grinding hooves. A gathering of starlings scattered in the courtyard, their wings flapping in noisy agreement.

CHAPTER TWENTY-ONE

Nashti zhas vorta po drom o bango.
You cannot walk straight when the road is bent.
Old Romany saying

Frozen leaves crackled under a horse's galloping hooves, and a sharp wind peppered Valentina's ears and cheeks. She winced, biting her lips to stifle the moan. Wisps of consciousness faded as shifting rays of sunlight penetrated her closed eyelids. A nightjar's song frittered in the trees, chirpy and cheery, hunting for moths.

She leaned back, luxuriating in the strength of a hard chest. Her body settled into the percussive rhythm of the powerful horse beneath her. She sniffed, catching a whiff of worn leather.

She opened her eyes and twisted in the saddle. *James.*

His heavy cloak swirled around them. His unkempt beard darkened his chin. Puffy, dark

circles dragged under his eyes. He stared ahead, solemn and silent, his gaze refusing hers.

She had thought she'd still been dreaming, only dreaming, when he'd appeared like a spirit and lifted her onto his horse. When he'd mounted behind her and closed his arms around her, she'd rested against him without hesitation and fallen asleep.

"Yolanda?" she asked, grimacing. Her head felt as if it were exploding.

"Riding ahead with Geoffrey," came the terse reply.

She strained past shadows of fatigue and spotted her sister's russet cloak whirling about her slight frame. She drew a relieved breath. "Thank you. We had—"

She thought he swore under his breath, and she stared down at her bare hands. She didn't want

to close her eyes again because her mind might swim with memories—of her time spent with James, her emptiness without him, the pain from her fall.

She focused on the stark branches of oak trees speeding by in ever-changing outlines.

An oncoming limb rushed at them, promising to

dislodge them both from the saddle if they didn't bend their heads. This time she ducked quickly.

She hardly remembered the earlier fall and what had happened after. Eventually, she and Yolanda had wakened to find the mare had run off and they were both chilled and wet from lying on the ground. She had lost all sense of direction, but some instinct told her which way lay James' estate. She and Yolanda walked for hours, and as darkness fell they saw a light from a cottage in the distance. 'Twas the home of one of James' tenant farmers and his wife and children. Too exhausted to do much more than sip some broth, the sisters had fallen asleep by the fire. Since James had found them there, she assumed the farmer had gone to the estate to tell him where she and Yolanda were.

Should she provoke the cold man whose chest she was leaning on, or talk rationally with that same caring man who'd carried her so gently onto his horse? She'd seen the worried, bleak light draw off his face when he'd bent over her and realized she'd been hurt. She thought of the day he had proposed to her in the stable, the way he'd tenderly kissed her in the rose garden when he'd reassured her that the hand of God was on her.

She knew James cared. However, he was angry because she'd left him without an explanation.

"Thank you for rescuing us," she whispered.

"I hope I didn't thwart your carefully laid plans.

Reginald finally confessed that you and your sister were on your way to London."

"I'm sorry. 'Twas wrong."

"Did your spirits advise you to sneak off in the middle of the night?"

"You know spirits aren't real."

"I don't know what to believe and not believe anymore."

Heartbeats passed, and they galloped across the final acres bordering James's land. Valentina drew in a sharp breath. Her body hurt everywhere.

As they approached the main house, her first thought was that the house looked the same as it always did. Candles flickered in paned glass windows, oil lamps were lit, and smoke meandered from the kitchen chimneys. However, as they rode nearer, she realized that the front courtyard and all the outbuildings were strangely quiet, devoid of any person or activity.

The horse slowed.

"Your home is defenseless and could be in jeopardy. Where is everyone?" Her thoughts marched through her mind in tense formation. "Suppose you were attacked?"

With deadly composure, James replied, "An enemy worth half his salt would throw himself off London Bridge before he attacked an estate struck by influenza."

Fear trickled through her, and she forced herself up straight.

They rode across the courtyard, and James reined in his horse. He dismounted, handed the reins to Tobias, and helped her down. Once her feet hit the ground, James was quick to release her.

"Thankfully, Yolanda wasn't injured." Valentina pointed toward her sister who was rushing already toward the stables. "She must be searching for Reginald."

James began striding across the lawn.

"Slow down," Valentina shouted as loudly as her tortured lungs allowed. "I said, Yolanda is searching for—"

James turned. His somber stare he gave proved far more furious than reassuring. "Yolanda won't find her blacksmith in the stable nor the forges. Reginald departed for Wales, along with most of the servants."

"James, wait. There's much I need to explain."

"Not now."

"Thank you for coming for Yolanda and me. The mare ran off and—"

At first, he ignored her. Heated, silent fury reined. He exhaled slowly, a nerve in his jaw vibrating with fury. He met her stare once more and replied curtly, "Don't thank me again."

She had to reach him. She had to go back to the

beginning so he'd understand. She spread out her hands, an attempt at an explanation.

His gaze raked over her. "Knowing you were injured, I came to extend my help. Fortunately, you weren't far away." He paused a second too long, although not before stark, bleak heartache ripped across his face.

"James, what's the matter?"

He folded his arms and looked past her. "My son is sick."

Jeremy. Nay. Her mouth opened and closed. She could find no words. She pressed her hands to her temples to calm the dizziness ringing through her skull. "How sick, James? How sick?"

He closed his eyes, and she knew.

Influenza.

Jeremy. Sweet and kind, gentle and innocent, the precious child she loved.

She leaned over, her hands on her thighs, and pulled in a tortured breath. "What can I do?"

"I'd appreciate your prayers."

Abruptly, he pivoted and strode up the wide stairs to his home. She caught up with him as he started for the hallway stairway, matching his swiftness, stride for stride. "Did you attempt my Romany cure?"

He rubbed a hand through his dark hair, his expression bordering between frustration and sadness. "I've come to believe shaking trees requires only your clever Gypsy skills. And, as we've both ac-knowledged, your Romany remedy didn't work."

Tenderness welled in her heart. A wrench of compassion made her lips shake. "May I pray with you?"

"Aye." He mumbled something in Welsh. "I lost one child, I cannot lose another."

"You won't lose your son," she vowed. "God will listen to our prayers." Valentina hoisted her gown and girded her loins. She'd become a prayer warrior, fighting for Jeremy's life.

CHAPTER TWENTY-TWO

Te na khutshos perdal tsho ushalin.
Try not to jump over your shadow.
Old Romany saying

With Yolanda behind her, Valentina edged into Jeremy's cramped chamber. Richard, the vicar, was there, along with Elspeth and Clare. Valentina pressed her palm against Jeremy's flushed forehead. "How are you feeling, little man? Your father said you're unwell."

His over-bright gaze fixed on hers. "Mam?"

For the child's sake, she steadied her shaking hands. Sinking onto the bed, she swabbed his sweaty brows with slow, careful massages across each tiny hair. The image of her brother's dark Romany face merged with Jeremy's light, cherubic features.

She rested her head on the mound of pillows by Jeremy and prayed. It wasn't enough, she

knew, although she was learning that God's grace was enough.

Hours passed, and inky-blackness deepened the chamber. The handful of servants who remained kept hovering in the doorway.

"Jeremy is afraid of the dark. Beatrix was afraid too." James' impassive statement belied his words, making them all the more frightening because they were filled with desolation and despair.

"'Tis a natural fear," Valentina said. "Everyone is afraid of the dark on occasion."

She recalled Luca's warning whenever their caravan camped near a new town. "We are safe for now, although beware of the dark."

"My son cannot speak," James was saying. "Who will help him if he cried out?"

"You will. I will. For as long as he needs us. Believe in a miracle."

"A miracle," James repeated quietly.

Minutes went by. A sliver of moonbeam lit the dark sky and streamed into Jeremy's chamber.

Valentina and James spent the remainder of the night pacing the floor on either side of Jeremy's bed. Jeremy kicked off the covers when fever burned or clambered for blankets when his teeth clicked. He was a fighter, though, Valentina assured herself. Tough, like his father.

His slight body became a shivering cocoon. He tossed in his sleep.

But he was alive.

She closed her eyes to shut out the slightest distraction—the sputter of the curling flames in the fireplace, the mumbling of servants in the corridor, the grating creak of the carpeted floor beneath her footsteps.

James stared out the window at the night sliding past. "Jeremy, there's so much I want to show you. Wales. Do you remember our home there, and the sea? I can hear the drumming of the waves against the shoreline, taste the salt …" His gaze darted to the bed, his face spoke of panic. "Don't leave me, son."

Valentina studied the tall, enigmatic man standing across from her. Desolation filled his haunted features. Slowly and surely, he was being crushed by a sadness he couldn't control.

Other men might fear him in battle, but in this chamber, James was only a desperate father who'd sacrifice everything for his son. And his anguish ran as deep and shattering as her own.

He strode to Jeremy's bed and held his son's small hand, an attempt to infuse his strength into Jeremy's weak body. "I'll not allow you to die. You can't hear me, but God can."

Valentina approached and stood behind James. She wanted to touch his back, clasp his hand. Ordinary acts of kindness she knew he'd never accept from her. He kept his focus on his son and didn't acknowledge her. If the muscles in his forearms hadn't tightened, she might have thought he hadn't even noticed her nearness.

～

*T*he darkest hours of night slipped by.

With a weightless rap on the door, Geoffrey entered. "Mr. Colchester, I can watch over your son so that you may rest for a few hours. Sir?" Geoffrey raised his voice, for James seemed not to hear him.

"You expect me to leave my son?" James asked, as if he hadn't understood Geoffrey correctly. "I left Jeremy alone countless times when I was away at battle."

"You're of little use to anyone if you're exhausted. You haven't slept in days. Perhaps if you rest for a while—"

"Easy answer. Nay." James shook his head, allowing no room for argument.

With a heavy sigh, Geoffrey threw his hands up in the air. "Very well, sir. I'll be in the hallway. Yolanda and Clare are keeping watch also." Geoffrey retraced his steps and latched the door shut behind him.

Valentina stared at James until he made eye contact, keeping her tone firm. "*I,* however, will continue to stay."

"Stay. Go." He shrugged. "It makes little difference."

The chamber was shadowy, and the flickering fire in the grate burned low, mimicking the pensive mood of the room. Valentina sat on the floor at the foot of Jeremy's bed. James settled a feather pillow beside her, shaking his head when she opened her mouth to thank him.

She watched while he kept his vigil, his lips uttering prayer after prayer, although she didn't know all the words. What she did know was that the fever needed to break, and soon, or Jeremy wouldn't recover. And neither, she knew with the same certainty, would his father.

She knelt by Jeremy's bedside and prayed the same prayer countless times: "Please Lord, come into this chamber and take away this little boy's illness and pain. Let us feel your guidance and grace. Guide us, Lord, we praise you. Amen." She couldn't start with the way things were, so she focused on how He was a triumphant God who performed miracles.

At some point during her prayers, she pressed

her fingers to her temples to dull the headache she'd suffered since her fall and felt herself dozing.

~

*T*he door rattled. Valentina squinted at the first rays of dawn lighting the chamber. The aromas of warm ale and yeasty bread floated to her nostrils.

James bent to set a tray of food on the night table beside her. "There's little left to eat. Our supplies are low." He inclined his head away from her, preferring to restlessly pace the chamber than sit by her.

"Because the servants have left for Wales?" Blinking in confusion at how long she'd slept, she reached for Jeremy's bedpost and stood.

"Aye."

She clutched the folds of her gown while she attempted to drag enough air into her lungs to dispel the heavy knot of guilt. "How many hours did I sleep?"

"Not many." James added wood to the fire and settled his gaze on his son.

She had vowed to be strong, for Jeremy's sake. Bravery and faithfulness, she reminded herself. Between her and James, they had an abundance of both.

"You, little man, are going to fully recover." She busied herself with tucking the woolen blankets around Jeremy. "James, he seems more comfortable." To illustrate her point, she lifted a finger to her lips and stood quiet, noting Jeremy's raspy breathing had calmed.

James walked toward the bed. "I thought the same."

She shook her head. "I shouldn't have slept so long."

"We all need sleep."

"You don't."

"And in our many years together, since he was a young boy trying to escape the schoolroom, Mr. Colchester required a minimal amount," Geoffrey provided.

Valentina spun.

Standing in the open doorway, the elderly man acknowledged her with a slight nod.

"Geoffrey, you were so quiet I didn't realize you were here," she said.

He strode to the bed and assisted her in tucking the blankets around Jeremy. "Think of me as a guardian angel, silent and ever-present. I've stood in the doorway for a while now, despite Mr. Colchester's insinuations I should hang about in the hallway."

"Some things never change," James murmured. He leaned over and pressed the back of his hand against Jeremy's forehead. With a stiff nod, he swung back to the window and stared out at a colorless dawn.

Valentina hid a slight smile. "A guardian angel is a pleasant idea, Geoffrey."

"Excellent, because you have one also." Geoffrey turned a conspiratorial half-grin toward James, who stood with his back to both of them.

Another insistent knock broke the silence. Clare entered, curtsied, and kept her gaze nailed to the floor. "Mr. Colchester, Tobias insists he must speak with you, sir. He said 'tis urgent."

James scowled and strode from the room. Clare followed him.

Valentina assumed James' earlier position on the right side of Jeremy's bedside. Scattered fragments of sunbeams filtered through the window.

She bent and rubbed her cheek against Jeremy's forehead. His face wasn't as warm. Hope surged, filling her heart.

"Don't give up on Mr. Colchester," Geoffrey said. "He needs you."

She glanced bleakly in the direction of the doorway. "You couldn't be more wrong. He blames me, and for that I must bear his cold manner."

Geoffrey pulled up a stool. "Are you a person who enjoys stories, Valentina?"

The tiniest note of dread whispered between them before she answered. "Aye. Who doesn't? My mother spun many a tale."

"Good, because 'tis necessary you hear this one."

She pulled up a high-backed wooden chair beside Geoffrey. "What kind of story?"

"A story about the people you love."

She braced her hands along her thighs and took in Geoffrey's tight mouth, his sad eyes, his bowed spine.

He beckoned her to lean nearer. "When Jeremy and his sister were born, Mr. Colchester wasn't present for their births. While we were fighting on a gory battlefield, the babies came early."

Valentina gripped her hands in her lap, knowing this story's ending was plagued by grief. "His wife must have been frightened to birth two babies without her husband near," she murmured.

"Aye, and when we returned, Alyce ailed for months. She blamed Mr. Colchester for everything —the fact he was at war and not with her, the hard childbirth, and Jeremy's deafness. She took little interest in either baby, most notably Jeremy."

Geoffrey paused to gaze out the window at the somber treetops, groggy with tiredness, preserving the weariness of the night. Compassion etched his hard-worn features.

"And Beatrix's death is spoken about only in whispers," Valentina said.

"Beatrix was perfect." Geoffrey dropped his voice to a whisper and kept a guarded gaze toward the door. "She resembled her mother, all shiny blonde hair and violet-blue eyes. Unfortunately, the child was too curious for her own safety."

Valentina held the breath in her throat, afraid to exhale, afraid to disturb the fragile memories. Mumbles from the corridor grew louder, followed by James' voice giving rapid directions. Lightly, she touched Geoffrey's arm, encouraging him to continue.

"The day of the accident, Alyce insisted on leaving Jeremy at the main house and taking Beatrix for a walk. Elspeth offered to accompany them, although Alyce refused."

"Perhaps she wanted to spend the afternoon alone with her daughter," Valentina offered.

"Nay." He shook his head. "Beatrix loved sniffing the white roses growing wild along the hedgerows. Perhaps she went looking for them while her mother was otherwise occupied. She didn't realize the child was missing until later that day." Geoffrey concentrated on Jeremy's chest rising and falling beneath the bedcovers. "You see, Alyce met her lover. He is Mr. Wellsey's brother."

"So that's what this feud was all about," Valentina murmured.

Geoffrey paused and rubbed his temples. "And Alyce went into quite a state when no one could find Beatrix, although by evening, she'd confessed her tryst. Mr. Colchester searched all night for his daughter. I've never seen such crazed agony in a man. His frenzied search resulted in the horrific find of his little girl's body the following morning. She'd fallen to the bottom of the cliff."

Tears coursed down Valentina's cheeks. "A nightmare for him, for everyone."

Geoffrey reached into his waistcoat pocket and offered her a linen handkerchief, which she appreciatively accepted.

"As he often does, he blamed himself and grew quieter as the weeks passed. I saw him pray often and watched as he experienced it all—grief, anguish, anger, and a sense of desperateness." Geoffrey shifted, hesitated. "Are you aware Beatrix's death had been foretold a few months beforehand?"

"By whom?"

He let the question hang in the shallow breaths between them. "By you."

Valentina shoved back her chair and stood with a jerk. "Me? When?"

"The Colchesters had visited a traveling fair in a nearby village, Lowestoft, as I recall, where you read Alyce's palm."

Slowly, Valentina sank onto the bed beside Jeremy. "I remember. A distinguished woman inquired about her twin babies and insisted I read her palm. And a man stood a few feet away."

From the furthermost sealed corners of her mind, realizations rushed to the fore. Arms crossed, his back propped against a tree, a tall man with grey eyes had caught Valentina's gaze with nonchalance before letting go.

"Oftentimes, I worried that Mr. Colchester would never recover from Beatrix's death, and his wife carried on for months afterward," Geoffrey was saying.

"Surely she loved her daughter, and her son."

"In her own way, perhaps. Jeremy tried to be close to her. She acted ashamed of him, perhaps resentful because of Beatrix's death. One never knew for certain what Alyce was thinking. The boy clung to his mother. But the harder he tugged at her sleeves, the harder she shook him off."

Valentina's chest felt compressed as if in a vise. She clutched Geoffrey's handkerchief and dabbed at her eyes. James had assumed that Beatrix's death was proof that Valentina's predictions were accurate, and that was why he'd trusted her, despite his belief in God. Her heart broke at his desperation, which she'd betrayed without a care.

Geoffrey went on. "Mr. Colchester believed he should have been able to prevent the accident because of your frightening warning, even though he was skeptical of Gypsies. We all were, although we'd begun to—"

"If you're finished whispering, Geoffrey," James said abruptly as he strode into the chamber, "you may leave."

Geoffrey's sentence trailed off into silence. Stiffening, he stood. "I'll wait in the corridor, sir." With a loud humph, he quit the room.

"You shouldn't speak so curtly to your closest friend." Valentina swallowed to clear her parched throat. "He's concerned about you."

"No need for refined trivialities. Geoffrey knows me well enough." James removed his waistcoat and hung it by the door. He looked leaner than she remembered. His wrinkled linen shirt outlined the contours of his hard chest; the thin morning sunlight accentuated the ache flashing across his handsome face.

How would she ever understand this man? She veered between wanting to shout at him for the distance he'd effectively placed between them or sobbing her regrets against the sweat-stained sleeves of his shirt. She did neither, easing Jeremy's damp hair off his forehead instead.

Aye. The boy's skin was definitely cooler, the color returning to his pallid cheeks. Her hand stopped in midair. "James, the fever is gone."

Two strides brought James to the bedside. He clasped Jeremy's hand. "Are you certain?"

"Aye." Valentina kissed Jeremy's frail fingers through his father's strong ones.

James held her gaze. "Valentina, I've heard your prayers this past day and night, and you've heard mine. Will you join me? Prayers of thanksgiving are greater when said together."

"I've just begun learning your prayers."

"Then you know the words are simple." His hands closed over hers and he bowed his head. "God, please look upon my son with favor. Guide him to adulthood, so he may enable others to live a giving and full life. We pray for thy everlasting mercy." He squeezed her fingers before releasing them. A tear leaked from the corner of her eye. She could fight his anger, but his kind-heartedness would be her undoing.

"I prayed this prayer more times than I could count," he said.

"You display such a strong sense of faith."

"'Tis when I need the most encouragement. And I had a revelation while I prayed. There are some things that my own irresponsibility and despondency created, and I kept searching for a reason— someone to blame. Then I realized God is still with me, through my good decisions as well as my poor ones."

"Your beliefs never falter."

He studied her before he replied, a flicker of disquiet in his eyes. "Nearly never."

His convictions and integrity ran deep and wondrous, and he acted on them, his word true. And she'd never loved him as much as in that moment when he stood so near, yet so removed.

"Keep up your courage, for all of us." Tentatively, she rested her hand on his forearm.

His muscles tensed. "Perhaps you should rest awhile? You're still recovering from your fall." He didn't physically move, although she felt him retreat.

With a sigh, she let go of his arm and touched Geoffrey's handkerchief to her temple. The headache had abated. "Aye, for a few minutes," she agreed.

She stepped toward the door, changing directions for one more peek at Jeremy. The woolen blankets on the bed stirred, and his face peeked out from underneath.

Valentina stood mutely, one hand on the door latch, the other hand splayed across her heart.

"Ver-y ..." Jeremy wiggled into a sitting position. His smile seemed to light up the entire gaping chamber.

She hurried toward the slender boy, enveloping his body with hers. Warmness healed everything inside her that had earlier been cold.

"'Tis so good, so good, to see you smile."

"God was listening and answered our prayers, son." As she released Jeremy, his father hugged him, holding him so fiercely she wondered if he'd ever let him go.

She dabbed at her tears with Geoffrey's already damp handkerchief. "Our God is a God of faith. His presence in this chamber gave me purpose."

"Because praying works." For the first time since she'd returned, James smiled.

"Hungry." Jeremy pointed to his stomach and scrambled beneath his father's grasp.

"There's plain bread and warm ale." Valentina frowned at her forgotten tray of food. "Surely I can find something more appetizing for him in the kitchen." Thrilled at the healthy color already returning to the boy's face, she studied his father's haggard one. "He'll recover fully, James."

He wiped at his eyes. "Thank God."

Her chest lightened. She wanted to fling the tray to the ceiling, then wrap her arms around both James and Jeremy, kissing them with all the elation in her heart.

"He's with us wherever we go," she said.

"Emanuel." Joy flickered in James's gaze. "He showed up in the middle of despair."

"And He is here now."

CHAPTER TWENTY-THREE

Patshiv tumenge Romale.
This song was offered as a gift to worthy men.
Old Romany saying

*J*ames hardly noticed the amber-tinted sunlight filtering through the clouds lighting the winter landscape. Since Jeremy's recovery, he had spent the days tallying his accounts. Trade was paralyzed because of the influenza epidemic and rural England was hard-hit. However, a shortage of necessary supplies had forced his hand, and he was preparing to depart for Wales before the end of the week.

"Tad!"

James looked up from his seat behind his desk in the study. He gazed out the half-open window as his son ice skated across the lawn in his boots. Valentina ran close behind him.

Jeremy broke off his carefree wave to concentrate on his balance. "Eeek! Uh-oh." He fell into the slick grass with a squish.

"Jeremy!" James sprang from his chair, bounded down the hallway and darted outdoors.

Valentina had already hoisted Jeremy upright, sweeping the snow off his royal-blue cloak. "Your son wanted to learn how to skate on the snow." Her mouth creased into an easy smile and she dabbed at her wind-lashed nose.

"He did? Or you did?" His amused gaze flitted over her. Her gown matched the crimson of her lips, as rich and vivid as the vegetable rouge English women wore on their cheeks. She looked so attractive it took him several seconds before he could look away.

She laughed. "'Tis a splendid day and too agreeable to stay indoors. The physician said Jeremy is completely recovered."

"Aye. The remaining servants have burst into euphoric activity, readying for the journey to Wales."

"Euphoric?" she teased with a grin. "Still using fancy words, Mr. Colchester?"

She didn't call him *James* anymore, he noted. How long had it been?

"Are you impressed?" he asked aloud.

"You should speak in Welsh or learn a few useful phrases in Romany."

"Thanks to you, I've learned a number of colorful Gypsy curses. At least, I think they're curses. Is that a start?" Their smiles connected, and he was tempted to continue their friendly banter. He even debated asking her to join him for supper.

Nay. Never again. He silenced his tongue. His grin slipped away.

She licked the last trace of snow from her bottom lip. "You're doing it again."

"What?"

"Staring at me and scowling. Do you think I'm too old to play childish games in the snow?"

"On the contrary, I thought to join you. However, there's much I must attend to before departure."

"Some other time, then," she called out to him as he returned to his much-too-large home and endless responsibilities.

He inclined his head, neither agreeing nor disagreeing. It was easier this way—simply enjoying his son's devotion to her. Their squealing joy should have lifted his spirits. Their happiness should have been contagious. Instead, the emotions left him with impossible obstacles, bringing a genuine sadness to his chest.

Just when he thought he could walk two steps

without thinking of Valentina, lyrical Gypsy songs floated across the fields to resonate vivid chords in his heart. When he caught her expressive eyes staring at him, his heart lurched, his stomach tightened. And then he remembered her deceit—her deceit with her fortune-telling and how she had run away.

He paced his chamber each evening, any semblance of restful sleep evasive. Valentina had always stripped him of the skill to act reasonably. Why should these final hours be any different? He knew the servants were impatient to embark on their journey to Wales, but he told himself he had to be certain Jeremy was well enough to travel. However, that wasn't the only reason he waited. He was delaying telling her.

Truth be told, he was delaying telling himself.

⁓

James and Geoffrey dined together at midday, carrying their sparse meals up to James's private chamber. As he did every day, Geoffrey spread a woven tablecloth over the decorative wooden table and set their bowls on top.

"What I wouldn't do for a tankard of sweet Welsh ale and fresh venison," he said.

"Include a loaf of laverbread seasoned with bacon fat and a fistful of honeyed almonds while you imagine a perfect meal." James seated himself across from Geoffrey, eyeing the dirty smudge on his spoon before stirring the suspicious broth in his bowl. "Anything is better than what we've eaten lately."

Geoffrey picked at his half-cooked goose and took a tentative bite. He scowled, pushed the plate to the side and loosened the ring of his black leather belt to better fit his stomach's wide girth.

"No doubt Valentina will enjoy Wales," came his unasked-for observation.

James' spoon slid into the broth and disappeared. "I believe we were talking about food, not Gypsies."

"Our food may be inadequate, but our conversation can still be entertaining."

"Entertaining or disagreeable?"

"I only speak with your permission."

"And when did this start?" Getting up, James strode to a table in the corner and poured himself and Geoffrey a generous goblet of wine. "Please—eat, drink and speak your mind."

Geoffrey gave his best imitation of looking contrite, then shrugged. "When you were away, the household panicked after Roland's death. Your son was beyond himself with fright, and Valentina comforted him constantly."

James held the heaviness in his heart. "My place was here with my son, not on a battlefront fighting a war for an impetuous king."

"You had no idea influenza would strike while you were gone."

"Because I wasn't paying attention. Memories, sad memories, had taken hold of my heart. And because I was too interested in a Gypsy woman who dominated my every thought." James gazed through the window and surveyed the sweeping view of his estate, along with the emptiness of the late January day. The leaded glass pane lent a blue tint to the ringlets of smoke streaming from the kitchen chimney across the courtyard.

"Sometimes, the greatest gift comes from the greatest regret." Subjecting James to a brief perusal, Geoffrey added, "No disrespect intended, Mr. Colchester. However, you look like you haven't slept in a month."

James brought their goblets back to the table. "Has anyone ever mentioned that tactfulness is not your forte?"

Amusement glinted in Geoffrey's eyes before he turned his attention back to extracting a hunk of meat off the bone. Failing at the attempt, he sat back and downed a tidy swig of wine. "Valentina has capably reassumed her role as Jeremy's caretaker."

James took a long swallow of his drink. "Thank you for your astute observation, Geoffrey, although I already employ Elspeth, a calm and thoughtful nurse who has attended to him since his birth."

"Aye, she's a lovely woman, though as ancient as

Merlin the magician, and she's not Jeremy's mother." Geoffrey raised his goblet. "Every child needs a mother."

"His mother is dead."

"A mother is a woman who loves a child and will sacrifice everything for him. A woman who is also an equal partner for the child's father. Someone who's unselfish and gentle and ..."

Half-listening to Geoffrey's droning, James pondered a number of ways to politely dismiss his steward. Before the afternoon faded, James planned on confronting Valentina, and the afternoon was fading rapidly.

"Mr. Colchester, have you heard a word I said?"

"Aye. You refer to Valentina, and two months ago, I would have agreed with you." James grimaced at the whiff of a vinegary vegetable he didn't recognize. He fished his spoon from the broth and shoved the offensive food toward Geoffrey.

Sitting forward, Geoffrey inspected the broth with genuine interest. "And have you noticed—"

"I wouldn't want to deprive you of your two favorite pastimes, saying whatever is on your mind and eating."

Geoffrey made no attempt to cloak his grin. "Have you noticed Valentina's expression whenever you're around her?"

"As always, her tongue is tart and her manner insolent."

Her sparkling laughter had shimmered beneath his skin on one too many occasions of late. His body's reaction to her had blindsided him, a reminder she wielded power.

"She regards you with respect and admiration, oftentimes when you're not looking. And she sings every morning in her Gypsy language no one understands except Yolanda. Do you enjoy hearing Valentina's songs as much as I do?"

James started from his chair, then sat back down. He debated about whether to reply to Geoffrey's rhetorical question. No response at all might be taken as agreement. He gave a low whistle through his teeth. "I hear little else."

"She told me the melodies and words were lullabies from her childhood. Her voice is lovely."

"Aye." James lifted his goblet as if in a toast. "Lovely voice, lovely eyes and a lovely face."

"You cannot live alone forever."

"Your directness is laudable, Geoffrey. However, my son is perfect company."

"He's a child." Geoffrey blithely ignored James's unwavering frown. "You need a strong woman by your side, because a man like you will want more children."

"One surviving child is a blessing."

Images of olive-skinned toddlers with flashing grey eyes and tangled black hair skipped through

James' mind. Wishful notions, forever intruding and invading. He swallowed hard and cut them off.

Geoffrey kept his steady gaze on James. "You prefer the Welsh countryside to England. 'Tis isolated, and few people would give a second look to a Gypsy woman."

A beautiful Gypsy woman would draw stares wherever she went. Still, James found no reason to dispute the finer points of the discussion. Once Geoffrey formed an opinion, he held onto it like a cat that scurried around its owner's feet until it was fed.

James drained his goblet and grimaced, belatedly remembering how much he disliked sweet wine. "Have you forgotten what she did? I made one misstep in marrying a dishonest woman, and I won't make another."

"Valentina spoke a half-truth in foolishness and desperation."

James laid down his spoon and scraped back his chair. "Surely you don't expect me to forgive her?" Try as he might, James couldn't read Geoffrey's answer, well hidden in the depths of his steward's clouded blue eyes.

"Perhaps—"

James surged to his feet.

Geoffrey, on the other hand, remained relaxed in his chair. "You don't believe in Gypsy superstitions and fortune-telling. Forgiveness will release your heart from rage and resentment. Or you will grow to be an unreasonable old man."

"Like yourself?"

"I never regretted my decisions. Nonetheless, I'd loathe seeing you live your life alone, knowing 'twill be filled with sadness and regret."

"I will live in peace."

"A lonely existence is no life for a man in your position."

James leaned over the table to peer at Geoffrey. "Do you believe for one moment I didn't consider marriage to Valentina? I have thought of little else, my friend." He chafed his fingers against his temples. Memories recurred of the meal Valentina had offered to prepare for him. Pickled porcupine, or some such Gypsy dish, seasoned with hot black pepper. For a wedding, a Gypsy wedding, a feast comparable to any the English aspired to.

Geoffrey met James' stare with bullish determination. "Even a strong emotion is better than none."

Noncommittal, James hedged for a beat. "No emotion is best."

Geoffrey seemed to form his next words cautiously. "Will Valentina and Yolanda accompany us to Wales? Yolanda is eager to see Reginald. She inquires incessantly about him whenever I pass her in the halls."

"Reginald is a good man, despite his disloyal efforts."

"He displayed more courage than I ever suspected he had in him." Geoffrey sat straighter. "What *are* your plans for the women?"

James stared past Geoffrey, regarding the frost gathering outside the mullioned window. "Need I mention the fact I prefer silence over your insistent, prying questions?"

To James' annoyance, Geoffrey simply finished his goose and reached for James' broth. He skirted the broth out of Geoffrey's reach, then strode to his chamber door, opening it so wide the hinges whined. "My friend, you must be pondering the numerous preparations for our departure, and I won't delay you any longer."

Geoffrey grunted to his feet. "I've been more than ready to depart for a fortnight. In any case, I trust you'll come to the right decision." With an affectionate slap on James' shoulder, Geoffrey quit the chamber.

As Geoffrey's footsteps lumbered down the stairs, James sat back down in his chair and propped one booted foot over the other.

Valentina expected to travel to Wales come the morrow. He'd pretended not to see the quiet anticipation in her eyes, the questioning glances whenever he mentioned their upcoming journey. *'Twas easy to fake ignorance.*

Once, he'd believed her a woman of spirit and compassion, kindness and empathy. Instead, she'd misled him, all the while obediently complying with the rhythm of his household. Believing him an idiot.

Forgiveness. Remember Colossians 3:13. "Bear with each other and forgive one another if any of you has a grievance against someone. Forgive as the Lord forgave you."

A grudging laugh, a shake of his head. Nay, he couldn't, not this time. Valentina had taken away his expectations and dreams, and his disappointment ran too deep. Alyce had taught him well. He'd lost a valuable part of himself that he couldn't risk losing again.

He brought his rigid shoulders forward and stood. As if his legs were made of wood, he strode to the window. Hesitant, he slid his fingers over the cold glass and opened the bottom pane.

Valentina's laughter trilled upward. "Jeremy, you're thirstier than a lake with no rain. And nay, I won't go with you to visit the falconer because I loathe those awful birds. I'll walk through the garden and see if any herbs remain that I can salvage for the journey."

Jeremy chuckled before scampering off like a skylark. She'd probably made one of her absurd, silly faces.

At the vision, a streak of unanticipated joy flowed through James. In spite of his trouble-filled heart, he smiled.

CHAPTER TWENTY-FOUR

Kay zhala I suv shay zhala wi o thav.
Where the needle goes surely the thread shall
follow.
Old Romany saying

A few minutes later, James donned a heavy cloak and headed to the herb garden. For months, he'd thought of the herb garden as Valentina's garden. They'd strolled its flagstone path numerous afternoons when he'd overseen her planting efforts. Wheelbarrow in tow, she'd doubled the size of the herbal beds. The beds, arranged in neat, rectangular rows, stretched from the kitchen garden to the far side of his home. By June, sage, parsley, and thyme would bloom.

At least, that was the plan.

A whisper of wintry air tiptoed across his cheeks. He blew on his hands and tucked them inside his cloak. He checked on Jeremy first, who was with the falconer. Then, James continued on to the garden.

He stopped short when he reached her. For an infinite minute, he just stared.

Flanked by a garden spade and her yellow scarf, Valentina sat on a decorative iron bench bordered by shrubs. A burgundy velvet pelisse cradled her body and pooled at her ankles, and a large cashmere shawl covered her shoulders. Sunlight warmed her skin to ripe chestnut. Her lustrous hair flowed around her, reminding him of an ebony waterfall.

His breath came quickly. Even at this distance, she captivated him.

A layer of unmarked snow crunched beneath his boots as he approached.

She smiled at him. "Did Jeremy find the falconer?"

"Aye. And I found you."

"I'm not very hard to find these days. Seldom do I wander like I used to. Mr. Colchester ... James." She shrugged. "I don't know how to address you anymore."

"I'm the same man."

"Are you?"

"Who else would I be?" He walked behind the bench, unable to resist combing his fingers through her hair. "Address me whatever way you'd like."

She tilted her head back and settled her hands in her lap. "I like *James*."

"James it is, then." Despite his unsteady efforts, her hair crackled beneath his fingertips.

Her head rested on the garden bench, her face turned to the sky. "Why are you smirking?"

"Because you always say whatever you please, regardless of my opinion."

She looked up at him with her laughing, extraordinary gaze. "I try to think before I speak."

"Surely not when I'm near."

"You seem different. You've avoided me since I returned. Are you angry about something?"

"Why would I be angry?" He gave a cracked, hopeless laugh. Was that what this emotion was called—the one making his muscles clench and his face brittle?

Her wide-set eyes sparkled like the purest emeralds, blemished with a yellow speck of hesitation in the center. "Did you come to the garden to comb my hair?"

He smiled inwardly, because she knew him so well. "You may speak first."

"About what? *You* came to see *me*." She rose from the bench and turned to face him, forcing him to release her hair. "I have nothing to say, except 'tis freezing and I'm going inside." She straightened her shawl, lifted the hem of her pelisse, and started walking away.

He grabbed her hand, enveloped her in his arms and pressed her body close.

"I waited and waited," she said, "and I was beginning to think you no longer cared." Her tongue slid over his parted lips. Her hot breath tickled the prickly hairs of his beard. "I miss the walks we used to take together. I miss—"

No man could resist a woman like her, his melting mind rationalized. He kissed her, savoring her sultriness, stamping her skin with blistering, wild kisses.

His conscience nudged. *What was he doing?*

He'd sought to tell her of his decision, not to kiss her.

He dragged his lips from hers and took a rigid step backward.

"What's wrong?"

"Nothing." *She's a trickster. Remember?* Yet when he kissed her, he couldn't feel a trace of deceit in her response.

She folded her arms around his neck. "Thank you for being so tolerant. You're a good, forgiving man. I don't deserve—"

He shook off her hands. She probably hadn't told him the truth since they'd met.

And she'd never accepted responsibility for

what she'd done but had blatantly withheld the truth from him. He didn't believe in fortune-telling, although that wasn't the point. A lie by omission ... He had to be strong. He'd cared for her so much, fallen in love with her, asked her to be his wife and spend her life with him. Yet now when he gazed at her, he felt conflicted, his anger a constant reminder of her dishonesty. His gut split in thirds as infinite seconds passed. Her captivating eyes bore into his and she leaned in to kiss him.

He hadn't intended this. He'd come to say goodbye.

Recklessness warred with reason as he answered her kiss. His tongue probed. Her delightful mouth opened and gave.

Her moistened lips brushed his throat, and she inclined her head toward the pathway. "Someone might see us."

He kissed her earlobe and breathed in her ear, "We're concealed by the garden wall."

Her fingers burrowed into his back, her mouth feather-touched his. He tried to focus on the sunlight, the snow, the hazelnut trees—anything except her nearness. Her mouth moved urgently against his. Her silky eyelashes fluttered, a surrendering sigh across his cheek.

In the blue-grey glow of the winter afternoon, his tongue explored, voracious, like a starving beggar. "Valentina, I can never get my fill of you. Why? Why?"

Her hands twined through his hair. "Because we love each other."

He reclaimed her lips in one last kiss, branding her with possessiveness so that she'd never forget him. His gorgeous, irresistible Gypsy woman.

"Me kamav tut." She placed a light kiss on his chin, marking a path down his neck.

He grasped her face, stopping her. A blistering wind blew across his nape. He shuddered and

waited for the tremor to pass.

Floating silver crystals of snow outlined her flawless face, and her spicy scent heated the coldness around them. The tip of her tongue peeked beneath her lips. "Are we leaving for Wales come the morrow?" Her combination of innocence and sensuality kept him spellbound.

A war raged through him, the battle cry of betrayal. He stared past her, his resolve

slipping, his tidy piece of earth swept to the side. "Nay."

"When are we leaving?"

"Soon. There's something I intended to tell you first."

"First?" Her expression closed. "Before you kissed me, or after?"

If she didn't look so heartbreakingly gorgeous, if he didn't despise himself, he wouldn't be so torn.

Nay, he couldn't be weak. He needed to be in control.

Their gazes met, and for the first time in his life, he wasn't sure how to begin. She seemed so far away. He wanted to touch her again. He didn't. He wouldn't get hurt ever again.

"Unfortunately, all the women I've known in my life seldom speak the truth," he said.

Her fingers fumbled with the edges of her shawl. "My mother was truthful."

The air murmured by, a silent beat after beat.

"Women think they can dupe a man."

'Twas the beginning of a conversation with no end. She'd never understand. His words wouldn't matter to her.

"James." She reached out her hand. "Geoffrey confided about your late wife and how Beatrix died."

"My wife cared little about our daughter."

Stains of color flamed Valentina's cheeks, her emerald eyes shining.

Stay focused. Stay focused. She was a consummate street performer and would use all her feminine tricks to deter him. He grasped a handful of icy snow from the bench, hoping to numb his feelings.

Tendrils of black hair wreathed her face, frozen into wavy curlicues—calling to mind a provocative ice princess from a far-off snowy land.

He drew in the deadened air, tranquil except for ice tinkling against stark tree branches.

"If I'd stayed longer in your chamber that night," he said, "I might have asked where you intended to go once I left."

Her slim fingers tucked her hair under the shawl, exposing her birthmark. Moist with snow, it glittered like a miniature horseshoe.

Worry was overtaking her expression. Why had she deceived him and cheated them out of their love? Why couldn't she have been honest?

"Has the entire night escaped you?" he persisted. "If I hadn't been half dead because of my beating by a misguided Gypsy tribe, I would have woken and heard the creaking wood floor as you departed. Nonetheless, on a midnight breeze and a chestnut mare"—he snapped his fingers—"you and your sister trotted off. Only a person harboring a secret slips away when the hour is darkest."

Her hands fidgeted like dueling swords. "I never intended to hurt you."

"You have a dramatic way of accomplishing your goals."

"Your goals are my goals."

"My goal is to protect my son."

She bit down on her shaking lower lip. "You know I love Jeremy."

"And yet you left."

"If I'd known Jeremy was sick, I never would have left." Her tone rose and sliced the stillness. He recognized that tone. It reminded him of his late wife's high, teary voice whenever she was backed into a corner.

Tapping his fingers on the garden bench, he waited. An intense sorrow hit him at the loss to come, and he had no way to defend himself.

"Why did you leave, Valentina?"

"You're an honorable gentleman. I couldn't let you spend your life with the likes of me." Her expression was so vulnerable he had to physically stop himself from wrapping his arms around her to protect her.

He shoved away from the bench. "Why did you leave so suddenly?"

She snatched up her sodden yellow scarf from the ground. "You're making me feel as though you are peering down from atop your gentlemanly perch —judging and belittling."

"What were you running from?"

"Myself."

Her quiet breathing was sweet, filling the air.

The wind no longer howled. In a desolate garden, the normalness of an ordinary winter afternoon ceased. He counted the number of times she blinked before dropping her gaze. A tiny piece of blue embroidery lined the sleeves of her gown, and she fiddled with the lace at the cuff.

"The night I read your palm," she said, still looking down, "I didn't tell you everything. I'm sorry. Please forgive me. I was wrong and made a terrible mistake."

He gripped her forearms. "Mistake? Is that what you call it?" *She'd broken his heart.*

Tears flowed from her eyes. With a pang of self-reproach, he let her go.

"I'm sorry." She wrapped her arms around herself and wept. "Please accept my apology."

"Why?" He thought he repeated the question aloud, although he could no longer be sure.

Why? The question he'd asked himself countless times.

Because he'd been fastened to sadness and trepidation so long, he'd decided on his own foolish plan, relying on superstition and disregarding God. Because he'd felt God had abandoned him.

James peered up at the thick, sullen clouds, then down at the snow accumulating at their feet.

She lowered her gaze. "I want to be a good person. I try and I fail."

He folded his arms, driven by a need to be right. "What did you see on my palm that first night?"

"You don't believe. I don't believe."

"Indulge me."

Tears glinted. Strange that at this moment he thought of her lashes as luxuriant, velvety fans she could no longer hide behind. Stranger still, she attempted to conceal her tears from him. Most women used tears to their advantage.

Furiously, she wiped at her eyes. "I saw sickness."

He snapped his head to the side, as if she'd actually struck him.

"My son. He loves you." So calm, so numb, some other man must be speaking.

"I love him too. And by reading your fortune, we ventured into a place we shouldn't have gone. My spirits are false because there's only one true God. You knew it before I did, yet you asked."

"You're blaming me?"

Even as he spoke, he knew she was right. He'd been out of step with God, and desperation and fear had steered him far from the truth. He needed to follow God in the right order. There was no easy answer to his dilemma about traveling to Wales. It took prayer and prayer alone.

Her unmanageable hair clung to her face. He nudged the wet strands away before forcing his
hands down.

"You'll never understand how the rest of us struggle just to survive," she said. "When I first met you, that was my life. I knew no other."

Images flared through his mind, infinite bloody battles. "'Tis the life you're used to, as I am used to mine."

"I was obliged to you for every meal, every piece of clothing."

"You and your sister were welcome guests." Guilt stabbed like needles, numbing his frozen feet. Unnerved, he pushed out words wedged in his throat far too long. "I assumed you were happy with me and my son. Wasn't that enough, sharing a lifetime together? I would have given you everything I own, Valentina. Everything."

"We can still have our life together." Guarded hope shone in her eyes, the hope he'd once had,

that elusive shimmer of happiness. He could never get it back.

"I won't be a fool again." He locked his hands behind him and fixed his gaze beyond her on the bare branches of the trees. "I came to tell you I've made arrangements for you and Yolanda to be escorted to London. My son and I and the remainder of the servants will travel to Wales."

She drew in her breath with a loud gasp.

Life, his life, must go on without her. *Unthinkable. Unimaginable. No other course.*

Terrible regrets assailed him. To control her trembling, and in an insane effort to comfort her, he gripped her arms as if to give her courage against his words, against him.

Face pale, eyes proud, she coolly lifted his hands away from her.

A lonely existence, Geoffrey warned.

"I'm leaving." She spoke to herself, reflective, no longer hearing him. "Influenza may sweep throughout England soon."

"Your journey won't end in London. I've made

further arrangements for you and Yolanda to travel
to Scotland. You'll be safe there."

"Nay. We'll go where our tribe has settled."

"'Tis safer in Scotland until the influenza epidemic passes." In addition, he'd be tempted to seek
her out if she were any closer.

She took a low, shuddering breath. "'Tis so far
away."

"Gypsies are resilient. Better to escape an epidemic and be protected from exposure."

"You condemn Yolanda and me to a life of begging and stealing."

He shook his head. "I'll give you both a substan-
tial amount of money to live comfortably."

"You're sadly delusional if you believe we'd ever
accept money from you!"

"Your safety will be ensured by me and my acquaintances abroad."

"Are you paying to make amends and atone for
your indifference?"

He extended his hands, attempting to explain.
"I'm trying to do what's best."

"Yolanda counts the days until she sees Reginald.
This arrangement will break her heart."

"There are many hearts broken today, cariad."

"I thought you loved me." Her words came in
whispers. "I thought I meant more to you than one
of your endless possessions."

Uneasy determination propelled him. He needed

to ensure she loathed him so she'd never look back. "Perhaps you'll find another caravan in Scotland. Many men will want you as their wife. Your Gypsy friend, for one." The image of her with another man, any man, tore at his insides. He blotted the thought out of his mind, for 'twould surely kill him.

Ramrod straight, she clasped her shawl tighter. "Once, I believed you were an honorable man. A true gentleman caring for his lands and his tenants. How wrong I was, because you're an unforgiving man. Your son may be deaf, but you're blind."

"What you did—"

"I want to see Jeremy, to tell him I'm leaving and kiss him good-bye."

"'Twill be too difficult for Jeremy to see you weeping. Better he remembers you by your laughter than your tears."

James half-expected the snowflakes to keep falling, harder and faster, leaving them frozen in time. The snow had stopped, though, and a wan sun desperately tried to warm the air before it sank beyond the grey horizon.

"I'll arrange for Geoffrey and Richard to ride with you to London, as I realize you trust them. A servant will awaken you at dawn." Already the gravity of his decision wound around his heart like a shackle, and he feared his feet might root him to the spot behind the garden bench forever. A lifeless, ice-covered statue that had once been a man.

She rolled her yellow scarf between trembling hands. "Once I depart, don't try to find me. I'll disappear."

"Rest assured, I will not seek you, cariad."

An infuriated sob broke from her throat. "I'm not your sweetheart."

He didn't expect the glorious, defiant woman who raised her gaze to his. Chest heaving, she almost smiled when she snapped the scarf across his cheek, so sudden his head jerked to one side. She dodged a twisted hazelnut tree as she pivoted and marched through the snow in a flurry of ruined velvet.

He rubbed his sore cheek. "Valentina, if you knew how much ..."

Even from a distance, the slam of the heavy front door rang throughout the deserted garden. He retraced her small footprints across the whiteness of the fresh snow. When he reached the entry, he had the urge to yank the miserable door off its brass hinges.

Hours past sundown, James stood in the shadowy upper corridor of his magnificent home, lashing himself with the sound of Valentina's racking sobs. He leaned against her chamber door, taking in her sorrows, struggling to eradicate her pain. In hopelessness he whispered, "I'm sorry." He whispered over and over, empty words because the person who mattered most couldn't hear him.

She'd endured countless hardships, withstanding her burdens with bravery and grace. No one else he'd ever known had displayed a more splendid fortitude or stronger character. Tougher than any man, she'd been afraid to own up to her mistake because she'd feared his inability to forgive, his massive pride.

I thought you loved me.

He closed his eyes. He'd planned everything sensibly, carefully, wisely, because he was right and she was wrong. He was now free of resentment.

However, he didn't feel very free because he'd lost the only woman he would ever love.

CHAPTER TWENTY-FIVE

Mutato nominee, de te fibula narratu.
With but a single change of name, the story fits thee
quite the same.
Romany spiritual incantation

*I*t was the last cariad that had done it.

James' final Welsh endearment before
casting her out of his life.

The wood fire blazing in the fireplace did little
to warm Valentina, nor stop her persistent shaking.
She stifled her sobs into her pillow to drive out her
grief. Throughout the night, her emotions had spi-
raled. Then they disintegrated, leaving an empty
shadow of a person she once knew.

The first rays of morning prompted her awake.

She rose and shuffled to the basin on her bureau. Survival. Moving on.

She ripped off her muslin dressing gown and flung it to the floor. She splashed cold water on her swollen eyes and lathered herself with a shard of rosemary-tinged soap, the scent of pine burning her nostrils.

Kneeling, she groped through the trunk in the corner of her chamber where she'd kept her Romany clothes. All those months ago, she'd laundered and sewed her scarlet gown. Wisps of black pepper, comforting scents, and the roughness of homespun cotton soothed her sadness. She donned the scarlet gown and smoothed out the wrinkled seams.

Taking a deep breath, she descended the stairway and stepped outside. Blinking back tears, she greeted Yolanda, who wore a full-length coat and carried a beaded reticule, every inch the English lady.

Yolanda answered with a cheerful smile, an attempt to hide the sadness lurking in her deep, soulful eyes. It was everywhere, this sadness, Valentina thought, as Yolanda grasped her icy hands, an attempt to give Valentina a strength she couldn't accept.

Someday she would be competent again, courageous again, consistent again. Just not today.

The lawn spun, and the ice glinting from the

peak of James' home grew fainter. Yolanda shouted, although Valentina couldn't understand her because of the roaring in her ears.

"Are you unwell? Here, take my coat." Yolanda secured her full-length coat around Valentina's shoulders. "I'm bringing my jacket also."

Valentina tried to straighten, to act proper and strong for her sister. "Thank you."

The sight of Yolanda's solid expression brought feelings of unabashed pride. Yolanda had abandoned the man she loved to stand beside her sister. If Yolanda held Valentina responsible for taking her away from Reginald, she gave no indication. She only offered compassion and courage.

Together, they gazed upward at James' home.

"No different from any other wealthy landed gentry's home," Yolanda murmured.

A slight stirring shifted the ash-grey light in James' chamber window. Valentina's heart quaked, a flurry of hope he might still be there. He might glance out the window, extend a teasing smile.

Nay. A man like him couldn't love a woman like her. They were from two unlike worlds—poles apart. Hadn't she tried to read what lurked behind his silvery eyes? For an exposed second, she thought she'd glimpsed his pain. Now she realized she'd been mistaken.

I assumed you were happy with me and my son. Wasn't that enough, sharing a lifetime together?

"Do you know how much I love him?" she whispered to Yolanda.

Yolanda gave Valentina's trembling hands a reassuring squeeze. "Aye."

"*Valentina.*"

A little boy called out and Valentina peered through the morning fog.

"Jeremy! Little man, I'm here." Her gaze caught a round red checker jutting from the snow. She bent and slipped the checker into the folds of her coat, a precious keepsake for all she'd lost.

Yolanda extended a questioning glance, and Valentina shook her head, knowing she'd imagined Jeremy's voice. Only the woof of a stray dog pierced the quiet.

Geoffrey rounded the corner of the stables leading an enormous black horse. "I beg your pardon, Valentina. If you're expecting Mr. Colchester, he and his son departed before daybreak. Tobias and the others rode out with them." Geoffrey studied her. "You're so pale. Are you and Yolanda strong enough to ride? We can take one of the carriages."

"Of course. When have you known a Rom to be weak?" Unable to bear the elderly man's scrutiny, Valentina turned her head.

"I'm certain Mr. Colchester bids you a safe journey." Geoffrey checked the saddle's girth and then patted the horse's neck. Its ears pricked, and its bushy tail swished behind a squared-off body. James obviously had ordered the use of a military animal, one ridden for extended travel.

Her strength of mind rising with her chin, Valentina accepted Geoffrey's gloved assistance to mount the horse. Simple motions required greater effort, and her movements were labored.

Once she was seated, Geoffrey swung up behind her. She clutched the horse's wiry mane and focused on Richard and Yolanda mounting their own black and white steed. Hooves ringing, they crossed the cobblestone courtyard.

The two horses gathered speed. Geoffrey pushed the horse into a gallop, and Richard and Yolanda followed at a close clip. They reached the outer edges of James' estate, then followed a narrow path rather than the main road.

"We're going in a different direction than I expected," Valentina said.

"'Tis a shorter route."

The devastation in her chest broke into an inconsolable sob. James had wasted no time in ridding himself of her. The quicker, the better, he'd obviously told Geoffrey.

Her heartbeat dulled. If the pressure in her lungs ceased, she might be able to breathe.

Geoffrey broke the hush of the following three days by recounting a stream of ceaseless tales, albeit one-sided. He related the history of Mr. Colchester's estate, how many years he'd served Mr. Colchester's parents and the battles he'd proudly fought by Mr. Colchester's side. Carefully, he avoided using a certain man's given name.

Valentina replied to Geoffrey's long-winded epics in monosyllables. She welcomed their hurried pace since it helped her sleep at night.

Whenever they stopped and rested, Richard offered a tranquil prayer, and Valentina prayed with him. Richard spoke softly, a pious vicar, garbed in a black suit and white cravat. For the most part, Yolanda listened and nodded, as was her character.

On their fourth day of travel, Yolanda's loud exclamation woke Valentina from a fitful sleep.

London emerged, nay, *swarmed,* in front of them, and pigeons flew in scattered paths overhead. Haze cloaked the city's ragged edges, the crooked rooftops and spiked chimneys backlit by the pocket of an amber sun.

Valentina's head jerked up. On these twisted streets, Troka had sated his lust with her.

The sickening waves of horror erupted, as dreadful as that day long ago. She wiped the sweat off her hairline, slowed her breathing to a crawl, and clutched the horse's mane. Why had she assumed the passage of time would bury the memories? How isolated she'd felt, her worth as a person unraveling, along with her honor. That evening, the cold of a winter's night had snuck in, and Valentina had never felt so alone.

And all these years later, she still felt alone, and there was nothing for it now.

She stroked the horse's mane and wiped a strand of hair from her eyes. The awful stench of waste and garbage oozed from packed alleyways. Grimy, underfed children ran alongside Geoffrey's and Richard's horses, begging for coin.

Yolanda fingered the lining of her fine Spencer jacket. Then her gaze darted to a harried man, tugging and shouting obscenities, tugging at a herd of goats. A woman hunched over, gaze dull, dirty white cap untied, carrying a basket of soiled laundry.

All of London looked forgotten and tired.

"We lived here once, like these people, trying to survive each day," Yolanda said.

"We've changed, even if London cannot," Valentina replied.

For the first time since arriving in the city, she noted Geoffrey and Richard exchanging a faint signal. Catching her gaze, Geoffrey offered, "Mr. Colchester arranged for you and Yolanda to rest at an inn for a few days. From what I recall, the Smuggler's Purse is clean and serves a good meal."

"We'll not accept any more tokens from him." Valentina reluctantly commended James for his generosity, although her life and future was her doing from now on, not his.

Geoffrey handed her a generous amount of coin. "He insists."

She didn't argue. Instead, she beckoned to a particularly scrawny boy who'd followed them into the city and decided how best to use James' offerings.

~

*W*hy, James thought, avoiding another thatch-roofed village, did it seem like he'd never reach the Welsh border? He'd led his group through remote areas of England to avoid the influenza epidemic. Unending days of hard riding did little to settle his raging disposition, and his servants struggled to keep up with his breakneck tempo.

For most of the journey, Elspeth and Jeremy rode in a carriage behind him. The nurse sat rigid, stout frame upright, bending now and then to tend to Jeremy's needs. She doted on him, as a good nurse should, heedful of his frailness.

Jeremy's puppy had doubled in size in less than six months. Within fifteen seconds of departing, its continuous barking grated on James's already frayed nerves. The offensive dog had been placed in the carriage with Jeremy, to his acute delight and Elspeth's speechless dismay.

They rode for hours, days, in blessed silence. James used the time wisely—to dwell on his torturous memories of Valentina. Her lilting laugh, her impudent wit, her splendid fearlessness. He took in little of the sparse English landscape nor the icy paths beneath his horse's hooves. When he wished to force himself to the brink of madness, his mind burned with thoughts of her trembling words.

I thought you loved me.

Awash in those particular tormented reminders, he noticed dusk nearing.

He glanced to his left. In the cumbersome coach, his son snuggled beneath a nubby blanket, a wriggling dog on one side, a flustered nurse on the other.

James smiled at the trio, his first smile in days, before self-reproach stole the smile from his lips. He hadn't allowed Valentina to see Jeremy one last time. What had he done instead? Refused her, of course.

He uttered his preferred curse of the day at himself, grinding another spike into his sore joints by recalling her pale, dry lips and hollow expression.

The sky had blackened by the time James halted. In a grove surrounded by fir trees, the servants dismounted. For several minutes, his son ran along the compacted snow while the men built campfires. The hiss of wet wood filled the acrid, smoky campsite and James sniffed appreciatively, oddly calmed by the promise of warmth.

Days before, he'd explained to Jeremy that Valentina wouldn't be traveling to Wales with them. Jeremy had cried and called out for her. Since then, he'd folded his little arms and lifted his small chin in mute blame whenever he caught his father's gaze.

James understood his son's sadness and reassured him at every opportunity, wanting him to enjoy the naiveté of childhood. Still, his attempts to kiss Jeremy good night were met with an accusatory frown. Jeremy was neither happy nor reassured.

As a father, James had failed. As a husband, he'd failed. As a man on the brink of finding love where he'd least expected, he'd thrown it away.

Resting on top of a woolen blanket, he clasped his arms behind his head and stared at the silent winter sky. Come the morrow, his group should see the rocky peaks of Wales. To return to his homeland gave him a quiet joy and helped to quell the lonesomeness of his life. Sleep, as usual, eluded him, and his mind traveled to the sole place it cared to dwell—on his green-eyed angel and her beautiful smile.

Had he made the right decision by sending her to Scotland? That was only one of the nonstop questions with no answers that plagued him. After a few minutes of exhausting the same air in and out of his throat, he resorted to the finer torture of recalling her infectious laughter. Especially, he liked to recall those early days when they'd strolled the lawns of his home every afternoon, and she'd dined with him every evening.

All the while, she'd shrouded her love for him under the heaviness of her remorse. Because she'd feared confiding in him, afraid he wouldn't forgive her. She'd never asked anything of him, except his forgiveness.

Coldheartedly, he'd thrown her apology back at her, intent on assuaging his never-ending need to be in control—a cruel maestro. For his beginning bars, he'd interrogated her. For his repeat, he'd belittled her love. For a finale, he'd kept Jeremy from her.

Proof that he was, indeed, the cold-hearted gadje she'd called him on numerous occasions.

He closed his hands over his ears, attempting to block out the memory of her weeping. He focused on a brooding cloud to stop the sound of her heartache breaking through her chamber door and ferociously burrowing a hole in his heart.

"My brave, beautiful, girl," he whispered. "How did we end like this after the love we found together? I'd been so confident of our impending marriage when I'd stopped at that Gypsy camp before riding back to you."

Mercifully, the steady rise of a silver dawn broke, and James stretched his limbs and stood up. If the snow blowing down on them erased her image, he might be able to find his footing again.

Perhaps in Wales, a pert Welsh woman would make him shout with laughter at her witty retorts, or tempt him with sultry green eyes, a regal tilt of her head.

Any such idea died a quick and effortless death. There'd be no other woman.

Because no other woman tied an absurd bright yellow scarf around her neck, ensuring it never matched any garment she wore. And no other woman teased him about his singing or laughed at herself when she tried to learn the intricate steps of a fashionable and senseless dance.

Because no other woman was Valentina.

James rose, tended to his uncommunicative son, and prepared the camp for departure. He remounted his horse and gave the signal to resume. If they continued at a gallop, they'd see his beloved Wales by midday.

I remind you of a country?

Valentina would have loved the rough mountains and primitive coast of Wales as much as he did. Although she'd never see it, because now she was gone.

CHAPTER TWENTY-SIX

It's ushti bak to wellan a Rom,
When tute's a pirryin pre the drom.
When you are going along the street,
It's lucky a Gypsy man to meet.
Old Romany saying

*E*asy.

James planned to immerse himself in overseeing his Welsh estate as soon as he arrived in Wales. A simple plan requiring simple effort.

As he expected, the rugged landscape and wild gardens were neglected. Perfect. He'd engage in grueling physical labor and erase Valentina from his mind.

He rode with his group through a lively rain. He spotted his Welsh flag flying—the red dragon flapping on a green and white background—and the sight was like music to him. Finally, he was truly home.

Lowdie, one of his servants, greeted him.

Little things should've alerted him something was wrong—her skittish eyes, her agitated hands, her white face beneath her whiter bonnet.

The neigh of a Welsh pony distracted him.

He stared at his mansion house, the pockmarks in the stone, the moorlands in the distance.

Dismounting, he smiled. "Did you wish to speak, Lowdie?"

She stared at the ground, her shoes shuffling wet gravel into tiny circles.

Jeremy and his dog darted out of their carriage and slid into the mud, racing side by side. A befuddled Elspeth gasped and panted and scolded. James laughed at the mismatched threesome before directing his attention back to the voiceless servant.

Lowdie curtsied. Standing in the rain, she blocked his path.

"I assume you've been in Wales a while," he prompted, soothing his sweaty horse.

"We arrived days ago, Mr. Colchester."

He nodded and raised the hood of his cloak over his head. Brisk, salty dankness teased his nostrils, and he embraced the turbulent clouds, the scent of rye grass, the gritty soil.

Nearby, the sea's violent tide hurtled against the shore. For an instant, he thought he saw Valentina balancing on the craggy rocks, arms outstretched, a flock of seabirds swooping around her. She gave him one of her surreptitious smiles, followed by an insolent wave.

He almost raised his hand to wave back before he expelled his breath. He brought two fingers downward to glide across his lips and scratch his wet, bearded chin before his gaze returned to Lowdie. "You may speak." His voice rose to be heard above the persistent rain. "That is, if there's something ... anything ... of merit to say."

"Aye."

"Are all the servants here?"

Her unsteady sigh rose with the wind. "Most are settling into the household routine."

"Did Tobias ride into town for our supplies?"

"Aye." Lowdie curtsied again. "Mr. Colchester, 'tis something you must know."

At this rate, he'd never see the inside of his home.

"Speak your mind."

"Reginald is no longer here in Wales. He overheard one of the servants who rode ahead saying that Geoffrey was taking Yolanda and Valentina to London, then sending them to Scotland. There is a rumor in town that Scotland might be imprisoning all Gypsies who enter their country."

"These new laws are frequently discussed and then usually discarded." James handed his horse's reins to a stable boy. "When did Reginald depart?"

"Soon after he heard the rumor. He told Tobias that he intended to ride to London and find Yolanda. The next minute, Reginald saddled a horse and was gone."

The rain picked up, attacking from a black cloudburst. When he reached the front hallway of his home, he didn't stop to admire the beloved furnishings he hadn't seen in years, nor the stucco walls and poplar beams.

He yanked off his soaking cloak and threw it on a carved wooden chair.

He shivered. 'Twas so damp. He'd forgotten about the dampness. It was everywhere, seeping through the walls onto his clothing. He could even smell it.

As his booted footsteps echoed across the slate floor, he prayed the peace he'd hoped to find in Wales wouldn't elude him. He looked around. Little had changed. Even the hallway leading to Beatrix's sleeping-room, the one she shared with Jeremy, tucked away near their nurse's chamber on the second floor, was undisturbed.

Beatrix.

He fumbled with the chamber's latch, hesitating.

The door rattled when it opened. He stepped inside the tiny room and bent his head to avoid striking the slanted ceiling.

Rain buffeted the eaves, a driving staccato. The sound of the sea's stormy waves against the shoreline battered beyond the window.

Jeremy's bed stood on one side of the room. Beatrix's wooden bed stood near the wall, her favorite doll sat lopsided on woolen bedcovers. A picture book lay opened with several pages folded at the corners. Pictures of bedraggled, tawny kittens and lame, purple ponies. Beatrix had always loved to save the forlorn.

Grief and emptiness sliced open a wound in his chest that had never healed. Lightheaded, he leaned against her bed and gazed around the precious chamber.

Something was missing.

Where was her cloth ball, the one she'd played with for hours? She'd arranged her doll and ball together on the bed the day they'd departed for England.

"My toys for Wales, tad. They stay here." Her giggle had filled him with love and unconditional joy.

"Aye, darling," he'd promised. "They'll be waiting for you when we return."

Unsteadily, James crouched and lifted the bedcovers. Clouds of dust burned his eyes. He reached underneath the bed and grasped his fingers around her tiny pink ball.

He stood on trembling legs, letting them guide him to the window. He held the ball close to his face and inhaled a whiff of flowers. Wild roses, fragrant and wistful. Bouquets she'd pinned upside-down in her silky blonde hair, rose petals she'd dropped on the stairs when she'd pretended to be a countess.

"Watch me, tad," she'd call out to him as she skipped across the lawn like a grand lady.

Once more, he breathed in the pure fragrance of white rosebuds and childhood and closed his eyes. She was gone, his sweet baby girl. Helpless with grief, he whispered a psalm of comfort and hope. "Even though I walk through the valley of the shadow of death, I will fear no evil, for you are with me; your rod and your staff, they comfort me."

How can you tell me not to be discouraged, God? How can I be strong and courageous through such sorrow? He couldn't help his feelings, couldn't help feeling overwhelmed with grief.

Although God never said not to be sorrowful. Just because James felt those feelings didn't mean he had to carry his sorrow on his own. Surely, God was with him.

James examined the well-worn ball and squeezed it back into a semblance of its former shape. Ever so gently, he rolled the ball to the bed.

"I will always love you, darling. My perfect angel." He grabbed the wall and sank to the floor. His limbs had changed to sand.

He put his head in his hands and wept like a child.

Hours passed, and the light streaming through the window had colored the walls to a brilliant gold, deepening to purple. The Sleeping-room stood silent, traced in shadows.

Evening neared. James descended the stairs and found his favorite linenfold chair by the blazing hearth in the parlor. The chair creaked when he sat, and he changed positions a number of times never feeling comfortable. An unseen servant had placed a goblet of bragget on a side table. The honeyed Welsh ale beckoned, and a wretchedly empty evening awaited.

"Cheers." He lifted the goblet and saluted the fire. While he drank, he listed the many reasons why his former blacksmith showed an astounding lack of common sense, first and foremost by saddling up a horse and riding off to London.

Still, Reginald had displayed undeniable bravery, which was why James respected him.

He set the goblet on the table, swearing at the silence and lack of any servants about. Somewhere in the sizable house, a shutter banged open and shut, most likely caused by the howling wind. An odious mix of leeks and lamb coming from the kitchen made his nose wrinkle. Grimacing at the scent of *cawl,* his favorite soup up till a moment ago, he proceeded past the kitchen and up two flights of stairs.

When James reached Jeremy's chamber, he found his son huddled beneath woolen blankets, ignoring him, his *father*, and feigning sleep. James opened his mouth to bid his son good night and kissed his hair instead.

"Mr. Colchester, may I get you anything?" Elspeth stood in the doorway and displayed her usual half smile.

"Nay." Unwilling to engage in a second of conversation with anyone, especially his son's anxious nurse, James ascended another flight of stairs leading to his own chamber.

'Twas sleep he lacked. 'Twas why the day had seemed so endless and despondent.

At midnight, James lay awake in the middle of his four-poster bed, a stubborn fire refusing to burn out in the grate, an unceasing tirade of rain pummeling the window. Hands folded behind his head, he studied the cobwebs on the ancient ceiling.

"If I come for you, will you return with me, cariad?" he whispered. "You can teach me your Gypsy customs and I'll teach you about life in Wales. We'll have as many children as you wish, with eyes like emeralds who will speak in gentle Welsh brogues."

Impossible, his mind cautioned. He'd insured she'd hurl every Gypsy curse she'd ever learned straight at him if she ever saw him again. It would be better if she lived with her tribe. Anything was better than staying with him and his wretched inability to forgive.

In an effort to sleep, he tallied the ways he might strangle Reginald.

Each time James added something, memories flowed of Valentina's laughter, her carefree manner of living. Oh, how he missed her. The pure love that was theirs and theirs alone. He couldn't imagine what life could bring without her at his side.

So, what was he doing lying in bed counting cobwebs?

James surged to his feet and shoved on his boots. Quickly, he snatched his cloak and secured a precious necklace into his pocket. It wasn't the loneliness that prompted him. It was time, and he wouldn't lose another minute of it without her beside him. Valentina, he vowed, would never set one shapely toe in Scotland.

He'd been headed in the wrong direction when he'd met her. And then he'd blamed her. Although, in hindsight, he'd needed to meet her to turn him back around. God had had everything planned.

He strode to the window and jammed the iron latch until it opened. Heavy winds lashed an impressive sea against the rocks. Treacherous weather for travel. Perfect weather for travel.

He bounded down the stairs, spotted Clare asleep on a pallet and prodded her awake.

"Mr. Colchester?" Clare's lisp slowed her speech. The blanket she clutched slid through her hands.

James yanked on his damp gloves. "I'm riding to London and expect to arrive back in Wales within a fortnight. Tell Elspeth to tend to Jeremy. I leave immediately."

By moonlight, a groom saddled James' stallion. James flung himself on and lowered his head to escape the biting rain. Across meadows and mountains, he headed east toward London.

Despite the frantic pace, his shoulders eased. The downpour settled to a drizzle.

He focused on the rising sun, the beginning of a rainbow on the horizon, and laughed out loud.

Aye. He wanted children, four more, with the beautiful woman he loved.

CHAPTER TWENTY-SEVEN

Piri telemosa chi athadjol o kam.
The kettle that lies face down cannot get much
sunlight.
Old Romany saying

*A*ll color escaped from Yolanda's face, and she looked as though she'd seen a *mulo*. She skidded to a stop in the midst of a busy London marketplace, crushed her hand to her mouth. Her cry held a note of ... jubilation?

Geoffrey and Richard set down their bundles of gingerbread and shortbread and blinked simultaneously. They enjoyed the baked goods in the central courtyard of the inn, watching passengers being let down and horses changed.

Valentina cast a baffled, sidelong glance toward the baker's stand on the lively street corner. "Yolanda, how much white bread can you possibly eat?"

"'Tis not the bread." Yolanda broke into a teary smile. "'Tis Reginald."

Valentina dropped the biscuits she carried and spun.

Reginald rushed to Yolanda and embraced her, unmindful of the stares of passersby. "I feared you'd left for Scotland and I wouldn't find you in time."

"The rumors reached Wales?" Geoffrey asked.

"Aye."

"Rumors?" Valentina accusatory gaze landed on Geoffrey. "What rumors?"

"Richard and I heard the talk as we approached London. The Scots don't want Gypsies in their country, and we couldn't risk placing either one of you in danger."

"So that's why we've stayed in London a fortnight? I was wondering why 'twas taking so long for fresh horses," Valentina said. "Surely you should have told us this before now."

With his customary cordiality, Geoffrey replied, "I was unsure where to go next."

Reginal beamed, a contented man with Yolanda at his side. "When Yolanda and I marry, we'll make our home near Bury St. Edmunds. The lakes are beautiful and several of my brothers live nearby."

Yolanda crossed to Valentina and placed her cold hands in hers. "Reginald and I spoke of our plans often while at Mr. Colchester's estate. Please come with us. Reginald won't mind, will you, Reginald?"

He shifted his weight from one foot to the other. "Of course not."

If Valentina had met her sister's gaze, she might have considered accepting her kind offer. Instead, she focused on two farmers bartering over the price of a sheep. "I promise to think about it."

"I want you to be safe," Yolanda said softly.

"In that case, 'tis settled." Geoffrey shrugged, strode to Reginald and shook his hand. "The women will be well cared for, and Richard and I can be on our way to Wales."

Yolanda and Reginald, arms entwined, attached as twins joined at birth, headed to the baker's shop. Valentina stooped to retrieve her biscuits and wiped the tears from her cheeks. She smiled, an overwhelming clash of emotions filling her chest. Happiness for her sister's prospects; uncertainty about her own future. Although, one night when they'd traveled, hadn't the vicar said that peace might feel far away even when it didn't have to be? The decision was hers.

The wind grew stronger, depositing discarded refuse around their feet. For once, Valentina was grateful for the predictable torrent of rain, providing an excuse to dash back to the inn.

The next morning, she awoke to the indifferent first rays of the sun shining through the window of her spacious bedchamber. She washed and dressed in her scarlet gown and tied her yellow diklo in place. Thinking better of it, her hand stopped in midair. Instead, she gently woke her sister.

Yolanda thrust the bedcovers aside and slid from the bed. "You're up before dawn."

Valentina placed her diklo in Yolanda's hands. "Take this. I'm leaving London, traveling to Brighton and returning to the tribe."

Yolanda's smile faded. Her fingers froze around the diklo. "Mr. Colchester won't be pleased."

"Please don't tell anyone where I'm going." Feeling chilled, Valentina swung her cashmere shawl around her shoulders and blew her warm breath on her cold fingers. Several careful steps took her down the stairs. Bypassing the inn's front room and grimacing as a loud horn heralded the arrival of numerous coaches, she marched out into the light snow of a London morning.

~

James arrived four days after Reginald. Tearing through the noisy streets of London, he rode straight to the ivy-covered inn he'd arranged for the women's stay. He dismounted, tethered his horse, and strode inside. The innkeeper and a serving wench collided in their hurry to assist him. He dismissed them with a wave of his hand.

"Mr. Colchester, so good to see you ... I think," Geoffrey called from a corner of a private sitting room as James neared. "Are you in London to see some theatre?"

"You must be jesting."

"Are you under the weather?"

"Perhaps from not sleeping since I left England a fortnight ago, only to turn around and ride back." James perched on the edge of a chair near the room's large fireplace. He raised a sardonic brow at the innkeeper, who hovered nearby.

"The Scots might be making rash decisions," he added.

Geoffrey offered a thin smile. "'Tis the reason why Richard and I remained days longer than we intended. We'd planned on departing for Wales come the morrow."

"Glad I caught you before you left."

"Our plans were all sorted out with Reginald's help."

"Reginald is at the inn?"

"Aye. He arrived days ago."

James scanned the front room beyond, overcrowded with patrons. A server in a gathered skirt and low bodice appeared and disappeared with fragrant lamb pies and crisp apple tartes.

"Valentina—is she upstairs in her chamber?" he asked.

Geoffrey sloshed his tankard of ale and watched the foam run over the rim. "She's not here at the moment."

James sighed in grateful relief and removed his gloves. "Where is she? I want to give her something."

With an expression bordering on helplessness, Geoffrey eyed the diners seated at the next table, then a grease spot on the wall above James. "Reginald and Richard are searching for her. You see, Valentina seems to be missing."

James dropped his gloves to the floor. "How can someone *seem* to be missing?"

The clinking of spoons, the laughing diners, the raucous conversations in the room, all came to a standstill.

Geoffrey went to speak but paused. His blue eyes held James imprisoned, seeming to be appraising what James' next reaction might be. "She couldn't have traveled far. However, for now, she's disappeared."

James strode out of the inn, pushing past a wandering musician playing his recorder in the large cobblestone courtyard. Then he mounted his horse and sped away.

The fruitless afternoon search was a frustrating agony, for there was no sign of Valentina anywhere. When he returned to the inn, he immediately asked for ale, not even bothering to seek out the others. He'd been there only a few minutes when Yolanda joined him.

He stared at the yellow scarf tied around Yolanda's slim neck. Sighing, he averted his gaze. He couldn't, he wouldn't, look at that diklo.

Yolanda untied the scarf and placed it in his hands. "Valentina would have wanted me to give this to you."

"Thank you." He hesitated, gliding the worn fabric between his fingers. He brought the diklo to his lips, inhaling the guileless scent of pine and pepper and promises. He breathed it all in, swathing his face in the sheer heartbreak of losing her.

"She loves you very much," Yolanda said.

"Do you know where she is?"

Yolanda shook her head. "All I will tell you is that she's safe. I know Reginald and the other men want to find her, but after tomorrow, I will convince them that Valentina is secure in her decision and we should leave for our own homes."

"I hurt her because of my pretentiousness. Who am I to judge right and wrong? I've done nothing worthy to deserve her love." Just as it was written in Luke 6:41, he thought. *Why do you look at the speck of sawdust in your brother's eye and pay no attention to the plank in your own eye?*

"Your presence speaks of your devotion," Yolanda was saying. "Don't worry."

He raised his hands, trying to explain, then watched them collapse on his lap. "After she left me, I couldn't forgive her. And then the fortune-telling ... And then Jeremy got sick, and my temper blinded me to reason." James drank more ale, a hard swig.

"Valentina took her role in our tribe very seriously. Without her and Luca, we all would have starved." Yolanda touched a piece of fox fur that seemed to have been hastily sewn onto the sleeve of her fine silk gown. "She didn't want to leave you, although she knew you'd never forgive her. She always described you as an honorable, upright man."

"I was more interested in doing things my own way. I didn't listen to her. I listened only to my pride."

"Valentina is stronger and braver than anyone. Nothing in this world will be cruel enough to take her away from you a second time."

"Please tell me where she went."

A reassuring smile flicked across Yolanda's pretty face. "You'll realize soon enough."

Memories of Valentina, her wittiness, her kindness, rushed over him, and sadly, he smiled. She'd cared so much for him, putting him on loftier ground than he'd ever deserved. Yet her humble principles were higher than his.

Her strength, not his, pushed him to his feet.

At dawn, their group spread across the outskirts of London. Geoffrey and Richard searched to the north, and Reginald to the south. James combed the bank of the River Thames, riding past tall ships and rich merchants exporting their wool. He searched the inner streets, narrow and crowded, until all the wooden buildings of the alehouses and shops blended into the same brown canvas.

Indeed, Valentina had vanished. He knew that as each hour went by, the sadness he'd caused her would change her love to resentment. And if anything untoward happened to her, he'd never forgive himself.

In the encroaching dusk of a clambering city street, a thought struck him completely unaware. His hands tensed on the horse's reins before he brought his horse to a halt, staring into the bright cold air with a mixture of incredulity and relief.

"We're traveling to the coast, near Brighton," Luca had told Valentina the night he'd snuck into her chamber.

James charged back to the inn to leave word for Yolanda and the men. Nearly colliding with a horse cab, he thundered out of London and headed for the coast.

CHAPTER TWENTY-EIGHT

Zhan le Devlesa tai sastimasa.
Go with God and in good health.
Old Romany saying

*V*alentina pushed open the flap of her tent and leaned on the precariously fragile pole keeping the tent from collapsing. "Luca, you're tending to the fire all wrong. Blow on it carefully or our entire camp might burn to the ground with all these dried leaves underfoot."

Luca tossed a handful of grass onto the slow-burning campfire. "Green damp wood will never burn. Your fire will be useless for cooking. Heap dry branches onto the flames so the fire will get hot."

Valentina opened her mouth to tell him he was impossible, overbearing, and that she loved

him as a true friend.

He pressed his index finger to his lips, his smile broadening. "Just agree with me for once or you'll wake the elders."

"How did you know what I was thinking? Often, I've wondered if you were the drabardi." She lifted a clay pot filled with water, leeks, and parsnips and walked toward the campfire.

"Stop lifting these heavy pots." In a primal show of strength, he grabbed the pot from her and hoisted it over the open fire.

She waved him off. "Don't you have anything better to do than watch a woman cook?"

"I'll be back by dusk with two crows. If I'm lucky, I'll snare a rabbit too. The Brighton towns-people should be setting up their wares soon be-cause 'tis market day."

Valentina tried to disguise her mirth and disap-prove, although a chuckle broke out anyway. "They should willingly offer you all their small wild animals to save you the effort of stealing."

"'Tis my responsibility to provide food for our tribe."

She touched his sleeve. "Please be careful."

She might have imagined the undercurrent of desperation in his dark eyes. Perhaps the concern

was her own, because Luca never worried about anything. He survived by instinct. She used to be like
him, acting on impulse and not caring about the
consequences. A long time ago, in another lifetime.

With a mischievous grin, Luca retied the square
orange cloth around his head and wiggled his gold
hoop earring. In one heartbeat, his lean frame pivoted and blended into the woodlands.

She sighed and stirred the broth in her pot. He
might be overconfident and think himself invincible,
but he'd handled her mother's burial with dignity
and honor and had kept their tribe alive through
much of the winter.

Valentina blinked at the whitish sun, rising
steadily higher, assuring another day of mild temper-
atures, even though it was only February. As she'd
done for the past several mornings, she walked to
the edge of the caravan and kneeled at a small,
modest gravesite she'd erected for her mother.

"Daj, I have something special to tell you today. I
fell in love with a wonderful man. He's an Englishman, and very generous and fine-looking. He wanted
to marry me. Me, can you imagine? We didn't ... because ... Please be proud of me. I've learned a lot
about myself and—"

She stopped. How could anyone be proud of her?
She'd wronged the very people she'd loved. She tried
to continue to speak and decided to pray. Then she

cried until her temples throbbed and her throat was sore and she didn't have any grief left to spill.

When the sun sat directly overhead, she stared up at a brilliant blue sky. Strangely refreshed, she wiped her eyes and sniffed a whiff of wild primrose, an assurance of spring. Soon, the wildflowers would bloom, strewing blossoms of yellow and gold along the worn trails. Valentina tarried at the modest gravesite and noted the air. So calm, the oak trees hardly swayed. A sunny day meant she'd be able to hang laundry outside to dry, as well as tidying several unused wagons. The elders would be awake by now and finishing their pots of porridge. She was about to stand when a man spoke.

"Bury me kneeling, for I have been standing all my life."

The deep, familiar voice pervaded the tranquil air, speaking words she recognized, yet out of order. Warm hands stroked the back of her hair, then kneaded her shoulders in gentle, persistent circles.

James.

Her heart tilted. She gazed ahead at the tips of hazelnut trees bordering the campsite. She couldn't breathe. Nor think. Nor move. She clutched her jacket to stop her body from shaking.

Rest assured, I will not seek you, cariad, he'd said while her heart had split in two.

Nay, it couldn't be him. Not here. He wouldn't have known where to find her. No one knew except Yolanda, and Yolanda wouldn't have told anyone.

"Valentina."

She could never turn to him, because she'd never recover from the heartache of seeing his handsome face. If she wished to shout at him, how could she find air to utter the sounds?

"Valentina."

His deep voice was different, his tone strained to a whisper. And something else.

He no longer stood behind her, because he was lowering himself to his *knees* beside her. This proud man who'd never knelt to anyone except their king, who employed countless servants and tenant farmers, had dropped to his knees.

James. Memories squeezed and reminded. *Your presence would add a sparkle to every home.*

Slowly, she opened her eyes.

He held out his arms in a gesture of helplessness. "'Twill be easier if I can hold you."

She never hesitated, moving forward into his embrace because she belonged with him. She inhaled his agonizingly recognizable scents, the worn leather, the raw silk, the scent of fresh air.

He tangled his fingers through her hair and kissed her.

How she loved him. She didn't know how many minutes they held each other. She only knew the sheer delight of his embrace.

"I'll chain myself to you if I need to," he said, "because I'll not let you venture another day from my side." His words were so quiet, she tipped her head nearer. He kissed her with his lips, his eyes, his tender smile. "I'm sorry for all your hurt, all your pain."

Tears welled in her eyes. "I'm not worthy and need God's grace."

"I'm not worthy, either. I need the same grace as you." His solid hands were so gentle, caressing her face. "Please promise to stay with me."

She outlined his forehead with her fingertips. She couldn't bear to see his strong face so broken. "My days of roaming ended when a desperate landed gentry with a noble spirit showered me with more kindness than I ever deserved."

He rose and extended his hand, assisting her to her feet. "I have something I want to give to you." He grinned like an expectant schoolboy, reminding her of his son, a hopeful gleam in his velvet-grey eyes. "I've carried this necklace with me for far too many weeks." He lifted a tattered ribbon from the pocket of his cloak.

She gaped when she recognized the symbol, shiny gold coins hanging from a moss-green ribbon. "Where did you get this? 'Tis a pliashka."

"Aye." He brushed a kiss from her neck to her lips. "So I've learned from a group of Gypsy men who weren't at all happy to see me."

"You carried this necklace all the way from London?"

"I never had the chance to give it to you, although I wanted to many times."

She laughed through a constricted throat and smoothed her trembling fingers along the ribbon. "'Tis so beautiful. Thank you."

He rubbed his thumbs underneath her eyes to catch her tears. "Marry me and say you'll come to Wales. I asked you once before in a horse stable and waited for your answer. This time, I'm not leaving until you agree. And I have a son who misses you almost as desperately as his father."

"You stole my heart months ago when we stood on a hillside admiring your splendid estate."

"You threw the boots I'd given you into an abandoned field."

She laughed, then grew quiet. This affectionate man, this man with a wry sense of humor, had come for her. She snuggled her face near his chest. "Please keep your arms around me," she whispered.

He squeezed her closer, taking on her sadness. "*Rrwy'n dy garu di.* I love you. I love your bravery. I love your—"

"*Me kamav tut.* I love you." She turned her face up for another exquisite kiss.

"How could I have been so unforgiving?" he murmured. "I'm sorry."

"And I've forgiven you. Now you must forgive

yourself and realize you're as imperfect as the rest of us."

He secured the necklace around her throat, then leaned back to study her. "'Tis so unpretentious."

"More eloquent words." She smiled and stroked the silken ribbon. "You risked your life for this necklace."

"An understatement." He grinned wryly. He reached into the pocket of his cloak again and produced her mother's yellow diklo. "A gift to me from Yolanda. I intended to keep the scarf until I found you. Now 'tis where it belongs, with you."

They strolled arm in arm through sprinkled sunlight shining past hazelnut trees, returning to the cluster of ragged tents. Several elders sat on improvised stools and peered at James, their wilted dark faces curious.

James glanced down at his black cloak. "From my limited experience as a gadje, I don't think the Rom like Englishmen."

"Most likely they don't, though they may like Welshmen, so eventually you might be accepted." Valentina stopped at the campfire. She sniffed the clay pot, chiding the solid residue of scorched leeks and parsnips, as if the vegetables were to blame for burning. "We'll have to make do with soft cheese for supper tonight."

"I'd hoped we might enjoy a pickled porcupine for our meal."

"'Tis a roasted hedgehog, not a pickled porcu‑pine. And you'll have to wait until we reach Wales for me to roast a hedgehog, unless Luca manages to charm one from one of the hapless townspeople. 'Tis certain they must roll their eyes when they see him coming."

James frowned. "When I see him, I want to do more than roll my eyes."

Valentina placed her hands on both sides of James' face, forcing him to gaze at her. "No doubts or mistrust must ever come between us. Luca is a childhood friend."

"Who unfortunately has grown up."

She rubbed the ever‑present stubble on his cheeks. "'Tis you I love."

He led her to the outskirts of the campsite and spread his cloak on the ground. They settled and she shifted close to him. He lifted her hands, pressing them to his mouth, kissing each finger.

She spoke softly, trying to keep her voice from shaking. "I have something to tell you. 'Tis of great importance."

He linked his fingers with hers. "Have you dis‑covered that you must converse with a tree before you shake it? Or have you found another herbal cure? You must recognize every sprig gracing England."

She laughed. "Nay, although I'd like a garden in Wales." Fairly bursting, she couldn't wait another minute. "I want to get married in a church and raise our children as Christians."

He'd been lowering his head to kiss her. Now he paused. "God's timing is perfect, and so are you."

"I don't doubt that He controls the order of our events." As she gazed at him, a Romany word came to mind. She held the word close to her heart and snuggled into his arms. "I wish Yolanda were here to share our wedding news."

"I left instructions with the innkeeper at the Smuggler's Purse to alert Yolanda and Reginald where I was headed. I wouldn't be surprised if they all show up this evening with Geoffrey and Richard in tow."

"What will we feed them? There's no hedgehog prowling through the brush, and my scorched broth is hardly enough to feed the tribe, let alone four more hungry people."

"As I see it, we have two choices."

She smiled. "Please don't hesitate to share."

He kissed her leisurely and thoughtfully, covering every inch of her face. "We can either ride into Brighton for a meal, or we can stay here. The choice is yours, Mrs. Colchester."

"Let's see how the afternoon progresses, Mr. Colchester."

"Call me James."

Which was when the Romany word drifted to

her tongue. The word grew from a chant to a melody, singing through her soul.

"*Ves'tacha*," she whispered, gazing up at the face of the man she loved. She clasped his hands and held them close to her heart.

Beloved.

THE END

ACKNOWLEDGMENTS

An appreciative thank you to my patient husband, Dave, and our three wonderful children.

A NOTE FROM JOSIE

Dear Friend,

Thank you for reading *Seeking Fortune*. I hope you enjoyed it. *Seeking Fortune* is the first book in my Inspirational Regency romance "Seeking" series.

If you loved this Inspirational romance as much as I loved writing it, please help other people find *Seeking Fortune* by posting your amazing review here, as well as for the bundle: The Seeking Series.

Seeking Fortune is available in ebook, paperback, Large Print paperback, and audiobook.

The Romany Gypsy culture is complex and fascinating. After researching their traditions and beliefs, I wanted to write stories focusing on bigotry during the Regency era.

Valentina Rupa is a feisty Gypsy heroine.

James Colchester, an English landed gentry, is

the perfect hero—dedicated to his son, yet conflicted in his search for God's truth.

Amidst a time when bigotry was the norm, the vibrant folklore of the Gypsy people sets the stage during the panic of the influenza epidemic. One brash lie spoken in haste is the catalyst.

My hope is to fully touch and engage you with the story of James and Valentina. It is a story of betrayal, forgiveness and God's unconditional love.

The Romany Regency Inspirational romances continues with Charity and Daniel in Seeking Charity, and Luca and Patience in *Seeking Patience,* and Nash and Rachel in Seeking Rachel.

I'd love to meet you in person someday, but in the meantime, all I can offer is a sincere and grateful thank you. Without your support, my books would not be possible.

As I write my next sweet or inspirational romance, remember this: Have you ever tried something you were afraid to try because it mattered so much to you? I did, when I started writing. Take the chance, and just do something you love.

With sincere appreciation,
Josie Riviera

Want more Inspirational romances?

Regency:
Seeking Charity
Seeking Patience
Seeking Rachel
The Seeking Series

Contemporary:
A Love Song To Cherish
A Christmas To Cherish
A Valentine To Cherish
Romance Stories To Cherish bundle
Holly's Gift

RECIPE FOR ROASTED HEDGEHOG

According to Medieval experts, the hedgehog should have its throat cut, be singed and gutted, then trussed like a pullet, then pressed in a towel until very dry. Roast and eat with cameline sauce, or in a pastry with wild duck sauce. Note that if the hedgehog refuses to unroll, put it in hot water. The Rom would have dredged the hedgehog in black pepper after cooking.

Although I can't personally verify the results, here's the recipe modified from Medieval cookery:

Method:

Season the meat. Wrap it in long grass, first lengthways, and then tying more grass crossways to secure the green wrapping in place

Prepare your barbecue and place a large pot filled

with water on it. Cook the meat for two hours. Once the meat has cooked, remove the grass, then place the meat back in the barbecue to sear. Carve and serve.

Nettle pudding can be boiled in the same pot and served as an accompaniment.

(Sorry, I don't have a recipe for Nettle pudding.)

Enjoy!

ABOUT THE AUTHOR

Josie Riviera is a *USA TODAY* bestselling author of contemporary, inspirational, and historical sweet romances that read like Hallmark movies. She lives in the Charlotte, NC, area with her wonderfully supportive husband. They share their home with an adorable shih tzu, who constantly needs grooming, and live in an old house forever needing renovations.

To receive my Newsletter and your free sweet romance novella ebook as a thank you gift, sign up HERE.

Join my Read and Review VIP Facebook group for exclusive giveaways and FREE ARC's.

To connect with Josie, visit her webpage and subscribe to her newsletter. As a thank-you, she'll send you a free sweet romance novella directly to your inbox.
josieriviera.com/
josieriviera@aol.com

ALSO BY JOSIE RIVIERA

Seeking Patience

Seeking Catherine (always Free!)

Seeking Fortune

Seeking Charity

Oh Danny Boy

I Love You More

A Snowy White Christmas

A Portuguese Christmas

Holiday Hearts Book Bundle Volume One

Holiday Hearts Book Bundle Volume Two

Candleglow and Mistletoe

Maeve (Perfect Match)

The Seeking Series

A Christmas To Cherish

A Love Song To Cherish

A Valentine To Cherish

Valentine Hearts Boxed Set

Romance Stories To Cherish

Aloha to Love

Sweet Peppermint Kisses

USA TODAY
BESTSELLING AUTHOR

JOSIE RIVIERA

Seeking Charity

A Christian Historical Romance

This book is dedicated to all my wonderful readers who have supported me every inch of the way.
THANK YOU!

CHAPTER ONE

*W*ales, 1812

"*L*et's drink to a long and happy life for the bride and groom!"

Charity Weston stood at the edge of a smoky campfire with her Romany Gypsy tribe and raised her tankard of ale. Luca, the leader of their tribe, offered the toast in celebration for a *pliashka*, a betrothal agreement.

Miriah, the attractive bride-to-be, smiled radiantly at her intended groom, who grinned proudly at her. Both sets of future in-laws stood beside them. Miriah's dark brows and eyes dominated her features, accentuated by glossy ebony hair tied back with a vivid red headdress.

So unlike her own copper-colored hair, Charity thought, fingering her unmanageable ringlets.

As the tribesmen hooted and cheered, Charity joined in the chants of *sastimos*, good health, even as her cheeks flushed at the bawdy remarks laughingly called out to the couple.

In the glow of the firelight, she studied the Gypsy men and women assembled in a circle around the couple—the laugh lines etched in the corners of their mouths and the granite determination in their jaws, announcing their decision to live unrestrained from the constraints of 'civilized life'.

Several men with greying beards loudly shared opinions about where they should travel next and that they should leave within a fortnight. They'd stayed in one place long enough. In the meantime, Luca didn't respond as he bent to retrieve a bottle of brandy for the groom's father. The father then wrapped a handkerchief around the bottle as part of the pliashka.

These were the people Charity had grown to love. Their kindness, their traditions, their joy for life. They brought nothing with them when they traveled and simply adopted the traditions of wherever they made camp.

A clap of thunder reverberated, and the heavy

wooden wagons, packed with garments and jewelries, creaked in response.

However, weather changes didn't deter the revelers. Besnik, one of the elders, took up a pipe whistle and began playing, whilst another grabbed his fiddle. Kezia, an elderly woman who was considered the *phuri dai*, someone who resolved conflicts with honor, clapped to the music and sang off-key. The melody was spirited yet emotional. Since the tribe had settled in Wales, their music had taken on a decidedly Welsh, Celtic quality.

Charity finished her ale. Intrigued, she watched as Miriah's future father-in-law secured a necklace around Miriah's throat. Made of a satin ribbon with gold coins, the necklace was a symbol of the matrimony bond.

"Remember." Kezia stepped forward and focused on Miriah, "*Ajsi bori lachi: xal bilondo, phenel londo.*"

Charity grinned as she silently translated: "Such a daughter-in-law is good who eats unsalted food and says 'tis salted."

"Good advice!" A boisterous shout of approval came from the men and Charity gave her head a shake. Despite living with Gypsies for six years, the good-natured commotion and dust and brightly-colored gowns sometimes evoked a dreamlike blur of confusion.

And lately, it also brought a sense of detachment. The setting was so different from the proper English background of her childhood—high-waisted white muslin dresses, formals planned months in advance, country dances with their processional marches and ballet-style movements.

But that was all in the past.

Through a break in the surrounding woods, she peered toward a stone mansion, the Colchesters' grand country estate. The owners, James and Valentina, had invited the tribe to camp on their property. Mr. Colchester was wealthy landed gentry, and Valentina, a Gypsy woman. Despite society's rigid rules, they had fallen in love, married, and moved to Wales.

And it was marvelous here, Charity mused, scanning her surroundings. The rugged Welsh landscape alive with summer color, the sounds of the sea crashing to shore, the bright open sky shining at night with pinpoints of bright stars.

Why, then, could she think of little else than her former English home?

Lately, Wales induced a longing for her childhood she couldn't explain. She had spent many a summer in Norfolk by the sea when her mother was alive, she reasoned. Perhaps 'twas why these remembrances came with more and more frequency.

As the last of the tankards were emptied, she set down her own to refill an empty flask with more braggot, a honeyed Welsh ale. She handed the flask to Luca, who poured some into a tankard for himself, then offered the flask to the others. Grabbing a slab of bread, he glanced at her, a smile crossing his dark tanned features.

"Thank you, Charani."

As always, he called her by her Gypsy name.

With a nod, she turned, planning to assist the younger women roasting a hedgehog on a wooden spit.

"What is troubling you?" For such a commanding presence, he had the ability to move quietly and quickly. He'd come up behind her, and she hadn't noticed until he spoke. "This past fortnight, you are preoccupied."

She shrugged her bright-pink shawl tighter around her shoulders. The temperateness of summer promised another month of welcoming days, although the chill of a sea breeze hung in the air.

"'Tis nothing," she said.

He studied her face. "I watched you during the pliashka. Are you missing someone? Mayhap a man from a neighboring tribe? I saw you conversing with Petshah the last time we went to market."

"We met once and are only friends. Besides, isn't he at least thirty years my senior?"

And so heavy he could crush her. She didn't add that part.

"Age doesn't matter."

"Perhaps." She waited for Luca's response. She

was twenty years old, and would soon be labeled a spinster if she didn't wed.

"He's made it known he's interested in you," Luca said.

She shook her head and didn't respond, knowing she was no match for the bristle in Luca's deep tone, nor his persistence. She picked up a stick to turn the meat and began a casual conversation about the passing of summer and of Romany customs, particularly the pliashka.

Thankfully, the subject of spinsterhood wasn't mentioned, but her good luck didn't last. With a determined gleam in his dark eyes, Luca repeated his earlier question. "What troubles you, Charani?"

She turned her attention away from the hedgehog and faced Luca squarely. "Sometimes ..." Her voice dropped to a whisper. "I don't know where I belong anymore."

There. She'd blurted it, becoming more like a Gypsy every day. Gone were the days of well-bred protocol, the soft tone of an Englishwoman schooled to never share her opinions aloud. Conversely, within the tribe, she could speak her mind.

Luca nodded slowly, his gaze understanding. "I know the feeling."

The emotion in his admission struck her heart, making her ache all the more for things left behind long ago—a lavish home, a soft mattress, and sparkling clean bed linens.

Nay, she admonished herself. She was unappreciative for even thinking such thoughts. Luca's tribe had been benevolent, accepting her after the first Gypsy tribe she joined had moved to Scotland.

"How would someone like you, a Rom, know anything about not belonging?" she wanted to ask, although she said nothing. He was the head of the tribe for a reason. While brash, he took an interest in every tribesmen, listening intently, offering advice whenever asked. And although she'd heard rumors regarding his parentage, his past was never questioned.

He took several sips of ale and then lowered the heavy tankard. "Have you met Valentina?"

It was a strange change in subject, although Charity was grateful.

"Nay. Have you?"

"Aye. She was a childhood friend. Earlier this afternoon, I met her at the stables. She assured me we were welcome to remain as long as we wished."

"She's a proper lady now, married to landed gentry."

He shrugged. "She'll always be one of us, a Romany at heart."

Us. So Luca regarded Charity as a Gypsy. Noteworthy, because she looked nothing like them. Her skin was pale, her eyes a crystal-blue, the opposite of the tanned skin and piercing brown eyes of Luca and the others.

"Valentina is kind to allow us to camp on her husband's land," she said.

She waited for Luca's response. The smoky smells of wood campfires, cooking odors of fennel and garlic, hung in the air. Inside a crude stable, a spotted Welsh pony, small and sturdy, whinnied.

As always, Luca took his time, retying the green sash around his waist, running a hand along his buckskin breeches. It was his way, deliberating when he had something important to say. Years earlier, he had assumed the responsibilities of caring for the mostly elderly tribe without complaint, although he was only a young adult male himself.

"Would you like to meet her?" he finally asked.

"Valentina?" Charity scarcely noticed the encouragement in his tone, his voice nearly drowned out by several of the men near the campfire calling for more ale. "From the tales I've heard, she's a *drabardi,* a fortuneteller." She shook her head. "I don't want my fortune told. The Rom have taught me how to live in the present and trust myself and my instincts."

Although when she was younger, she had relied on God to carry her through the rough patches.

Nay. She corrected her thought. God had carried her through every patch, whether rough or smooth. When had she lost the faith she once held so strongly?

"Valentina's no longer a drabardi," Luca was saying. He sipped his ale, took a bite of bread, before continuing. "Valentina told me one of Mr. Colchester's English acquaintances is looking for property in the area. She's invited them to stay for a fortnight."

"And?"

"And you can join them for a meal, or a game of whist, or whatever the English do to while away their time." He shrugged. "More important, 'twill give you an opportunity to converse with English men and women."

"I'm happy here with the Gypsies."

Firmly, he shook his head. "'Tis exactly what you need to bring pink color back to your cheeks. You've grown paler this season, despite the sun." Another sip, another bite. "Certainly an English lady like yourself grows weary of our Gypsy customs."

She frowned, reflecting on all he'd said. "I don't know Valentina."

"I'll introduce you."

"I haven't been invited."

"You will be."

"I won't fit in." She regarded her vivid orange gown. "I haven't conversed with any Englishmen besides shop owners in years."

"You'll like Valentina. She's adapted to the English ways and no longer believes in spirits."

"I don't believe in spirits, either."

"Mr. Colchester is a devout Christian and

Valentina has followed suit," Luca continued. "You are a Christian too, aye?"

Aye. Once. Long ago.

Since arriving in Wales, she heard the peal of church bells every Sunday. She had contemplated attending services, but always quelled the thought. She was a Gypsy woman now, and she'd enough of her tyrannical father's heavy hand, all in the name of God.

"Although I don't agree with Valentina's interest in Christianity," Luca added, "they are happy, and I am glad for them."

Charity couldn't be happy or sad for the Colchesters because she didn't know either of them, but she appeased Luca by agreeing.

A grin touched his lips. "So, you will consider my suggestion?"

Wrapping her arms around herself, she stared at the grand estate in the distance, the smoke billowing from enormous chimneys, the torchlights lit, the flickering light of beeswax candles through the windows.

"Of course," she replied. Inwardly, she'd already made up her mind. She couldn't attend a fancy dinner in such a grand house. Not wanting to spoil the pliashka with a disagreement, she decided to wait and tell Luca her decision come the morrow.

He surveyed her, apparently considering her reply. "Good. 'Tis settled." Abruptly, he swung around to rejoin the merriment by the campfire.

Immersed in her thoughts, she stared into the camp firelight, the festivities forgotten. Memories best hidden broke to the forefront. When she had run away from home, she had vowed to never look back.

She'd even changed her name to be doubly sure no one from England would ever find her.

$\sim$

A few hours later, long after she'd gone to her tent to sleep for the night, Charity awoke to a nightmare. Her eyes snapped open. Her heart beat heavily in her chest, her breathing quick. Something had brought her from a sound sleep to acute awareness.

She shot upright on her floor mattress. Judging from the angle of the moonlight spilling through her canvas tent, 'twas the middle of the night.

She flopped back, trying to get comfortable. With the sharp, chopped straw poking at her, comfort wasn't something that came easy. Still, she was safe, and in her familiar tent, the tent she had lived in for the past six years. Relieved, she swallowed. Her mouth was so dry.

She rolled onto her stomach and scanned the shadowy possessions she'd come to treasure. A small washbasin sat in a corner beside a water pitcher, a wooden stool placed nearby. A basket of blueberries she'd picked earlier in the day perched on a bench.

Her gown was draped on a table made of rough-hewn wooden planks.

She planned to wear it to market. Luca intended for the tribe to pick up supplies, which meant haggling for fresh vegetables and eggs whilst the boys and girls from the tribe stole jewelry from unsuspecting rich ladies to sell for coin.

Although Charity didn't condone stealing, she understood the necessity when supplies were low and jobs for Gypsies were nonexistent. Perhaps someday, the attitude toward Gypsies would change. The Colchester marriage was certainly an encouraging beginning to ending all the bigotry in the world.

Sweat gathered on her brow. Understandable, she rationalized, considering the close air in the tent. But it was more. The nightmare had jarred her dreams, and more memories of her upbringing invaded her thoughts.

Why now? Wales had brought her great joy, yet the remnants of past fears sat on the edge of her consciousness. After all this time, she still felt her father's firm fingers pushing her down onto the cold stone floor of the linen closet. She still felt his hand strike her with such force, the air was knocked from her lungs.

When he punished her, which was often, her mind had gone over and over her mishaps.

Why was she being punished? Was she really that bad?

She did ride her horse for hours, but that wasn't a reason to be disciplined.

Daniel Hayward, a longtime friend from her village, oftentimes accompanied her on his horse. Those were carefree, happy times, she thought. Indeed, her father must have realized she and Daniel oftentimes lost track of time, laughing and racing each other through the woods and pastures that surrounded their respective homes.

She smiled, her heart swelling with the heartening remembrances. She and Daniel had talked endlessly, of their childhood dreams and childhood pursuits.

Where was he now? she wondered. When she had left, he'd been eighteen, four years older than she. Despite that age difference, they got along wonderfully well together, although she sometimes overheard gossip in the village. Even Daniel's sister told Charity she made a fool of herself when she was with him, especially since she hunted him down to come riding with her.

That wasn't true. Daniel had always sought her, and he had clarified that fact on more than one occasion with his sister.

However, it *was* true that Charity couldn't help

glancing at him whilst they rode. He was tall and good-looking, possessing the easy charm of the affluent, well-bred gentleman. She'd seen him grow from a lanky boy to a man, his shoulders broadening, his muscular legs clearly outlined in tightly-fitted leather breeches. And his eyes—a soft silver-grey, frequently sparking with mirth. He was handsome and self-assured, and she developed a crush for him. Although, of course, he never knew, for at the age of fourteen she was plain-featured, overly tall, and self-conscious.

She sighed. Hadn't they vowed to be best friends forever? She wondered if he remembered the day before she decided to run away. It had been her birthday, and she had chosen to spend part of the day with Daniel, riding horses and enjoying a picnic with friends and several chaperones.

After they returned to her home and before he left for his, Daniel leaned against an oak tree, so close to her she was afraid he could hear her pounding heart, and teased her that he'd beat her fair and square whilst they'd raced home.

"Please never forget me," she suddenly said.

"Why would I?" He raised his dark eyebrows. "You're not intending to leave me, are you?"

How had he known?

She hadn't answered, gazing up at the face she knew so well, hoping she could memorize it forever.

Lightly, he'd touched her cheek. "Where are you going?"

Away, she thought, briefly squeezing her eyes shut. *I don't want to leave you, but I must.*

On impulse, she stood on her toes and kissed him. In response, he'd stepped away and joked about how he would always beat her when they raced. She'd responded to his bantering with laughter.

At that point, her memories went from good to bad as she recalled her "transgressions," as her father labeled her wrongdoings. Oftentimes, he caught her dozing in church. When accused, she argued her good reasons because the vicar droned on for hours. Certainly her father would understand.

But he never did.

Instead, he forced her to kneel and recite Bible passages. Hadn't he known that by forcing her to recite a beloved verse, she would turn away rather than toward God? Hadn't he known she missed her mother as much as he did? She saw the telltale sorrow crossing his face whenever her mother's name was mentioned.

And her mother's name was also Charity. Many people commented on their resemblance. Charity had her mother's same unaffected beauty, hair color, and fiery, headstrong nature.

She pushed a strand of her unruly hair from her face. That was where the resemblance ended because, unlike her mother, Charity was an independent woman, relying on no one but herself.

Resolutely, she turned her thoughts from anything having to do with the English and her former life among them.

Closing her eyes, she courted sleep. A passage from Proverbs came, uplifting and encouraging.

"'Trust in the Lord with all thine heart; and lean not onto thine own understanding. In all thy ways acknowledge Him, and he shall direct thy paths.'"

She hadn't recited that particular Bible passage, or any Bible verse, in many years. Yet somehow, the prayer had drifted easily to her lips.

CHAPTER TWO

*D*aniel Hayward assisted his sister, Penelope, into her carriage whilst she complained endlessly about the new cook she'd hired. A crisp morning breeze cooled the air, and the thistledown moving gently across the fields meshed with the scent of pine floating down the tall fir trees. In addition to their carriage, another coach carrying trunks, valises and Penelope's maid followed, along with two outriders, one riding in the front and the other bringing up the rear.

Daniel was staying for a month in Wales with Penelope and her husband, Theodore Huckabee. They'd been married for many years and were childless, a fact that bothered neither of them. For the most part, they lived completely separate lives.

Briefly, Daniel wondered how his parents would

have felt about his sister's marriage. Years earlier, he'd overheard their quiet prayers that Penelope and Theodore would find true love. When they were alive, they often expressed their desire for grand-children.

Their prayers hadn't been answered—neither by Penelope and Theodore, nor by him. At four and twenty years old, he had no desire to marry and sire children anytime soon.

"So, Daniel, what do you think of the property Theodore and I are looking at?" Penelope settled into the carriage and gathered her teal-blue satin gown about her. "Shall we purchase the estate or not?"

Theodore and Penelope had sought Daniel's ad-vice concerning an investment property in Wales. The place had a shabby quality, having fallen into disrepair, and Theodore intended to purchase the home at a low bid, pay for some repairs, and then resell at a profit. In the meantime, Theodore and Penelope were renting a summer home nearby.

"The home needs work," Daniel began, smiling at his understatement. He took a seat across from her in the carriage, and the driver guided the pair of greys out of the Huckabees' drive.

"That's your assessment?" A look of sorely strained patience crossed his sister's pretty face. She shook back her long blonde curls, sending them trailing over her shoulders. A pearl comb kept the tresses back from her face.

"Your husband has a greater say. 'Tis merely my opinion."

"'Tis your professional opinion. Considering the wealth you've accumulated, Theodore values your insight." She sighed. "Although I rarely see him now. He's hauled me off to Wales and then prefers to spend time alone in his study."

Drinking brandy, Daniel knew.

"'Tis unfortunate he couldn't join us for our fort-night visit with the Colchesters," Daniel said aloud. "We've both known James for years through our London acquaintances."

"He said he might be able to come for the last few days. He's a busy man, you know."

"Aye," Daniel agreed, although from what he knew of Theodore, he was the opposite of a busy man.

Crossing his arms, he stretched out his long legs and leaned back, admiring the dramatic Welsh seascape from the window as the carriage wound along the road. He hadn't visited Wales since his youth, and his gaze wandered over the familiar foot-paths leading to the sea. Everything here was the way he remembered, only better, and for the first time in years he allowed himself to relax. This was a working holiday, and he intended to enjoy the holiday part.

"Daniel?" his sister asked shortly. "You're overly engrossed with Wales. Most assuredly you've seen better views than this one."

"London is dirty and overcrowded of late. Thus, the country scenery is a welcome change."

Penelope pinched her thin lips together. "I'll ask a second time. What is your opinion of the investment property?"

"Perhaps when the bushes are pruned and the rotted wood repaired, 'twill look more like a home." Daniel chose his words carefully. He didn't want to sway them either way, for the decision was ultimately theirs. "And the inside is dark and dreary. Have you considered adding mullioned windows after your purchase?"

"We can't invest a fortune if we intend to make a profit." Penelope turned a false smile to him. "Unlike you, coin doesn't multiply in our hands as it does in yours."

He refrained from enumerating the reasons why coin didn't multiply in the Huckabee household, although they were threefold. First, Theodore's gambling had resulted in accumulated debts. Second, Theodore hadn't worked a day in his thirty years, opting to live off his father's inheritance. And third, Theodore had developed a fondness for the drink.

With feigned casualness, Daniel commented on the stunning scenery because a neat change of subject was in order. The last thing he wanted was a discussion with Penelope about how he'd managed to double his wealth in the past six years, handling investments and meeting weekly with his solicitors. Hard work, he thought, coupled with long hours, a drive to succeed and an almighty God.

Gratefully, he lifted praise, because the Lord had blessed him, and Daniel was grateful for each and every blessing in his life. He grinned, eyeing his oftentimes difficult older sister. Even the blessing of Penelope.

After traveling over two hours, Penelope pointed to a scattering of makeshift tents and wagons near a patch of woods. "There's the Gypsy camp. I can't believe Mr. Colchester actually married a Gypsy woman. 'Tis the reason why he settled in Wales, you know."

Daniel quirked an eyebrow. "And that reason is?"

"To hide his new Gypsy wife from everyone in London. Do you realize the rumors surrounding this marriage?"

Daniel gave a heavy sigh and tapped a finger against his thigh. Ordinarily, he would've shrugged off Penelope's words, for he was well-acquainted with her judgmental character, as well as that of her husband. In fact, he wondered if the real reason why Theodore hadn't joined them was because of his prejudice toward Valentina Colchester.

In any event, Daniel refused to let Penelope's biased comment slide. Perhaps if she were confronted, she would realize the wrongness of her intolerance.

"Hide Valentina from exactly whom in London?" he challenged. "James Colchester is well-educated and a good Christian man. Besides, who wouldn't want to settle here?" He gestured toward a cottage covered in ivy surrounded by green hillsides and lush farmlands.

"Here? In this desolate country? Surely you're jesting." The look she gave him suggested he'd lost his reason.

He tried to look disinterested, managing a nonchalant smile. On several occasions, especially of late, he had considered moving from London to a quiet, peaceful place teeming with waterfalls and lakes and mountains.

Perhaps Wales was the place he was seeking.

"English society will never accept a Gypsy," Penelope continued. "And Theodore agrees."

"I'm sure he does."

His sister fixed on him the glare he expected. To lighten the mood, he provided a broad grin. "English culture, which is so driven by the church, should take a studied look at our narrow-mindedness and read the Bible for insight."

"We do read the Bible!"

"Do we?" he asked, studying her scowl. If nothing else, he had gotten her to at least think about her narrow viewpoint. "In the end, aren't we all from the same race?"

He paused, catching sight of a woman near the Gypsy camp. She held a woven basket and was picking blueberries. His eyes widened. She stood out because of her reddish-brown hair and fair skin, so distinctive from the black-haired, olive-skinned women picking blueberries alongside her.

He leaned forward to peer out the window. Tall and slender, she wore an absurdly brightly-colored orange gown, a pink shawl draped over her shoulders. Assuredly, this beautiful woman wasn't a Gypsy. In contemplative silence, he held in a breath and just stared. Surprisingly, she resembled someone he knew from his youth.

Charity. Charity Weston.

He gripped his fingers together. Nay, it couldn't be. Charity was dead.

They'd been childhood friends, attending church together, riding their horses at a gallop through endless fields. She'd been light and skillful in the saddle, managing her horse at a breakneck speed. She'd secured her unmanageable waves into a knot, her face alive with exhilaration. Her sense of adventure outmatched even his.

He grinned, recalling their exploits. Her half-hearted attempts to play the pianoforte, plinking away with sighs of impatience, had resulted in her father declaring she didn't have a modicum of musical talent. Daniel remembered a recital performed by her and several other eleven-year-old children in a stuffy music room. Charity had forgotten her piece midway through but kept on playing, improvising with her head held high.

He'd been the first to stand and applaud when she finished, and she caught his gaze and smiled at him. She'd stood self-consciously, smoothing her ill-fitting dress and then bowing to the audience. She'd been all thin arms and skinny legs at the time.

Right then, he could've cheerfully boxed the ears of the other audience members, children, adults, and her overbearing father, who had sniggered during her performance. In his chest, he'd felt a deep, affectionate protectiveness toward her that, at the age of fifteen, had troubled him.

The last time they'd been together was the day she reached her fourteenth birthday.

Near her home, she'd stood on her tiptoes and kissed him. He'd been startled at first, and made sure he didn't reciprocate, for she was too young. Beforehand, she'd said something that had haunted his memory ever since.

Please never forget me.

He hadn't understood, assumed she referred to a time when they grew older, and married, and moved away from each other. Unquestionably, with her generously curved lips and skin as velvety as the finest cream, he knew her extraordinary beauty only needed time to develop before men would seek to court her.

In response, he'd asked her where she was going, then turned a humorous joke to tease her. Her musical laughter resembled carillon bells. That is, when she laughed. Her smiles had become rarer as the years passed, although her mischievous nature remained intact.

And then she was gone from his life.

To clear his mind, he shook his head as the carriage curved up the drive leading to the Colchester estate.

"Whatever is the matter?" Penelope peered at him. "Are you ill? You've turned white."

He cleared his throat, still gripping his fingers together. "Do you remember a girl named Charity Weston?"

"Didn't she suddenly disappear? Her father said she died unexpectedly."

"Aye. I well remember the day of his announcement."

Daniel had taken Charity's death hard and the ache in his chest hadn't gone away for months afterward. Had she known she was going to die? Was it premonition, or a cruel fate? He prayed to God, seeking answers. God hadn't responded.

Through it all, though, he kept his faith, though he refused to believe she was gone. His heart had been too filled with feelings he could neither contain nor comprehend.

Please never forget me.

"I think I just saw her," he said quietly.

His sister drew up short. "And I think all this garden-fresh Welsh air is making you a bit mad. The girl died six years ago. Obviously, you're mistaken."

Was he? He'd seen her so clearly. He peered out the window again, gazing across the fields, although he'd lost sight of her.

He tore his gaze away. For lack of knowing what to do, what to say, he folded his arms and kept his gaze on a point above Penelope's head, focusing on the cushioned seat.

In his mind, more remembrances echoed.

Frequently, he'd been present when Charity's domineering father chastised her. A mere slip of a girl, she would face her father, undaunted, and fire a plausible explanation that sounded more like an argument. Although he'd seen her father react to her rebellion with anger, Daniel always silently applauded her courage.

"I recall very little about the girl," Penelope said, "although you spent a good deal of time with her, and she was obviously keen on you." She threw him a meaningful look.

"What's that supposed to mean?" he demanded. "She was four years younger than me." Even with the age difference, though, they'd gotten along brilliantly. She had a smile that lit his heart, a giggle so infectious, she would set him to laughter, and it would go on for hours. However, what he appreciated most about Charity was she chose honesty above all else. And her faith in God had been steadfast.

In response to his question, Penelope shrugged. "I didn't mean anything. I do know that since Charity's death, you've escorted more women to the theatre and opera than I can count. Never forming an attachment to just one woman. Although now, of course, there's Lady Lydia."

"Aye." With a reluctant nod, he agreed.

Lady Lydia was the woman his family and acquaintances expected him to wed, and a different rumor seemed to be spread every week about news of their betrothal. Somehow, he hadn't been able to make the commitment yet. Perhaps he never would.

Because at some point in his life, he stopped believing in love, sharing instead the viewpoint of many of his peers. That love was elusive, and he'd never been able to grab hold of it.

Mayhap it had happened when Charity disappeared.

Nay. He shook his head. Absolutely not.

Nonetheless, remembering the affection and love his parents freely shared with each other made him sometimes long for that same attachment.

Their carriage stopped near the front steps of

the Colchesters' stone mansion. A distinctive Welsh flag, a red dragon on a green and white background, flapped proudly in a cold rush of air. Clouds were gathering. Mayhap a storm brewed nearby.

Penelope prepared to alight, wrapping her paisley shawl around her reedy shoulders. Not one to let any subject drop without the final say, she remarked, "As for you believing you just saw Charity, what would a dead English woman be doing cavorting in Wales with a band of dirty Gypsies?"

CHAPTER THREE

The following morning, Daniel awoke before dawn and spent several minutes praying. He always began and ended his days in prayer.

"Lord, guide my steps today," he said. "Help me to stand strong and choose only your ways above all others." He added a treasured Bible verse from 2 Timothy: "'For God hath not given us the spirit of fear; but of power, and of love, and of a sound mind.'"

He hoped the prayer would give him the insight he needed for the days ahead, for certainly time spent with Valentina and his sister's bias would prove challenging.

After he uttered a final amen, he washed, shaved, and cleaned his teeth. He didn't need a manservant, he decided, to pull on his white muslin shirt, striped waistcoat, and breeches. After a glance in the mirror to smooth back his unruly dark hair, he pulled on leather boots and decided to take the opportunity to explore the Colchester estate. He strode quietly down the hallway stairs whilst the rest of the household slept.

He assumed the day began for the others by eight o'clock in the morning, because Valentina had assured them the night before that a light meal of toasted bread, jam, tea and coffee would be served at nine. He reached into his crescent pocket and pulled out his gold fob watch attached to a chain. 'Twas half past six, giving him plenty of time to explore.

He stepped outside and enthusiastically inhaled the scent of rye grass and crisp air. His stride was sure along the gritty ground as he made his way to the sea.

Dinner the previous evening had proved a sumptuous feast consisting of three courses, his favorite being chicken with mushrooms and tender leeks prepared in a butter sauce, and baked apples for dessert, all served with wine and braggot—a honeyed malt ale. Valentina and James had fulfilled their roles as host and hostess with casual grace. Fun-loving and bantering throughout the meal, they frequently gazed at each other with an affection Daniel had rarely seen between a married couple. And it had given him hope that love truly did exist.

Their son, Jeremy, James's child from his first

marriage, was adorable. He hadn't spent many hours
with them because, as was the custom, his nurse Elspeth put him to bed before dinner. James explained
that Jeremy was deaf, and that Valentina was an attentive, loving stepmother. Daniel also learned Jeremy had had a twin sister, Beatrix, who died a few
years earlier in a tragic accident.

Penelope had been careful not to insult their
host's wife, although she pleaded fatigue and disappeared into her guest chamber shortly after the meal
ended.

Daniel dragged his thoughts from dinner and
squinted at the climbing sun. The morning air was
cooler than he'd expected, and he'd left his gloves in
the guest chamber. Although he started toward the
sea, he changed direction and made his way toward
the Gypsy camp instead. Shrugging his hands into
his waistcoat pockets, he hastened his pace.

Of course, if he were truthful, this was the path
he'd intended to take all along, and the reason he left
the house before the rest of the household stirred.
Thoughts of Charity had kept him awake much of
the night, and his restless imaginings had blurred
with visions of her—as a girl and as a woman.

He followed a footpath and stopped when he
reached a row of blueberry bushes. He knelt and
probed through the bushes, well aware a stranger
would view his behavior as utterly insane. He could
only imagine what Penelope would say.

Why was he chasing shadows and searching for a charming fourteen-year-old girl who no longer existed? Because, he reasoned, seeing the grown woman had aroused the same ache in his chest as when he was a young man. Charity had been his dearest friend, and losing her had filled him with an unexplainable loss.

As he straightened, a Gypsy man strode toward him from the opposite direction.

His muscles tightened. The Gypsy had come from nowhere—though how could he have missed a man dressed in buckskin breeches, a green sash about his waist, and a bright-orange scarf tied around his shiny black hair?

When the men came to stand face to face, the Gypsy's dark brows drew together in a suspicious scowl. "Are you a guest of Valentina's?" he asked.

He was tall and stood at Daniel's height.

"Aye, my sister and I arrived yesterday afternoon," Daniel replied.

"I saw your *grand* caravan when you passed the camp and went up the drive."

Did the Gypsy intend a slur when he'd emphasized the word *grand?* Daniel let the comment pass. With a close-lipped smile, he extended his hand. "I'm Daniel Hayward."

"Luca Boldor." The Gypsy accepted his hand and they shook, but then Luca quickly dropped his hand. He looked toward the sunrise, a pure, scattered light crossing the fields. "'Tis unusual for an Englishman to rise early, aye?"

"Oftentimes I awaken at daybreak," Daniel replied.

"What brings you here?"

With supreme effort, Daniel managed to keep the emotion out of his tone. "I'm looking for someone. Yesterday, I saw a woman picking blueberries."

"Is it against the law to pick blueberries?"

"I didn't say it was."

Luca's jaw hardened. "Before you intend to cause trouble for the Roma, Valentina gave her permission for us to enjoy the Colchester land as we see fit."

"'Tis not my intention to insult you. I came this morning to see if she was still here."

"Why?" Luca let his question hang in the ensuing silence. "All the Rom women are spoken for. I suggest you find an Englishwoman." With a curt nod, he gestured toward the stone mansion.

"The woman I seek is English. Her hair is the color of copper, and her name is Charity Weston. We were ... good friends when we were young." He swallowed an unexpected lump in his throat, a sadness that refused to let go.

A muscle jerked in Luca's neck. "Were you now? Good friends with a woman in what way?"

Daniel's conscience nagged. Shouldn't he tell Luca the truth—that the woman he searched for had died? Despite his wish that she still lived, he couldn't ignore the indisputable logic that she'd been gone too long.

Telling himself he had no choice, he admitted, "We were best of friends."

Luca scrutinized him, his face becoming an unreadable blank. "There is no woman here who goes by the name of Charity," he said flatly.

"Aye, she is dead," Daniel admitted. For some reason, his heartfelt response brought a derisive gleam to Luca's eyes.

"Mayhap she is a woman dead to the English."

Daniel pondered the man's reply. And his tone, which was a suspicious mixture of amusement and disdain.

"Although somehow," Daniel whispered, half to himself, "I hoped she might still be ..." He scrubbed a hand over his face. "Wishful thinking, I suppose." He turned on his heel. The pleasant vision of Charity was obviously not becoming a reality.

"Bid Valentina a good day when you see her," Luca called out as Daniel strode away.

"Aye," Daniel muttered without slowing his pace. He intended to walk back to the house and then continue on toward the sea. This had been a fool's errand, a small wish for a miracle. But only God created true miracles, his faith reminded.

He had not gone far when he heard a woman speak to Luca, asking when they would be leaving for the market.

Daniel stopped. He'd recognize her voice anywhere. He forgot everything else in the world as he pivoted.

Standing beside Luca was a beautiful woman with piercing blue eyes and hair the color of crimson. She turned from Luca to him, and for a moment the very air around them seemed to still. She sucked in a breath, then covered her mouth with her fingers. All color drained from her face.

"Charity." He reached out his arms. She was only footsteps away, and all he wanted was to embrace her, although the shock of seeing her again kept his legs paralyzed. "'Tis really you?"

"Aye." She extended her hands.

"Thank you, God," he whispered. For a moment, he closed his eyes. She was alive, and lovely, and God had brought them together in Wales.

Luca was watching them, frowning. Seeing Luca's frown, she dropped her hands and clasped them together. "What are you doing here?" she asked Daniel, shuffling backward.

"Go back to the camp." Luca's sharp command was unmistakable. "Tell the others we leave for the market as soon as I return." Quickly, he stepped between Daniel and Charity. He was obviously not caught in the same hold of paralyzing incredulity as Daniel.

"Get out of my way. I must speak with her." Daniel recovered from the surprise of seeing her and attempted to thrust Luca aside. He was met with a furious glare as the Gypsy stood firm. Slowly, Luca pushed up the sleeves of his muslin shirt.

A clash with Luca was the last thing he wanted, Daniel thought, as he frantically reviewed the alternatives.

"Shall we let the lady decide?" he asked. He peered past Luca and fixed his gaze on Charity. Appealing. Praying. Hoping.

"Daniel, please ..." Her eyes met his, and she lifted her hands palms up, a plea for understanding. "I can't."

"Don't you remember all the days we spent together?"

Did she know how long he'd grieved when she'd disappeared?

"I'm sorry." Her gaze softened, her expression yielding. And it was for him, he knew it was. Now if only Luca would permit them to speak alone.

Daniel studied the man, sizing him up, weighing the probable outcome of a skirmish. Perhaps it was the best way to settle this. Luca, meanwhile, was helping himself to a handful of blueberries, taking his time, keeping himself between Daniel and Charity. The disdainful look on his face banished the last of Daniel's patience.

Anger surged as he firmly shoved Luca aside and strode forward.

"Charity, you disappeared on me once, and 'twill

not happen again." He reached her and firmly put his hands on her shoulders. She squirmed, although she didn't move away. "All this time, your father said you were dead."

At the mention of her father, her blue eyes iced up, and her entire demeanor changed. Gone was the yielding smile, the warmth in her gaze.

"I am very much alive and will speak plainly." Her spine stiffened as she stood straight and faced him squarely. "Please don't come here again. I am dead to anyone from my past."

Then she twisted free and ran toward the Gypsy camp.

CHAPTER FOUR

*D*aniel Hayward. It couldn't be.

In the solitude of her tent, Charity sank onto the wooden bench. Her skin was still tingling, her hands shaking from their encounter. She cried off going to the marketplace, knowing Luca wasn't pleased with her decision. However, it couldn't be helped.

As if she had last seen him on the previous day, she mulled over the years she'd spent with him. Aye, she dreamed about him more often than she admitted.

And then he had appeared from her dreams to reality—his eyes the same entrancing silver-grey, his muscular frame filled out with the promise she'd seen in the young man. His deep voice when he'd called her name was achingly recognizable. Instinctively, she'd extended both hands to him before seeing Luca's furious expression.

Why would Daniel be in Wales, of all places? Mayhap he knew Mr. Colchester, because wealthy gentlemen were well-acquainted with each other in their exclusive London circles. She recalled Luca mentioning Mr. Colchester had investments in London, although he conducted most business from Wales.

Very likely that was the connection, she mused. Daniel had always been interested in finance and had excelled in math studies. Unlike herself. She held a smile. How often had he helped her when she couldn't make sense of the formal columns of numbers, despite her tutor?

Or, she reasoned, there was a chance it could all be a mere coincidence he was here.

Satisfied with her rationalization, she swung around and swung up the basket of blueberries she'd picked the day before, intending to cook them over the outdoor fire. If sugar was brought back from the market, she could add a glaze. 'Twas better, she reasoned, if she kept her mind and hands busy.

Before she reached the opening of her tent, she stopped in midstep. Her feverishly working brain had offered up another, more pressing reason why Daniel was in Wales. She set down the basket and caught her breath.

Assuming her father had been looking for her all

these years, could he have somehow made the connection between Mr. Colchester and the Gypsies? Could he have found out she'd joined a Gypsy tribe after she ran away? And then, because her father knew she trusted Daniel, could he have asked the boy who used to be her friend to come for her and bring her back to England?

Nay. She contemplated the logic with a sinking heart before dismissing it. Daniel would never betray her, because friends didn't betray each other, did they? And although she'd never spoken of her father's abuse aloud, surely Daniel had detected the pain in her voice, the anguish in her movements whenever it was time for her to leave his house and a servant escorted her home.

Despite her attempts to keep the remembrances at bay, her father's biting comments regarding her lack of musical skill, her unladylike antics as she climbed trees or used a slingshot, bubbled to the surface. She'd been a great disappointment to him.

And then she remembered the time she'd spent in Daniel and Penelope's home. Their parents were loving and kind toward each other, their interest in their children genuine and unmistakable. She had longed to live in Daniel's house, to spend her days in an atmosphere of harmony and tranquility, following God with a tenacious faith that had abandoned her long ago.

She sighed. She'd always regarded Daniel as her

blessing from God, her guardian angel who cheered her days despite her unbearable home life. And she had missed him, missed seeing him. Certainly, it wouldn't hurt to speak with him one last time. Indeed, there was no harm in conversing with an old friend.

Making up her mind, she glanced at herself in the small mirror beside her washbasin. She splashed cool water on her face, changed into a jaunty yellow gown and tucked her corkscrew curls into a makeshift bun tied with a yellow ribbon. With her chin lifted in resolve, she opened her tent, breathed in a lungful of fresh country air and stepped outside. The camp was quiet, as most of her tribesmen had accompanied Luca to the market in town. Some remained, giving her a brief nod before returning to their chores.

Kezia, stout and bent over with age, stood over a pot on the campfire stirring soup. The air around her was thick with the pungent scents of black pepper and garlic.

"You look exceptionally lovely, Charani." The dark lines in Kezia's face told the story of a harsh outdoor life.

"Thank you." Intending to keep her pace brisk, Charity continued walking.

"*Shuk tski khalpe la royasa,*" Kezia said. She placed the spoon beside the soup on a wooden bowl, then picked up her sewing, which was never far from her side. Today, she was mending holes in a pile of brightly colored blankets.

"Aye." *Beauty cannot be eaten with a spoon*, Charity silently translated, and nodded in response. But what exactly did that mean? Wasn't a woman allowed to fuss with her appearance once in a while? Or did it mean something else? She didn't dare ask, for Kezia was known to talk nonstop if the subject interested her.

"Where are you going?"

Charity had made it to the edge of the camp and turned back to Kezia. "I'm going for a walk."

The old woman retied the bright scarf around her snowy-white hair. "Which path are you taking? I prefer the path to the sea—except all that sand and some of the rocks are slippery. However, a hike up one of the many mountains in this country might be preferable, although then the rocks are the size of boulders and difficult to get around. I prefer—"

"Thank you, Kezia. I have a certain destination in mind, so I know which path to take. Mayhap we can chat later, by the campfire."

Determined to end the discussion, Charity turned and hastened her steps. Even as the camp grew farther away, she still heard Kezia's voice instructing her about path preferences.

A smile drifted across Charity's lips. Kezia was a good woman and beloved by the entire tribe. If she enjoyed chatting, then she'd certainly earned the right.

Tipping her head up, she shaded her eyes and peered at the sun. Years ago, she and Daniel had agreed they favored riding in the afternoon, when the weather was warm. So, she'd check the Colchesters' stables first.

Daniel, she thought, wiping her cold clammy hands along her gown. *I'm coming.*

～

The stables were surrounded by a white-painted fence. Beyond them, a path led to steep mountain ranges. Wales was a country of rare beauty, for another path led to the rough sea and a beach mostly made up of stones and rocks.

As she approached the stable, she appreciatively stroked the glossy neck of a chestnut horse standing at the fence. "You're magnificent, aren't you? I expect you're one of Valentina's favorites."

A groom came out from around the fence and introduced himself as Andrew. He was short and thin, his hair greying at the temples. "Are you Mr. Haywood's sister?" he asked.

Charity chuckled. "Nay, I'm—"

"Charity?" Daniel stepped from the stable, a riding crop tucked beneath his arm. "I heard your voice ... I thought I might be imagining ..." He looked around, his gaze narrowed. "Is your Gypsy guardian hiding behind a blueberry bush, impatient to pick a fight with me?"

"Luca?" She laughed and shook her head. "He's not my guardian. He's just a little overprotective of his women."

"A little?" Daniel flashed her a look and then frowned. His grip on the crop tightened. "Are you one of his women?"

She met his gaze, which had gone from warm to cold. "Of course not. Gypsies don't have harems or anything like that. They marry one person."

"So the man is married."

"Nay. He doesn't have time and he's more interested in keeping the tribe alive than any one woman."

"Aye, except he is a man and—" He seemed to want to say more, but paused and thought better of it. He handed Andrew his crop and Andrew stepped back into the stable. Coolness was still in his gaze when he turned back to her. "Then why are you here, Charity?"

"I remembered you used to go riding at this time of day ... I mean, we went riding ..."

"Congratulations for at least remembering something about us," he said impersonally.

She realized she was staring at him and, despite his coolness, felt herself melt a little. He was so handsome, even more handsome than she remembered. She passed an admiring glance over his flawless white shirt, open at the collar, and blue riding jacket. Black riding breeches and leather boots hugged his strong legs, and she couldn't help noting the tiny crinkles around his eyes.

Six years, Daniel, she reflected, and held in a breath. She'd carried off a cool outer bravery with the Gypsies, but had also bottled up excess emotion. Now, looking at him, she choked back tears for all the time they had lost because of her impulsiveness ... because of her desperation to get away from her father.

A breeze ruffled his deep-brown hair, the color of dark chocolate, and she imagined running her fingers through the thickness.

Nay, she told herself.

But another voice answered, *you know you want to.*

She averted her gaze, afraid he'd see the longing in her eyes.

"We think alike, we always did," he said. "When I came to the stables earlier today, I thought of you. Then when I saw how splendid the horses are, I knew you would love them as much as I did." She looked up as he walked toward her, interest replacing the earlier coolness in his expression. "Are you here because you want to go riding?"

"I hadn't intended to ride."

"And yet here you are at the stables." His eyes

sparkled with challenge. "You haven't forgotten how to ride and race, have you?"

She drew herself up straight. "I've ridden ever since I was a young girl. You know that."

"Well, you've obviously been around the Gypsies a long while. Mayhap you're out of practice." He gestured toward the stable, grinning. "You can choose a tame horse. Perhaps Old Biscuit. He's quiet and agreeable, and you'll enjoy a merry promenade whilst he sniffs the rosebushes every few feet. I promise I'll give you a head start."

"Your memory is apparently faulty." Her lips twitched with laughter. "I used to beat *you* when we raced."

"Did I declare a race? If so, I probably should share my secret with you." He shrugged, then looked away. "I meant to tell you a long time ago."

She plunked her hands on her hips. "And that secret is ...?"

"Oftentimes I let you win because 'twas the gentlemanly thing to do."

"You didn't let me win. I beat you!" She took a step forward, intending to pass him and walk into the stable to choose her horse. "If anything, you cheated."

"Me?" He beamed a charming smile, his white teeth gleaming. "A Christian man?"

"You always were impossible, and now you're using Christianity as an excuse." She attempted to render him a stern glare, although her shoulders spoiled her efforts by shaking with laughter.

"So 'tis agreed? We'll ride together, just as we used to."

Aye, just as they'd done years ago, although everything was different now.

He was quiet, apparently awaiting her reply. When she didn't speak, he said her name and touched her shoulder lightly. Her heart did an unexpected flip in her chest as uncertainty collided with want. Debating, she fixed her gaze on the row of boxwood hedges lining the edge of the fencing. Considering Daniel's teasing tone and the fact she hadn't had the opportunity to ride for pleasure in many years, she took the bait and agreed. Or mayhap 'twas because of the way her pulse raced whenever she looked at him.

Nay. Certainly not.

In any event, she quashed her feelings and justified that time spent with him was the surest way to discover if he was a spy sent by her father.

Daniel's steps were sure as he strode beside her into the coolness of the stables. He'd grown a couple of inches and now stood half a head taller than she, still lean and splendidly fit. As he showed her around, one part of her wanted to throw her arms around him and breathe in the warm masculine smells of worn leather and fresh air. The other part wanted to stand back and reproach him for suddenly appearing in Wales and setting her emotions in turmoil.

After admiring the horses, she chose a magnificent sturdy bay. The horse poked its nose through the stall and nuzzled her hand.

"Will he do?" Daniel asked. "His name is Chester."

She stroked the horse's black mane. "Aye, Chester is perfect."

The groom saddled the horse and led Chester outdoors to the mounting block, where Daniel assisted her onto the sidesaddle.

"Will you ride Old Biscuit?" she couldn't resist teasing. "Or maybe Twinkle Feet?"

He laughed out loud. "My horse's name is Bandit. He's the one I rode this morning and he will do nicely." He nodded to a black stallion being led out of the stable by Andrew. After swinging up onto the horse's back, he drew his horse abreast to hers and then took the lead. She guided her horse and followed Daniel to a quiet corner of the pasture.

She viewed the golden sun streaming through the leaves of the trees. "Now that you've brought me here, shall we wait until twilight to ride or is there something I'm missing?"

"I wanted a moment to be sure you were real— that this moment is real. I wanted to take the time to appreciate it."

She smiled at him, at his honesty. He always had the ability to speak his mind.

Once, when she asked how he always seemed so sure of himself, he told her it wasn't him. He relied on God's grace to keep him steady. More than anything, she was starting to believe that it was through God's goodness that they had been reunited.

He nodded, apparently thinking the same. He had also always had the ability to read her thoughts.

Vaguely, she took in the sights of a splendid summer afternoon. Squirrels skittered up and over tree branches, a group of plump pheasants wandered nearby. Unable to stifle her contented sigh, she savored the peace enveloping her heart. It had been a long time since she'd felt so serene.

"Dare I suppose your smile indicates a softening of your initial reaction toward me?" he asked. "In the blueberry patch, you didn't seem at all pleased."

"You're mistaken," she lied. "I've never had a reaction to you one way or the other."

She knew her cheeks had colored. Whenever she was around him, she struggled to hide her innermost feelings to no avail, thanks to her fair, telltale complexion.

He guided his horse nearer and ran his hand along hers. "On the contrary, I think you have a strong reaction to me, as I have to you." Very quickly, very lightly, he leaned over and pressed a kiss on her temple.

She fixed her gaze on the pheasants, not him. Reflexively, her fingers tightened around her reins.

"Charity. Look at me."

She took judicious note of the tenderness in his tone as she met his gaze. Slowly, he bent his head. She knew he was going to kiss her.

"Are you set then, Mr. Haywood, Miss ...?" Andrew shouted from the stable. She picked out his thin form as he gestured toward them.

"Her surname is Weston," Daniel called back, then returned his gaze to her. "I assume you're not married, Charity. Or is there a Gypsy man who's interested in you?"

"There is one. His name is Petshah, although he is old and cranky, and always looks tired because of his heavy eyelids. When we met, I couldn't tell if he was sleeping or awake."

His expression darkened. "Has he woken up enough to declare himself?"

She shook her head. "Not yet." And if Petshah ever did, she'd run as hard and as fast as she could to avoid him, despite Luca's apparent approval.

She hesitated before asking Daniel, "And you?"

"The right woman has eluded me."

Until now.

He hadn't said the words, yet she heard them in the silence just the same.

She tried to think of a quick rejoinder, but he'd already swiveled in the saddle. "Ready?"

"We're racing? Now?" She took a moment to digest this, to calm the steady pounding of her heart and then tighten the yellow ribbon around her hair. "How much of a warning will you give me?"

"None! I cheat, remember? First one to reach the stone wall wins." He pointed to a wall a good distance ahead of them. With a laugh, he broke into a showy trot, then full gallop.

He didn't give her a choice. Chester tossed his head, impatient to join the race.

She leaned forward. "C'mon, let's beat them!" With a joyous laugh, she galloped after Daniel.

CHAPTER FIVE

*W*hen Daniel glanced over his shoulder, apparently gauging his lead, she estimated he was five lengths ahead of her. Her horse's hooves thundered over the hard ground as Chester strove to close the distance. Quickly, she gained back the five lengths and assumed she'd reach the stone wall first. At the last second, Daniel's horse edged past hers and won by scarcely a hairsbreadth.

She laughed, exhilarated by the hard ride. Refreshing breezes cooled her cheeks and revived her spirits, and she felt more animated than she had felt in years.

"I've always loved to ride horses," she said as she slowed Chester. "The faster, the better."

"And I've always loved the privilege of watching

you ride at full speed, although my heart was often in my throat."

"Then and now?"

"Aye."

"Whatever for?"

"I was fearful you were sometimes too careless, despite the obstacles." He grinned when she frowned and held up a hand. "Sometimes. I said *sometimes* and please take it as a compliment. Even when you were twelve, you were an expert horse-woman." He swung down from his horse, assisted her dismount, then tied their horses' reins to a birch tree. On the far side of the stone wall, a meadow led to a burbling stream. Skylarks twittered from the trees.

"May I remind you I won our race today?" Daniel asked triumphantly, tickling her under the chin.

"May I remind *you* that you cheated? If I'd had a five-second lead like you had, I would've easily beat you."

"We'll have a rematch come the morrow. Your riding skill against mine."

Motivated by the challenging flicker in his eyes, she took up the gauntlet and agreed, soundly warning him not to cheat again. Only afterward did she realize he had successfully maneuvered her into seeing him again.

"If I am with you," he said, "than I'm the obvious winner, no matter how fast you ride."

She regarded his boyish grin. Despite his joking, she again heard the tenderness in his voice, saw it in his gaze.

"If we walk to the stream," he said, his tone casual, "we'll have a view of the entire estate."

He took her hand, and they strolled through a fragrant meadow blooming with wildflowers and tall grass, until they found the pathway to the stream. She blew back a wisp of hair that had fallen onto her face. As they climbed, she retied the yellow ribbon holding back her unruly ringlets.

When they reached the stream, he shrugged off his jacket and spread it on the bank. Standing beside him, she gazed at the splendid view of the Colchester grounds, unmatched by any she'd ever seen in England. In Wales, the landscape was forever wild and untamed.

Daniel pointed out a garden in the distance, explaining it was Valentina's herb garden. There, he explained, Valentina tended plants used for healing sicknesses—dandelion root and flaxseed and coriander. Because Kezia used many of these same plants, Charity was familiar with the herbs' benefits.

"Shall we rest here a while?" he asked.

She nodded. Having his strong hand clasped warmly around hers brought a gentle, jubilant harmony to her heart.

Whispers of their youth—chaperoned picnics by a lake as smooth as glass while they watched a group of swans gliding past, the sun warming their faces, the varying shades of wildflowers when he picked her bouquets. All these memories were so joyful.

Although, she reminded herself, she hadn't yet confronted him about her father. But then she shook her head. Not today. The afternoon was too perfect for such unpleasantness. Besides, it wasn't in her nature to be churlish and blame Daniel for a suspicion that might not be true.

He was watching her, and she wondered whether she should stand or sit. She opted for letting go of his hand and sitting on his jacket.

To break the silence, she remarked on the stretch of good weather as she settled her gown around her. She went on, explaining how she planned to boil the blueberries she'd picked with a sugar glaze when she returned to camp.

He listened without interrupting. When she finished, she glanced up at him. Her subject matter had seemed to amuse him for he was grinning.

"So you believe you'll beat me come the morrow, aye?" he teased, gazing upward. Wispy clouds floated across a gloriously blue sky. "Even if it rains?"

She grinned. "I can beat you in a downpour if I rode a chicken."

He chuckled and sat beside her. "In all the years I've known you, I've always found our conversations so ..." He paused, seeming to grasp for the words. "So joyful."

She grinned at his choice of the word *joyful,* the same word she'd thought a few moments earlier.

"How long have we known each other?" she asked. "It seems like we've been best friends my entire life."

"I remember the first time I saw you. Our families had known each other for a while, and we were sharing a mutual tutor. When you left the tutor's house, you put on an absurd hat that seemed to have foxgloves growing out of it." He sat back and propped his shoulders against a thick tree trunk. "I recall you and your father arguing about that hat because he insisted you wear it."

"That sounds like our relationship."

She reflected on the day when she first realized Daniel was her champion. It had started that day. He'd paused to speak with her father, discussing finance with the knowledge of a forty-year-old seasoned investor. She'd yanked off the hat and hid it behind the tutor's boxwood hedges. After her father had finished his discussion with Daniel, they'd left the tutor's house and departed for home. And her father had forgotten all about the hat.

His gaze shifted from her face to her hair. "I still remember that hat. You looked lovely."

"I looked anything but lovely." She waved her hands dismissively. "However, you saved me from wearing a silly purple confection and I was eternally grateful. Did you know foxgloves can grow to over six feet tall?"

"Aye, and I feared they were actually starting to sprout, so I had no choice but to come to your rescue." His gaze slid meaningfully to her lips, and the obvious interest in his grey eyes was clear. "I don't believe you ever thanked me for saving you from that hat."

Instinctively, she scooted back. "Of course I did." Under different circumstances, she might have laughed. However, sitting so close to him, feeling the warmth of his breath brushing against her cheeks, tender memories made her want him as strongly as he obviously wanted her.

Nay, she told herself. *You're no longer an adolescent girl with a crush on a handsome man.* She was now a grown woman who'd lived among the Gypsies for six years. However, that didn't mean she was experienced around men. Although Luca was her friend, most of the men in her tribe were elderly. And Petshah, the man Luca had suggested for her, was a giant of a man, balding, with a mouthful of teeth resembling a picket fence.

She situated her gown primly around her legs and sat up straighter.

If she thought that would deter Daniel, she was mistaken. He whispered her name, a smile lurking in his voice, and then, without warning, his lips gently descended on hers. She kissed him back, yielding to her desire to be closer to him. When he lifted his mouth, she was trembling.

He drew her closer. His lips brushed against her temple while his gaze canvassed the landscape. "'Twill be time for dinner soon," he said. "'Tis time we leave."

For some reason, she wanted to finish their conversation, to start taking down the barrier she'd erected between them.

"When you saw my father and me at the tutor's house," she said softly, "he was merely doing what he always did—attempting to browbeat me into becoming a proper English lady."

Daniel's gaze narrowed. He drew back his head and studied her face. "You mean he used force?"

"Aye." She winced, remembering. "And I resisted."

"Charity." Caringly, he cupped her face in his hands. "*Force* and *resisted* are two words that alarm me, especially when they concern you. Tell me what happened."

He deserved an explanation, although she was ashamed of the way her father had treated her. And then she had done a very un-Christian-like thing and run away from home.

He tipped up her chin. "Why did you leave? Your father said you were dead."

A flush crept up her cheeks. "You could never

understand. Your life at home was so different from mine."

"Try me anyway."

For an interminable moment, she hesitated, then met his sympathetic gaze straight on.

"My father was cruel. I don't know why. Mayhap he didn't love me." She caught the sob before it welled in her throat. "Mayhap he was resentful."

"Why? You were his only child—his only family."

"And I was a girl, not an heir. To add to the wound, my mother died birthing me."

"Surely you don't blame yourself for her death."

She gazed up at him, amazed again that he was sitting beside her, so handsome and so caring. "I don't know what I believe and don't believe. My faith in God is no longer strong, either."

"God is just and always with us."

"Mayhap with your family. He certainly wasn't anywhere near mine." She stretched out her legs.

Although still watching her intently, he dropped his hand.

"Your family prayed often, displaying their faith publicly," she said. "When I dined at your house, I remember bowing my head and I even remember the blessing." She took a deep breath. "'Lord,'" she began, "'thank you for the food set in front of us, the loved ones sitting beside us, and the love we have for each other. Amen.'" As she recited the simple verse, Daniel joined in with her.

She sighed. "'Twas wonderful, the feeling of be-longing in a loving household."

"Faith is meant to be more than a supper bless-ing, more than a feeling."

"What is faith, then?" She tilted her head back to regard him. "I don't understand."

"Faith is difficult, yet easy to explain." He leaned back on his forearms. "You can examine faith for-ever and have endless discussions about it, but you don't have to be exultant or even appreciative to have faith. Faith simply means that whatever the storm, you're going to get through it."

His words hung significantly in the stillness.

She studied him. He had turned his head to gaze at a red deer in the woodlands. The deer stood ma-jestic and at frozen attention, staring back at them.

"Do you remember any Bible passages?" Daniel asked.

"I recited multitudes of Bible passages as I knelt on a cold stone floor when I was being punished for acting unladylike, or whatever the transgression my father chose to accuse me of that day." She shivered, recalling the heavy closet door falling shut behind her, latching into place as her father locked her into the dark linen closet for hours.

Sadness and regret shadowed Daniel's eyes. "Charity, I didn't know. Why didn't you tell me?" He shook his head. "I should've known," he whispered.

"How? I certainly never told you." She drew in a

shaking breath. "Whenever you asked if anything was the matter, I'd accord you a brief dismissal. You weren't a seer."

"But I knew you. And, deep in my gut, I knew something was wrong." He pulled her to his chest and gathered her close. "I'm sorry. I'm so, so sorry. I should have protected you. I always vowed to myself that I would keep you safe."

She placed her hand on his chest. His heart beat warm and strong and alive.

"None of this was your fault," she said. "Truly, you were the anchor safeguarding my days and your kindness empowered me to get through my sorrowful nights. I wish I had my faith to lean on, as you have yours. But 'tis too late. I have too many doubts now."

"'Tis where you are misguided." He took her hands in his and gently squeezed. "Having doubts doesn't mean you don't have faith. Faith is the conviction that God is real. You remember Hebrews 11:1?"

"Aye. 'Now faith is the substance of things hoped for, the evidence of things not seen.'"

"And you, my beautiful Charity, are most assuredly a woman of God."

His words were directed straight to her heart.

"Sometimes I long to return to church," she said. "I hear church bells ring out from whatever towns we're camped near on Sunday mornings. Not long ago, I sat outside one of the churches to listen to the service."

"Would you come with me to church on Sunday?"

She took a deep breath, watching the shy hares hopping through the grass, this way and that, as if they weren't sure where they were going.

"I would like to attend with you," she finally said.

"Good."

She gave him her full attention. "Luca might not approve ... Although I think you'll like him once you get to know him. And the tribe ... Everyone is so fun-loving, good-hearted and—"

"I can hardly wait to meet them and pray they're more hospitable than Luca." Daniel's long fingers moved up her arm in a delightful caress. "Although if someone told me I'd be visiting a Gypsy camp after I arrived in Wales, I would've assured them they were mad."

She grinned. "And now?"

He bent his head, and a flurry of nervousness rose from her belly.

"Daniel, I—"

He pressed his forefinger to her lips, halting her words. "And now I believe 'tis high time you thank me for saving you from wearing an outrageous hat. So, I'll accept your gratitude now." With that, he took his time and tenderly kissed her.

When he released her, she snuggled her head

against his shoulder. "When I came to see you, this was not how I envisioned our encounter was supposed to go today."

"'Tis exactly the way it should've gone. 'Tis perfect." He kissed her again, his mouth firm and sweet. "Charity, I've missed you so much."

After the kiss ended, he assisted her to her feet, brushed the leaves off his jacket, and wrapped it around her. Taking her hand, he led her back through the meadow where the horses waited. Sunlight bathed the fields, lighting everything in its path. For a moment, it seemed that heaven and earth touched.

Her eyes brimmed with tears, although these were grateful tears. The day had dawned, the afternoon complete as they rode back to the stables.

And Daniel Hayward was at her side.

Just as he'd always been.

As if she had never left.

CHAPTER SIX

In her tent, Charity sat on the wooden stool by her washbasin and critically appraised herself in her hand mirror. She combed her burnished-copper locks into a low bun and tied a lavender-colored velvet ribbon around them. Her dark-purple gown with flowing bell sleeves fit her to perfection. Encouraged by Kezia, she had purchased the fabric at the village market. Kezia had sketched the garment, then her nimble fingers had gone to work as she sewed the gown to Charity's measurements.

It had hung in Charity's tent for several days, sending a trill of excitement through her pulse every time she beheld it. For 'twas the gown she planned to wear to a formal dinner at Valentina and James Colchester's house.

Standing up, she turned and Kezia fastened the back buttons of the gown. Then she twirled. The gown, tight-fitting at the waist and widening at the hem, cast gay whirling shadows across the canvas tent. She fingered the diamond necklace at her throat, a gift sent earlier in the day from Valentina and delivered by a footman, and watched it shimmer in the candlelight. Tiny matching earrings completed the effect. Once again, she was a regal English lady.

Kezia clasped her hands together and took a step back to survey Charity's appearance. "You are the most dazzling princess I've ever seen, Charity," she declared.

Of late, Charity had overheard the Gypsy men murmuring that she was comely, despite her fair skin and red hair, and she smiled. Finally, she'd been accepted, at least somewhere.

"Thank you." She acknowledged Kezia's compliment with a smile. "Although I'm far from a princess ..." Pausing, she grasped Kezia's shoulders. "Wait a minute. You haven't called me by my English name since I arrived. Why now?"

"Because the tribe is traveling south and I won't see you anymore." Kezia patted Charity's back with her small hand. "And because you're taking a new step—away from the Rom—and toward the future where you truly belong."

Charity leaned back to regard the elderly

woman. Kezia stared back, her dark gaze dancing beneath thinly arched eyebrows. As much as her mind denied Kezia's words, her heart said otherwise.

"I'm both excited and nervous about tonight," she admitted. "Does that make sense?"

"Perfect sense." Kezia stood on her toes and pressed her rough cheek against Charity's smooth one. Her wise voice whispered Romany words Charity didn't understand, but she knew they were meant to encourage and embolden her.

A fortnight had passed so quickly, Charity reflected, and come the morrow Daniel and Penelope were leaving the Colchester estate to return to Penelope's summer house that she'd rented in Wales.

Since the first day she'd chanced upon Daniel at the blueberry bushes, they'd ridden their horses at breakneck speed, watched incredible sunny days pass, and, most important, shared memories. They stole away every hour they could, kissing by a secluded pond, lingering over lavish picnic spreads the Colchester servants served—cold chicken and sliced ham and buttered biscuits one day, bread pudding and pigeon pie the next.

Despite her frequent inward rebuttals, she knew she was falling in love with him, just as she had when she was a girl. It was against her better sense, of course, for a wealthy man's future didn't lie with a woman who'd become a Gypsy and therefore had nothing to offer—no dowry, no fancy

London lifestyle, and a decided lack of ladylike mannerisms. Yet when they spoke gaily of shared reminiscences, or had spirited discussions about God, her heart refused to listen to her logical mind.

She soon learned that Daniel's mathematical intellect was as brilliant as ever, and his wise London investments frequently paid off handsomely. He was remarkably perceptive, balancing his knowledge with sensible ventures, and he had accumulated wealthy reserves in just a few years. One day he casually mentioned he didn't need to work in London anymore, and had considered purchasing property in Wales.

It was the first time he'd brought up the subject of a future, and she carefully sidestepped the discussion. Besides, she hadn't confronted him about possibly working with her father to bring her home, and she'd vowed never to return to the life she once led.

Two nights before Daniel was slated to leave, Luca greeted the news that she was dining at the Colchester home with as much enthusiasm as if he'd been told she planned to dine with highwaymen.

"I thought you wanted me to dine and converse with the English," she countered. "Daniel's sister Penelope is staying with the Colchester's, and I distinctly recall you telling me that English company would be good for me. Something about bringing back the pink color in my cheeks."

"Did I, indeed?" He quirked a dark eyebrow. "I don't remember."

She burst out laughing. Typical male, remembering only what was convenient.

"And since when do you listen to anything I say, anyway?" he continued.

"I'm here, aren't I?" She plunked her hands on her hips. "I traveled with your tribe all the way from England, and that trip took months because of all the rain and mud."

"A minor detail." He shrugged, and she couldn't tell if he was joking or serious.

Kezia, however, made no secret about wanting to meet Daniel.

"He's Charity's young man," she boasted to the tribesmen one evening as they shared a meal around the campfire. Pivoting to Charity, she predicted, "I guarantee you'll wed him by summer's end. We will be gone by then, so be sure to tell him he must jump over a broom with you. 'Tis a Romany wedding tradition and good luck."

Charity had refuted Kezia's prediction, though she smiled at the broom reference. Because Romany weddings were not recognized by the church, they were forced to marry through nonchurch rituals. A broomstick ceremony involved the couple jumping over a broom placed in the doorway to a home, signifying sweeping away the old life and jumping into the new.

Now, seeing Kezia's bright smile, Charity knew this past fortnight, lighthearted and joyous, was the beginning of something that was hard to put into words. Or mayhap she didn't want to put it into words, for fear her happiness would disappear.

During the hours she and Daniel spent apart, she missed him, then felt foolish for missing him. She'd been without him for many years. Why would their reunion make her want to see him more, not less?

Kezia poked her head outside the tent. "He should be arriving soon, aye?" she said gaily, another prediction.

Charity sent her a reassuring smile. "Aye."

Moments later, both women turned at the clip-clop of horses' hooves.

"He's early." With a smug smile, Kezia held out her hand. "He obviously can't wait to see you and a lady never keeps a gentleman waiting. Come."

Although the Gypsy camp was less than a mile from the main house, Daniel had insisted on borrowing a carriage from the Colchesters so Charity wouldn't have to walk.

She snatched a paisley shawl to wrap around her shoulders. Hand in hand, she and Kezia stepped from her tent and walked toward the carriage, elegant and lacquered a gleaming moss-green. The hood of the carriage was raised, and two midnight-black horses tossed their heads and whinnied.

Daniel stepped down from the carriage. Carrying

a bouquet of wildflowers, he hastened to meet her halfway. When they stopped, face-to-face and a foot apart, he cast a puzzled glance at the tribesmen surrounding them.

Charity sent him a reassuring smile. "This is my dear friend Kezia," she said.

"I've heard a lot about you." Daniel turned a genuine smile to the woman.

"And I about you, young man." Her thick lips wreathed in a smile, Kezia dropped Charity's hand and stepped to the side.

"You look beautiful tonight, Charity." He came nearer, and his gaze smoldered as he regarded her. "And you've achieved something quite remarkable."

"Something remarkable?" she repeated.

"Aye, my love." He closed the distance between them. "You're even more gorgeous than when you were fourteen."

She felt the warm flare of color in her cheeks. He'd never called her *my love* before.

He handed the fragrant flowers to her. "These are for you."

"Thank you." She smiled and sniffed them—the scent of greenery and sweetness, reminding her of days spent with him that she had cherished in her heart.

"Just like old times, aye? Oftentimes in the past, I traipsed through many a meadow to pick you a bouquet after you told me you loved wildflowers."

She said nothing, for what could she say? She was caught in the enchantment of his captivating eyes, the wonderful memories his tender voice evoked.

He shifted closer, bending his head.

Just behind her, Luca cleared his throat. Kezia, speaking in a voice loud enough for everyone to hear, declared, "*Kon del tut o nai shai dela tut wi o vast.*"

Charity stifled a laugh.

At Daniel's look of perplexity, she translated, "It means, 'He who willingly gives you one finger will also give the whole hand.'" She added, whispering in his ear, "Although I may not be exactly correct. When it comes to Romany sayings, I'm never sure."

"I understand the significance of the words." He pulled her to him and she squirmed, knowing they were in full view of her tribesmen. "It means, I will give you anything in my possession, whether big or small. And I willingly give you my heart." He spoke quietly, with deep emotion. He was a man who wasn't ashamed to show his feelings. He was a man who would always protect her.

Although Luca and Daniel had previously met, their greetings were stilted. Luca deliberately used Charity's Gypsy name, Charani, rather than her English name.

Other tribesmen followed suit with overformal introductions, keeping a respectable distance and eyeing Daniel, whom they considered a *gadje*, with suspicious interest.

For the first time, she noticed that several of the wagons had been packed and numerous tents were down.

At her quizzical glance, Luca shrugged and replied, "We'll be traveling again soon."

She realized Kezia had said the same thing in her tent, as she helped Charity dress. She hadn't put much weight on her words. "I thought you liked it here," she said to Luca.

"We are a wanderlust people, Charani. You know that."

Daniel interrupted, saying that they needed to go. She handed the flowers to Kezia for safekeeping, and then Daniel assisted her into the carriage. She felt the solidness of him as he settled on the seat beside her. Her gaze wandered sidewise, appreciating his good looks—strong legs clad in shiny leather boots and sandy brown breeches, a buttoned white muslin shirt, and brick-colored waistcoat.

With a contented sigh, she leaned back against the velvet seat. In the deepening dusk of a glorious August evening, she gazed at the tranquil night sky.

"What's a *gadje*?" Daniel asked, as he gave the lively horses the prompt to start.

Her gaze shot toward him. "Why do you ask?"

"Because I overheard Luca and the other men talking and assumed they were referring to me."

"'Tis a Romany word. It means you aren't one of

them. In your case, 'tis because you're English. As am I."

"So, you're a gadje, also."

"Aye, although when I mentioned this fact to Luca, he stated most emphatically that because I've lived in the tribe so long and adopted to the Gypsy ways, I'm not considered a gadje anymore."

"So, a gadje is an insult?"

"Aye, most assuredly. And when I reminded him I didn't believe in spirits, Luca stated that being a gadje was about more than religion. 'Twas a mindset and way of life. I didn't agree with his observation but thought it best not to tell him."

"And your Gypsy name ... is Charani? That explains why Luca feigned ignorance when I asked him about a woman named Charity." He shook his head. "Convenient."

"He was only trying to protect me." At Daniel's frosty glare, she groped for a safer subject. She wished Luca hadn't used her Gypsy name so noticeably.

"Charani is a Gypsy name and it means bird," she added.

"Really? Then you are a bird? A bird who prefers to fly away?"

She hesitated. She didn't want their last evening together to be spoiled by something as unimportant as a name. Desperately seeking their earlier pleasantries, she remarked, "Thank you for taking me to church services on Sunday."

"My pleasure." His glance met hers, along with a grin that all was forgiven. "The vicar's sermon was one of encouragement and faith."

"And wisdom. I appreciated when he said everything that happens in our lives—all the bad, all the pain—enables us to fully appreciate the good."

"Aye." He urged the horses into a trot. "Although we can't see around a corner, God can, and we should embrace his knowledge with grateful hearts."

She turned to him, studying the sharp features of his chiseled profile. "Thank you for helping me find my faith again. I'm learning our God isn't a small God. 'For my thoughts are not your thoughts, neither are your ways my ways, saith the Lord,'" she quoted.

Daniel accorded her a nod of approval as he guided the magnificent horses farther away from camp. They clattered across a wooden bridge, then turned on a forked road leading to the Colchester estate. "Isaiah 55:8. I've always loved that passage."

"Me too," she agreed with a smile.

She caught his look of pleasure, and held onto her smile.

He released the reins with one hand to briefly squeeze hers. "I am so pleased you agreed to meet Valentina and James. And all it took was a fortnight of refusals before you finally accepted a dinner invitation."

"One of the reasons I accepted this particular invitation was because I knew my time was running out."

"For what? To come up with more excuses?" he asked. "Why wouldn't you want to meet the Colchesters?"

"I'm ... I'm not a proper lady anymore." She glanced at him. "I'll forget how to act, what to say—"

"Be yourself. You're everything a lady should be —considerate and kind, and a woman with a sincere heart." He held up a hand when she shook her head. "And you're modest. But what I most love about you is that you're an original."

She shook her head. "I'm not worldly or sophisticated."

"A coquette feigning a blush never interested me."

Her heart hammered. So, he had now declared his interest in her, although of course she'd already assumed he was interested because of all the hours they spent together. She just hadn't known how much.

But he hadn't said he was in love with her ... or had he?

She lowered her lashes, but not before she caught the gleam in his eyes as his gaze roved over her. He was bent on using charismatic ways to enrapture her, and 'twas working. Her cheeks were turning pink, and she didn't know where to look. She decided to inspect the toes of her boots.

'Twas easier to deal with him when they bantered, she decided, than when his expression heated with affection.

"What is your other reason?" he prompted.

"Other reason for what?"

"Refusing to meet the Colchesters despite my encouragement."

Her head jerked up. Her first impulse was to joke about his excellent memory in continuing their earlier conversation. In its place, she astonished herself by blurting out the truth. "You are leaving come the morrow, giving me no other choice."

"Your last chance to reenter English society?"

My last chance to be with you, she thought, although she merely nodded.

He guided the horses around the last bend, granting them a splendid view of remote hills and abundant, uncultivated moorlands. The carriage rocked comfortably beneath an arch of gnarled tree branches on the long driveway leading to the mansion.

As he pulled the horses to a smart stop at the entrance, he turned to her and beamed. "We're here."

Charity blinked rapidly. The grand house blazed with hundreds of flickering candles, and smoke billowed from the chimneys of numerous fireplaces. Pockmarks in the exterior stone walls boasted the resilience of enduring a harsh climate. In the distance, she heard the sound of waves hurtling against the rocky shoreline.

"Well, I'm hoping my news is good," Daniel was saying.

He was grinning, and she wondered what she'd missed as she'd gaped at the house. Her gaze narrowed with suspicion. "What news?"

"Penelope is leaving come the morrow. However, I decided to stay a while longer. Perhaps indefinitely."

"Why?"

"Why do you think, Charity?"

She contemplated him. His former amusement had been replaced with a look of such profound affection, it took her breath away.

Silence reigned for a beat as her brain processed the information.

He was staying because of her.

Feeling faint with happiness, she tipped her head back and drew in a deep breath.

He reached out to tip up her chin, and his gaze locked with hers. "I lost you once and I can't lose you again." Slowly, he bent his head, and his lips parted hers for a long kiss. Without thinking, merely reacting, she twined her hands around his nape and welcomed his lips.

He responded to her yielding, kissing and cuddling her. When his lips finally left hers and their breathing slowed, he rested his forehead against hers. The heat of his body melted against her, and she felt love lighting the recesses of her heavy heart.

She touched her fingers to his beloved face and smiled into his eyes.

He smiled back. "Ready to reenter English society?"

Her stomach gave a funny little lurch. There was no mistaking the tenderness in his voice. And she'd repay him for his kindnesses by showing him she was truly the lady he believed her to be.

That is, if she could step out of the carriage without her legs collapsing beneath her, she thought, thinking about the formal evening ahead of her.

She again inhaled deeply, staring toward the house. "What if—"

"What if you dazzle them? Most assuredly, you will." He went around the carriage, caught her by the waist and helped her down. A fine penetrating mist prompted her to wrap her shawl closer around her shoulders, a reminder that summer waned and fall quickly approached.

A footman bearing a torch emerged from the house, followed by a young servant, who bobbed a curtsy and introduced herself as Clare. A lisp slowed Clare's speech as she welcomed them.

Daniel inclined his head to thank Clare, then put

his arm around Charity to give an encouraging squeeze. "My sister is anxious to see you, and James and Valentina are eager to meet you. I've spoken of you often."

So she'd been a subject of conversation. Could she live up to their expectations?

She turned a desperate look on him before she forced herself to think sensibly. Penelope was Daniel's sister. James Colchester was a London acquaintance. She could do this.

Nonetheless, would Valentina accept her as a Gypsy or Englishwoman? And what about James?

And Penelope? Charity had always felt Penelope disliked her. And from what she recollected, Penelope harbored a disdain for Gypsies, avoiding them by purposefully crossing the road if she spotted any. Perhaps she had changed. She had managed to stay at the Colchester home with Valentina for a fortnight.

Resolutely, Charity dismissed any negative thoughts while Daniel tucked her hand in the crook of his arm. Together, they walked up the mansion's stone steps, and their boots echoed on the slate floored hallway. She paused to admire the stucco entryway, the thick poplar beams, the portraits of Colchester ancestors hung on the walls. Truly, the home was one-of-a-kind.

She fought to keep her nerves under control, reminding herself that Valentina and James were

Christians. If she faltered in conversation, surely she could talk about the Christian faith.

And Daniel had mentioned that James's son Jeremy was deaf. She was eager to meet and communicate with the little boy, although she assumed his nurse had probably already put him to bed.

Some other time, she hoped.

"Ready?" Daniel asked again.

"Aye." She squared her shoulders, hoping the cluster of nerves in her stomach would dissolve before she reached the parlor.

CHAPTER SEVEN

*I*n the hour before dinner, Daniel sensed Charity's tenseness begin to ease as soon as she and Valentina exchanged appropriate greetings. With a wide smile, Valentina led her into the parlor, where she introduced Charity to her husband, James, and then settled into a linenfold chair beside her.

Penelope, already seated, offered only a faint inclination of her perfectly coiffed head. "So, the woman who caused her father so much grief has reappeared," she said. "Hello, Charity."

Visibly, Charity stiffened at Penelope's malicious remark, and turned to Daniel, her face pale, her expression strained.

"Don't be ridiculous," he snapped at Penelope, who met his cold stare with sham puzzlement.

"In my home," Valentina said, "judgements against others are not allowed." She threw a look of unwavering dislike toward Penelope. "We are all Christians and surely you know this Scripture from Matthew: 'Judge not, that ye be not judged.'"

To Daniel's disgust, his sister didn't apologize, nor even bother to agree with Valentina. Instead, she merely glanced at a servant waiting in the doorway and indicated she wanted more sherry.

For Charity's sake, Daniel broke the uncomfortable silence by announcing that one of the dishes being served for dinner was cawl, a typical Welsh stew and ideal for a late-summer evening.

"And 'tis one of my husband's favorite dishes," Valentina said. "'Tis a stew made from meat and carrots and leeks. I've grown fond of it, just as James has grown fond of Romany roasted hedgehog." She glanced at her husband. "Aye?"

James chuckled imperturbably. His grey-eyed gaze lit with warmth as he looked at his wife. "Aye."

Spurred by Charity's agreement about the deliciousness of roasted hedgehog dredged in black pepper, Valentina bubbled on, recounting her childhood living in a Gypsy tribe with her sister, Yolanda, then her years as a drabardi, a fortune-teller, and how she became a Christian.

"Sometimes I believe God sent an angel to bless me. I thought I was powerless, but 'twas just the opposite. He gave me so much grace I became

stronger, not weaker." Valentina cast another affectionate smile toward her husband, who stood with
one shoulder propped against the fireplace. He
raised his goblet to her, affectionately smiling at his
radiant, ebony-haired wife.

Appearing a little bemused, Charity replied, "An
angel is a wonderful idea, Valentina."

"We all have one, and your angel happens to be
standing a foot away from you."

Valentina peeked sidewise at Daniel. "In fact,
I've noticed that your angel never takes his eyes off
you." She leaned over to whisper in Charity's ear.
"And he never stops talking about you, either."

Daniel grinned, overhearing Valentina's words.

His sister didn't appear nearly as enraptured by
the women's conversation. Instead, she leaned back
in her chair and took swallow after swallow of the
excellent sherry.

When dinner was announced, Daniel guided
Charity into the dining room. The room was suf-
fused with the delicious aroma of cawl stew.

Their host, James, sat at the head of the dining
room table, with Valentina on his right and Penelope
on his left. Charity sat next to Penelope, and Daniel
took a seat across from Charity.

After they bowed their heads and said grace, the
servant set bowls of the stew in front of everyone.
As they began eating, Daniel gazed around the long
dining room table, formally set with white damask

linens, and then focused on the breathtakingly beautiful woman seated across from him. Glowing beeswax candles created a golden ambiance in the room, and Charity had never looked lovelier. Tonight, she was draped in a soft, deep-purple gown. Her burnished ringlets were pulled back and framed her exquisite heart-shaped face.

As servants refilled wineglasses, and silver clinked against soup bowls, all five people seated at the table focused on the stew, except for him, because his gaze kept seeking Charity.

After six years, he thought, she was still slender, although her figure had blossomed. Her movements, always graceful, had become even more so, and her curves were enticing. Nature and the years had worked closely to produce a woman of extraordinary beauty. Thick black lashes edged her extraordinary eyes, reflecting crystal-blue when she was angry or indigo when she was sad.

Yet there was an elusive quality about her, as if she were a bird ready to take flight.

Charani, the Gypsy name that meant *bird,* was most appropriate. But even when she was younger, seemingly delighted with nature and everything life had to offer, she would land only long enough for a lively discussion with him. At the slightest risk of being captured, she'd become distant, her responses evasive. *And she'd fly away*.

All because of her father. Just thinking about the

abuse she'd suffered at his hands made Daniel's fingers tighten around his wineglass. If only he'd known so he could have done something about it.

Nay, he silently chastised himself. He *should* have known something was wrong. He and Charity had been best friends. He had loved her then, a Christian-like love as well as the love of a friend, and he now felt incomparable sadness at the abuse she'd suffered.

He tried to concentrate on his meal, but again his gaze was drawn to her. Everything about her flowed like an unforgettable melody humming through his veins.

Because he loved her. They were soulmates. They were meant for each other.

His spoon stopped halfway to his mouth, as surprise and acknowledgement forced him to pause. This was more than a love for a friend. This was real.

James's voice caught his attention as he offered up a toast to Charity. Daniel raised his goblet, warmth radiating through his chest. Aye, he was totally and unequivocally in love with her.

She caught his gaze and smiled. He nodded reassurance and added a grin and a wink. They had been meant to meet again, here in Wales. God had brought them back together.

When the main course was cleared and the tablecloth taken away, sweetmeats, fresh fruit and ice cream were served.

Daniel leaned back in his chair and refused the sweetmeats. "No baked apples on the menu this evening?" he teased Valentina.

"Not tonight. You have told me often enough that baked apples are your favorite dessert. Shall we plan on dining together tomorrow evening and I'll add them?" She gestured to Charity. "Will you join us? If you can come earlier in the day, you can meet Jeremy."

Charity vacillated, and Daniel was surprised. He assumed she would readily agree. Then again, his sister's icy silences, broken only by thinly-veiled insults at Charity, had cut through the meal's conversation. He assumed Charity had shrugged off the remarks, for she offered no rebuttals. From years past, she would have known Penelope's manner was difficult.

When dessert was finished, they rose and all complimented Valentina on an excellent meal. The men prepared to enjoy their glasses of port wine in the dining room, and the women to chat in the parlor. Afterwards, they'd come together again for tea and more conversation.

A perfect evening, Daniel mused. He'd be able to spend more time with Charity.

Penelope strolled to the dining room window, pushed back the heavy draperies and gazed at the nighttime sky. "Theodore will not be joining us after all," she informed the group. "He sent word he's no longer interested in the Welsh property, and we're returning to England immediately. If you'll excuse me, I'll take a walk by the garden and then retire. 'Twill be an early morning and I need a restful sleep." With that, she bid them a stiff good night.

Valentina, always the gracious hostess, met Penelope's moody stare with a smile. "I hope you enjoyed your stay here in Wales."

Silence reigned so thick that all movement in the room was momentarily suspended.

"Of course," Penelope finally replied.

"I'll walk in the gardens with you," Daniel said to his sister, as Valentina took Charity's hand and led her toward the parlor. "We won't be seeing each other for a while, as I'm intending to stay in Wales."

"You are welcome to stay here as long as you like," James said, and Valentina concurred.

Penelope didn't answer.

Daniel took her elbow in a firm grasp and steered her outdoors. He intended to upbraid her for the rude and unkind remarks she'd hurled at Charity. They were uncharitable and most uncalled for.

"Nay, Daniel." Penelope frowned at his hand on her elbow and drew back in the entryway. "I've changed my mind and have decided to head straight to bed."

"Nonsense. A stroll in the night air is ideal for a good night's rest." Tightening his hold, he pushed open the front door with his other hand, propelled her toward the garden, then abruptly dropped her arm.

"What was all that about in there with the Colchesters and Charity?" Fortified by his wrath, he raised his voice. "You were extraordinarily rude."

Outrage flew across Penelope's face. "You've become blind to reason, rhapsodizing about Wales ever since we arrived. And I blame that ...that heathen woman. She's turned your feelings inside out and you're acting like a besotted fool."

"I already told you what Charity told me—she was forced to run away because of her father's cruelty."

"Mayhap." Penelope's fists clenched and then unclenched. "But by doing so, she caused him great harm. So much so that he lied about her whereabouts and said she was dead. What kind of Christian woman would do that, and then live like a vagrant all these years?"

CHAPTER EIGHT

*P*enelope was wrong, of course.

Blind with anger, Daniel shouted that her tongue was venomous and he almost expected snakes to slither beneath them while she spoke. Then he stormed away, leaving her standing in the garden in speechless silence.

The hush of an ageless tomb settled on the carriage when he brought Charity back to the Gypsy camp later that evening. Throughout the ride, he tried to convince her to go back to England with him and resume her previous life there. She stated, clearly and without reservation, that she'd never return.

"I'll see you come the morrow then," he said when he walked her to her tent. "We'll go riding."

Activity around the campfire was absent as he returned to the carriage and departed. In his frustration at his sister, at himself, and at Charity for not listening to reason, he failed to notice that the camp was almost empty and something was amiss.

At least, that was what he told himself when he returned late the following morning, filled with regret at the way he and Charity had parted the night before. When he rode his horse to the Gypsy campground, the tribe was gone. No tents, no wagons, the campfires cold.

In disbelief, he stared around at the empty place where the active tribe had stood with him the previous evening, when he'd come to bring Charity to dinner. A group of people couldn't simply disband and leave everything in their lives that quickly. Could they?

He scratched his chin, reminding himself the Rom carried everything they needed with them. They hadn't left anything behind. Except him.

Where could they have gone? Surely not far, as they must've departed only hours earlier. He shaded his eyes and peered north, then east, south, then west. But in what direction were they traveling?

He swiftly rode back to the Colchesters' and strode into the house. The entry door slammed behind him. Alone in the parlor, he closed the door and considered the possibility that Charity had gone off with another man, that Gypsy. Daniel couldn't recall his name. Something about a pet. That contemplation was an unbearable and exasperating one. He couldn't believe she'd actually wed anyone but him.

As the minutes ticked by, he stood at the far end of the parlor and stared out the window at a rapidly fading afternoon.

"I thought you cared about me," he said into the empty room. His voice rose. "I thought you loved me! Why did you leave me again?" He shook his head. By insisting she move back to England, he had caused her to fly away again.

He strode to the sideboard and poured braggot into a goblet. He sipped, tasting a harsh defeat. What in the world was Charity doing, wandering all across Wales? Gypsies lived hand-to-mouth, and she'd once enjoyed a comfortable English lifestyle. Wasn't she better off in England? Why, her behavior was infuriating and hardly made sense.

He took a long gulp of the braggot and then turned as the door behind him opened. He set the goblet on a side table as Valentina entered. She shut the door and then rushed to him, placing a hand on his arm.

"I know Luca's tribe departed this morning."

She didn't say how she knew, although as they'd talked one day at breakfast about Gypsy customs, she mentioned that the tribes relied on a *vurma,* a woman who knew the exact whereabouts of all the tribes. Now if only he knew where to find the *vurma.*

"Aye," he answered and looked away, unable to conjure up his usual ease with her.

Her hand tightened on his arm, forcing his gaze back to her. "I presume Charity went with them?"

Drawing a long breath, he curtly nodded.

"And you miss her?"

With a ragged sigh, he whispered, "Aye."

"Then I will come directly to the point. Why aren't you out looking for her?"

"I don't know where to look," he said quietly, trying not to flinch at the stabbing pain of loss in his heart. "This time she's disappeared for good. Last night when I took her back to the camp, I tried to force her hand and convince her to return to England." He trailed off, reached for his goblet and drained the braggot. "Why would God be so cruel ... to bring us together, only to rip us apart?"

"Mayhap what you believe God is doing to torment you is really using your circumstances to transform you. Sometimes God uses closed doors to lead you to the doors that are open."

He stared out the window as her words revealed the enormous mistake he'd made. Ever since he'd found Charity again, he'd assumed she wanted to resume her previous life in England. Despite the abuse she had revealed to him, he had believed she would welcome a return to the comfortable lifestyle she'd known—a fine house and plentiful food, parties and the opera, dancing in spacious, well-appointed drawing rooms. He hadn't stopped to consider that a simpler lifestyle suited her—as it suited him.

Valentina's voice drew his attention back to her. "Luca said he intended for the tribe to go south, where the warmer weather will last longer. He usually gravitates toward Swansea. 'Tis a market town, so he'll be able to barter any wares they've lifted from the townspeople here."

Daniel raised an eyebrow. "You must mean any wares they were *gifted* from the townspeople."

"Nay, I meant what I said. Lifted." Valentina met his gaze directly. "Soon, when you spend enough time with Charity, you will learn of the Rom's desperation. No one will give them work and so they must resort to stealing. You will realize they are not at fault." She subjected him to a long scrutiny. "Remember when we quoted the verse from Matthew last evening? There is another verse that has always been dear to my heart, because I stole many, many times, along with my fellow Rom when I lived with them."

"You stole?"

"Aye." Tears sprang to her eyes as she quoted,

"'Judge not according to the appearance, but judge righteous judgement.'" She retied a bright-yellow handkerchief around her neck and walked to the parlor door. Opening it, she said, "Now go and find her."

~

*T*he ride to Swansea, which Valentina had predicted would take three hours, took Daniel two and a half. Although the daylight hours of summer were long, a purple dusk was deepening as he reached the outskirts of the city.

He and Charity had been apart for less than twenty-four hours, and he missed her so much his chest ached.

'Twas more than her beauty that appealed to him. A captivating exuberance surrounded her, a mischievous approach to life despite her hardships. His mind understood the harsh reality of her absence, but his heart refused to accept a life without her. Even if she rejected him, he had to try.

When he found the Gypsy camp, they were still unloading heavy wagons and setting up tents. He tied his horse's reins to a tree, then wended his way around canvas and long poles and wooden trunks, searching for one head of red hair among the dark-haired Gypsies.

Luca greeted him with a quick nod and no friendliness. Other men regarded Daniel with stony expressions despite his courteous salutations. Kezia, however, rushed over to him and threw her arms around his waist.

"What took you so long?" she asked.

Although numerous replies formed on his lips, he stated the truth. "At first, I didn't know where to look."

Kezia's tiny fingers squeezed his arm as she guided him toward a tent located away from the others. "Charity has been so despondent this entire trip, I feared she'd never stop crying."

"She was crying?"

"Aye."

Feeling a pang of guilt so great he couldn't breathe, he lifted the opening to Charity's tent.

She sat on a wooden bench with her hands in her lap, her head bent. Wrapped in a gown of lavender wool, she looked like an angel, her shining copper-colored hair tumbling over her shoulders.

"Daniel?" Her crystal-blue eyes widened into huge orbs as she rose. Her generous lips parted into a slow smile.

He stepped forward. "Did I ever tell you that your smile lights up a room?'

"I don't know. Mayhap." She tilted up her chin. "Why are you here?"

"Because you're coming with me."

Her smile was replaced by a hurt, determined look. "Nay. I told you I'm not returning to England."

"Good, because neither am I."

Her hand was at her throat. "I—I don't understand. Exactly why are you here again?"

"I'm here because I love you." There. He felt better now that he'd said the words he should've spoken to her a fortnight ago.

He blew out a breath and waited. He also had to accept the fact that she may not love him.

She bit her lip in a combination of what looked like shyness and thoughtfulness, although he knew Charity would soon grow weary of cowering. She always confronted her reservations head-on.

He reached her and ran a forefinger over her delicate cheek. "I want us to make a life together."

She stepped back, shaking her head. "I can't return to my father, and you can't force me."

"Force you?" His hand stilled. Her face was so gorgeous, her expression so vulnerable, that he questioned himself for the thousandth time. How could he not have known of her mistreatment? Tenderly, he resumed caressing her cheek. "Your father is dead, Charity. He died soon after you ran away."

"Dead? My father ...?" Briefly, she closed her eyes and drew in a shuddering breath. "You're not here to haul me back to England, to him? He did not send you to find me?"

His hands slid up and down her arms. "I'm here for only one reason. I love you. I've always loved you."

In the flickering glow of three lit candles on a wooden table, he saw expressions flit across her face —disbelief, sadness, and relief. "Daniel, I apologize for misjudging you." She tilted her head up, offering her mouth for his kiss. "I've always loved you too."

He kissed her, long and lingering, with all the desire and love he held in his heart. "Will you marry me?"

At his lips' urging she kissed him back, placing her slim fingers along his cheeks. "Aye," she whispered. "Aye."

"When? When will you marry me?"

She continued her exploration of his face and traced her fingers over his mouth. "A proper English wedding takes months to plan." She grinned at his frown. "Whereas a Romany Gypsy wedding takes only a day."

"I've waited six years." He fingered her curls, his pulse quickening at her nearness. "One more day is all I can manage. Who performs the ceremony?"

"Well, sometimes the leader of the tribe ..." Her long fringe of black lashes flew up, and she regarded him with her clear blue eyes. "So, Luca—"

"As long as he doesn't cut my throat, then 'tis agreed. We can send for the Colchesters to attend the ceremony."

"Of course."

Appeased by the fact they'd wed come the morrow, he wrapped her in his arms. "And I hope you'll agree to live here in Wales. I've grown to love the country."

She slid her arms around his neck, molded herself to his length, and lightly kissed him. "As do I."

"Good. I've made a decision to purchase a country estate. 'Tis a three hour ride from Swansea, and the property needs a bit of work."

Aye, a neutral phrase for a grand undertaking, he thought.

She grinned. "Sounds perfect."

He gazed at his beautiful bride-to-be and thanked God. He had separated them for a while, but He'd also given them abundant grace and made them stronger. They had realized a deeper love, as well as an appreciation for each other that they would never have known otherwise.

"Daniel?" Charity was asking. "So you're agreeable to a Romany wedding ceremony?"

"Of course," he murmured. He kissed her again. He couldn't get enough of her.

"Do you even know what a Gypsy ceremony involves?"

"Nay." Distracted by her stunning smile, he grazed his lips over hers, savoring the exquisite taste of her.

"You'll learn of the ceremony come the morrow then," she said. "Do you have a broomstick handy?"

HE END

RECIPE FOR TRADITIONAL WELSH CAWL STEW

Ingredients:
Approximately 2 ½ lbs. lamb, beef or ham
1 chopped onion
6 peeled and chopped potatoes
3 peeled and chopped carrots
2 peeled and chopped parsnips
2 washed and peeled leeks
fresh parsley
vegetable stock
salt and pepper

Place meat in large pot, cover with water and bring to boil. Let simmer for 3 hours. Leave in refrigerator overnight to cool. The following day, skim off any fat.

Cut the meat and return to stock. Add potatoes,

carrots and parsnips. Simmer until done and season with salt and pepper. Add shredded leeks and parsley just before serving.

Enjoy for lunch or dinner with crusty bread.

A NOTE FROM THE AUTHOR

Dear Friends,

Seeking Charity is the second book in my Inspirational Regency romance "Seeking" series.

Charity Weston, with her copper-colored hair and crystal-blue eyes, is a complex heroine. Running away at a young age, she joins a Romany Gypsy tribe.

Daniel Hayward, the hero, is a wealthy Englishman, and a devout Christian with a kind heart.

My hope is that this story will make you believe again in second-chance love and God's grace.

The Romany Regency saga continues with Luca and Patience in *Seeking Patience*.

Please help other people find this book and post a review.

Thank you!

Josie Riviera

P.S. *Seeking Charity* is available on Audiobook, Large Print paperback, and ebook.

ACKNOWLEDGMENTS

An appreciative thank you to my patient husband, Dave, and our three wonderful children.

ABOUT THE AUTHOR

USA TODAY bestselling author, Josie Riviera, writes Historical, Inspirational, and Sweet Romances. She lives in the Charlotte, NC, area with her wonderfully supportive husband. They share their home with an adorable shih tzu, who constantly needs grooming, and live in an old house forever needing renovations.

To receive my Newsletter and your free sweet romance novella ebook as a thank you gift, sign up HERE.

Join my Read and Review VIP Facebook group for exclusive giveaways and ARCs.

To connect with Josie, visit her website and sign up for her newsletter. As a thank-you, she'll send you a free sweet romance novella.
josieriviera.com/
josieriviera@aol.com

ALSO BY JOSIE RIVIERA

SEEKING PATIENCE

SEEKING CATHERINE

I LOVE YOU MORE

OH DANNY BOY

A SNOWY WHITE CHRISTMAS

CANDLEGLOW AND MISTLETOE

A PORTUGUESE CHRISTMAS

HOLIDAY HEARTS

A Love Song To Cherish

A CHRISTMAS TO CHERISH

A Valentine To Cherish

1-800-CUPID

MAEVE

SEEKING FORTUNE

Aloha to Love

Sweet Peppermint Kisses

1-800-CHRISTMAS

1-800-IRELAND

Irish Hearts Sweet Romance Bundle

The 1-800-Series Sweet Contemporary Romance Bundle

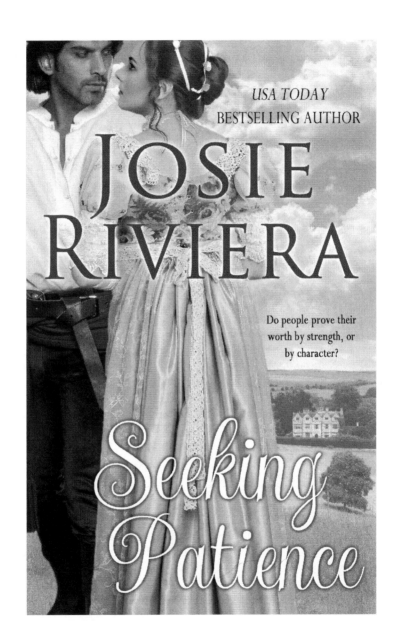

USA TODAY
BESTSELLING AUTHOR

JOSIE RIVIERA

Do people prove their
worth by strength, or
by character?

Seeking
Patience

This book is dedicated to all my wonderful readers who have supported me every inch of the way.
THANK YOU!

PRAISE AND AWARDS

USA TODAY bestselling author

READER REVIEWS: SEEKING PATIENCE

"Seeking Patience was an incredible book - it's a must read! I recommend it to all romance lovers - they will love it!"

"Once you start reading you won't be able to put this novel down."

CHAPTER ONE

*E*ngland, *1813*

*L*uca Boldor had made a mistake—a *big* mistake.

"May God strike you all," he swore under his breath at the murderous band of rival Roma tribesmen gaining on him, ready to attack. He'd merely been looking for food for his tribe.

He pulled his ragged overcoat around his shoulders and made his getaway through the snow. Snowflakes fell thick and heavy, twice as fast as earlier that evening. Wind carried the drifts in wayward, wispy circles and thankfully concealed his tracks.

He could escape unseen. He'd become good at that.

Slipping on a patch of ice, he stumbled and hit the ground face first.

His voice broke in agony. He stifled a scream, because a man never screamed. Certainly not a Roma man.

Relying on sheer muscle to raise the lower half of his body, he dug his elbows into the gritty, wet snow and crawled forward. Aye, a man didn't crawl, either.

But sometimes a man made exceptions to his own rules.

Advancing shadows split the stretches of dull white snow. Desperately, he searched his surroundings, knowing he was too easy to find. His body ached with the pain of a cruel beating. His breath, so cold a moment ago, burned in his chest.

Give up. But the thought was so inconceivable that Luca pushed it from his mind.

Instead, he envisioned the elders of his tribe foraging for food. They'd starve without his hunting skills and perish in a sennight. If he could only get them through another winter, he could improve their lot by moving them to the coast. Food was more plentiful by the sea and they wouldn't need to steal to survive.

Heavy footsteps crunched through the snow and Luca risked a swift glance over his shoulder. Marko, the leader of the rival tribe, and his men drew closer.

Blind panic rushed through Luca's limbs.

Past a swell of blackthorn trees, he spotted a ravine. He dropped to his knees and burrowed into the snow. Faster. Deeper. His nerves pinched in short, silent spasms.

Curse the frost for numbing his fingers. Curse his senses for deserting him. Curse the whole, damn, uncaring world.

He lowered himself into the hole and threw brittle tree branches on top. Then he peered through the branches and waited. The bleary figures of Marko and his tribesmen approached. A glimmer of moonlight lit the darkness and threatened to expose Luca's meager covering.

A persistent voice whispered in his mind. *Run. There's time. They won't see you.*

He grimaced. His restless body shifted. His battered leg stiffened, a reminder of his helplessness.

"Luca won't escape me." Marko's rough tone severed the cold night air. "He claims he disappears like a spirit, but he's just a man."

A few men snickered uneasily and Luca recognized their voices. Killing was a sport for them. Despite the numbness, tiny hairs on Luca's nape stood on end.

Marko's booted toes stopped within a few feet of Luca's makeshift hole. The stench of his unwashed body filled Luca's nostrils and he held his breath until he thought his lungs would burst. His eyes watered from the cold, but he kept his gaze on Marko.

"Nadya is my woman and they've been meeting secretly for months. She was hiding our food and giving it to him." Marko didn't speak, he growled. Despite the cold, he wiped his sweaty face with dirty gloves, then kicked the blackthorn trees, rustling the brittle branches of Luca's covering. "No one betrays me. Nadya learned her lesson quick, and he will, too."

In silent rage, Luca squeezed his eyes shut to blot the unsettling images racing through his mind. If he'd known that Marko was going to beat Nadya, Luca would've stayed and tried to protect her. When Marko and his men had stormed into Nadya's tent, Luca had fought them, then gotten away. He knew his strength would be no match for a tribe of enraged, jealous Roma.

Luca tightened his fists, defying the impulse to shake off the burdensome branches and pummel the rival lord's head into the snow. He'd not allow Marko to escape punishment for senselessly abusing a woman.

Nay. Not now. He swallowed to quell the pain feeding his anger.

He was a half-breed—half-English, half-Romany. And when his strength returned, he'd seek justice the Romany way—swift and sure.

At thirty years old, he was a leader. A legend to fear.

"Nanosh," Marko shouted to one of his men, "We'll resume our search at sunrise. It's too dark to continue." Marko's footsteps receded. His men obeyed without complaint.

Luca waited an interminable minute before he pushed the branches off his snowy covering. He heaved his body out of the hole and sucked in a sharp groan at the needle-like pain piercing his leg. Then he crawled away from Marko and his men like a helpless, despicable cripple.

If he didn't find shelter soon, he might lose his leg. Then he'd no longer command the respect of his tribe. Then he'd sink deeper in his English father's eyes—if such a thing were possible. Then...Hell, then he might as well die, because there'd be nothing left if he were a broken and helpless cripple.

Every few feet, Luca stopped to catch his ragged breath and control the shivers wracking his limbs. He tried to flex his fingers but they had no feeling, stiff and frozen sticks that hardly moved. Wryly, he thought about the leather hawking gloves, an unexpected treasure he'd found on a dirt road months before. The English dandy who'd dropped the gloves in a busy London marketplace never missed a step, never bent to search for them. Just kept walking, probably to Bond Street where he could spend more coin, while his rich, ruby cloak billowed behind him.

Those precious, warm gloves. All smooth black leather and cream silk lining.

Luca had left the gloves back at his camp for an elderly tribesman to wear.

Wryly, Luca shook his head. He'd assured the tribesman he wouldn't need the gloves, but foresight had never been his forte. Throughout the night, he'd pondered the ironic joke the fates had played on him as he blew on his cold hands.

He crawled, then limped through the snow, grabbing a tree branch to steady his gait. Beyond, a large, ungated home loomed. He focused on the flicker of oil lamps in the windows, the tall chimneys standing as sentinels on either side of the house.

He'd reached the outskirts of Ipswich.

He gripped the tree branch tighter, the icy bark biting into his fingers.

He should never have led his tribe here. This town always brought bad luck, much as it had brought bad luck to his Romany mother.

A weighty sigh brought an unanticipated heaviness to his chest. His mother would've loved being a proper hostess in a fine house such as this, serving tea with hot, buttered buns to her guests while she sat on a cushioned settee. Why hadn't he been able to give her these things?

The wintry wind swirled his cloak around him. He slumped against the tree, his torn boots sinking into the snow, soaking his feet. He wiped the wet snowflakes from his cheeks.

He still remembered his mother's fragrance, bergamot and roses, the precious oils she dabbed on her wrists each morning. Her soft voice still resonated in his chest, whispering of love, and beauty, and happier days. And then she'd died, abandoning him, and he'd struggled and sparred his way to adulthood.

"A plague on the English," he whispered, knowing the haughty aristocrats living in the grand home couldn't hear him. He loathed the idly rich and the privileged life they led, the desperation giving him no choice but to seek their favor.

"Luca."

His legs gave out. Dropping the tree branch, Luca fell to his knees and peered upward. The voice above him sounded youthful, deep, and familiar. He clawed through his hazy thoughts, trying to remember the child's name.

"I followed you out of Marko's camp. I know you were trying to get food for our tribe."

Luca kept his attention on the boy, his dearest friend since the boy was a child. "Pulko?"

He heard his own voice, slurring, sounding weak.

Tears streamed down the boy's face, despite a hasty swipe at his cheeks.

"Stop crying." Luca didn't have the strength to give the boy his usual friendly cuff because he needed to lift his arms, and his arms prevented his upper body from collapsing.

Pulko mopped the scraggly whiskers on his chin with his ragged blue cloak. "No one saw me. I'm fast and stayed hidden in the trees."

"Circle back to the tribe. Your mother will worry if you're missing."

"She's asleep." Pulko crouched beside Luca. "I'll stay with you."

Luca's palms flattened into the snow. "Your foolishness endangers the entire tribe. You'll give away my position."

"I won't abandon you," Pulko said. "I'll protect you."

"Protect the tribe. I don't need anyone."

Pulko hunched into his overcoat, his long dark hair flapping in the blustery weather. He paced, making a line of large footprints in the snow. "Marko will kill you if he finds you."

"Brush away your tracks and go. I'll seek help at the English mansion from one of the stable boys. Otherwise, Marko might capture us both and then our tribe would be lost." Luca grappled for the tree branch. With painstaking slowness, he braced his weight on his good leg and wobbled to his feet. He'd known Pulko all his life, two young males caring for an elderly tribe, bonded by shared responsibilities.

Refusing to meet Pulko's dark eyes, Luca drew his face taut against the wind and stared straight ahead. "Stay low and out of sight. I know what's best," Luca said.

He waited for the boy's brisk steps to wane, then forced a grim smile. Pulko knew better than to disobey. Luca was the tribal leader and his decisions, whether good or bad, safe or dangerous, weren't questioned.

When he was certain Pulko was gone, Luca leaned on his makeshift cane and wrenched his muscled body toward the estate. His temples thudded with the effort.

The woods thinned, exposing a field coated in ice.

Bone-chilling cold. Water soaked through his clothes and penetrated his skin. He sank to the ground. His dreamlike state numbed his wits and tempted him to curl into a locked ball.

His shoulders rose in a shrug of anger. Never. No man would ever find him in such a pathetic position.

Calm shrouded the air. He glanced at the sky. Soon it would be early morn.

The stable looked deserted and he pushed on. Bottomless purple clouds framed the imposing English home, the wood strangely weathered and neglected at closer range. A wide arch boasted an entryway. He doubted he could reach it.

～

F̶ight. But his body wouldn't stop shivering, his arms wouldn't stop shaking.

His heartbeat weakened, faded. Hopeless images of his tribe flashed across his mind, then images of happier times before the endless poverty and starvation.

Times such as Pulko and his sister running across a field, chasing a shiny, red ball they'd stolen from an innkeeper's barn. Pulko's sister had loved that ball, clutching it ever so tight. When the fever struck her small body she'd wanted the ball near, turning it round and round with her tiny fingers while she sweated and moaned in pain.

They'd buried her with that red ball, setting it beside her in the small wooden casket.

Joy was elusive and fleeting. If a person didn't appreciate it, joy slid through one's fingers as soon as one looked away.

Luca focused on his shallow breathing, one breath, another, another. The pain in his leg receded, becoming a dull throb on the fringe of nothing. He crawled the last few feet to the entryway of the large, English home and lost his struggle for consciousness.

CHAPTER TWO

*P*erched on a wingback chair near a cozy, crackling fire in her bedchamber, Lady Patience Blakwell sewed a row of uneven stitches along the ripped seam of her wool scarf. A simple task, requiring little thought and littler effort. She did a poor job, knew it, and didn't care, for no one inspected a wool scarf. But she tried to behave like the other ladies, at least a little, and every woman she knew sewed.

A wisp of stubborn hair loosened from the long, curly ringlets on her forehead and fell into her eyes. She blew the strand back with a huff. Her thick hair never cooperated with even the simplest style. She poised the needle in midair, tucked the offending strand beneath her mob cap, and peered out the window at the vast acres of her late husband's estate.

"Lord Bertram Blakwell, what a quandary you left me to sort," she said aloud.

The frustration rising in her throat spilled over, choking her.

If she remembered how to cry, she would have, although she hadn't cried since she was thirteen, and she had no intention of crying eight years later. So she did what she always did. She swallowed her feelings and buried them at the bottom of her heart where nothing could hurt her.

She glanced out the tall window, framed by sheer white curtains. A pink sunrise lit the blanketed, wintry fields. Perhaps the day would turn bright now that the snowstorm of the previous night had passed.

Patience accidentally pricked her thumb and put down her sewing, tormented by thoughts of her tyrannical late husband's endless speeches and lewd manner. When he was red-faced and yelling, she'd prayed fervently for strength.

At sixteen, her father had forced her to marry Lord Bertram Blakwell, the Earl of Orwell, assuring that the earl would give her prosperity, security and children.

Five years after the marriage she had neither prosperity, nor security.

Nor a husband. Nor a child.

With a weighty sigh, she set the wool scarf into the sewing basket beside her chair.

So much for neat stitches. She'd never liked sewing, anyway.

Voices from the hallway below halted her musings and she frowned. Unexpected visitors in the early morn didn't bode well.

She couldn't call for her lady's maid, Amelia, to assist her in dressing, as Amelia was visiting an uncle in Bucklesham. Struggling with the buttons, Patience quickly changed her muslin morning dress for a white satin slip and black mourning frock.

Oliver, her devoted lapdog, settled closer to the hooded fireplace and absorbed the scant warmth remaining in the bedchamber, the rest being carried away by the drafts. The old dog cocked his head, sniffed, and tucked his nose between oversized paws.

Patience stepped to him and affectionately scratched his ears. "Little help you'd be if I ever needed protection."

A rap sounded on her bedchamber door. Penham, the head butler and a trusted servant, stepped in and filled the room with his booming voice and portly body.

"Pardon, my lady. You're needed downstairs. There's a man in the hall."

"Another creditor?" she asked.

She was a dowager countess, although the title meant nothing. The responsibility, however, weighed heavily on her. How was she supposed to maintain her estate on the miserly monies her stepson, Lord Crispin Blakwell, allowed?

Oh, if only she were done with this groveling. By dower law, she was entitled to one-third of her late husband's estate, but Crispin threatened to formally charge her with murdering his father and withheld the monies. She was forced to rely on Crispin's benevolence and live in her dower house, one of the lesser properties, until she proved her innocence.

And how likely was that? She was a woman, and a poor one.

"The man in the hall is a Gypsy, and Digby wants to send the Gypsy on his way. I told your steward that you're compassionate and gentle, and you've always cared for beggars."

Patience crinkled the pleats of the black gossamer dress hanging loosely over her hips. "If my stepson, Crispin, didn't force me to keep Digby on, I'd have discharged Digby a fortnight ago."

Penham nodded and gave a slight bow. "I wouldn't have disturbed you but—"

"You were right to come to me." She filled her lungs with a fortifying whiff of warm air. The aroma of fresh baked bread from the kitchen wafted through the bedchamber.

Her stomach growled and she shook her head. She couldn't control her hunger of late.

Walking to the bedroom fireplace, she carefully stepped over her sleeping dog. In two rapid breaths, she blew out a row of stubby beeswax candles on the cupboard.

Penham shifted. "This man downstairs, he's not well."

She tied her paisley cashmere shawl around her shoulders. "Show me to him."

He offered a slight smile. "Of course, my lady. You're a fine and brave woman."

She followed Penham's long, flapping waistcoat through the hallway and a hint of vinegary herbs assailed her nose, reminding her of her late husband and his unending medicine vials scattered throughout the house.

Patience reached the bottom of the oak stairwell, then jostled past several kitchen maids crowded in the hall.

A lifeless Gypsy man huddled near the entryway. He was rough looking, with strong, angular features, lying helpless in filthy clothes.

A cutting reminder of her late husband's battered body six weeks earlier returned in a rush and her breathing hastened. Perhaps the men who'd killed her husband were the same men who thrashed this Gypsy.

She rushed to the Gypsy's side, lowered to her knees, and lifted him by his forearms.

He groaned and crumpled against her, heavy, dirty, and pale beneath dark skin. Fearing she might drop him, Patience settled his head in her lap and lightly touched his wet hair.

Digby, her steward, regarded the raw-boned Gypsy with undisguised disdain. He sniffed and arranged the puffing of white linen at his wrists. "Rather appalling, my lady. A Gypsy beggar isn't the sort of person Lord Blakwell allowed on his estate. May I suggest that 'tis best if this man crawls back to where he belongs."

Patience halted the disdainful servant with a glacial glare. "This Gypsy cannot walk, let alone crawl. I'll not allow this man, nor any man, to freeze to death outside my door."

She pressed her ear against the Gypsy's mouth, reassured by slow, faint breaths. His lower arms were bare where the ragged tan cloak fell away, exposing a well-muscled arm covered with black, silky hairs. Her gaze lingered on his large hands, masculine and scarred. So different from the shaking, gnarled hands of her late husband, or the smooth, pampered hands of her late father. Callused and rough, the Gypsy's hands were those of a rugged hunter.

A dangerous hunter.

Her fingers lurched. She had the fleeting urge to pick up her skirts and tear from the hall. But that was utter nonsense. With his brutal injuries, he could no more hunt than she could sew.

The Gypsy's eyelids snapped open, revealing a black gaze that stared straight through her. His nearness caused her overwrought nerves to crackle in awareness.

He jerked his gaze from hers, then swung back. Their eyes locked.

"Help me." His voice—an urgent twinge woven into a rich, low timbre.

She studied his set jaw and sharp profile. From the little she'd heard, Gypsies led perilous lives full of bluffs, brawls, and violence.

She hesitated, chastising herself for debating whether to aid him. He was badly injured and desperately poor, and she'd done all the cowardly things she could do in one life—bowing to the commands of cruel men who'd cared only about themselves.

She placed her warm hands on the Gypsy's cold ones, praying her decision didn't jeopardize her servants by placing them in danger. Most were house maids and possessed neither the skills nor experience to fight off an unexpected attack by ruthless Gypsies.

"With God's mercy, of course I'll help you," she said.

He closed his eyes. His long black lashes cast a straggled shadow on his cheeks.

Patience turned to her servants. "Penham and Digby, please lift the man to his feet."

Aching with sympathy, yet prudent enough not to let anyone see her concern, she stood and offered a reassuring smile to her recoiling housemaids.

"Allow us to pass," she said.

Patience straightened to her full height of five feet and pointed Penham and Digby toward the stairwell as she walked alongside. The Gypsy's lips whitened beneath his dark skin as he sagged against the sneering Digby.

No man would endure all this suffering in a guise to steal her insignificant assets. She almost opened her mouth to tell the Gypsy as much, but gave herself a hard rational shake. Life required choices. Hers was to walk with God and help the less fortunate.

Patience hurried ahead. "Bring this man upstairs to a spare chamber."

No footsteps followed and she wheeled around.

The Gypsy resisted the servants' attempts to move him. He groaned, a soft grasp for breath. "I'll not go upstairs. There's no time and I must leave. You cannot fight—"

Her gaze jerked to the Gypsy's face. "Fight? Fight who?"

Lines of pain etched into the corners of his mouth. "Tend to me here."

"Who is there to fear?" she asked.

"Tend to me here." The fierceness of the Gypsy's demand made her stop in mid-step.

"This is my house and I choose where to care for you. Upstairs is safer because it will be harder for them to find you there."

"Nay. Cruel men search quickly—"

She stood ramrod straight. "The lawmen in the town will protect us."

He laughed, or snickered, she wasn't sure. "Fifty lawmen in fifty towns aren't enough."

"I have servants," she said.

The Gypsy shook his head. His straight black hair fell across his face. "Not enough."

He repeated the same warning twice, and both times the warning made little sense. This was a civilized England ruled by the Prince Regent, George, Prince of Wales.

"The citizens of Ipswich are law-abiding and honest, the town prosperous. The barristers and constables keep order and peace." Her shoulders went back. "I'm not afraid of anyone."

"You should be."

She narrowed her eyes at the sharpness of the Gypsy's tone. Several of her servants fell back amidst a murmur of disapprovals.

Digby's jaw was a hard, distinctive line. "My lady, may I suggest—"

"One more suggestion and I'll no longer require your services, no matter what my stepson says," she countered.

That quieted him. That quieted the entire room.

The Gypsy weaved twice as the servants hauled him up the stairwell and along the far end of the hallway. The oil lamps swayed and flickered as they passed.

Once in the chamber, Penham half-carried the Gypsy to the four poster bed.

Patience squinted into the dim light. Her late husband's vinegary medicines still lined the top of a mahogany wardrobe. Ultimately, he'd died from his beating, not his long illness. She tried inhaling through her mouth because the smell brought back memories she'd rather forget.

She shuddered and wrapped her thick shawl closer about her shoulders.

With flint and tinder, Penham lit a fire in the fireplace and two candles on the night table. Another servant bolted the tall, narrow window more securely to keep out the wintry morning air, and added a screen to lessen the draft.

A brown quilt lay folded on a stool beside the wardrobe.

Patience piled the quilt in her arms, brought it to the bed, and tucked it about the Gypsy.

"Who are you?" she whispered.

No answer. He was obviously penniless, although he had a noble look about him. She brushed her hands up his cloak, prompting convulsed shivers to rattle his body.

"You'll freeze to death if you stay in these stiff clothes," she said.

She turned. "Penham, begin removing this man's

wet clothes. Digby, instruct the housemaid to fetch hot tea from the kitchen. The drink will warm the Gypsy."

Digby rooted himself in the doorway. He tilted his head, his gaze cold. "May I suggest, my lady, that you supervise Cook in the kitchen so that I, or one of the other male servants, may attend to this beggar properly."

"I'm assuming you didn't forget my earlier reprimand regarding your suggestions," she said sharply. Either Digby had a poor memory, or he didn't respect her authority.

She hung her shawl by the doorway, then twisted to face him. "I've treated countless injuries and have the skills to care for this man. Go and tell the housemaid to bring the tea."

"Perhaps—"

She raised her chin. "Perhaps you didn't hear me?"

Digby's thin lips folded in as he trudged from the bedchamber.

Patience pulled a stool by the bed. Lowering the overcoat off the Gypsy's shoulders, she gasped at the bruises along his neck. "Whatever happened to you?"

He didn't reply. His breathing was soft, interrupted by jagged gasps.

Carefully, she removed his tattered cravat and the green sash tied at his waist, then tugged off his worn boots and placed them on the floor. Penham raised the Gypsy's upper body and Patience lifted off a worn leather pouch strapped around the Gypsy's waist. His thin linen shirt and the orange scarf around his head followed. She winced at the fierce scar cut across the coarse hair on his chest, an old injury among his recent ones.

"How many brawls can one man be in?" she asked softly.

His eyes opened, but his gaze was dazed and unfocused. He moistened his lips. "Over a hundred."

Penham settled a pillow under the Gypsy's head, then folded the clothes and placed them on the wardrobe. "Lady Blakwell, I can finish here."

"I'll fetch clean cloths and hot water while you undress the man," she said. "Then I'll see to his injuries."

Penham's gape turned owlish. "Are you certain, my lady? Perhaps we should discreetly call for the physician?"

She met her elderly servant's gaze directly. "My uncle was a physician. I assisted him many times."

Patience hurried through the entry and closed the door. When she returned, Penham nodded toward the Gypsy on the bed, restless beneath a heavy quilt. With the subtlest of scowls, Penham withdrew from the chamber and latched the door behind him.

The logs in the fireplace sparked. The air was heavy with the scent of dried blood, as hard as iron.

A hush filled the bedchamber and she shifted uneasily. Quiet moments needed to be filled with chores and chatter or unwelcome memories rushed to the surface.

She regarded his buckskin breeches, folded with his other clothes on the wardrobe, then turned to study his face. Just his face.

His full lips twisted cynically, even in sleep, although his rugged features softened as his breathing slowed. The fire warmed the room and drops of perspiration lined his forehead. He opened his eyes and attempted to speak, but his eyes closed as quickly as they'd opened and his expression shut down.

She touched his forehead. "You've endured much, but by God's divine power you'll be strong again."

Patience went to the hearth and gathered two pieces of linen. She dipped one in the warm water, the other she kept dry. Grateful that she stored her sewing notions in every corner of the house, she started for her needle and thread. She washed her hands, then the needle, then brought the needle to the fire in the fireplace to sterilize the tip.

By candlelight, she threaded the needle and went to the bed, then raised the bottom hem of the quilt to expose the Gypsy's torn leg.

She kept her gasp to herself while she eyed the gashes and washed him with clean linens. She blew on the cuts, then the needle. "Your wounds are deep and starting to fester." She bent her head and made a firm attempt to control her trembling. "Fortunately, I am...somewhat of a seamstress. You can trust me to stitch your wounds."

Her husband's sour herbs blended with the smells of the Gypsy's sweat and blood and unspeakable injuries. Her stomach roiled. Her hands shook as she lifted the needle.

"I'll do you no harm," she said, adding with an attempt to lighten her panic, "as long as I don't teeter to the floor in a swoon and miss the wound completely."

She choked gulp after sickened gulp as she forced her stitching through the tender, raw parts of his skin. She bound the dry linen cloth over his stitches and covered his lower body with the quilt. When she finished, she ran her hands over his muscled arms, his massive shoulders and bronzed chest. A tremor wracked his body.

"Father," he murmured.

"Do you call for our Father in heaven?" she asked.

The Gypsy shook his head. *"Gadje, Gadjensa, Rom, Romensa."*

"I don't understand. Shall I fetch your father?"

"English with English. Rom with Rom." The Gypsy opened his eyes, his gaze so intense and full of hatred that it tore through her stomach like a broadsword.

She grabbed for the moistened cloth and swabbed his forehead and gashes as gently as her fingers allowed. His head tossed on the pillows. He rambled in his strange tongue, mysterious and indistinguishable Gypsy words.

"Ssh, try to sleep," she whispered.

"Marko." He grabbed the sleeve of her frock. His eyes darted, black, smoky fireballs that refused to rest. "I must leave."

"You cannot. Your leg—"

"Nay! Not my leg!" He screamed a hollow denial, ravaging her insides. He yanked back the quilt and tore at the bound linen cloths.

Her heart wrenched and she clutched his restless hands. "You won't lose your leg. I sutured the nastiest of the gashes. You just can't walk on it for a while. With time, you'll heal with few scars."

He stared down at his leg and his face hardened. "You've taken away my chance to escape."

"I saved you and you should be grateful." She released his hands, grabbed the quilt, and bundled his legs.

An ornate, ruby-red ring glimmered from his forefinger. Why did poverty-stricken Gypsies indulge in such colorful clothes and expensive jewelry? Perhaps it was a way for them to enjoy the small, beautiful things in life amidst all their hardships.

"I can't endanger you further," he said solemnly.

"You can't endanger anyone if you're just lying here. Don't fret. I'll protect us."

His mouth slipped to the slightest of smiles. "You don't look old enough to protect a puppy."

"My, you're such a flatterer."

His head fell back against the pillows and his hand found hers. He jerked her fingers to his face. "Is there something to quell the pain?"

There was laudanum, but she refused to use it. The medicine was too powerful and oftentimes deadly.

"Nothing will help for long." She spoke quietly, fighting for a balance of calmness and honesty, groping for believable reassurances. "The first few hours are the worst, but I'll not leave you. Give yourself time to heal."

"I have no...time." His voice faded, the suffering naked on his face.

Humming seemed to soothe him, so as the morning passed, all the English songs she'd learned as a child passed through her lips. Songs of fair maidens and faraway kingdoms—all dreams that be-longed to other people's lives.

Over and over she ran the moistened cloth along the stubble of hair on his chin.

And she prayed. "Please, Lord, heal this man and take away his pain."

She squeezed the Gypsy's fingers, stroked his cheeks, wiped the sweat from his forehead.

He grasped her hands and held tightly.

The grayish morning pushed on in a blur. His moans quieted. His breathing came easier. She stretched out her cramped legs and rested her cheek on the pillow beside him. Just for a few minutes, she told herself. Then she'd retire to a nearby chair.

His warm face dozed on the pillow next to hers. "Am I dying?"

"Nay." Lightly, she touched his chest. "God won't let you."

"Your God doesn't know me," he whispered.

She felt the Gypsy slipping back into his own, private limbo.

CHAPTER THREE

"*L*ady Blakwell, the only tea the housemaid found was green tea. I took the liberty of adding milk and sugar to the brew and decided to bring the tea up myself." Digby's voice came from the doorway of the bedchamber. "The scullery maids are a lazy lot, and the maid-of-all-work doesn't know a sliver of Pears soap from a slice of fresh fruit."

Patience blinked to rapid awareness. The Gypsy's heartbeat thudded beneath her fingertips in a slow, steady rhythm. His skin was cooler. She swiveled, taking in the brightness of the bedchamber. The time was well past noon.

Digby's disapproving face greeted her, and any remaining semblance of dignity she held was in shreds. Digby could easily report this to Crispin, and

Crispin's opinion was crucial to her future. She jerked up and climbed off the bed so rapidly the stool overturned.

The servant flashed a cold smile, then raised a white porcelain teapot in one hand and two porcelain cups in the other.

Patience kept her back straight as she marched to the doorway. "Green tea is perfect, Digby. Thank you."

The steward lowered his chin. His gaze was shuttered. His mouth pinched. "Will there be anything else for your Gypsy? Hot water, more linen—"

Her Gypsy—comparable to her dog—like an animal she threw scraps to from her table.

"Nay." She accepted the teapot and cups from Digby's outstretched hands and set them on the tea table near the window. "Close the door as you depart and when next you enter, knock first."

The bedchamber door slammed, followed by Digby's footsteps stomping down the hall.

Patience turned to the bed and her gaze collided with a pair of perceptive black eyes.

She stiffened and clasped her hands together, polite and ladylike.

Absurd, considering the circumstances, a naked man on her late husband's bed, covered by little more than a brown quilt, his breeches draped on the wardrobe. If she accorded him the opportunity, she scarcely envisioned the tales he'd divulge. She only had to glance at his rough face to know he was a man of mystery and experiences better left unspoken.

"I didn't think you were awake," she offered.

~

"*A*ye, so it seems." Luca heard the weariness coloring his voice. He chased the weariness away with a ragged cough and choked groan. His mouth was dry, as if he'd been eating sand. He clutched the sides of the mattress until the quavering in his forearms subsided.

"How are you?" the woman asked. She looked so slight, so fragile, her huge blue eyes glistening with worry.

"Thirsty."

She smiled, an understanding beam lighting her heart-shaped face. "I have tea."

"Good," he managed, although ale would've been better.

He winced at the sunlight streaming through the window and squeezed his eyes shut, trying to shake off the cobwebs, thick and scratchy, blurring his brain.

She brought a porcelain teacup filled with tea to the bed and angled him to a sitting position. He felt her gaze on him as he drank greedily.

"Who's Marko?" She turned to the night table and refilled the cup. "Is he your father?"

Luca stiffened and opened his eyes. "Why do you ask?"

She placed the cup in his hands and steadied it. "While you were feverish you called out for Father. At first I thought you meant our Father in heaven, our God."

"You mean *your* God." Luca accepted the cup and shrugged off her hands. "And my earthly father is dead." Dead to me, he amended to himself.

"You dreamt of him," she said.

"'Twas a nightmare." Despite her questioning gaze, Luca refused to say more. It was the same nightmare that had tortured his sleep for years.

He'd walked with his father, at night, going on a fox hunt. One didn't walk on a fox hunt at night, one rode a fine horse during the day, but such was the nature of nightmares. He was three years old, but he'd assured his father he was old enough to catch the fastest fox in the forest because he'd made his own slingshot. They'd held hands, but his father let go and Luca was left alone. A fox lunged at him, its hot breath and sharp teeth nearing his face. Luca's heart raced, his hands shook as he'd tried to climb a tree. He'd screamed for his father, but the skeletal tree limbs far beyond his small hands ridiculed him by their distance.

"My father will search until he finds me," he'd assured the trees. "He'll not leave me to be mauled by a fox."

Luca always cried in his dream, despising himself afterward for his weakness. He could never shake the fear, the panic that gripped him afterwards, the emptiness of abandonment, nor the shame of defeat.

"Do you miss your father?" the woman asked.

Luca stared into his empty cup as though it might offer a plausible answer.

"'Twas simply a nightmare and it will fade," he said.

"I have nightmares sometimes." Those enormous blue eyes studied him.

He averted his gaze, handed her the teacup, and searched for a reply to appease her. He'd heard her voice while he'd slept, coming from a long way away. He'd doubted the voice was real, the tone so kind, so reassuring. No one had ever spoken to him like that. No one had ever reassured him that all would be well. Certainly never an Englishwoman.

"In your nightmares, do you fight off the evil villain?" he asked.

"Of course. The honorable are always victorious over the wicked."

There wasn't a hint of alarm or misgivings or disgust on her expression. Never in his life had an aristocratic lady looked at him thus. To the English, he was a dirty Gypsy, a person to loathe, a person beneath them. She could easily have let him die outside in the cold rather than rescuing him, but she'd courageously chose to save him.

If they'd met at another time, a time of less peril, he might have told her how much her kindness meant to an injured, weary man. If he could find those types of words.

She might have returned his compliment with a soft, self-deprecating laugh.

But he had naught to offer except his presence, which was the last thing she needed because he placed her in grave danger.

Briefly, he closed his eyes, disgusted with himself for tarrying so long. "I must go. Help me stand." He attempted to swing his legs around the bed, wincing when a blast of pain split his side.

"I will not." Her spine straightened, and something changed in her expression. The gentle caregiver had vanished, and a stern opponent had appeared in her place.

He attempted charm. "I remember hearing you'd attend to my leg. Then you approached with a long needle and I passed out."

That brought a grin to her freckled face. "Hopefully not at the sight of me?"

"Nay. 'Twas your needle at fault."

"I sutured your leg as best I could. I'm not a physician, but I am a bit of a seamstress."

He ran a hand through his hair. "Are you trying to reassure me?"

"Aye." She leaned over the bed and smoothed the blankets. "Lay back so I may clean the gashes on your arms again."

"Promise you'll not hurt me." He smiled, just a little, but he wasn't jesting. He couldn't afford any further injuries if he wanted to leave quickly.

"You're hurt enough for one day," she said. "But by the grace of God, soon you'll heal."

He eased back onto the bed. Just for a moment, he allowed himself to believe her. Just for a moment. "Then I put myself in your care," he said.

She examined the wounds on his arms. Her expression sobered as she dipped the linens in the clear water. His blood stained the water. The levity passed.

"You slept a good while," she said, tending to him with the solicitousness of a mother cat hovering over her kitten.

His eyelids lowered, his arms felt heavy. "Shall I recite my dreams?"

"You're hardly able to keep your eyes open, much less speak about your dreams, although your speech is eloquent for a Gypsy."

"I studied at the finest schools, with the finest tutors."

"And I don't believe a word you're saying."

"The lovely vision tending to me is very real," he added.

"That part was a dream," she murmured. "Because, I assure you, I'm far from a lovely vision."

He gave in to the luxurious sensation of closing his eyes. "My strength often leaves me, but always returns."

"In the meantime, even the strongest men require rest."

He forced his eyes open. She was grinning at him, and he wasn't amused.

He lifted the quilt and examined his leg, neatly stitched and bound. How could he walk, much less run, without opening the sutures? He caught her anxious stare. Their eyes clashed.

"If there's one look I cannot abide, 'tis one of pity," he drawled.

"You mistake my expression. 'Tis one of disquiet, not pity. I've seen thrashings before, but yours was one of the cruelest."

He shrugged. "I can bear more than ordinary men."

Her blue-eyed gaze danced in the flicker of the candles. "And I can bear more than ordinary women. The secret is to think pleasant thoughts to fool the mind. I think of heaven."

"What is heaven?"

She hesitated, his question seeming to weigh on her. "Heaven is everything you love." Crisply, she smoothed the quilt over his leg.

Who was she, this aristocrat with the red scar

across her cheek, wearing a black mourning frock? Her white English hands spoke of pampering, yet her eyes spoke of hardships. Whatever cruel accident had befallen her pretty face wouldn't prepare her for the kind of violence Marko would deliver if he found her with Luca.

"I must return to my tribe. Please. They need me," Luca said.

Please. He couldn't remember the last time he'd spoken the word aloud.

～

*P*atience fetched a linen cloth from the basin, but his urgency made her hesitate. She studied him, his dark handsomeness, his confident profile. And his manner, downplaying his injuries, gazing at her directly as he spoke, tilting his head as if to listen to her more intently.

He resembled a proud Gypsy lord, if there was such a man. He reminded her of nobility by the aristocratic jut of his jaw and the authority when he spoke.

Although that was mad. He was only a Gypsy.

Her fingers trailed the fringe of bed linens. This man, by his strong presence and good-looking features, made her self-conscious in her own home. Images of holding him, touching him, being touched, dreams dormant for so long that she'd forgotten such feelings, appeared. But she refused to let the images take hold. She shook them away, for they were as foreign to her as he.

His eyes captured hers. "Will you see to the gashes on my arms?" he asked.

That same stubborn strand of hair fell from her mob cap and half-covered her face. She pushed it back in place as unwelcome warmth started up her face and seared her ears. The man was hurt and all she thought about was her own discomfiture.

"'Tis impossible for a mere human to heal someone in a few hours," she murmured.

"Make it possible," he said.

From the foot of the bed she retrieved a silk pillow and tucked the pillow beneath his head, wondering why she didn't stride from the room like a sensible woman and direct a male servant to finish the task of attending to the Gypsy.

She stole a cautious perusal at the medicine vials lining the wooden wardrobe. Two fortnights ago she'd done just that—counted on a servant, left the bedchamber, and consequently lost her husband.

Perhaps the Gypsy read her thoughts because he grabbed her hand to stop her movements. His hold was different than before, now more self-assured and bolder. No longer was he the feverish man squeezing with an intensity born of survival, in search of a lifeline.

His generous smile flicked a tremble down her spine. "*Kamadiyo*, I want you alone to tend to me."

She tipped her head nearer his mouth, expecting an explanation for the strange word. When one wasn't forthcoming, she said, "Sir, I wish to learn your name."

"Luca Boldor." His hand lingered. An overwhelming silence filled the air, as if he'd told her too much about himself, although he'd only said his name.

"Allow me to finish tending to your wounds, Mr. Boldor." The unfamiliar name drifted on her tongue, shadowy and unsafe.

"What is your name, *kamadiyo?*"

She permitted herself to peer into his fathomless eyes, although the warmth in his gaze threatened to dash any attempts at reason.

"Lady Patience Blakwell," she said. "I'm a widow."

"Lady Blakwell, the young widow." He smiled again, but this time it came slow and hinted of insolence. "I'm in the company of a true English lady. Shall I bow, or kiss your hand, or offer my sincere condolences?"

She reexamined the wounds on his arms. "You may stay quiet and do nothing."

Keenly responsive to his grimaces and sharp intakes of breath, she gentled her touch.

"How bad?" he asked.

"Your skin is dry and the wounds are clean."

"Shall I be grateful you're not the type of woman to swoon at the sight of a gash?"

"Swooning is for naive English damsels. I'm years past that nonsense."

"Lucky me."

"And unlucky me, for having the likes of you drop unconscious on my doorstep." She exerted light pressure on one particularly angry welt on his forearm. "Try to hold still."

His face grew drawn. He seemed to make a concerted effort not to flinch.

"The gouge on your leg is ghastly," she said. "Your stomach and chest are dreadfully bruised, although not cut." She spoke evenly to divert his attention from the pain. "'Tis too soon to determine if your leg is broken or badly sprained, since it looks to have taken the worst of the blows. Who did this to you?"

"No one you know."

The smoothness of his voice unnerved her. "A secret?" she asked.

He half-smiled. "I want you to be safe."

Heat vibrated from his body. Her hands fidgeted. He was all secrets and little information.

"Be calm, Lady Blakwell. I'm the one hunted, not you."

"And I have a hunted man in my home."

"And that is why you must hurry. My tribe will

perish without me." Propped against the pillows, he seemed so confident, although they both knew he was very weak.

She shot him a dubious look and pulled up the stool. "You shan't travel far, so your tribe will have to wait."

"They can't wait long. They need me."

She frowned. He expected her ministrations to heal him quickly and her skepticism didn't seem to deter him. Before she could turn up the plain long sleeves of her frock, raging male shouts resounded from the hallway below, both harsh and unfamiliar.

Patience gave a momentary scan of the bed-chamber door. "Who—"

Luca snared her wrists. "Marko and his vile men are here, searching for me."

She tried to yank her hands away and press them to her stomach, where her fortitude had quickly dissolved. "Marko is the man who thrashed you? Is he your secret?"

Luca held her hands firm. "Instruct them to depart before your servants reveal I'm here. I'll not perform a dance of death for my enemies, and neither will you. I was offered food for my tribe by someone trying to help me. I did nothing wrong."

His jaw tensed as he spoke and her mind sorted the facts beyond Luca's declaration of innocence. He was too injured, too anxious. He'd say anything, do anything, promise anything, to get back to his tribe.

"I'll not lie," she said. "Speak to these men as one reasonable man to another."

"Marko?" Luca's laugh was gruff. "He's a barbarian. He'll kill everyone in your home if he suspects you took me in. You must lie, for my sake as well as yours. Deter him, find an excuse for him to leave. I'll protect you if things turn bad."

Perhaps he could protect her if he could walk. Patience looked around, grateful she hadn't said the words aloud. She glimpsed more than a twinge of unease in Luca's pleading expression.

Her gaze slid to the sunlight slipping through the bolted window while she contemplated her decision.

She stood. "I'm going downstairs," she announced.

"Please lie to Marko," he repeated.

Luca's demeanor had changed, now more serious, bearing little resemblance to the soft-spoken, teasing man of a few moments ago.

He expected her to do his bidding. On his terms. In her house.

She kept her voice steady. "I'm a very poor liar." She cinched the high waistline of her frock and straightened the demi-train. For the second time that day, she clicked a bedchamber door shut and quickened her steps to the hall.

CHAPTER FOUR

*P*atience reached the bottom of the stairs and held her breath. Two filthy Gypsy men stood silent. Their colorful cloaks were caked with dirt and stretched to span bulky arms and hulking bodies. Two pairs of bloodshot gazes impaled her across the length of the hallway.

She clutched the baluster and reared back. The wooden floorboards creaked as she scanned the drawing room. Digby, his posture stiff behind a straight-backed chair, flashed her a cold smile.

Beyond, in the dining room, honey cakes and tea were set out for a light midday meal, the scent of ground ginger and saffron unmistakable. Cook, Penham, and several servants stood near the kitchen doorway.

Digby stared at Patience with a hard squint, then

adjusted his fancy waistcoat. "As you can see, we have visitors, my lady."

With a cursory nod, she acknowledged the larger of the two Gypsies, a frightening looking man with a long, stringy, black beard.

"I heard the disturbance from upstairs," she said to the large Gypsy. Despite her efforts, the quake in her voice betrayed her nervousness. "What is your interest, sir?"

"We seek a Roma man, my lady. He's injured and we believe he's here." The man's polite words didn't match the derisiveness of his tone, nor his gruff, unwashed appearance.

She linked her hands in front of her. "You're mistaken." She swallowed her inquiry as to what had prompted his suspicions and stayed silent.

The bearded Gypsy advanced through the drawing room in four bold strides and stopped within a foot of her. He blotted his perspiring forehead with a wrinkled handkerchief and kept his stance wide. "No one lies to Marko."

Marko. The barbarian. The killer. Patience's blood ran like an ice-cold stream through her veins. She raised her shoulders, repositioning her body as a barrier blocking the stairwell.

"You're not aware of this man's whereabouts?" Marko shouted.

"Should I be?" she asked carefully. Her calves scraped the blunt ledge of the bottom stairs. She swayed but held firm.

He drew closer, forcing her to take in the uneven scar on his jaw, the odor of his rotting teeth. "His wounds led us right to your door. This man bedded my woman, then convinced her to give him food for his tribe."

Patience pasted her lips into a steely smile and mentally ran through the situation. Luca's battered body, his brave demeanor despite his injuries, his desperation. Maybe he'd bedded Marko's woman. Maybe he'd accepted food for his tribe that this woman had freely given. Or maybe Marko was believing that Luca had stolen the food, Marko's version of what had really happened.

In any case, Luca had obviously risked his life for his tribe. And Marko was obviously cruel in his beatings. In addition, Marko's manner towards her was threatening and abrasive, whereas Luca had been concerned about her safety, his manner polite and soft-spoken.

"The man you seek must be elsewhere," she said.

"Shall I summon the others, Marko?" the second Gypsy shouted from the hall.

"Don't call for your men, Marko. Leave at once." With a quick mouthful of air, she counted the cluster of servants huddled near the kitchen. Adding herself and Penham, they totaled six against two Gypsies, giving her and her servants the decided advantage.

Marko thumped his fist into his palm. "I command, little lady. Not you."

Patience tried not to flinch, although her heart beat so loud surely everyone in the house heard. She glanced around. No one moved.

She was much stronger than this, she chided herself.

"You issue no orders in my house." Her stomach knotted with fear although the outward breath she drew was brave. Her gaze sifted through the rooms, looking for one valiant servant willing to meet her eyes. In response to her silent appeal, Penham nodded and lurched forward.

In contrast, Digby's darting dark-gold eyes, like a frenzied fox, met hers. "Don't be foolish." He mouthed the words.

She glanced at the door. The other Gypsy man, face impassive, arms folded over his pot belly, barricaded the entrance.

Marko's glower narrowed on Patience. "Where is he?"

She stalled, refusing to draw back although Marko's chest was within a foot of her.

"Stay away from me," she challenged, throwing down the gauntlet. A portrait of Luca blazed through her mind. His feverish moans, his hand tightening around hers. He was a brave man caring for his tribe, not part of this group of repulsive men.

Luca's manner carried authority, coupled with gallantry and courageousness.

Marko goggled the high neckline of Patience's mourning frock, stared at her face, and broke into a lecherous chortle. "This man hides wherever there is a woman—any woman will do, even a face on a stick."

She bridled at the insult but didn't rise to his sneers. She was far from beautiful. Her body was scrawny and a thin scar ran along her cheekbone.

Long ago, her adolescent declarations of love and clumsy attempts to please her smooth-talking cousin had brought only laughter and disdain from him afterwards. That, and his cruelty, for he'd burned her face with a tallow candle as a remembrance of their first and only night together. She'd endured the snickers and resulting scandal by building a tidy wall around her feelings, so high and so thick that no one could penetrate her heart.

"The man you seek isn't here," she scoffed, realizing a small dose of gratification when Marko's laugh faltered.

Marko's mammoth hand seized her shoulders. "I'm never wrong about my enemies."

She squirmed, refusing to cry out. "I told you to be on your way."

Penham charged forward. "Leave us as Lady Blakwell commanded."

A tide of servants surged. Flashes from Marko's silver dagger and splitting blows erupted.

One of the Gypsy men's heavy fists smashed into Penham's nose. Penham staggered and fell to the floor. He wiped the blood from his nose and looked up at Patience. With calm focus, he said determinedly, "Be brave, Lady Blakwell. 'Tis a small injury, and nothing that I can't tend to later."

Before she could respond, another servant plowed to the fore, head down, fists drawn. Marko sent the servant reeling with an unpitying ram to the servant's jaw.

Patience heard herself scream. Time surged, slowed, surged again. She never should've let her foolhardy pride endanger her servants.

Marko brushed his palms together—a man ridding himself of numerous nuisances. She countered his bloodthirsty glare with her own dispassionate one.

"You have no business here," she said.

"This man is my business." Marko's tone, without emotion, chilled the hairs on her scalp. He peered over his shoulder. "Nanosh, open the door."

The entry door flung open and three Gypsy men converged into the house and up the stairwell, knocking Patience and her servants aside as they passed.

"Where is he?" Marko howled as she reached the top stair. Her gaze fixed on his booted feet, the cracking of door after door as he stormed down the wide-planked hallway.

"Stop! Leave us!" She launched at him and wrenched the seam of his cloak. "I'll notify the constable of this outrage."

"The constable owes me money. He'll look the other way."

One swipe of Marko's sizable knuckles snapped her head back. Her chin crashed against the wall in an explosion of white agony. She swallowed the bitter taste of blood and slid to the coolness of the floor. Her fingers crammed into tight-fisted pellets and she counted to ten through a swell of cramps shooting through her stomach.

She peered upward. A malicious grin crept across Marko's mouth.

Glaringly aware she had less than an instant, she curled her arms around her head and lifted her legs. She prayed she was strong enough for the unforgiving kick she planned to strike to his knees.

As quickly as her legs lifted, Marko caught her ankles. His thick lips swam above her, his terrible voice belting his fury. "Show me to him or my men will bar all the doors in your miserable house and set every chamber ablaze."

"Please. Please wait." Patience tried to say more but she was shaking so badly her words locked in her throat.

Marko dropped her legs to the floor.

Slowly, she pushed to her feet. The stucco ceiling pulsed and weaved as she struggled for balance and she groped the wall to steady herself. Beyond, Luca's bedchamber door squeaked open, swinging back and forth.

Marko snatched a clump of her hair. Her pinned ringlets loosened and unraveled, sending auburn waves fluttering over her shoulders and her mob cap falling to the floor.

Marko dragged her past her private bedchamber. She prayed that Oliver's keen bark didn't sound from wherever he might be hiding. She swallowed, longing to glimpse the sight of her dog's pricked ears, knowing she couldn't reach him. He was so small, so loving, with huge trusting brown eyes. She couldn't protect him now. She couldn't protect anyone. Not her servants, not Luca, not herself.

Marko's bulbous shape and Patience's slight one cast a shadow on the floor as they entered the last bedchamber in the hallway. Luca's bedchamber.

For an entire morn, she'd tried to save him, a man she hardly knew. All for naught.

These men would show no compassion when they found Luca lying helpless on the bed. Everything had gone mad and he was at the center of the madness.

Gradually, her eyes adjusted to the watery sunrays lighting the bedchamber. An afternoon wind howled and cold air whistled through the unbolted window. One lone, discarded pillow lay bunched on the floor.

Incredulity stopped Patience from breathing. Open-mouthed, she dragged her gaze to the empty bed. Luca had vanished.

Marko released his grip. "Where is he?"

She heard his voice from a long way off. Strange. She never swooned, but her knees shook, her ears buzzed, her blood surged. She groped the top of the wardrobe, sweeping her late husband's medicine vials to the floor. She knew she was falling, heard the shattering of glass around her. Her thoughts swirled white, then black, shouting far-off denials.

Luca had quit the bedchamber.

Impossible.

CHAPTER FIVE

*P*atience forced her eyelids open, licked her cracked lips, and stared up at Marko.

He wrested her from the oak floor. She stumbled and landed against the wall.

He threw the draperies open and the window wide, then leaned over the ledge. "Indeed, 'tis a cold month to keep your window unbolted, little lady."

If Marko spotted Luca's body far below, he gave no sign. He stood motionless and grappled the windowsill. After an eternity, he whistled a frustrated curse through his teeth, slammed the window closed, and swerved round.

To hide her trembling, Patience stooped to brush pieces of broken vials to the side of the room. Could Luca have crept out the window in his condition? Gypsies were notorious for their spells and curses, but even Luca couldn't get dressed, leap out the window, and float into the forest on empty air. He could hardly move, let alone walk.

Or could he?

Her gaze flitted to the half-open doorway and her heart plummeted. Nanosh and the other three Gypsy men prevented her servants from entering the bedchamber. She looked for Penham, but he wasn't there. Nanosh gave an ugly laugh and lifted a pistol from his overcoat, an apparent toast to her entrapment.

She rose and faced Marko in a worthy imitation of indignation. Her pride didn't permit her to remain hunched over like a servant. "As you can see, no one's here," she said.

Somehow, she withstood the impulse to shove past Marko and scan the fields, hoping, praying, to glimpse Luca vanishing into the woods alongside a hobbling Oliver.

Marko bent and examined a telltale speck of blood on the floor. He lifted his head and assessed her, intent on a truth she prayed wasn't emblazoned on her forehead in screaming scarlet.

He stood. "Who was the knave in this bedchamber?" he demanded.

She pinned a cast of annoyance on her features. "No one."

With a quietness belying their size, the Gypsy

men strode into the bedchamber and encircled her. So casual. So menacing. So dangerous.

She balled her icy hands at her sides and gulped back the fear inundating her.

"A scullery maid cut herself in the kitchen several fortnights ago and used this bedchamber to convalesce," she lied.

"A scullery maid sleeps on a pallet in the basement. I know your grand English ways."

"And I pricked my fingers while sewing in this bedchamber." She spread out her fingers, forever jabbed by needles. "I'd forgotten."

The Gypsy men hung back, no doubt waiting for her to throw herself at Marko's feet and scrawl a confession. Marko tried to scare her by bragging that he could control the lawmakers. But he still needed information about Luca's whereabouts, and she could play a game equally as perilous.

She cast Marko a look of seemly resignation. "I tire of your degrading insults and threats."

Marko shrugged, turned toward his men, and ordered them to block the doorway.

She picked up the silk pillow, along with a piece of slivered glass from the vial. The glass felt sharp, finely honed, and polished. Sharp enough to deter a brutal man and protect herself.

Clutching the vial beneath the pillow, she stood on legs she hoped wouldn't abandon her.

Marko turned from his men and sauntered

nearer her. "I expect payment for stretching my men to exhaustion." His tone lowered, sending an awful sting of warning along her spine.

She kept her lips sealed and hugged the vial and pillow to her chest.

With lightning speed for such a large man, he grabbed her shoulders.

"You filthy monster," she spat, shaking him off and landing a sturdy, knee-jerk to his thigh. "Release me!"

"English witch!" he thundered, whether from astonishment or pain she wasn't sure.

She clinched her hands beneath the pillow and accidentally jabbed her forefinger on the broken vial. A drop of blood seeped through her fingers.

Marko's gaze veered toward the bed. He yanked off his cloak and hurled her onto the bed so violently, the pillow and vial flew from her hands and scattered across the floor.

He eyed the broken vial. "Trying to kill me?" He laughed and fumbled with the ties of her frock.

A sheer black quake ended her final bit of sanity. Bile heaved in her stomach. "I demand you leave," she cried.

"Shut up." He wrapped his hands around her neck, crushing and squeezing. Her eyes closed to blot out his vile breath and mottled features while her teeth chattered and her senses dulled. Pervasive, sickening odors invaded her nostrils. She tried to distance herself, tried to ignore the Gypsy men's snickers by the doorway, tried to hold onto reason. A quiet moan, a woman's gasp, but it couldn't be hers, for she couldn't breathe.

"Marko."

A gruff voice broke through her horror and revulsion. Marko twisted to the side and swore at the large Gypsy man barreling into the bedchamber.

"One of our men spotted footprints leading to the river," the man shouted.

Marko released her and plowed to his feet. "Luca!"

Patience didn't swallow, nor move, nor adjust the ties on her frock.

Marko whipped around, sneering at her while he pulled on his overcoat and knotted his purple sash. A black line of hate ran across his face.

"I'll search these grounds until I find him," Marko said.

She thought she reacted to his threat with a short nod, although she wasn't certain.

She heard Marko and his men drive her servants down the hallway, although she didn't lift her head. She quivered from shock and degradation like the shattered, adolescent girl she'd once been, helpless beneath her smooth-talking cousin.

She rubbed her tear-filled eyes. Then she

climbed off the bed and found herself crouched on the floor, searching blindly for a useless, shattered vial.

CHAPTER SIX

*P*atience attempted to walk the short distance to the bedchamber door, although her body refused. Sharp tremors stilted her movements. With a groan, she sank onto the bed and huddled, her face in her hands. Perhaps she'd passed beyond fear and outrage. After all, unreality surrounded the entire day.

Footsteps rumbled downstairs. Several minutes later, the babbling of servants intermingled with Marko's fading shouts.

The front entry door slammed and all was silent. Wretched, wretched silent.

Shakily, she stood and shuffled to the doorway. She needed to reassure her panicked servants that she was unharmed. Instead, she secured the door, leaned against it, and allowed the door to prop her up. Her hands still trembled. Her lips were still dry. Her feet shambled back to the bed, scattering snow and dirt from the Gypsy men's boots in wayward directions, exposing sprinkles of blood. She floundered to her knees and inspected every drop. Slowly, ever so slowly, she followed the trail of blood to her unused sewing closet adjoining the bedchamber. She rocked to her feet, pushed aside the wooden chair hiding the latch, and wrenched open the closet door. Slivers of dust floated through the air.

Oliver looked up at her.

Patience gaped into the darkened area. How had her dog gotten into the closet?

She blinked once, twice, and tapped her shaky hands on her thighs. She'd thought her dog was dead, swallowed into the forest alongside a floating Luca. However, Oliver's body waggled, all ardent adoration. In four tiny leaps, the dog reached her. Alert, shiny eyes and a rough, wet tongue reassured her that Oliver was very much alive.

Reason fought to reappear. She stroked Oliver's satiny nose and sank her face into his brown fur. "I'm so relieved you're safe." Clutching the dog close, she twirled in a circle, then stopped to view the small closet. Spools of thread overflowed the open lid of a large wardrobe, crammed with sewing supplies.

Odd. She always kept her thread tidy, even in a storage closet she hardly used.

Sighing, she shook her head. "Oh, Mr. Boldor, I think I know where you are." Her voice came like a sing-song. She couldn't remember the last time she spoke to a closet, or sang to a door for that matter, but she was giddy as her nerves eased. The danger with Marko had passed. Her dog was unharmed. Her servants were safe.

She stepped over scraps of colorful fabric and entered the closet. Oliver squirmed from her arms and padded on her heels. She heaved the wardrobe to the side and exposed the hidden door leading to the unused servants' quarters in the attic.

Her laugh of disbelief had an edge. "Mr. Boldor, while you were climbing these stairs to hide, I could've been raped, then killed." She went back into the bedchamber to light a candle, then marched through the sewing closet and clicked open the door leading to the attic. Her dog led her quickly up the stairs.

CHAPTER SEVEN

*P*atience reached the highest step leading to the attic and closed her fingers around the latch. She steeled herself for the sight of Luca. He might be unconscious, his gashes open and bleeding.

If he were alive.

She took a deep breath and flung open the door. A whiff of damp buckskin and green tea filled the air.

Luca was slumped on the floor. Sunlight glinted through a small paned window and the light reflected the shininess of his black hair. Her dog raced ahead and rubbed against Luca's legs, then found a comfortable spot beneath the rafters. She braced one hand on the doorway, the other on the lace at her throat.

"*Kamadiyo.*" His bass voice wove around her as relief turned her legs to silt.

In what appeared a Herculean effort, he pulled himself to sit upright. He was dressed in his breeches and linen shirt, his green sash tied around his waist, his orange scarf folded on his lap.

So engrossed in rushing to him, she didn't stop to consider her question when she burst out, "Mr. Boldor, how did you climb the stairs with your terrible injuries?"

His face grew so brooding she wondered if he'd heard her.

"I was carried," he finally said.

She set down the candle and took a place on the floor beside him. "Carried by whom?"

Derisive amusement touched his lips. "Penham, I believe, after he found me outside."

"You climbed out the bedchamber window?"

"Aye."

His movements were alarmingly slow and blood from his leg seeped through the tight buckskin. She ran a jerky hand across his knee and felt the stickiness. Her stomach twisted in a thick band of apprehension. "And then?"

"And then I don't remember anything except Penham carrying me up the back stairs, through the guest chamber, and to the attic."

"Many people are carried by God during times of

trouble. You were merely carried because of your injuries," she said.

He stretched out his long legs and grimaced. "I'd presumed your attic boasted feathery beds for your servants, but the hard wood floor will have to do."

"This is an unused attic, not a fancy inn."

He laughed, a warm, rich, mellow laugh. "A pity, as I enjoy sliced cottage bread and warm leek stew served on a silver tray in my bedchamber."

She didn't expect his warm laugh nor his wit. He'd seemed so unapproachable. Apparently, his difficult life hadn't vanquished his sense of humor.

"I'm certain your Gypsy tribe furnishes warm meals and feathery beds," she assured.

He shook his head. "You describe your English heaven, not any Romany tribe of mine."

"English and Gypsy heavens are quite similar."

"Gypsies don't go to heaven," he said quietly.

"Of course they do."

Luca's expression darkened, his gaze unwavering. "Did Marko hit your chin?"

The disquiet in his voice was too intense. Patience pulled her gaze from the storminess invading his eyes and focused on her dog sleeping beneath the rafters.

"Aye," she said quietly.

"You shouldn't have suffered on my account."

"The swelling will subside and besides, my injury is naught compared to yours." She eyed the slight bump on the bridge of his nose. Attempting to divert his attention from her chin, she asked, "Did you once break your nose?"

"When I was younger."

"Were you in a brawl?"

"'Tis the injuries done to you"—his voice caught for a moment—"which concern me."

"Mr. Boldor, if we compare injuries, you're the obvious winner."

"This is a contest I prefer neither of us win." Luca tried to rise, appeared to think better of it, and nodded in the direction of the door. "You can assist me down the stairwell."

"Marko is keeping watch. If you want to rest in a lower bedchamber in plain view and place us all at further risk, you'll receive no help from me."

"*Kamadiyo*, you are angry because I ask for assistance?"

She was relieved he was safe. She was relieved he was alive. Nevertheless, with relief came fury at the danger he was in, *they* were in, which he'd brought about by stealing from another tribe.

Her long-suffering composure cracked. "We could've all been killed."

"I will protect you."

She arched a brow. "Really? So far you've done a terrible job. I've protected *you*."

An understanding smile played on his features.

"Someday you'll need my protection and I'll be there. However, for now, I need you."

He *needed* her. Even more alarming, his words made her feel safe and reassured, and that all would be well when his wounds healed.

"A brave, protective Gypsy knight isn't a part of any English folklore I remember," she murmured.

"Gypsies are the bravest knights of all, Lady Blakwell. We have nothing to lose, so we have nothing to fear."

She shook her head. "Not when a blackguard like Marko is around."

Luca gripped the black gossamer fabric gathered at her wrists. His mouth knitted into a frown. "I count the days until I can fight Marko."

"I prefer to solve disputes rationally because wrath leads to cruelty. English people solve their disagreements in a civilized fashion."

Imperceptibly, Luca's grip on her sleeve closed tighter. "Say you won't betray me if Marko returns."

"Of course not." She knew her laugh was sardonic. "And I'll do this in exchange for you bursting into my home."

He sat there, ruggedly handsome, yet vulnerable. "You give me more credit than is due," he said. "I didn't burst into your home, I collapsed at your doorstep. Asking for help isn't the usual way of my life."

She jerked her wrist from his grasp. "Indeed, 'tis

the only course you seem to know—demanding and demanding more of me each time."

Briefly, she closed her eyes. Somewhere in the mayhem of what she'd once called her emotions, it occurred to her that she'd never been so aware of a man. Her tongue clicked the roof of her mouth, eager to inform Luca that men wreaked havoc in an orderly life, and, for a woman, matrimony was a lifetime sentence. All in trade for security, while a man took whatever he pleased, tiny bits and pieces until a woman was no longer whole. She'd never trust a man again.

She opened her eyes to Luca intently watching her, his dark brows drawn together, offering her an understanding nod.

As before, this indescribable man with the hypnotic voice and horrific injuries made her wonder how he was so perceptive.

"Forgive me, sir. I've endured several difficult weeks since my husband's passing," she said. "He was ill, although a violent thrashing ultimately caused his death and the murderer hasn't been found."

She used Luca's rumpled orange scarf to blot the blood staining his breeches and firmly clamped her lips together. At this rate, she'd become a stuttering henwit who forgot her own name by sunset and spouted inane observations regarding her cruel husband and loveless marriage. And she could sprinkle in her stepson's wrongful accusations, all of which were of little importance to a Gypsy fighting for his life.

Luca halted her agitated fingers and forced her to gaze at him.

"In my tribe, 'tis said that I heal quicker than any man. Some say I am a legend."

She couldn't help but smile, assuming he was trying to lighten her mood. That is, until his voice lowered to a conspiratorial whisper.

"And I heal best in a comfortable feather bed," he said.

Cleverly, he was asserting control, conveniently forgetting he required *her* assistance to reach that very same feather bed.

She dropped the blood-stained scarf on his leg. "If you're not satisfied with the Blakwell lodgings, feel free to sprout wings and go elsewhere."

"Perhaps I should fly away like a pigeon."

She plucked the unlit candle beside her and stood. "Godspeed. Have a safe journey."

The space between them grew silent. A shadow of doubt crossed his features. "Lady Blakwell, why did you lead Marko directly to my bedchamber, thinking I was helpless?"

Coupled with his brusque tone, his eyes had turned as cool and dark as a winter stream.

"You interrogate me like I'm a common criminal. You were safely hidden in the attic by the time

Marko and his band of criminals *found* your bed-chamber. You obviously didn't hear what went on because you were outside with Penham, but your friend is impossible to deter."

"Marko's not my friend and I instructed you to lie about my whereabouts."

"Mr. Boldor, I did lie. I didn't want to, but I did, in order to protect you."

"And what does your God say to that kind of lie?" Luca asked.

She faltered for a moment. "Matthew in the New Testament says to show forgiveness and store up treasures in heaven."

They fell into quiet. After a few moments, Luca said softly, "Gypsies don't go to heaven, remember?"

"Of course they do."

She watched his chest rise and fall, the hesitancy and flash of hope in his face before he shook his head. "I'll leave tonight," he said.

She rewarded his objection with feigned indifference. "Stay. Go. I shan't take the blame when you collapse in the middle of the stairwell." Half to herself, she muttered, "Of all the homes in Ipswich, why did you choose this one?"

"Believe me, the home of a *gadje* was the last place I wanted to be."

"I'm almost afraid to ask the meaning of the word."

"A stranger to the Roma. A person who's not one of us."

Their gazes met—his escorted by a grudging smile, edging her to grin. The absurd notion of their conversation and his blunt response surrendered any hope of a serious quarrel.

She laughed outright. "Then we're in complete agreement. You don't want to be here, and I don't want you here. But assuming you're staying, I'll send Penham, my trusted servant, to help you attend to your personal needs in the bath adjacent to the bedchamber below. Then please, please, please return to the attic."

"Aye, but only because you beg so prettily."

With an exasperated shake of her head, she added, "My dog can stay with you. I'll check on my other servants, who surely must think I've forgotten them. Later, I'll send Penham up with a loaf of bread and some nutmeg pudding. In the meantime, don't venture far."

Luca bestowed a mockery of a bow. "For tonight. I'm your submissive patient."

She refused to throw her hands up in frustration, nor deign to reply. Quickly, she quit the attic and descended the stairs. Halfway past her sewing closet, she sniffed and hesitated. Surely the servants hadn't roasted the salted deer without her consent. She'd hoarded the meat for the remaining sparse winter weeks ahead.

She clutched the neckline of her black frock and hastened her steps. Acrid smoke assaulted her nostrils. Dread tingled up her spine. She kept walking, quicker now.

Her disjointed thoughts broke into fragments.

Fire!

The realization wrenched the bottom from her stomach. She dropped the unlit candle, leaving it in pieces on the floor. Her legs raced of their own accord. Reaching the guest bedchamber, she ran to the window and wrenched it open.

Her gasp of shock swept the rooftops. A cloud of smoky blackness blew perilously near the house. Her servants scurried through the snow covered grounds toward the stables.

Patience curled her fingers around the windowpane. Her first cry of panicked denial closed her throat. She dashed through the bedchamber and descended the stairs two at a time. As her feet touched the bottom stair, a low groan told her to glance back.

At the top of the stairs, Luca gripped the balustrade and locked his gaze with hers.

"Why are you running?" he asked.

She tried, but the answer wouldn't come. She was too afraid.

CHAPTER EIGHT

*P*atience allowed Luca's question to hover in the stairway between them.

She reached the entry and Penham was upon her, his arms gesturing wildly. "My lady, the Gypsies set fire to an abandoned stable. Marko shouted that he wanted gold coins for his trouble and that he'd return."

She hardly heard her butler. She nabbed her wool pelisse and bonnet by the door, stepped into her overshoes, and pulled on her gloves. She hurried outside, doubling her strides.

"When did the fire begin?" she asked.

"A short while ago. I crept to the drawing room window, saw Marko torch the stable roof, and heard his threats. The stable boys doused the blaze," Penham said.

"Marko lit the fire to frighten us." She shaded her eyes from the late afternoon sun and peered through the steeple of her hands. A vaporous stream of smoke thickened the sky. A dozen geese flapped their wings, walking and honking across the lawn, their slickly rounded bodies herded together in an effort to escape the confusion.

She headed nearer the smoldering stable. Several yards away, heat forced her footsteps to flag and she blinked and wiped her stinging eyes. In the smudged air, a myriad of servants heaved buckets of water into the dying embers of the burned down stable. Digby mopped the cinders from his forehead and considered her with chilled features.

Lifting her chin, she ignored Digby and asked Penham, "Is anyone injured?"

"Nay, my lady."

"Thank the good Lord for keeping everyone safe." To be heard above the din of splashing water and panicked shouts, she spoke in a loud, calm voice and addressed her servants. "The fire caused little damage and we English don't scare easily." She pushed closer. "I'm confident the Gypsy men are gone."

Her reassurances rang in the scorched air, reassurances even she, the one uttering them, didn't accept as true.

Apparently intent on reading her thoughts,

Penham chimed, "Although I fear they'll soon return."

The best response to an alarming statement was no response at all. Saying nothing, Patience regarded a fat hedgehog prowling through the bushes.

Another servant, a young housemaid, called out in a voice as earsplitting as the Ipswich town crier. "Lady Blakwell, where's the injured Gypsy man you took in this morn?"

Patience fingered the fox fur trim at the neckline of her pelisse. Her overshoes sloshed in puddles of snow, and she walked four more paces before coming to a standstill.

Shouting back 'What Gypsy man?' would hardly do. She treated her servants with respect and answered their questions honestly, although the direction of this question was unacceptable. She couldn't tell this housemaid the truth because the housemaid was loyal to Patience's stepson, Crispin.

Patience whirled to the young housemaid and planted her hands on her hips. "The Gypsy man departed. His injuries weren't as severe as I thought and I sent him on his way."

She glanced at Penham. He scuffed the charred ashes in the snow with the toe of his boot and wouldn't meet her gaze.

Patience shook her head. All she did since meeting Luca was lie for him.

She walked over to Penham. With a good-natured smile, she whispered, "I'm thankful for your allegiance."

"'Tis my pleasure, my lady." Penham met her smile with a slow, toothless grin, reminding her that he was an elderly servant, in service to her for many years, and could keep a secret.

~

For the next several hours, Patience performed her role as dowager countess to a fault.

Admirably. Calmly. Efficiently. Nonetheless, she glanced up the stairwell each time she passed, imagining a pale and weak Luca standing there.

When a supper of capon, beets, and a small salad ended at seven o'clock, Amelia, Patience's lady's maid, flung open the entry door. With a flourish, she deposited her traveling trunk in the hall.

"Here I am," Amelia declared, as if she were the Regent King of England waiting for his subjects to applaud, rather than a servant to a soon-to-be destitute dowager countess. Amelia hung her pelisse by the doorway, shook her black muslin skirt, and spread open her ample arms. "I returned a day earlier than planned. From the looks of the rubble in the field, I'm back just on time." She frowned. "My lady, your lip is swollen and your chin is bruised."

Patience rushed to her maid's side and extended

Amelia a sincere hug of affection. She regarded Amelia as her only family, her personal lady's maid. Neither young nor French, as was the custom, Amelia was old and proper and English. Opinionated, aye, but kind-hearted and faithful in her walk with the Lord.

"'Tis nothing," Patience said. "How fares your uncle in Bucklesham?"

"He's as tight as a drum, foxed as usual, and refused to provide so much as a spare shilling to help you."

"My dearest maid, thank you for trying to help."

"Can you contact your cousin, Faith, in Whitehaven to help?" Amelia asked. "She and her older sister and brother are said to live prosperously."

"I haven't corresponded with them in years, and heard there was a scandal in their family recently. They never answer my letters."

Amelia's voice fell to a whisper. "Surely your stepson cannot charge you with such a terrible sin as murder without proof, my lady?"

"I have faith that my stepson will eventually give up this nonsense. I was a devoted wife to my late husband and no one can claim otherwise."

Amelia shot a look around the empty hall. "You endured more cruelty than any young woman should bear in one lifetime."

Heat crawled up Patience's cheeks. She stepped

back. "You knew? What my husband did? When we were alone?" The humiliating intimacies increased tenfold by the knowledge that her maid had been aware of what had happened. Every night of Patience's loveless marriage she'd breathed the same vinegary sourness on her late husband's sweat-stained pillow.

She shivered and wrapped her arms around herself. She could still feel his gold rings bearing down on her shoulders.

"Most of the servants knew that Lord Blakwell was a vile man." Amelia extracted a white, embroidered linen handkerchief from her sleeve and dabbed at her eyes. Then she stuffed her handkerchief in her bodice and glanced at the door. "Smoke lingers in the fields. Servants are creeping about and whispering of an injured Gypsy disappearing out the window." Amelia's gaze quickened to the housemaids entering the dining room and clearing the dinner dishes, wiping their hands on their white, ruffled aprons. They set hazelnuts, grapes, and walnuts in a silver bowl on a mahogany side table.

"Did I miss the meal?" Amelia asked.

"Before you eat," Patience said, "I must speak with you in private first." Effectively silencing her maid's habit to prattle on without a breath, she guided Amelia to the drawing room. They settled on a settee near the bay window and pianoforte. Patience kept a firm watch to ensure no servants wandered near.

"Gypsies attacked this morn and set fire to an abandoned stable," she said.

Amelia yanked the handkerchief from her bodice and clapped it to her lips. Her eyes widened like two hazel orbs. "I heard tales of a tribe of Gypsies camped by the river near Ipswich. Why would they come to your dower house? We're far removed here in the country."

"These particular Gypsies seek a man."

"Gypsies roam all the time, and with all that wandering, they shouldn't be surprised to lose a man every so often."

Patience extracted the handkerchief from her maid's hand and waved it like a matador to attract her attention. "They're desperately serious to find him."

"Desperate Gypsies steal and pillage." Amelia's amiable face changed from one of worry to one reddened with conviction. "We should notify the law, the constable, the Prince Regent!"

She placed the handkerchief back in Amelia's hands.

"No law is forceful enough to outmaneuver a cold-blooded man like Marko. He and his tribe intended to kill the man they were seeking, as well as anyone who kept him hidden."

"Thank our gracious God this isn't our concern."

Patience focused on Amelia's adamant tilt of her head and the silver wisps of hair escaping from her mob cap. Like Penham, Patience knew she could trust Amelia. Both servants were with her before she'd married her husband, whereas the other servants had been hired afterward by her husband.

Patience squeezed Amelia's hands to soften the next bit of information. "The Gypsy man they seek is convalescing in our attic. I hid him there."

Amelia's handkerchief slipped silently to the floor.

Fearing she'd reduced her maid to speechlessness, a state she'd never seen her in before, Patience relied on Amelia's Christian spirit to overcome her objections.

"He's severely injured and in pain," Patience said. "I need your help to care for him properly and secretly. Within a fortnight, he'll be mended and on his way."

Amelia's brows puckered.

Patience stood before her maid voiced any protests. "Come and meet him."

～

A reassuring peek in Luca's empty bedchamber prompted Patience's heart to skip in relief.

He'd actually listened to her advice. With a half-smile, she tugged Amelia through the sewing closet and up the stairs to the attic.

Patience was aware of him before she saw him. He dozed in a corner beneath the eaves, his stained orange scarf draped around him. His face, like bronzed satin, absorbed the winks of moonlight peeking through the tiny, paned window. The muscles in his arms bunched as he leaned on one elbow. His long legs sprawled lengthwise, his worn leather boots set haphazardly beside him.

Patience latched the attic door shut without a sound.

He jerked up. Quicker than a panther, he unsheathed a dagger from his boot and raised the shiny blade.

Amelia shrieked.

Patience stepped in front of the maid. "Mr. Boldor, what are you doing?"

Slowly, he lowered his hand. His wrist shook. He was still so weak.

He sat heavily against the wall and frowned. "'Tis a habit to always be on guard for an unwelcome visitor."

"I live here, remember? And whom did you expect—a night watchman? Put the dagger away." Patience extended her hand. "Better yet, give it to me."

"This I cannot do." He sheathed the dagger and

slipped it into his boot. His well-muscled body, though injured, conveyed authority, like the fighter he surely was. A life spent living outdoors had hard-edged his features and creased his forehead into tiny lines.

"I trust the fire from earlier this afternoon was doused?" he asked.

"Aye, although the stable is reduced to ashes. Marko must have a brother named Hades."

She expected Luca to smile at her jest. He didn't.

"When I'm strong, I'll right the injustices done to you today," he said solemnly.

"Please, no violence. Thank the good Lord no one was harmed."

"If it were not for my injuries I would have—"

"You would've jeopardized everyone on the Blakwell estate if you'd stormed onto the fields with a bucket of water in your hands," Patience said.

He smiled, and his jaw lost some of its stiffness. He glanced in Amelia's direction, as if he'd noticed her for the first time.

"Who's she?"

"My personal maid, Amelia. She's a very patient caregiver."

Ignoring Amelia entirely, Luca stared at Patience, his black eyebrows in two upraised arches. "You will not care for me, *kamadiyo*? Do you leave all the difficult tasks to servants?" His voice matched his expression, both bland, as if his opinion of her had lessened.

She prickled. "I sewed your wounds and washed your gashes, remember? And tended to you since you've arrived. You're the one who should be chastised. Amelia is a trusted servant and most compassionate."

Never at a loss for words before, Patience's indignant maid stood surprisingly thunderstruck. Indelicately, the maid coughed several times into her handkerchief while blasting glower after glower at Luca as she waddled toward him.

Patience's dog cocked his head and considered Amelia's coughing spasm with a lid twitch.

Luca bestowed on her maid the most charismatic smile Patience had ever seen. "My lovely Amelia, you woke Lady Blakwell's dog, if not the entire household, with your raspy cough," he said. "Consider downing a generous cup or two of stinging nettles... to loosen the cough."

Her maid rent him a critical glare. "Mr. Gypsy, if you're such an expert on sickness, then you can easily look after yourself." Apparently reunited with her voice, she added, "Because I refuse to attend to a dagger-wielding savage!"

Patience closed her eyes and hoped, when she opened them, that Luca might have dozed off, or Amelia might have disappeared. She opened her eyes to find Amelia with her mouth open in poised position, and Luca very much awake.

Meeting Patience's gaze, his mouth lifted so faintly she wondered if the smile was intentional.

"Aye. I see what you mean." His shoulders seemed to shake in silent laughter. "Your maid is most compassionate."

CHAPTER NINE

Fortunately, Patience's stepson, Crispin, lived in London, and her handful of servants, save for Penham and Amelia, didn't know that she hid a Gypsy in the attic. The servants went about their daily duties, then returned to the servants' bedrooms in the basement. Several had worked at the Blakwell house for less than a year, which was typical because servants were fluid. They rose early, stopping when Patience awoke, then completed their tasks in the evening. They were expected to remain out of sight and be silent.

Penham and Amelia slept in separate wings in small garret rooms in the attic. They were elderly, devoted servants and remained supportive of Patient's decision, providing discreet help in caring for Luca.

Still, Patience was a dowager countess, and she knew that many people would surely disapprove. This reasoning, and the attraction she felt whenever she came within two feet of Luca, kept her well away from the attic.

Amelia settled into the daily routine of tending to him. She brought him plates filled with baked eggs on toast, roasted chicken livers, and boiled ham sprinkled with paprika, proclaiming that all Gypsies liked liberal doses of paprika. On several occasions, she and Penham managed to sneak up a metal hip-bath and fresh water for Luca to bathe.

The days progressed, and Amelia grudgingly muttered that Luca proved a most cooperative patient. For a Gypsy, he never got riled. Furthermore, he was extremely courteous, even though she knew he was in terrible pain whenever she rubbed her special liniment into his raw gashes.

Four days after he'd arrived on Patience's doorstep, Amelia whispered to Patience after dinner that Mr. Boldor would be departing the following morn. In an abrupt and astounding gush of apologies for being unable to see him off, the red-faced maid brandished her ever-present handkerchief and bid Patience to wish him a safe journey.

"I have a midnight meeting on the outskirts of Ipswich," Amelia declared between bites of apple tarte, brushing her frock free of the last bit of crumbs. As she hurried from the dining room, she donned her pelisse and secured the frog fastenings.

Patience blinked in confusion, an empty platter arrested in her hands. "What sort of meeting convenes at midnight?"

White streamers askew from her maid's cap, Amelia bustled into the kitchen and out the pantry door. "A meeting of utmost importance."

Patience peered out the bay window of the drawing room just as Amelia bobbled through the moonlit fields. She towed a large travel bag, her pelisse flailing in the night breeze. She'd declined the use of a driver and carriage, preferring to walk.

Walk? On a cold, dark night? Amelia never walked anywhere during the day, let alone at night. Perhaps she'd planned a meeting with a secret gentleman. Patience accompanied that thought with a negative shake of her head. On more than one occasion, she'd witnessed Amelia vocally lashing a suitor whom she'd deemed below her station. And any wealthy aristocrat above her station wouldn't traipse about Ipswich at midnight.

Patience wandered through the rooms of the house, dawdling in the dining room, feigning interest in imagined particles of dust on the rims of each serving piece. All in a futile effort to keep her hands busy and her wits occupied until she bid Luca farewell.

As evening shadows deepened, the servants finished their chores and retired. At nine o'clock, a housemaid went to Patience's bedchamber to draw the heavy curtains and set a cup of tea on Patience's nightstand. After the housemaid left, Patience hurried to the kitchen and wrapped several green apples and a slab of brown bread in a knapsack. With one last guarded look over her shoulders, she hid the knapsack beneath her paisley shawl and climbed the stairs.

She stopped in her second floor bedchamber to unfasten her mob cap and release her waist-length hair. Comb in hand, she pulled her hair up so tightly her eyes watered, then secured the crown with a plain white ribbon. She sipped her tea and stared at herself in the mirror. Hardly widow-like, her auburn hair curled in ringlets below her shoulders.

She reached the attic stairs with her knapsack and reminded herself of how relieved she'd be when Luca was gone. Amelia's opinion might've wavered, but Patience worried that beneath Luca's rugged appeal was a practiced rogue, a vagabond at best.

But there was another reason why she wanted him gone. There was a connection between them that was unexplainable and disconcerting. Her brain warned avoidance, but a quiet nagging in her heart encouraged her to confront her emotions.

So here she stood, on the top step leading to the attic.

Taking a deep breath, she knocked once on the door and entered.

Luca sat beneath the paned glass attic window with his legs drawn to his chest. He was fully dressed in his linen shirt and buckskin breeches. His worn leather pouch hung at his side. The air smelled of him, dark peppery spices and leather.

He clutched a quill pen and scratched on a piece of paper perched on his knees. When their gazes joined, his eyes reflected a mischievous smile. He raised the quill pen. "You caught me."

"'Tis hardly a crime to hold a pen."

From the questioning look on his face, she assumed he wanted an explanation for her unannounced visit.

"Amelia said you're to depart in the morning," she said. "I came to bid you a safe journey." She eyed the pen inquisitively, then him. "There are no signs of Marko and you look well. Have you given any thought to leaving tonight instead of tomorrow?"

Luca set the quill on the paper and rubbed a thumb across his unshaven chin. "A splendid idea. You shall finally be rid of me."

Patience walked to several stools stacked against the wall and retrieved his cloak and cravat. "You purposely misunderstood me." She came toward him, closing the distance, then lurched back at the resentment leaping from his eyes. He truly was the most proud, overconfident man she'd ever met.

"I worry for your safety," she admitted quietly. "You're not that strong, although I know you're anxious to return to your tribe."

Luca picked up the quill again, scraping ink against paper, thoroughly ignoring her.

Taking his silence as acquiescence, she motioned to the quill. "You have a long journey ahead of you knowing that Marko is skulking about, yet you while away your last hours of safety by sketching?"

Ink against paper. Ink against paper. Scraping. Scratching. Rubbing.

"Mr. Boldor?" She held his cloak out to him. "Are you fit to travel this evening? You'd be better escaping detection at night."

The seconds of silence ticked while she watched his closed expression. He squeezed the tip of the quill and his strokes came swift and firm.

Unhurriedly, he lifted his head. "Where do you imagine I travel, Lady Blakwell?" he asked silkily. "Perhaps a filthy camp by a nameless river?"

"I don't judge you by where or how you live."

His earlier smile faded, the spark in his eyes snuffed out. "You performed your honor-bound deed and saved a poor, homeless beggar. Your conscience should be clear."

"Amelia is a fine caregiver."

"And I heal quickly."

She heard the underlying resentment in his tone, and without understanding why, felt deflated. Under his fixed stare, she shifted his cloak from one arm to the other and fingered a patch of rabbit fur haphazardly sewn on the sleeve.

"I didn't realize Gypsies could write," she said.

A muscle twitched in his jaw. "Do you assume all Roma are illiterate?"

Her breath wedged in her throat and she forced out a 'nay.' "You rummaged through numerous trunks in the attic to search not for a traveling bag, nor a spare blanket for your journey, but a quill pen?" she asked.

"I carry my pen and paper with me."

He carried a quill pen. And paper. And a silver dagger.

A Gypsy, a nomad, a man who wasn't supposed to be able to read, much less write.

She gestured to the paned window. "Why did you move to the other side of the attic? Is the light better?"

He set the quill and paper on the floor. "I refuse to sit facing a portrait of a dead man. 'Tis unsettling." Luca motioned to a dusty painting hung crooked on a far wall.

Lord Bertram Blakwell.

The colors had faded with time, but the crafty blue eyes and distinguished white beard still managed to make her feel afraid and chilled and sick to her stomach.

"I doubt any man, dead or alive, could unsettle you," she said.

"'Tis your late husband."

"How did you know?" she asked.

"I read as well as write. Lord Blakwell's name is clearly etched in the corner of the frame."

Her glance fell to the portrait and back to Luca. In a vigilant attempt to change the subject, she asked the first question springing to her tongue. "Why are you using a quill?"

"Perhaps I'm writing a letter to my tribe to ask how they're faring without my protection. That is, if I can string five words into a sentence." Luca waited a long time before continuing. "In my letter, I'll ask the elders if I should trust you, an Englishwoman, and journey tonight. Or, should I wait until morn as Amelia suggested? Is your eagerness for my departure a deathtrap in disguise?"

Patience dropped his cloak at his feet. "If I wished this, wouldn't I have refused to help you when I first found you in my home? And I didn't mean to belittle you nor your people."

"Perhaps not intentionally."

She heard his irritation. He'd remembered their conversation, despite his pain, despite his feverish moans. And because she'd been preoccupied with tending to him, he'd assumed she'd been disinterested in his ways and his tribe.

"Some Englishmen believe that Gypsies are uneducated. Be assured these are not my beliefs," was all she said.

"The Rom are savages, if I remember correctly."

"Amelia's words," Patience corrected.

"Whereas the English are—what was the word you used—aye, of course. The English are gentlemen."

"Civilized," she said.

Unable to contain her curiosity, she bent to view the paper and her gaze froze midway between awe and incredulity. No black marks were illegibly scrawled. The likeness staring back at her mirrored familiarity and such lovely features that she caught her breath.

"This woman's face is so serene, so life-like."

"'Tis you."

She jerked to her feet and retreated. "Me? I'm not this woman. She's young, perhaps sixteen years old. I'm one and twenty, soundly past the age of a maid, although I recall my sixteenth year clearly." She hesitated, terrible memories roiling through her. "'Tis the year I married Lord Blakwell."

"A young girl betrothed to an old man."

Self-respect made her stand taller. "I had no choice."

"A hard-hearted choice, if we tallied your English ways compared to the Rom. Is marriage to a wealthy old man perfectly respectable for a young English lady?"

"I wed whomever my father chose because my marriage protected the decent name of my parents and ensured their welfare."

Luca's mouth downturned. He shook his head.

"People have sanctioned arranged marriages for centuries," she said.

"An impressive speech, Lady Blakwell, but most ineffective." He pushed to his feet while he tied the green sash around his waist and fetched his cloak and paper off the floor. "And from the dueling swords your pretty eyes flash, shall we consider this conversation a draw?"

"You're not above reproach," she said. "You told a falsehood by allowing me to think you were writing a letter."

"You came to your own conclusions."

She glanced at the paper, at the wide blue eyes of her youth, shining with excitement. "Your sketch isn't a true depiction of me."

"I sketched what I saw. You display such sweet innocence."

Briefly, she closed her eyes. "I'm a widow and anything but innocent. If you wish to compliment me, you do a poor job. In any case, I'm immune to compliments."

He genuinely smiled. "All women enjoy compliments, Lady Blakwell."

"And because I'm a widow, you assume I'm ripe to your trickery and silver tongue."

"I'm a Roma. You describe my specialty."

She shook her head. "No woman in her right mind would ever fancy your flowery words."

He placed one hand to his chest. "You're breaking your patient's heart."

"Better than your leg."

Despite their attempt to make light of his grim situation and imminent departure, the mood sobered and her heart gave a funny lurch.

He came nearer, reminding her of his overpowering height. In one hand he held his cloak and pouch, carelessly thrown over his shoulder. In the other, he clutched the paper. He suppressed a groan when he put weight on his leg, and she grabbed his forearms before he could take another step.

"Mr. Boldor, wait and leave in the morning. I'm sorry that I suggested you leave tonight. Each day you'll grow stronger," she said.

"I'm accustomed to the pain in my leg." With scrupulous politeness, he extended the sketch to her. "Please accept this humble gift for saving my life."

She released her grip, stepped back, and ran a hand along her gown. "I cannot accept a gift so personal."

He cupped her hands and urged the crinkled paper into her palms. "I'm indebted and want to repay you, as 'tis the way of the Rom. Close your fingers around my sketch and say *'nais tuke.'* Thank you."

She couldn't. She wouldn't. She'd be vulnerable if she accepted such a personal gift, and vulnerability frightened her, because she'd become weak and defenseless. She couldn't trust that a man would only want to thank her with a small gift, even if his demeanor and mannerisms were kind and thoughtful. He'd want more.

She rolled the paper between her fingers and shook her head in refusal. "Nay."

"Wrong word and wrong gesture." Luca took her hands and folded them around the paper. "I will not leave until you grant me the favor of accepting my gift."

Perhaps it was his sincerity that kept her fingers gripped around the paper. Or perhaps it was the earnestness in his dark eyes.

"Grant me the favor of accepting my gift. And say '*nais tuke*' in return, *kamadiyo*."

Her gaze drifted to his firm lips. A pale hidden smile reminded her that many women's heartbeats might flutter around him, but she wouldn't permit hers to be one of them.

"*Kamadiyo*," she said quietly. "Your mysterious word with no meaning."

"Aye." The engaging, utterly charming grin he gave triumphed over her misgivings. He knew it would. Just as he knew his voice was so compelling that she'd forget her own name if he kept speaking.

The sketch was a simple gift with neither obligation nor hidden meaning. A gift meant acceptance and appreciation, as wondrous as a new cloth doll had once been at Christmas. She needed to give him nothing in return. He was simply expressing his appreciation.

Clasping the paper, she murmured, "Very well. Thank you."

"*Nais tuke*," he reminded.

"*Nais tuke*."

He dropped his cloak and pouch and gazed at her. "When last I saw you, your lip was swollen from Marko's cruel hand." He lifted his fingers. "May I?"

She nodded. "Aye."

Lightly, he traced her lips. "The swelling is gone."

"Because I heal quickly," she said.

"Then we have much in common." Bending his head, he brushed his lips across hers. She closed her eyes and heard her own sudden intake of breath. *Stop this madness* some part of her implored, but not the part she listened to. Logic reeled. This man was neither a barbarian nor a savage. He was a gifted artist.

"This was not part of our arrangement," he said in an undertone, as if arguing with himself.

He placed his arms around her shoulders, holding her as gently as a precious jewel. Yet memories of her late husband's hands pitiless groping made her jerk back.

Luca dropped his hands. His thumbs moved to

her shoulders, tenderly, carefully, pushing down her panic.

She shook her head. "My life has no room for this."

"Make room." He nestled her close to his chest and her cheeks rubbed against the cool linen of his shirt. Near him, she knew exhilaration and peacefulness, two differing ends of an unbending spectrum.

His clear gaze probed hers. He was seeking something, and, while seeking, he threatened to usurp every secure boundary she'd carefully erected around her heart. And when he tired of her, he'd leave with nary a backward glance.

She leaned her head back and offered an intentionally careless smile. "Have you discovered a new technique to aid your healing? Sketching your caretaker and then kissing her?"

"I believe that you are my true caregiver. The urge to sketch and kiss Amelia never occurred to me."

Her disloyal pulse quickened to triple time. "Amelia mentioned you ate heartily these past few days. You have a large appetite if my empty pantry is any indication."

"Amelia is a veritable chatterbox who never takes a breath," he said dryly. "She doles out an opinion on every subject that ever graced England's shores."

He glanced toward the window and frowned.

Patience slipped from him and reached for the

knapsack. "I brought you a slab of bread and some apples for your journey."

He cast a quick appraisal at the fare, then back at the window. "You were right. I must go tonight. I've stayed too long and I don't belong here. This is an English world." Still frowning, Luca picked up his cloak and swung the pouch over his shoulder. "I'll use the back stairwell. Once I reach the woods, I'll follow the river. Amelia explained the route in excruciating detail and I didn't have the heart to tell her that the Rom have traveled these paths for centuries."

Patience searched his handsome face, now disengaged and preoccupied. He was leaving and the realization hit in a rush. The razor thin stillness was punctuated with no explanations. Effectively, he'd sliced a clean division.

"It's probably better to leave when it's dark, after all. Goodbye, Mr. Boldor."

"Good night, Lady Blakwell. I'll keep watch and listen for information regarding Marko's whereabouts while I travel. If I hear he's headed back here, I'll return. I assure you that you'll be safe." Luca turned on his heels and left her standing in the middle of the attic.

Without preamble, he reached for the latch, then closed the door behind him.

She clutched his sketch in one hand and the knapsack in the other. He'd forgotten the food. She

stared at the door, mindful of the dull ache com-
pressing her chest, the heavy loneliness constricting
her breath.

Wind scoured through the cracks in the rafters,
bringing a whiff of peppery spices. Somewhere outside, footsteps crunched through the snow and a
tree limb snapped. She held the knapsack close and
found her control hidden beneath a choked swallow.
No tears, of course. Only a heavy, nagging ache in
the hollow of her chest. He'd bid her good night as if
nothing significant had occurred between them.
And he'd left with nary a backward glance.

CHAPTER TEN

*L*uca glared in mounting irritation at the tall, broad-shouldered lad in yellow breeches scampering far ahead. He'd discovered Pulko behind a tree almost immediately after departing Lady Blakwell's house.

Normally, Pulko never outran Luca. Now, Luca's leg allowed him no more than a sluggish limp through an icy, moonlit countryside while he trailed a boy half his age.

Pulko wielded a sackful of food and seldom glanced over his shoulder. Before sunrise, he slowed and doubled back across the fields. "I see some tents," he called out. "We're almost home. Hurry."

With each labored step, Luca's thoughts grew stormier, especially when Pulko feigned absorption in the brightening sky instead of Luca's uneven gait.

Luca clamped his teeth together and hoped the throbbing in his leg ceased once he'd reached his familiar tent.

"Have you decided to allow me an extra minute to catch up?" he asked.

The boy peered dully over his shoulder. He heaved his sack to the ground and plopped himself on top. "You cannot help your slowness. You tire easily because of Marko's thrashing."

"Very understanding," Luca said sardonically. He pulled his attention from his discomfort to the questions burning at him throughout their journey. Trying to keep his manner non-critical, he studied Pulko's impish face, the black straggles of Pulko's mustache, and weighed his words. "Why did you reappear at Lady Blakwell's house hours earlier than I expected? Amelia told me you weren't due back until early morn, after she met you by the river with supplies for our tribe."

The boy shrugged. "The tribe required more food. I raided the countess's kitchen pantry one last time."

"By climbing onto the rooftop of her house? I looked out the window and expected to see the sky, not a flash of a blue cloak. The roof is steeply pitched and you could've fallen. If you expect me to commend you, 'twill be for your foolishness, not your daring. And if you expect me to believe you, I'm disappointed you think me such a fool."

Pulko swung his legs down from the sack. "I stood on the roof of Lady Blakwell's house to be sure that Marko wasn't about."

"I don't need a young scoundrel to look out for me. I take care of myself."

"Marko's out for vengeance. He'll find you. 'Tis rumored he's still in Ipswich," Pulko said.

Luca considered Pulko's words. There'd been no sign of Marko, but Lady Blakwell would be vulnerable and in danger if Marko was still sniffing around Ipswich.

He sighed and rubbed his face. His tribe had been waiting several days for his return. They needed to break camp and head for the coast. They'd exhausted their food and supplies, and he couldn't leave them in the hands of young Pulko without checking on them.

He eyed Pulko's mop of dark hair, the heavy, dark brows offset by a roguish grin. Although Pulko's voice had deepened and his chest and arms had filled out within the past year, Luca still considered Pulko a child.

Aloud, Luca said, "We must break camp and journey toward the sea immediately."

Pulko's face brightened. "An excellent idea because the tribe grows tired of Ipswich and Portman's meadow. The farmers are wary of us and there's little left to pilfer. The elders say you lead us back to Ipswich every year because your English father might still live here. Why don't you confront him and tell him who you are?"

"My father's a cruel man. He deserted me and my mother and he's dead to me." The words stung as Luca uttered them. He released a deep breath. His father wasn't a part of his life anymore and Luca had been raised by a kind, caring tribe, which was more than enough for any man.

From sheer habit, Luca scanned the forest bordering the riverbank, looking for enemy Rom or English intent on harming Gypsies. Daylight spilled across the field, glistening the frost to shiny white dust and showing no foreign footprints.

Luca crooked his index finger and beckoned Pulko nearer. "So then, why were you spying on me while I bid goodbye to Lady Blakwell?"

The boy rose taller, almost to the height of Luca's shoulders. "We depend on you, and you stayed in the Englishwoman's house far too many days."

"I was recuperating, and this matter isn't for you to decide."

"You were with a *gadje,* a stranger. *Gadje Gadjensa, Rom Romensa. Gadje* should stay with *Gadje, Rom* with *Rom.*"

"My mother once said that I resembled my English father more than a Rom." Luca's words were disjointed, as if stuck in another place.

"Some of the elders said that she spoke highly of your father," Pulko said.

Something, Luca added to himself, he never intended to do. The familiar aloofness closed his heart and a long-forgotten memory flicked across his mind. His beautiful, dark-haired mother standing near their tent, cupping a tiny finch in her hand, laughing softly when the bird sang. Remembering his mother added to his loathing for the absent nobleman who'd used her, then cast her and their young son off when he grew disinterested. She'd died heartbroken and alone.

And then there were whispers of Luca's twin brother, a baby who'd died at birth. Some tribesmen had mentioned the baby's death was a result of Luca being born too strong and rebellious, taking all the air in his mother's womb, whereas his brother was born stillborn, too frail to survive.

Quelling the ever-present guilt, Luca nodded curtly at Pulko. "Lady Blakwell's maid, Amelia, is a *gadje*. You seemed to get along well with her."

"She gave me food. I didn't venture too close, though, or she would've contaminated me." Pulko lowered his voice to a conspiratorial whisper. "I saw you kiss Lady Blakwell. You're definitely contaminated."

"So you *were* spying on me. When you grow older, you'll want to kiss a woman, especially a beautiful woman."

Pulko reached into the sack, pulled off a fistful of bread, and stuffed it in his mouth. "Girls are needy nuisances."

"I taught you well, but some women are virtuous and brave."

Like Lady Blakwell. She'd deterred Marko single-handedly. A rare woman indeed, she'd managed to squeeze Luca's cynical heart with an affection he hadn't known existed. She spoke of Christian ways, of kindness, and consideration, and a true caring for others.

He closed his eyes to focus on her skeptical smile when he'd told her she was sweet and innocent.

'I'm a widow and anything but innocent. If you wish to compliment me, you do a poor job.'

With a noiseless groan, he opened his eyes. Better to expose his heart to his worst enemy than a prim and proper English noblewoman. No matter how kind she was, the English he'd known proved cruel and uncaring.

Luca and Pulko resumed their pace, their strides taking them to the top of the clearing. Hardly visible through the blackthorn trees, a scattering of recognizable *benders*, tents, came into view, along with an assortment of dilapidated brown carts and three-wheeled wagons.

Luca stamped the snow off his boots and stood silent. He cupped his hands and blew into his palms to warm them. There was much to do—greet the elders, ensure everyone had food, and then prepare for the tribe's departure. Afterward, when his tribesmen were settled around a sputtering, smoky campfire, he'd mention Lady Blakwell's courage and kindness.

His mind flashed to how she'd looked before he'd quit the attic—grappling a knapsack for him in one hand, which his pride had refused to accept—and his sketch of her in the other. He visualized her high, wide cheekbones overshadowed by glorious sapphire eyes and curly auburn hair.

He owed her his life, although he'd never see her again. He had a tribe to care for, she had an English society to live in.

Wending his way into camp, he yanked off his orange scarf and waved it high. Diverted by lively howls of delight, he breathed in whiffs of singed game, undiluted wine, and finely ground hot pepper. Amidst welcoming handshakes and relieved embraces, utterances of '*Sar shan,*' and 'how are you', his grin overtook his face.

He was needed. He was where he belonged. He was home.

CHAPTER ELEVEN

*S*tanding near the entryway to his *bender*, tent, Luca shifted and braced for the blast of pain sure to follow. He tried to think of something, anything, to stop the sudden knifelike agony. Only a lovely English woman came to mind, and he focused his thoughts on Patience's delicate face. Behind her tranquil smile, she was a lady with more pluck and honor than a man four times her size. Her valor for saving his life had nearly cost her own.

When he'd kissed her, her formalness had fallen away. She'd tried to suppress her feelings under light quips and lighter banter, despite her lingering smile and softly parted lips.

But now he was back with his needy tribe.

And Marko was angrily stalking about somewhere.

And Patience was alone and unguarded.

Luca's left knee buckled, and he struggled to adjust his weight to his right leg. He leaned heavily on the walking stick he'd devised out of an oak tree branch to keep the pressure off his bad knee. Fourteen days and nights of continuous dampness had prevented his injuries from healing properly.

He viewed the early streaks of daylight, the flicker of intermittent campfires. He sniffed appreciatively, although the tang of moist earth and cloves and wood smoke did little to raise his mood.

Wintry rain coated the branches of blackthorn trees and a faint tinkling of sleet hit the ground. Waterlogged, his tribe's camp stood draped in a soggy mist. Squeaky wagon wheels groaned deeper into a thick sludge of mud and snow. Every day that passed, each drop of icy rain that fell, made attempts to break camp more and more difficult. He glanced at the crude stable and the two dapple-gray horses Pulko had stolen several months earlier. The old horses would have a wretched time lugging the wagons if the sleet and rain continued.

When their tribe left a place, they had nowhere in mind, no place to walk, no place to push their carts. But still they'd walk, still they'd push. And in each new village, Luca hoped his heart would find a home, that this was the place he truly belonged. He winced, a slight heaviness in his stomach. Would his feelings of restlessness never cease?

A fierce split of thunder broke his musings in half, and he shook his head at his inability to control the weather, his tribe's inability to leave, and the vulnerable position Lady Blakwell was placed in on his account.

He closed the flap of his tent and retrieved his cloak and pouch, then limped through a clump of slick leaves to Pulko's *bender*. For balance, Luca depended more and more on his walking stick. He hated the wretched thing.

As Luca approached, Pulko poked his head from the opening of his canvas tent. "Are we leaving for Colchester today?"

"Unfortunately, the miserable weather fails to cooperate."

The canvas flapped open and Pulko's mother, Fabiana, emerged. At a height close to Luca's, she faced him eye to eye. The center of her black gaze gleamed like a new pair of leather boots.

"How's your leg?" she asked.

There was little use in lying to a woman who knew him better than a son.

"The pain has worsened," he admitted. Intent on the icy rain cooling his overheated flesh, he raised his cloak, and showed them his wound. He'd slit the leg of his breeches so he could roll up the pant leg.

"*Prikaza.* Your luck is bad because your wound is taking so long to heal, although the stitching looks neat and clean." Fabiana knotted her bright pink shawl around her shoulders and clucked. "I'm impressed at the good care you got from a *mahrime*, an unclean and impure English woman."

"She gave me excellent care." Luca clarified as he draped his ragged woolen cloak closer about himself. He glanced toward Fabiana's tent. "Perhaps a cup of hot tea will help ease the soreness in my leg."

"No tea, only water from the stream. You're not in a rich English manor anymore with a cook and steward." With a hmph, Fabiana reentered her *bender* and poured the water from a jug, handing the cup to Luca.

Luca smiled as he accepted. He drank, then lowered the cup, circling the rim with his fingers. He glimpsed one of the elderly Rom's campfire through a patch of woods and walked toward it, crossing a stream and rotted wooden fence.

Several large open wagons piled with clothes and trinkets stood beneath a covering of trees. Shaky carts missing several wheels, creaked with the wind. Two thin, dark-eyed children swung upside down on a crude hammock tied to the trees. They smiled and waved as he passed. He bent and playfully mussed their hair, then reached in his cloak and offered them an apple to share.

A group of older women danced on a cracked barn door that they'd used for a floor, swaying their large hips in time to rattling tambourines and ascending modes.

Four of the elders seated around the campfire studied Luca with narrowed eyes as he approached. The gaiety ceased. The music stopped. All the tribesmen, Luca's tribesmen, were wary of his association with Lady Blakwell, the Englishwoman, despite the fact that she'd helped him.

One of the elderly men, Besnik, stood as Luca approached. His worn-down face boasted shriveled cheeks and no brows. "Pulko said we're to break camp and leave Portman's meadow."

"As soon as the weather cooperates," Luca replied. "Our tribe will find food by the sea."

"Will living by the sea keep us safe from Marko's men who want vengeance, or from the English who hate us?" Besnik pressed. "Or shall we assume the English are now our friends?"

A lean dog sniffed at Luca's heels as he knelt by the campfire and warmed his hands. Flimsy tents rocked in the slight breeze, as if sensing his tribe's unrest.

"Lady Blakwell showed me that not all English are as cruel as I believed," he said.

The men didn't seem persuaded. Their faces remained impassive. Silently, they shared a jug of brandy and wiped their mouths on their sleeves after each guzzle.

Luca stood. "May I join you?"

They shrugged and made room for him on a spongy log.

Luca refused the brandy jug as it was refilled and passed, smiling politely. Though few in number, these were his people, and they needed him as their leader. Proud, enterprising, and self-sufficient, they worked at whatever tasks were available to them, selling fruit and mending bellows, weaving baskets and harvesting crops.

His thoughts moved to Lady Blakwell. Aye, she employed servants, yet he worried for her safety. She couldn't protect herself against the likes of Marko and his men.

He sighed, deeply. He was only one man and couldn't be in two places at the same time.

He belonged here in the forest by a campfire, not in her upper-class, stiff English dining room. Besides, she deserved an upright, honest, and wealthy Englishman as her protector, not a dark-colored thief.

He sat quiet, reflecting. He and Patience were so different. He'd lied his way through life in order to ensure his tribe didn't starve. What would she think if she knew his past, the brawls too numerous to count, the stolen chickens numbering in the hundreds, the clothes and jewelry and coins pilfered from purses of unsuspecting noblemen?

Misha, one of the crinkly bearded elders, brought Luca back to the present with his bellowing voice. "Nadya is marrying a lord of one of the richer tribes. She's through dallying with Marko, and with you, too, apparently."

"My tryst with Nadya ended a long time ago," Luca clarified. "I wish her much happiness."

"She'll marry the rich lord for his money." Misha took another swill of brandy.

Gazing at the campfire, Luca said, "Nadya's parents are both dead. What male relative will speak for her at her wedding?"

"Her older cousin. If both sides agree, then we'll witness her betrothal ceremony, the *pliashka*," Misha replied.

Luca grinned. "I haven't been gone a decade, Misha. I know what a *pliashka* is."

The insistent clip of horses' hooves stopped Luca from continuing. He raised a forefinger to his lips and stood without making a sound. "Ssh. Someone's coming."

CHAPTER TWELVE

"Highwaymen," Misha came to his feet alongside Luca. "They're in the wrong place. There's nothing to rob here."

Before Luca could reply, a stocky, imposing man wearing a black cloak, ambled across the stream in the direction of the small group. The women on the barn door screamed and dashed for their tents. All the elders except for Misha fled.

Another hulking man, even larger, emerged from the forest, his movements measured and deliberate, his cold, flinty gaze pointed at Luca.

Luca's heart pounded in double time. He fingered the sheath of his dagger concealed in his tall, brown boot. "What do you want?" He kept his tone calm as he scanned the forest for more attackers.

"We were told there were Gypsies camping in this area," the stocky man said.

"Now that you've seen us, you can move on," Luca said.

He glanced toward the children on the hammock and nodded to one of the women. She grabbed the children and ushered them to the fringe of the camp.

"Where's this dog's collar?" the stocky man asked, jerking his chin towards the lean dog. He snorted. "You're all dogs. Where are all your collars?"

Luca stiffened. The air had turned predatory in a blink. The insults he'd heard so many times before, he was tired of them, tired of protecting his people, good people, from bad English men.

The stocky man sauntered closer to the campfire where Luca and Misha stood. "You're damaging the grass beneath the snow."

Luca swallowed and focused on holding his temper in rein. "Keep your distance," he gritted. Legs a foot apart, shoulders rigid, his stance shifted to one trained for fighting. If these men were waiting to see him or any of his tribesmen fall, they'd be sadly mistaken.

Luca glanced at the tents and the numerous pairs of black eyes peering from the openings.

Then his gaze locked on a set of ham like fists.

"Do you have anything of worth that you've

stolen?" The other, bulky man regarded Misha. "Gold coins can aid us in keeping yer secret of encroaching on other people's land and owning dogs without collars."

"This is forest land and belongs to no one," Luca said before Misha could speak. "When the weather breaks, we'll leave peacefully."

The stocky man grabbed a branch from the ground and snapped it at Luca. "We can find you dirty Gypsies anywhere because of yer smell."

Luca reached for his knife. Nay. He didn't want to fight these men. He didn't want to carry the guilt, the knowledge that what he did was wrong. The bulky Englishman skulked closer, together a vibrating haze of hostile mouths and bloodless eyes.

Luca grasped the handle of his dagger. He had no choice, because the tribe needed to be protected. "Don't do anything you'll be sorry for," Luca warned.

"The law wants to be rid of Gypsies littering our land, moving around so quick to hide your criminal activities."

"Leave us alone," Misha shouted.

The stocky man lunged at Misha. "Stay out of this, old man."

Misha surged forward and rammed into the stocky man's beefy chest. The man crumpled and a rickety tent collapsed beneath them both.

Without warning, the other, bulky man leapt forward and struck Luca in the groin, knocking Luca to his knees. Luca jerked in nauseating pain and let go of the dagger. Fury at his own foolishness for not being on guard pushed him to his feet. He risked a glance behind to be sure the tribe was safe. The saucer-eyed faces of the elders stared back at him.

The hulking man struck a heavy jab into Luca's chest. He threw Luca back to the ground, his heavy boot landing on Luca's leg.

"Worthless Gypsy," he tsked, eyeing Luca with brutal disinterest. "Where are all the men from your tribe? Are they cowards like you?"

Luca rolled to the side and willed himself to his feet. Every muscle on edge, he rubbed his split lips, wringing a silent rasp from his throat. There were two men. Both had attacked. If there were any more, he wouldn't be able to defend the tribe.

With an inhuman roar from the stocky man, a sharp-edged pair of steel boots lifted and smashed into Luca's right thigh. Luca's legs caved. Distorted shouts rumbled above him.

Bile hardened in his throat. He braced for the fiery stab of a jagged knife or the ball of a pistol shot into his ribs. He couldn't make sense of his mangled thoughts.

"My friend told you to leave." Through the cacophony of English jeers and curses, Pulko's deep voice rose above the din with a sharpness that Luca had never heard before.

Slowly, Luca raised his head. Pulko stood solemn,

aiming a pistol directly at the stocky Englishman. In unison, the two Englishmen raised their hands in surrender.

"Don't say a word," Pulko cautioned. "Just go."

The men didn't nod, didn't acknowledge that they'd heard Pulko. They scurried through the underbrush and into the forest. Soon the sound of horses' hooves clipped rapidly away.

Sprawled on the wet ground, Luca kept his eyes open, aware of the pain mushrooming in his skull. His leaden leg throbbed. Slush and dirt invaded his nostrils. A loud groan pierced the silence. His own damn, helpless voice. He glided his fingers down his cloak for the dagger in his boot, to be sure it hadn't been taken in the struggle.

Squeezing his eyes shut to control the pain, he staggered to his feet. He squinted through the tree limbs to focus on Pulko, but his vision wouldn't cooperate. Overhead, a murky stream of stars obscured the twilight.

"Where did you get the pistol?" he managed.

"I stole it," Pulko replied evenly.

Luca braced both hands on his knees. A penetrating jolt of agony shot up his leg, humbling him. Fog clouded his brain, but one message from the English screamed in his ears.

Be gone from England. Gypsies don't belong here.

CHAPTER THIRTEEN

Two more weeks passed. Two more weeks of rain and dreariness and dread of being attacked again. Adding to the dread, Pulko mentioned that Marko had been spotted at the outskirts of Lady Blakwell's property.

Luca felt his muscles tense. Arms folded across his chest, he peered at the hills surrounding the camp. He waited a minute to speak, trying to best phrase his thoughts to Pulko and Fabiana, who stood nearby.

"I'm returning to Lady Blakwell's estate for a visit because I don't want her vulnerable and in danger from Marko," he said.

In truth, he couldn't stop himself from going back to see her.

"What about us?" Fabiana asked.

"Pulko can begin leading the tribe to Colchester when the weather breaks and I'll join you shortly."

Fabiana's thin eyebrows formed two distinct arcs. She opened her mouth, but Luca raised his hand to continue. "I cannot lead our tribe wisely when my senses are slowed by continuous pain. Lady Blakwell's maid had applied a special liniment made from a white powder that relieved the throbbing in my leg. I should've brought the liniment with me when I departed, but I didn't."

"A Roma's liniments are more powerful than any English."

Luca leaned toward Fabiana. "This particular liniment eased my discomfort. Since the English's recent attack, my leg aches worse than ever."

Pulko held out his arms to push Luca and his mother apart. "You're leaving because of what I told you about Marko being spotted near Lady Blakwell's estate."

"'Tis only a short visit," Luca said.

Fabiana fingered a cord of tinkling bells tied to her bodice. The inky pouches beneath her eyes swelled as her gaze narrowed. "Pulko's too young to be left alone and lead the tribe."

Pulko put his large hands on his hips. "I'm not too young."

Luca took in the muscles in Pulko's arms. Pulko seemed to grow stronger with each passing day.

Noncommittal, Luca accorded his dripping

bender another glance. The hazel twigs holding up the roof looked in danger of caving. A film of green mold grew at an astounding rate up the side of the canvas.

He directed his gaze to Pulko. "When you depart, follow the cattle path along the coast and travel south towards Colchester where the weather is warmer. If you need me for any reason, you can find me at Lady Blakwell's."

Fabiana grabbed Luca's cloak. "Don't let your impulsive nature steer you on another disastrous course. Less than three sennights ago, you allowed hunger and desperation to cloud your judgment. The spirits were furious as a result, you could've lost your leg, and Nadya was also brutally beaten. Nevertheless, you tempt fate again for a woman. An English noblewoman."

She spit at the ground.

"'Tis perilous for Lady Blakwell to be alone," Luca said. "She's defenseless."

Luca and Fabiana scowled at each other, two stubborn Roma from different ages, quarreling beneath a soaked, torn canopy. "I'd appreciate a pair of Pulko's woolen hose, if you can spare them."

Fabiana retied her peacock blue scarf around her head and gave the ends an infuriated yank, then reached into her tent and slipped Luca the hose. "Be careful," she said.

"Aye. Thank you." He accepted the hose,

scooped his pouch from the ground, and snatched his walking stick.

Luca walked to Besnik sitting near his tent. "Can I borrow my hawking gloves?" he asked.

"Going hawking, are ye? Coming round to the English gentry, although they nearly killed us?" The old man's frown went so deep Luca imagined he could fit a shilling in the wrinkles. With a humph, Besnik rubbed his gloved hands together, then wrenched off the gloves and threw them to Luca.

Luca pulled them on, flexing his fingers into the layers of black leather, brushing his thumb against the fine gathering of fringe on the cuff. He admired the painstakingly embroidered initials in gold thread. E.H. The initials certainly weren't his, nor anyone he knew. He shook his head. There was such extraordinary wealth in England, such extraordinary poverty.

"I'll take great care of E.H.'s gloves," Luca replied wryly, then swung toward the woods.

Oddly, the throbbing in his leg subsided with each measured step. Rather than declare his astonishing recovery to Fabiana and Pulko, Luca trudged past the campfires, past the tents, past the crude stable. He headed west, leaving behind his cherished tribesmen and an uncomfortable silence.

∼

*T*wice, Luca considered abandoning his decision to visit Lady Blakwell's estate while leaving his tribe unguarded. He even feared his attraction to her might've blurred his common sense. But he couldn't stop himself from returning. He needed to see her, be with her, regardless of the fact that he could never live a foreign, English life.

Briefly, he closed his eyes and rubbed his forehead, weighing the pros and cons of his decision. He didn't consider himself a hero. He considered himself an ordinary man, trying to accomplish not-so-heroic feats. He felt split in two—trying to guard both her and his tribe.

Aye, she was brave and had more than her share of spirit and mettle, but hidden beyond the façade he detected vulnerability. She possessed neither the ability nor resources to fight off a vengeful Roma lord a second time. Save for Penham and Amelia, her houseful of servants proved eerily inept.

Perhaps Luca could ask Patience to join his tribe, and she could live there safely with him.

He blew out a breath and shook his head. Unfortunately, many in his tribe would wish harm upon her and wouldn't accept her. It was ridiculous to think they could ever share a future together, even if he did have English blood flowing in his veins. Besides, Amelia had told him about Patience's stepson's threatened murder charge. Her stepson would lay charges for sure, and the law would come after Patience.

And why, Luca wondered matter-of-factly, did she bring about this protective urge in him? After more than two decades of hating the English, he, a Romany clothed in rags, was off to an English estate to protect an Englishwoman in a silken black mourning dress while abandoning his tribe in the process.

The afternoon warmed. Lulled by the tap-tap-tap of a steady rain, Luca managed to cover the distance to Lady Blakwell's estate in half the time he expected.

Perhaps she'd missed him when she wasn't occupied with her many responsibilities. Overseeing an estate was complicated, especially for a young widow. He'd never known a beautiful female who could juggle more than a few tasks without dissolving into tears. The dowager countess, a refined Englishwoman, accomplished her challenges with a calmness and devout faith belying her small stature.

He pictured her expression when he arrived at her doorstep. She'd surely rush to him.

The thought made him smile.

At the riverbank bordering her property, he paused to take in the vastness of the estate, the open, barren fields, the fences surrounding them, a wooden bench long abandoned. Etched into a limestone wall was the silhouette of a cross with heavenly creatures floating above with great white wings. His gaze rose from the arched entry to the large chimneys.

The house seemed different now. So welcoming.

He reached the kitchen herb garden a few minutes later and viewed Amelia through the window. She bustled in the kitchen with no other servants about. He rapped on the door and braced himself for the maid's receptive squeal of joy. She'd become an unanticipated friend and ally.

The door swung open. Wide-eyed, Amelia reeled. "Mr. Gypsy, what are you doing here?"

Unconsciously, he massaged his throbbing leg. He set his walking stick on the threshold and retied Pulko's hose around his knee. "'Tis a rumor that Marko's prowling about Ipswich and I won't leave Lady Blakwell vulnerable to danger."

And, he realized, he just hated not seeing her.

He glanced about the pantry and the kitchen beyond, inhaling the warm and welcoming smell of buttery biscuits.

Amelia clasped her hands together, a strained smile on her plump face. "Lady Blakwell isn't here. She's in town, meeting with a solicitor, giving him details about Lord Crispin's murder charge. The solicitor will then hire a barrister to represent her case before a judge. She should return with news of her meeting by later this evening."

"Lady Blakwell is innocent of murder," Luca said.

He thought of their previous conversation when Amelia had tended to him in the attic. Amelia had told him that Patience's evil stepson was coercing her cooperation in the matter of the estate with a threatened murder charge.

"Aye," Amelia said. "However, her stepson is tight with legal types and he'd be able to make the charges stick. In any event, she'll need funds to try and fight this case. Funds, unfortunately, that she doesn't have."

Again, Luca revisited the thought that if it was just a matter of being at the economic mercy of her stepson, Luca could ask her to join his tribe. However, his tribe wouldn't approve, and the law would surely be at her heels.

Despite that thought, his breath came easier as he swung his arms and entered the hallway. He'd see her later that evening, when she returned. Then they could discuss the matter further.

CHAPTER FOURTEEN

*L*uca headed to the attic to hide from the servants.

He'd assumed that Patience would be overjoyed to see him. And she was.

Except that she'd seemed preoccupied and quiet regarding her meeting with the solicitor, stating that the solicitor hadn't been encouraging that she'd win her case. She'd looked tired, and defeated, and Luca had encouraged her to retire early with promises that they'd talk in the morning.

Consequently, Luca had been unable to bring up the subject of her returning to his tribe with him, nor come up with another plan to protect her. And, he hadn't wanted to worry her regarding Marko so he'd said nothing except that he'd returned for her maid's liniment (partly true), and to ensure that Patience was safe.

He'd spent the remainder of the evening, hidden and out of sight, combing the outer fields of her estate. There'd been no signs of Marko nor his men.

Patience and he had both agreed that any moments together were risky and that Luca should stay hidden in the attic. Lord Crispin would charge Patience with scandalous, inappropriate behavior if he'd heard she'd harbored a Gypsy in her home, which could be used against her in his murder accusations.

And if all of this weren't bad enough, Luca's leg pained him worse than ever, although the pain didn't stop him from combing the woods one more time late that evening, searching for an absent Marko.

Instead, Luca met up with a *vurma* who'd told Luca that his tribe had quit their previous camp and had begun traveling along the cattle path en route to Colchester.

"A *vurma* is a Roma woman who keeps track of the Romany tribes and knows where they travel, because Roma have no addresses to speak of," Luca explained patiently to Amelia.

Although the hour was late, Amelia had returned to the attic to tend to him, rolling up his buckskin breeches and examining his wound. The linen cloths around his leg were tacky, the largest gash festering. With a worried frown, she'd admitted that her special liniment was proving ineffective and Luca needed a more powerful cure. Rather than the physician in town that everyone knew, she suggested a barber-surgeon several towns over who was a friend of hers and wouldn't divulge that Luca was hiding out in Lady Blakwell's attic.

This particular man cut hair and shaved beards. And dressed gashes, pried out teeth, and severed limbs from a man's body.

Luca swore he'd never allow a barber who also posed as a surgeon to come anywhere near his leg, or Luca would run the barber out of England, thus shortening the man's diverse trades.

The tension in the attic escalated. Amelia seemed to sense his aggravation and kept a respectable distance.

"I'd like to spend some time with Lady Blakwell before I depart tomorrow," he said.

Amelia assured him that Lady Blakwell would come to the attic to see him.

Luca waited, standing by the attic window and scrutinizing the surrounding fields, searching for any sign of Marko and his men.

He eyed the pallet and rubbed his sore leg. Perhaps he should sleep for a few hours.

~

*L*uca awoke with a start as Amelia clattered in.

"How are you this fine morning?" she asked cheerfully, disregarding the sullen clouds hovering beyond the attic window. Amelia carried a tray laden with roasted pork and a pot of coffee. Luca's stomach railed at the beastly smell of shriveled, overcooked meat.

"What time is it?" Luca stretched the kinks from his muscles on the ridiculously small pallet Patience had provided. His gaze didn't stay centered and he blinked, not knowing where to focus. Amelia's face smudged into two indistinct Amelias, with distorted red features and perpetually crooked knitted shawls.

He chafed his hands across his whiskered chin, feeling quick-tempered and lethargic. "Tell Lady Blakwell I'm returning to my tribe by noon," he said. "Did she visit me last night?"

"Aye, but you slept so soundly she didn't want to wake you." Amelia paused to take a breath. She set the tray beside Luca on a small oak table, knelt on the pallet, and touched his brow. "My word, you're feverish." She raised her eyes upward and whispered a silent prayer.

Then she threw off the assortment of heavy quilts he'd bundled around himself when he'd grown cold during his sleep. His green sash and orange scarf were next, leaving him clad in his wrinkled linen shirt and breeches.

Amelia ran the back of her palm across his cheeks and frowned. "Pulko came by earlier, riding a gray mare that has seen better days. He didn't want to disturb you as your sleep was fitful. He tethered the horse in the fields so as not to be seen by the servants and I provided him with provisions." Amelia smiled reassuringly. "He said he'd circle back within the sennight after the tribe makes camp."

"I'll return to the tribe before then." Luca shook off her hand and fairly growled. "Yesterday, I was unable to hike any farther than the boundary of the woods without tiring, yet Pulko came from near the coast and back in one day."

"He didn't walk as you did, he rode a horse and drove the horse hard. He's a very capable young man, as quick and sure-footed as you'll soon be again."

Luca shifted to ease the numbness. "My tribe needs me."

"Impatience hinders your recovery. I will pray. You will rest."

"I intend to repay you and Lady Blakwell tenfold for your kindnesses."

Amelia aimed a stern glare at him. "You can repay me foremost by confessing to Lady Blakwell what Pulko has been up to these past few sennights. Indeed, I cannot believe he talked me into being a part of such a shameful plan. Lady Blakwell doesn't mind sharing whatever food she has, but she'll be very unhappy when she discovers that Pulko has been stealing from her pantry with my permission."

Luca massaged his leg. "Pulko isn't stealing, merely borrowing, until I can provide adequately for my tribe when they reach the coast. I'll tell her myself what Pulko's been doing."

"She'd forgive you anything." Amelia hoisted to her feet and pulled up a stool. Using shears, she cut a heap of clean linen cloths and stacked them in a pile. "Draw your breeches to your knee." She covered the stool with her stout body and unbound the old cloths from Luca's leg.

Together, they eyeballed the ghastly sight of his inflamed wound.

Luca winced, the cloths weighty and wet as they slid down his leg.

Without an outward sign of emotion, Amelia said, "I need to call for the barber-surgeon or a doctor."

"Nay. No barber. No doctor."

"Awright, then," she demurred, holding up a vial of white powder. "We'll try my special liniment one more time."

"No liniment." He viewed the tray and shuddered. "No food, either."

"Drink the coffee. I ground a twinge of toadstool in the brew."

Luca leveled her with a baleful gaze. "Toadstool is poisonous."

"Toadstool will help you sleep."

"I slept enough. I'm leaving." He sipped the pungent, hot brew to appease her, until his throat refused to swallow another drop. His limbs felt weak. Perhaps he could rest a few more minutes.

"My lady will come to check you," Amelia said.

He thought he smelled panic in her voice.

＄

Somewhere between the twilight of sleep and wakefulness, Luca felt heavy quilts tangling about his legs. He heard hurried footsteps on the attic stairwell, doors creaking and slamming, distraught whispers somewhere nearby. He cried out in frustration, trying to escape the nightmares of chasing something he could never reach, no matter how hard nor how fast he ran.

He raked a hand across his face and tried to force himself awake. "'Tis only a dream," he told himself. "Only a dream."

His breaths came short and shallow. His heart pumped too fast. In his native Romanes tongue he cried out, but no one heard him, because the louder he cried, the more silent his shouts became, an empty scream leaving him sick and weak.

Whenever he nodded off again, worse dreams,

ever more terrifying, swelled his thoughts. Before his paralyzed eyes his leg withered to a small stump, like the end of a rotted cat's tail. Then his leg fell away, a never-ending freefall down a bottomless moat. He dove into the frigid, filthy water to find his leg, felt his chest burning to breathe, and dove deeper. He thought he saw the elders of his tribe at the murky bottom. At last he found them. He needed to save them. But his strokes were never strong, his breaths never powerful enough to reach them.

Other body parts fell off as well—a foot, a finger, an arm. He watched, helpless, sinking deeper, drowning alone in a watery grave. He couldn't swim, he shouted. He couldn't swim.

He awoke in a spasm of coughs and gasps, surrounded by Romany spirits of the night. The dreaded *martiya*.

Luca yanked the quilts from his leg and tried to focus, ensuring he was still whole.

What time was it?

Calm, he told himself. Stay calm.

When next he woke, the light glinting through the window was no longer the paleness of morn, nor the gray-white gleam of a winter afternoon. It was past twilight and a bright, full moon lit the sky.

He wasn't in his *bender*, his familiar tent. Nor was he outside, for the air wasn't refreshing and cool. He breathed deeply and concentrated on the familiar quilts bundled around his legs, the row of fat candles flickering in their sconces on a table nearby, the thick wool rug added to his pallet atop the blankets.

Lady Blakwell's attic. He was in her attic, awaiting her return.

He visualized her sweet face and sank back. His dreams came easier.

~

Through a burn of sweat, Luca realized a woman knelt beside him. She'd been there a while, for he felt the warmth of her body. Her curly hair was loose about her shoulders, a fringe of refined red in the moonlight.

Patience.

He moaned, tried to grope for his walking stick to stand, tried to recall where he'd last set it down. His injured leg hampered his movements. He didn't want her to see him so powerless and feeble, like a pathetic cripple.

"Go away." He tried to speak, but his voice didn't comply.

Her hands grasped his shoulders and eased him back down to his pallet.

So tender. So kind. So compassionate.

"Save your strength," she whispered.

He attempted a protest but his mouth was dry and he was too tired to object. He kept his eyes half-closed and heeded the tears pooling at the corners of her eyes and streaking past her cruel scar.

"*Kamadiyo*," he whispered, struggling to smile. "You're crying."

I don't have the strength to race from the room to avoid your tears.

She sniffed and dabbed at her eyes with her fingers. "These aren't tears."

"Don't lie. I'm not dead yet."

She averted her face and sobbed, quietly. "You'll not die. Promise me."

"I never make a promise I cannot keep."

"Promise."

"For you, *kamadiyo*, I will try," he whispered.

She bent and dabbed a moist linen cloth to his wound. His back arched with the pain of it. She tried to be gentle, he knew she tried. He clenched his jaw, an effort not to moan as agony roared through him.

Her hands shook as she wrapped a clean cloth around his leg. "Amelia will come to the attic with her gingerroot brew. The herb cures most afflictions."

"The herb will not cure a corrupted leg." Luca tried to breathe deeply, great heaves to absorb the purity of Patience's air into his lungs. "Tell Amelia to send for Pulko. I want a report on the tribe's journey and need to know they're safe." Luca's head fell back on the pallet. The throbbing of the gash was incessant and rhythmic and weakened his heartbeat. Poison filled his insides with venom. He felt it, saw the poison blighting each tiny pore of his skin.

The early morning hours elapsed in vague silhouettes and murky shadows.

Sometimes he felt nothing, a freedom from his body. He was a spongy cork, light, free, bobbing in the air, watching himself from the ceiling. He hovered in a place that protected him from more pain than his body could handle.

Patience sang, her melodious voice easing him. He recognized bits of Latin although he'd never set foot in a church. Endless Kyries and Agnus Deis, sacred hymns of prayers.

She talked when she wasn't singing, clear and reassuring words, and he'd forsake this safe dreamlike state for the reality of her fingertips squeezing his hands, the warmth of her comforting breath on his cheeks.

She was an illusion, a sparkle of decency with a heart of grace. Surely she wasn't real, for there was little good in the harsh life he knew. But he sought her touch, her hymns and her prayers, for her cool fingers revived his fevered body and flawed soul.

He must've dozed, for Patience shook him awake.

"Mr. Boldor, Amelia added more toadstool to a fresh cup of tea to lessen your fever."

He tried to surface from his dreams, to become a

part of Patience's world. "I cannot swallow," he protested. He forced himself to open his eyes. "Amelia is trying to kill me with toadstool."

Patience leaned over and held a dainty blue teacup steady. She smiled, the smile that told him to fight for his life.

He slept a while, awakening once more to the cup urged to his lips. Patience was agreeably close, her lavender fragrance filling the stench of the oppressive air. He never realized how much he liked lavender. Purple fields of lavender, rows and rows of sweetness. This was his life, a life full of unpredictable turns and purple lavender and dainty blue teacups.

She lightly kissed the bridge of his nose where it had once been broken and held out that damn, dainty teacup. "Drink."

"I don't like coffee with sugar in it," he said.

"Good, because this is tea. It will give you strength."

She offered falsehoods, her, a Christian woman. He'd never regain his strength, never again be physically able, because there was no remedy powerful enough to stop the venom that would kill him in a matter of hours. He felt the decay spreading through his body, breaking it down, bit by wretched bit. First rotting his useless leg, then his arms, then flowing through his blood until his heart stopped beating.

"You're doing splendidly." Patience brought the cup to his lips again.

His teeth chattered, making a light, sharp noise on the porcelain cup. He bit down on his dry mouth, licking the metallic taste of blood mixed with the potency of toadstool and tea with milk and sugar. His lips felt like charred pieces of bread scorched by a never-ending flame.

She dabbed a cool cloth to his forehead, whispering words of a prayer.

His head pitched back. Shadows dueled with awareness, darkness with light.

~

*S*unlight poured through the attic window when Luca next opened his eyes. Patience knelt on the floor near him. "Mr. Boldor," she said. "Penham snuck your friend, Pulko, here."

Luca licked his cracked lips and swallowed. "How did you find Pulko?"

"Amelia told me about a *vurma*," Patience teased. "We're learning your language. Aren't you proud of us?"

"Infinitely proud." Luca blinked to awareness and twisted up too fast from the depths of a comforting dream, although he couldn't remember the details. Tiny flares erupted behind his eyelids. The attic whirled, his stomach rolled. He grabbed for Patience's fingers to steady himself.

Pulko gaped down at Luca. His cheeks were ruddy with vigor, his sable eyes awash in sadness and concern.

With Patience's assistance, Luca sat up. "How's the tribe?" he asked.

"Everyone's well. We made camp near the sea." Pulko pushed aside his frayed cloak, which fluttered strangely. With a triumphant flourish, he raised a scratching and clacking black hen. Skinny claws hung from Pulko's fingers, a pointed bill pecked at his wrists, and black wings flapped furiously.

"I brought you this hen," Pulko said.

"So I see," Luca said skeptically.

"My mother said that a black hen will help you get well."

"Did your mother want the hen to peck a sick man to death?"

"Amelia will boil the hen and split it in two. All you have to do is eat it."

"Black hens cost far too much coin."

Pulko shrugged and held the flapping hen high. "I stole the hen so I used no coin. The *gadje* farmer didn't need the hen. He had two."

Luca glanced at Patience. He expected her eyebrows to converge, her frown accusatory for Pulko's crime of stealing. Instead, she pointed to a tray holding three jugs of water. "After you eat the hen,

Fabiana wants you to drink some water from the stream."

"And here's some wood." Amelia stepped forward from the eaves of the attic with several hazelnut branches. "We must throw these into the fireplace to keep you warm. Pulko and Penham will assist us in moving you back to your former bedchamber, and we shall make fine use of the fireplace."

Luca's bones trembled with the effort, but he agreed, feeling the first measure of hope in days. He couldn't help but grin, watching a squawking, pecking hen and dry hazelnut branches waggling in his direction.

Patience held him upright, her small fingers clamped around his forearm.

"Do you believe in Romany ways for healing sickness?" he asked.

She gave him a cheeky perusal. "I have the greatest confidence in anything Gypsy. This will ease your mind, and we'll add prayers to God."

"I made a poultice of butter and onions for your leg," Amelia added. "And I'll cleanse your wound mornings and evenings with a salve made from vinegar, although it may burn a bit. Between your Gypsy remedies and God's mercy, I predict you'll spring from your bedchamber within a fortnight."

"And I'll be good enough to eat," Luca said.

With effort, Pulko and Penham steadied Luca on the pallet and carried him down the attic stairwell to the guest bedchamber one floor below. Then, Pulko assured that he'd slip quickly from the house to return to the tribe.

Slats of a mid-winter sun pushed through the window and brightened the room. Luca's eyes feasted on the sight of the familiar bedchamber and the heartening blaze in the fireplace.

Penham assisted Luca with his private needs and helped him bathe. Once Luca was settled on the bed, Patience set a tray before him, a steaming trencher of boiled hen enhanced by a touch of rosemary. She fed him several morsels of cooked hen, giving him sips of water from the jugs after each swallow.

He lifted his head like a broken bird. Chewing, swallowing, helpless. After interminable bites, the bedchamber whirled, and Luca sank wearily onto the feather mattress.

"I'll eat more in a while," he assured, noting the protest poised on Patience's lips. He refused her cup of water. He intended to doze.

A few minutes later, he heard Amelia and Patience speaking by the fireplace.

"He constantly fears he'll lose his strength," Patience said.

"Between the wormwood and gingerroot I stirred into his water, he'll sleep for several hours," Amelia said, then sighed. "Unfortunately, in addition to the healing effects of the potions, there may be other difficulties."

Patience stopped, dried hazelnut branch in hand. "What sort of difficulties?"

"He may forget what occurred last evening. His nightmares, his screams of pain. The body has ways to blot out suffering." Amelia slanted a kindly glimpse in Luca's direction. "His wits may be slowed until he makes a full recovery."

"I'm inclined to favor his health over any temporary lack of wit," Patience said.

"On the other hand, he's strong. Perhaps he'll rally with no ill effects."

"He's endured enough pain for twenty men. He came back to be sure that I was safe and ended up suffering because of his tiring journey." Patience pitched the last of the hazelnut branches into the fireplace. She wiped her hands along her black frock and retied the knot of her paisley shawl. "I'll see to dinner preparations, then return to him for the evening."

"I'll come downstairs shortly. One more dose of water and he'll sleep through the night like a newborn babe," Amelia said.

Patience clicked the bedchamber door shut, her footsteps scurrying down the stairwell.

Amelia tweaked a piece of gingerroot and wormwood from the plants she'd placed by Luca's bedside and crushed the herbs into the water. She held the cup up to the late afternoon sunlight streaming from the window and stirred a second time.

She stepped on the stool, and leaned over. "How's my favorite Gypsy patient?" She blinded him with a bright, toothy grin and swished the water. "Feeling better?"

He fixed her with a slow-burning glower so threatening that she dropped the cup and spilled the water onto the wooden floor. She flew from the stool and grabbed some linen cloths by the bed. When her gaze finally bounced back to his, he snapped, "I feel in excellent health. However, I'll never be able to tolerate the sight of another black hen."

"Aye," she agreed. "But water's just the thing for—"

He pushed to a sitting position on the bed. "If you're waiting for me to drink another drop of your tainted water, then pull up a cushioned stool and fetch a great deal of knitting, for you'll be waiting a long, long time."

CHAPTER FIFTEEN

A fortnight had passed since Luca's feverish night in the attic. He'd made a full recovery thanks to a Romany cure of hazelnut branches and a black hen.

He smiled. Honesty prompted him to shake his head. His recovery was because of Patience's prayers and ministrations.

He'd wanted to be up and gone at least a sennight before now, because his tribe needed him. However, Amelia and Patience had disagreed, asserting that Pulko was handling the day to day activities of the tribe, and that Luca would hinder his recuperation by doing too much, too soon, and consequently suffer a relapse.

Worn out from a morning of digging holes and

repairing fences, Luca leaned on his shovel and stared at the grounds of Patience's estate. He'd worked in a field at the edge of her property to ensure that none of the servants could see him.

All his bones ached, and he wiped a dirty hand to push the hair from his forehead. He'd climbed to the top of the knoll, which gave him an impressive view while he searched for an absent Marko. The hills were open, the midday sun melting the snow that earlier powdered the lanes.

The hedgerows, a plush green, threaded through the moorland and separated the pastures. White sheep and black cattle grazed the highlands, a sleepy halcyon scene of salt and pepper.

He took in a bracing whiff of fresh air, thin and clear. A fine day, and uncommonly pleasant. He drove the shovel into the ground and turned up his breeches. Sweat poured from his temples and he wiped his brows. A good sweat, from hard work and warm sunshine. He cast off his cloak and rolled up the sleeves of his linen shirt.

"Mr. Boldor!" Patience shouted, effectively replacing his thoughts of her with her actual self. Her body seemed, fuller, rounder, which meant that she was healthy. With one hand lifting the hem of her berry frock, she emerged from a clearing of willow trees at the bottom of the knoll. She waved and made her way around a rusty pond, stepping along the wet ground.

"No more digging. You're not one of the servants."

Luca rubbed his bottom lip and briefly closed his eyes.

He wasn't a servant. He was a dirty Gypsy. Hated by most, looked down on by all.

He opened his mouth to correct her, but thought better of it. No need to begin their conversation with a disagreement, for she'd surely become indignant and gush about him being a man of honor, of virtue. A *bulibasha*. A lord of his tribe.

His tribe, he thought grimly. His care for their welfare was most delinquent. He wasn't an honorable, virtuous man. He was a neglectful lord, thinking naught of others, only of himself.

He had to get back to them.

He wiped his dirt-stained hands on his breeches. In truth, he wasn't ready to leave Patience. He had to be near her, near her convictions, near her truth.

Patience trudged through the mud, her velvet frock raised enough to expose the tips of her black boots beneath pantaloons. Her fur-trimmed pelisse was dark green, swinging open as she walked, a velvet belt tied above her waist. Her hair was completely hidden by a tight-fitting linen mob cap, leaving her freckled face exposed. Her cheeks were pale beneath the flush of exertion.

"Are you mad?" she asked as she reached him. "You're still weak. Amelia said you bathed this morn and you might catch a chill if you stay outdoors." She wiped at the smudges of dirt on his forehead with her gloved fingertips.

He took her gloved hands in his. "I'm hardly working and I'm hardly weak."

"You've been digging in these fields since early morn. This is the first day Amelia pronounced you healthy enough to venture outdoors, but she meant for you to go for a walk, not dig a ditch."

"According to Amelia, I'm better. According to me, I was better a sennight ago. I spent my days peering out the bedchamber window at these forgotten fields."

He looked in the direction of the fields and grimaced.

Patience followed his gaze. "The fields are neglected. With no dower, I can hardly pay the servants' wages. Only Lord Crispin benefits from any Blakwell fortune."

She'd misunderstood Luca's grimace, thinking he didn't approve of the sorry state of her fields, although he was grateful for the change in subject.

Luca stroked the knuckles of her hands. His gaze rested on the dark circles beneath her eyes, the paleness of her complexion. "You look tired of late."

"I suffer nausea whenever I smell vinegar."

"Amelia rinsed my gash with vinegar over a sennight ago."

"The tart smell lingers along with bad memories."

"Not bad memories of me, I hope."

Her eyebrows knit into a frown. "Nay. I breathe my late husband's medicine and the vinegar forces me to remember your suffering."

She was extraordinary, always worrying about him. She was the fragile English rose blooming in a spring garden, fresh and fragrant, lavender, mixed with the floral breeze of wildflowers.

He thought about kissing her, forsaking all boundaries of propriety. He tamped down his thoughts by focusing on his surroundings—the chirping of a nightjar, the gentle wind on his face, the drone of the first honeybees of the season.

He took in a long breath until his heartbeat slowed.

A knowing smile wreathed her face. "Obviously, you've recovered."

'Twas the Romany in him, he rationalized, his instinctual urge to kiss her outdoors under a vivid blue sky. But Patience was exquisite and delicate. She deserved to be courted wearing silk and satin, in a room decorated in fine lace and velvet.

He shifted. The longer he stayed in the *gadje's* world, the more accustomed he became to their comforts. He risked forgetting his own Romany world, and all that the tribe had done for him.

He met her doe-eyed gaze and smiled. He'd

fought his way through life as a man in pursuit of goodness and fairness. He'd never come across either, but here they stood, wrapped in a cloth of English respectability, while his Romany obligations pulled him away.

Amelia called from beyond the hill. She and Penham sprang from a small wagon carrying several wicker baskets and a table.

Patience grinned. "If you're up to it, I planned a picnic, far away from the prying eyes of the housemaids."

"What's a picnic?" Luca asked.

"'Tis enjoying food outdoors, " she said, "especially on a lovely day like this."

"I've eaten outdoors all my life and the Rom never called roasted rabbits on a spit a picnic."

She chuckled, childlike in her enthusiasm, as Amelia approached and assisted her with the baskets. "We'll not be eating roasted rabbit. I prefer tea with cream and rolls with butter."

Luca peeked inside the basket, grabbed a braised chicken leg, and grinned apologetically at Patience.

Amelia set the makeshift table with plates and silverware. "There's cold roast beef and plum pudding too."

"And a tin of biscuits," Penham added.

An hour later, the midday sun had turned the sky into a painting, an array of blue and pink punctuated with white clouds. Luca sat on the ground with his back against an oak tree.

"I like picnics," he said.

Patience stared at the open sky. "I'm glad."

"What's so interesting?"

"I look up and try to take it all in. The vastness of creation humbles me."

Luca stared upward, then back at the leftover chicken legs packed in the wicker baskets. "Your English picnic is an excellent idea. Next time I'll tell Amelia to add Rom food, perhaps a roasted hedgehog."

Next time, the assurance of another time, of a promise that he'd share another picnic with Patience in a setting as perfect as this one.

She laughed. "A roasted hedgehog doesn't sound very appetizing."

"You can fry it in butter, but roasting is better."

Patience glanced in the direction of the wagon and nodded at Amelia. "We should return to the dower house before it gets any later."

He helped the servants dismantle the table. At the sight of Patience's raised eyebrows, he grinned teasingly. "Did you think that I wasn't able to clean up after myself? Roma men are known for their neatness."

They weren't and they both knew it, and they both laughed.

With a curtsey and a bow, Amelia and Penham

finished wrapping the food, carried it back to the wagon, and departed.

"Where's your walking stick?" Patience asked as she and Luca made their way back toward the dower house.

"'Tis burning in the guest bedchamber fireplace," he said sharply.

"Suppose you stumble and fall? I'll make you another one."

"I walk well on my own two legs and don't need a third."

"Because you think that relying on others makes you less of a man?"

"Because I'm a legend." He placed his hand in hers as he guided her down the slippery knoll and along the broken flagstone paths. So easy they strolled together, talked together, joked together.

He'd hated the English all his life, but this woman was good-natured and intelligent, not a pampered, helpless creature. She was loving, compassionate, and giving. Someone who took joy in every aspect of life, whether she was bent over her ledgers which she'd brought to the attic, although the ledgers never seemed to add up correctly, or sitting by the paned glass attic window, her dog snuggled in her lap.

They slid onto a slushy trail while she pointed to the sodden meadows and wide expanses of land. "Soon the wildflowers will take over these fields in all manner of delightful shades."

She seemed blissfully unaware of his thoughts as she continued to name every species of plant to ever grace England's shores, including many he had any interest in ever learning.

"Spear and thistle, thyme and chamomile," she was saying, "in addition to asters and violets and goldenrod." She pointed to a row of hawthorn hedges. "The walled garden beyond is crumbled, but once was filled with butterflies."

"And newts." Luca directed his gaze downward.

"Such disagreeable creatures. They resemble lizards." She lifted her feet, avoiding a gray newt darting past her feet, two distinct rust-colored blotches highlighted its jutting ribs. The brush of its long tail slid along the hem of her frock. She shrieked and held tightly to his arm.

"I dreamt of newts when I was ill," Luca said. "They're extraordinary creatures with an astounding ability to grow new limbs, new jaws, and even new eyes. A newt wouldn't have to endure the nightmare of losing a limb."

Patience squeezed his forearm in a fierce, shielding gesture. A fortnight ago, when he was ill, she'd held his hands in the same way. And when he'd first collapsed at her doorway, broken and discouraged, she'd knelt beside him. His woman of prayer, guarding him from all harm.

"Don't speak of nightmares for they're not real." Her shoulders straightened, as if every fiber of her was being prepared for an imaginary battle. "If you'd lost your leg—"

"I wouldn't be a man," he said.

"No limb, nor lack of a limb, defines you as a man, nor a burden."

He glanced at her, with her jaw set firmly, her gaze focused on the muddy trail ahead.

"A Roma man without the ability to run and hunt is no man at all."

She scoffed. "You spout foolish male arrogance."

As they neared the outskirts of the property, the laundry maids boiled clothes and hung them to dry.

Luca paused, pulling Patience behind a row of trees so that the laundry maids wouldn't see him. "I admit my male arrogance may be overbearing sometimes," he said.

She leaned into him, her body light and weightless. "Sometimes?"

The afternoon faded into streaks of orange as the sun lowered, wrapped in a scarf of amber. A squirrel jumped madly from branch to branch, rustling the trees while foraging for nuts. A tree swallow twittered, diving for insects. A songbird courted his female with a warbling mating call.

Feeling more lighthearted as the minutes slipped by, Luca laughed aloud. Patience stood on her toes and tipped her head back to peer at him.

"You're happy?" she asked.

"For the first time in a long while."

Her mouth curved into a smile. "As am I."

He couldn't help his grin because a lifetime's worth of affection lurked in her answer. And he was England's biggest fool for being attracted to a woman he had no right knowing, much less falling for. *Romni*. The thought came unannounced. His woman.

"My beautiful lady." Lightly, he touched the infinitesimal dimple peeking from the corner of her mouth. He'd ask her tonight to join him and travel back with him to his tribe. Damn the consequences.

Through an orchard of apple and pear trees, they walked the last few steps to the house's side entrance.

Their walk was interrupted by Pulko. His clothes were rumpled beneath his muscled, strained forearms. He wiped at his over bright eyes, his gaze darting to Patience, then Luca.

"Luca, my mother is ill," Pulko said. "She...she wants to see you."

Luca felt his heartbeat race. Although they'd often quarreled, Fabiana had raised Luca since childhood. She'd been good to him, cared for him. He wouldn't refuse her request.

"Anything serious? Fabiana is never ill."

Pulko shook his head. "Nay, but she said 'tis time for you to return to the tribe. She told me to tell you that I can't hunt and fish and do everything on my own."

"We'll leave together at first light. Make camp and hide in the fields." Luca ran a jerky hand through his hair, then turned to Patience. "Fabiana is Pulko's mother, and the woman who raised me. I must leave. But before I do, I need to discuss something with you first."

CHAPTER SIXTEEN

*P*atience and Luca ate dinner together in the attic in silence. Amidst piercing thunderclaps and a ceaseless downpour, she swirled brown gravy around a crispy lamb cutlet, ate two spoonfuls of pea soup, and declined the sweet vanilla pudding topped with strawberries and meringue.

When dinner was cleared, Amelia and Penham retired for the evening.

"At last we're alone. No Amelia and no Penham," Luca said.

"Amelia is never far away," Patience replied.

Before she had the chance to cross the length of the attic, Luca had latched the attic door. Patience sat on a worn bench near the window, her fingers working rapidly on a piece of needlework. She closed her eyes, hearing his slight limp and the boyish urgency in his stride. She smiled at the out-right stubbornness he'd exhibited in refusing to rely on a walking stick.

He was the most overwhelmingly handsome man she'd ever known, with his swarthy good looks, the ever-present ruby ring glimmering from his forefinger, his worn linen shirt billowing from his broad shoulders. Most important, he was healthy. With him, she felt out of harm's way and...cared for. He'd never told her as much, at least not in elaborate words. Surely his actions of ensuring her safety, his interest in her, spoke of emotions deeper than a passing fancy.

She gazed through the window's paned glass. His reflection behind her was a tall outline of rough edges and strapping shadows.

His fingers wrapped around her shoulders. "What are you thinking, *kamadiyo?*"

"I'm thinking of you," she replied honestly. "And that you'll be leaving again."

"I'll visit you when I can to be sure that you're safe."

She set down her needlework, stood, then placed her hands on his. Together, they stared into the darkened countryside lit by a full moon and the river beyond. She inhaled his nearness, the mysterious scent of moss caverns and oak forest floors.

"Ours is indeed an unusual...friendship," she said.

Her throat ached, wanting to replace friendship with courtship.

"*Kamadiyo*, you're beautiful," Luca said. "And I care about you more than you realize."

Now where had that come from? Nevertheless, the words sent a trembling up her spine. Aye, she cared for him, too, this man who couldn't be more wrong for her. Or more right.

Luca curved her round to face him. Merely inches separated them—but in reality there was a rift of diversity—two different social classes and life-times apart. Reality forced her to realize that it would take more than murmured Gypsy endear-ments to meld the gap.

"Pulko was agreeable about leaving at first light," Luca said.

"I hope he's comfortable sleeping in the fields."

Luca gazed out the window and said absently, "Aye, the fields are perfect."

Patience glanced at him. She enjoyed looking at him when he gazed elsewhere, for it gave her time to study him at leisure. She admired the expanse of his shoulders and his remarkably firm jaw. He gave her a sidelong glance and smiled. Of course, he knew she watched him. His black eyes were warm, a burning of charcoal in their depths.

"Do you need to sit?" she asked.

"Only if you're with me." He touched the knee of his breeches. "And if you fear for my health, my leg has never been better." Completely contradicting his assurance, sweat gathered above his lips.

Patience calculated the pain he must be experiencing multiplied by the hours he'd spent working in the fields. "'Tis time for you to rest before your journey on the morrow." She felt her chin tremble at the thought that he'd be leaving in a few hours.

His eyes lightened with amusement. "How much did you miss me last time I was gone and tending to my tribe?"

She gave her best attempt at a nonchalant smile and didn't answer.

Miss him? She dreamt of him. All the while thinking she meant nothing to him, convincing herself it mattered naught when he'd abruptly left her that night in the attic.

She rubbed the back of her neck. Weary from the strain of the past two fortnights when he'd been so ill, she gave up trying to analyze this mystifying man. Or his motives. Or her response to him.

He touched his lips to hers and whispered strange Gypsy words she didn't understand. She only understood that the realization of his departure brought an unforeseen twist to her heart.

He often compared her wealth and privilege to his hungry, destitute tribe, but the wealthy were just as starving for love as the poor. She swallowed to dispel any silly notions of a future with him, any false expectations or fanciful daydreams. With a sigh, she drew back from him and stared down at her empty hands.

~

*L*uca noted Patience's stooped posture. Her eyes were lowered, her velvety eyelashes sweeping along her cheeks.

"When I'm in the English world, I feel like a knave who'll be charged with stealing something valuable," he said. "'Tis why I wanted to ask you...something."

Her posture straightened and she nodded, slowly. "What is it?"

He cleared his throat. "Would you...could you...travel back to my tribe with me when I leave in the morning? That way I know you'll be safe. You can stay as long as you'd like. I don't have money to offer, but I'll take good care of you."

He watched her hesitate, a wistful look in her gaze, before shaking her head. "I can't. You know I can't. My responsibilities are too great, and I must face my stepson's murder charge and fight back. I know that Amelia has discussed this issue with you."

"Would you come with me, were it not for his murder charge?" he asked softly.

The silence ticked by. He held his breath, waiting for a reply.

She focused on a point beyond him. "Perhaps."

His gaze found hers and she averted her eyes, as if she'd said too much. As if he'd seen more vulnerability than she'd wanted him to see. And he had. For he saw her fear, raw and exposed, on her face, in her voice, in the slight drop of her shoulders. The fear of rejection, and the shy admission of believing that she could trust him enough to be with him.

Her small hands fluttered about like two small birds, fumbling with her sleeves, smoothing her gown. The heady scent of her lavender soap on her skin was like a drug, a craving for all things Patience. He wanted to placate her with tender affirmations, but he'd never been one for elaborate words.

"You saved my life. In my haunted dreams, you were my hope," he said.

"You always make me feel protected and—"

Loved. His chest tightened. She hadn't said the last word, but he knew she was about to. He couldn't answer, nor fill in her sentence, because he'd never said the word to anyone.

He checked her fluttering hands. "Ssh," he whispered, which was all he could offer.

He prayed to God to help him, and wondered if God heard him, for no answer came.

He knew enough about women, this kind of woman, to know she'd never feel the same about him if he left and decided that he wouldn't return. And there was nothing for it, nothing he could do to stop the sadness, the realization that they could never be together.

He couldn't stay. He didn't belong here among the hated English. They'd been cruel, and unforgiving, and would never accept him.

A rousing white noise roared in his ears as he kissed her forehead. Perhaps they could live this way, die this way, hidden in their own, private attic without the interference of the outside world. The desperate thought passed through his mind. And then his mind stopped thinking when he gazed down at her beautiful face and the aching affection in her eyes.

Gently, he kissed her again. "My precious *wuzho*," he said. "Pure and untainted."

He held her, knowing he should let her go. He brushed an untamed, auburn curl from her cheek. The moonlight shining through the window transformed her creamy features to a burnished glow. How could he leave her? How could he stay? How could he abandon his tribe and lead an English life?

Patience stirred in his arms. She fulfilled him in a way no woman ever had. With her, he felt humored, his restiveness calmed, his spirit comforted.

Shyly, she smiled. "I want to show you something before you go." She whirled to her sewing basket and retrieved a sheet of paper beneath the colorful threads. She beamed as an excited child, her face lit by a maze of candlelight. "I have a gift for you."

His throat felt pinched and he swallowed. "I've never received a gift from anyone."

Patience gestured to the chair, pulled a stool next to him, and handed him the paper. Her earlier smile melted away and she peered at him beneath light, silky lashes. "Grant me the favor of accepting my gift and say thank you." She adopted the same low, persuasive tone he'd used in the attic two fort-nights earlier.

He unraveled the paper. In a simple drawing with black pen, she'd sketched him, remaining remark-ably faithful to his features. He sat astride a lion with a thick mane and powerful haunches.

Luca held the sketch up to the candlelight. "You took great pains to keep the lines straight."

"At first I sketched you on a horse but the animal wasn't grand enough. I think of you as Richard the Lionheart."

"The pious English king?"

"Aye, although he spent little time in England. King Richard composed poetry and was an adven-turous man with a sense of honor."

"I never sat on a lion, nor composed poetry."

"You have a sense of honor like King Richard, and you're a noteworthy hunter."

"Did you save *my* sketch ?" he prompted.

"Of course. I kept the two sketches together where I could look at them while I went about my day." She returned to her sewing basket and retrieved his sketch, tied carefully in a blue silk ribbon. "I've stared at it so often that the ink is starting to wear away."

A rustling outside the doorway made him pause. He set both sketches on a side table. "You should ask Amelia to prepare your bedchamber so that you can retire. Otherwise, I'm certain her ears shall burn off from eavesdropping."

"I'm not eavesdropping," Amelia's voice came from the other side of the attic door.

CHAPTER SEVENTEEN

*E*arly morning splashed into Patience's bedchamber and flooded her eyelids. Her mind was languid. Hazily conscious, she scrubbed her half-closed eyes with her fists and peered around her bedchamber.

Luca stood by the window, fully dressed in his linen shirt, breeches, and green sash. His overcoat was slung over his shoulders. Tied at the knee, the worn breeches exposed his well-muscled legs. His injured leg sported a thick linen bandage that looked as if it was recently cleaned and re-bandaged. His arms were crossed over his chest, his eyes focused on the fields.

She sat up in bed and yanked the comforter to her chin. "'Tis most improper to be in my bedchamber. A servant might see you. And how did you get in?"

Keeping his gaze toward the window, he said, "I wanted to ask you, one last time, if you'd come with me and live in my tribe."

She tucked the bed coverings securely around her and tried to reveal no emotion on her face.

The window was ajar and the sounds of servants shouting to break the ice on the well were answered by the bark of a familiar dog. The pleasant, refreshing breeze through the window hinted of spring. Soon, the estate would come alive in brilliant color. Not everything passed away. Life was a never-ending cycle of promise and bright prospects. The thought comforted her.

He turned, his dark gaze intent and probing. No apologies for sneaking into her bedchamber and watching her sleep. Only the same question, which she'd answered the previous evening.

She wanted to avoid his question, for last evening she'd almost asked him, begged him, to do the same for her. *Please abandon your tribe, your people, your way of life. We'll find a way to fight Crispin.* Dear God, please understand. The more she was with Luca, the more she was beginning to realize that she needed him more than they did.

The previous evening in the attic, she'd been relieved that they'd been diverted, for if Patience had divulged her fears, of humiliation, and loneliness, and sadness, then the walls she'd erected to protect herself would indeed come tumbling down as the walls of Jericho, and Luca might feel obligated to give her more than he was able. She couldn't be another duty for him.

She drew a shaky breath. "You said you may visit again?" she hedged.

"Aye."

Then why couldn't he meet her eyes?

He shook his head, a denial, and seemed to struggle to find the right words. "Although I could never make a permanent home here."

Across the distance of the bedchamber, his words tolled matter-of-factly, like the harsh peal of a funeral clapper.

Her throat clogged with tears. "I never expected you to give up your obligations for me."

"My ties are to my people. I must travel where they travel because I owe them everything. They accepted me when I was alone and abandoned."

"Why this endless journey having no beginning or end?" She tried to mask the guarded hope in her voice. "Where is your home? What are you seeking?"

He strode to the bed and pressed a kiss on her cheek. He spread out his hands and surveyed her bedchamber. "This life, your English life with its endless rules, is the dreaded life of a *gadje*."

She tore her gaze from his. Wrapping the bedcovers around her muslin nightdress, she refused his hand of assistance and slipped from the bed. He turned and walked to the fireplace while she pitched her wrinkled berry frock over her head. When she was finished dressing, she walked to him. "There's no need to explain." She caught herself from saying more, knowing she'd sound clinging, besotted, like that adolescent girl who'd sought love so desperately that she'd begged her smooth-talking cousin to hold her after he'd hurt her.

Patience pushed back her shoulders, mentally encouraging herself. She was a dowager countess, for heaven sakes. She kept herself vigilantly composed, hands folded together at her waist, hardly moving.

"I know you were married once. I'm assuming you'll not be interested in any other man in my absence," he said.

She blinked. "What gives you the impudence to think you can control me when you offer nothing? Only the assurance of your absence."

"I said I'll visit whenever I'm able."

She rubbed her fingers along the neckline of her frock. "You spout an arrogant demand followed by a poor promise."

Under the stream of brash sunlight filtering through the window, Patience put a hand against the wall. She'd felt sick to her stomach since she'd awoken. She leaned her forehead on her hand.

"Go and live wherever you please," she said, with bracing sarcasm.

He grabbed her cold hands. "Suppose I want to stay right here but know that I can't because of my duty to my tribe?"

His voice was low and adamant, causing flashbacks of their hours together. His quiet whispers in his foreign tongue would forever resound in her mind. Attached to all those memories was the fact that she wanted him standing beside her in order to be complete. And she wanted him to feel the same.

Luca nodded slightly. As always, he read her thoughts. He brushed the hair from her face and brought her nearer. This was mad. They'd just quarreled.

Her fingers twined through his silky-smooth hair while his lips kissed her forehead.

Still, she felt a sense of dread. She ascribed the feeling to weariness. a weariness she'd suffered for many weeks.

"You heard Pulko. His mother said the tribe's lack of food necessitates my hunting skills as he can't do everything alone."

"Pulko can hunt. Pulko can guide."

"Not alone. And Pulko's young, only fifteen years old."

Her vision blurred. Her pulse rang disturbing screams of caution.

"What if something disastrous happens here while you're away?" she asked.

"From my exhaustive searches across your land, I'm assuming Marko gave up his need for vengeance and has gone back to his tribe in the south of England. I've seen no signs of him nor his men. If you need me, send Penham and I'll immediately return. He'll find the *vurma* on the cattle path along the sea and she can direct him to my tribe's camp." Luca's eyes warmed as he squeezed her hands, prompting her heartbeat to skip and skip and skip.

~

A few minutes later, she slipped out of the back door with Luca and walked with him to the edge of the estate. Pulko bid her farewell and began the journey to Colchester, with the assurance that Luca would join him shortly.

The morning was chilly and blustery and Luca pulled on his black leather hawking gloves. She stood with him in a field of new meadow grass, on the trimming of the rusty pond overlooking the crofter's cottage. Luca had placed two stone urns flanking the doorway of the cottage and replaced the thatched roof. He'd promised to fill the urns with violets when the weather turned warmer. Another sign that he'd return.

Looking every bit the Gypsy, Luca tied his orange scarf around his hair, his ruby ring glinting from his forefinger. His cloak was slung over one shoulder, the patch of rabbit fur sewn securely to one sleeve. His swarthy complexion glowed robust and healthier than he'd looked in weeks.

He caught her in his arms and locked his lips to hers. She slid her hands over the familiar black bristle of his beard and rested her palms against his chest. His heart pounded beneath her fingertips, reaching inside her to a secret, heartbreaking place.

"Don't forget to change your bandages. I packed you several clean cloths. And please, be safe," she said.

Grinning, he patted his pouch, filled with linen cloths, sliced brown bread, and a favorite Bible verse she'd written on a sheet of paper.

Romans 12:12: *Be joyful in hope, patient in affliction, faithful in prayer.*

She shivered in the bitter breeze and he secured her pelisse snugly to her chin. It was these thoughtful acts, a gentleman concerned about his lady's comfort, all the reasons why she cared so much for him.

He neared the woods, his strides devouring the ground. His limp was slight. Several times, he walked backward and gave an exuberant wave. He was hindered by his injury but she never doubted his deftness. With chiseled features and a stubborn, angled chin, he was a man riddled in complexities and strange customs and never-ending duties.

And with each passing day, she was realizing more and more that he was the man who completed her.

When he assumed she no longer saw him, his gait slowed, his limp more distinct. In the harsh daylight, in the harsh breeze, he tried to hide it from her, the fact that his leg hadn't completely healed. When he was in pain, and she knew he always was, he disguised it under an indulgent grin and nonchalant shrug.

She swung from the woodlands and shuffled to the dower house. Determinedly, she blinked through a pall of unshed tears. Desolation spilled like a virus, taking hold, until she stopped to take great gulps of cold air. The clean, cutting snap of wind reminded her that winter still held a grip on the land.

How could she survive a day without him, let alone a fortnight? He was a man of principles, of obligations, she reminded herself, and she'd await his return proudly, patiently.

She fastened the belt around her pelisse and increased her pace to the house.

A stack of mending filled her basket that she'd neglected since his arrival. Better to keep her fingers busy throughout the long, lonely days.

CHAPTER EIGHTEEN

Several hours after Luca and Pulko had departed, Patience retired to her bedchamber for an afternoon nap. She hadn't meant to glance out her bedchamber's window when she awoke. She was simply walking from her closet to the bed, deciding on which frock to wear the following day. Black mourning clothes, perhaps with a green satin bow beneath her mob cap to contain her unruly waves.

Tawny sunlight crisscrossed the bed hangings, heralding the onset of evening.

A cold breeze came through the window, apparently left ajar by one of the servants. She walked to the window and decided to leave it open for a few minutes. The breeze freshened the stale air of a long winter.

The sun set quickly, encircled in one last bright hue of yellow, although a crack of thunder boomed in the distance. She sniffed. Rain was in the air.

Penham trimmed the lamps and lit the torch lights. Gazing at the flickering fires, she pondered how English society would view her relationship with a Gypsy, if and when she was found innocent of Crispin's murder conviction. Most likely, the English would look at Luca with pronounced disdain and distaste.

She went back to her wardrobe, stopping to light two beeswax candles from the dwindling ashes in the fireplace. She set the candles on the mantel and wiped the blurriness from her eyes. She'd been exhausted from her walk to the croft cottage with Luca to see him off and had hoped that a nap would refresh her. Instead, her brain was foggy and she felt light-headed.

Thinking of Luca again, she smiled. A Gypsy artist. A good man. An honorable man, conflicted by his responsibilities. He'd said that he'd return to visit her whenever he could, and to call upon a *vurma* to summon him if Patience suspected she was in any danger.

The flickering lights of the candles warmed her with a quiet thankfulness. Tonight, she'd enjoy a good meal and sleep soundly.

She washed leisurely and pulled a clean black frock over her head, debating whether to call for

Amelia's help to button the small pearl buttons at the top of the neckline.

A noise outside her window, the crunch of unfamiliar footsteps starting and stopping, caused her to pause. The servants scurried downstairs from kitchen to dining room, making last-minute dinner preparations. Lamb cutlets, fresh green vegetables, and thick sweet strawberry pudding for dessert made Patience's mouth water. Her appetite, thankfully, hadn't been deterred by her tiredness.

Unfamiliar footsteps outside. Again?

Her hands stopped at her throat. Perhaps Marko and his men watched her dower house all this time, giving her a false sense of safety, all the while planning an attack.

She grabbed one of the candles on the mantel, hurried to the tall bedchamber window, and peered out. Dusky shadows had turned the sky to black and the wind had picked up. Her white sheer curtains billowed outward, sucked through the open space of the window.

She set the candle on the wardrobe and grabbed the sash, intending to close the window before rain left puddles on the wood floor.

There. Near the trees. A blinding flash of lightning lit the ground. A large man with a stringy black beard stood beneath a row of hedges. He mopped his forehead with a rumpled handkerchief, his demeanor dark and menacing.

She froze. Heavy rains slit against the window pane. She shoved the window down, too shocked to move away. Her heart thudded madly. She jerked against the wall and pressed a hand to her chest. A Gypsy man. He looked like Marko, but she couldn't be sure.

She drew to the side of the window and carefully lifted the curtains to peer out.

Perhaps she was still dreaming from her earlier nap, for Luca had scoured the fields endless times and assured her that Marko was nowhere in sight and probably had gone back to his caravan weeks before.

Thunder rattled the windowpane. Lightning flared.

Through a blur of white sheer curtains and blinding rain, the large man raised a fist at her.

She gasped and jerked back from the window, her hands clutching the curtains.

She gathered her breath and peered out, one more time. Surely no one was there.

And no one was.

A scant few hours earlier, Luca had instructed her. 'If you need me, send Penham. He'll find the vurma on the cattle path along the sea and she can direct him to my tribe's camp.'

Nay. After spending so many days with Patience, Luca had only just begun his long journey back to his tribe. They needed him. Fabiana needed him. He'd been away too long.

Patience pressed her lips together. She refused to interrupt him within a few hours of his departure because of her wild imagination, showing herself as a pitiable, needy, dependent woman who couldn't last one day without him.

She lifted the curtains, one last time.

Aye, just as she'd thought. She'd imagined Marko.

CHAPTER NINETEEN

wo days afterward, Luca arrived in Colchester. Pulko had gone on ahead. Evening neared, and an exuberant chorus of exclamations from his tribe greeted him as he approached. The teeming scents of timber fires and crackling meats drew him to the center of the camp.

"*Misto*! Welcome!" Fabiana hailed.

"You're apparently feeling better," Luca observed.

Fabiana waved a dismissive hand at herself. "All I needed was rest and some good, fresh fish." She eyed Luca warily and kept a scrupulous frown on his limp. "Did your fine countess and her hard-working maid fix your leg properly this time?"

"Properly and completely," Luca prevaricated. "And Pulko found us food along the way and made a *bender* for us to sleep at night while we traveled. He took well care of me. Your son will become a fine Roma lord someday."

"'Tis too much responsibility for a boy so young."

"He's older than I was when I became a lord." Luca looked around. "And where is this boy who's like a *plal,* a brother, to me? I couldn't keep up with him."

Fabiana grinned. "He returned a couple of hours ago. Presently, he 's stealing from a noble who owns far too many horses. Pulko is taking a chestnut mare off the *gadje's* hands as we speak. *Yekka buliasa nashti beshes pe done grastende.*"

Luca translated in English, "With one behind you cannot sit on two horses." He strode to his *bender* and Fabiana's voice followed him.

"The *gadje* are greedy and selfish," she said.

Proud of her Romany heritage—speaking from seasoned knowledge regarding the despised *gadje*— the always practical and ever opinionated Fabiana never kept her views on life to herself.

Luca rested on a log near the campfire and stretched out his legs. "Are you referring to any *gadje* in particular, Fabiana?"

"Aye. Your fancy English countess." Fabiana tromped through the sand, carefully avoiding the marsh orchids, and lingered near the campfire. "How many days will you remain with us before you return to her?"

"How many days, weeks, years, do you expect me to stay before my debt to the tribe is repaid? I appreciate that you raised me and cared for my mother when she was ill, but now I'm a man with other interests."

"Other interests besides your duties?" Fabiana peered up at the sky, her countenance forbidding, as though she appealed to the heavens for guidance on how to steer an unruly, unappreciative child who'd insisted on giving the wrong answer.

"Have I not cared for the tribe since I was little more than a boy?" Luca persisted.

"Aye, and with no complaint until now. But don't play the long-suffering martyr, for Pulko has kept us abreast of your growing attraction to Lady Blakwell."

Luca rubbed his jaw and gazed at a flock of gulls screeching overhead. "You speak of my interest as if it were a hideous crime."

"The English nobles refuse to help the Rom and they attack without an excuse. They won't spare so much as a coin, even when we starve and beg for work. Can you not recall how much your mother suffered, all because she loved an Englishman? The Rom helped her when she was alone and birthed two sons. Where were the English? Where was your father?"

"How can I ever forget? You've reminded me a thousand times."

"Are the Rom, your people, an obligation now that you've gotten a taste of a grander life? A duty you want to rid yourself of as quickly as possible?"

He trained his stare on the wet leaves and twigs scattered in the sand.

Fabiana twisted her fingers through the fringe of her bright pink shawl. "Nadya has healed, and the scars on her face from Marko's thrashings are noticeable only on her forehead, which she hides with her beautiful long hair."

Luca didn't glance at Fabiana. There was no need to see her expression, for he felt certain it was grudgingly pleasant now that she spoke about a Romany woman.

"Nadya wanted me to send word when you arrived," Fabiana continued. "Will you see her?"

"Of course," Luca agreed. "But first, I'll meet with Pulko to discuss our provisions."

As if on cue, Pulko appeared at the edge of the camp, sliding on a slick patch of muddy grass and landing at Luca's feet. Despite the mud streaming down his face, Pulko raised two cackling chickens for the tribesmen to admire.

"Are you not a clever thief?" Luca laughed. "You go to steal a horse and come back with two chickens."

Fabiana scooped the chickens and Pulko hoisted himself to his feet.

"I'll steal the horse come the morrow," Pulko said. "The chickens will feed us tonight."

"Aye, along with the pantry provisions furnished by Lady Blakwell," Luca said.

Two spots of bright red appeared on Pulko's whiskered cheeks. He swiped the mud and jutted his chin, looking for all the world like he'd been grievously misunderstood. "The elders needed food."

Luca restrained a grin as he peered into Pulko's fire-breathing eyes. "'Tis a habit of yours of late," he couldn't resist baiting. "Whenever you see me, you carry fowl in your hands."

Later in the evening, Luca took a place with the elders in the marshy grass by the sea. A comet streamed across the black sky, its tail shimmering. The men put down their tambourines and waited for the comet to pass. Luca knew Fabiana would predict the event as a bad omen.

He stretched out on the grass, feeling the salty air on his face, tasting it on his lips.

Black pepper and garlic sizzled from a pot over the campfire, and several women roasted the two charred chickens on a spit. Crisp green beans simmered in a vegetable broth. Fried bacon flavored the air. Some of the old men and women jangled tambourines and sang in the familiar Romanes language, sparked by a tinge of Indian and English accents.

Withdrawing paper and a pen from his cloak,

Luca sketched the scene—a scene he'd observed hundreds of times. Through the years he'd accumulated stacks of sketches from his nomadic life, the everyday trials of his tribe, the little he remembered of his slim, dark-skinned mother. One of his sketches was her standing beside their crude tent. She held a gleaming gold bird cage and gazed fondly at the tiny brown finch perched on a stick in the cage. The bird chirped and trilled and she'd laughed aloud.

'There's such beauty in this world,' she'd said.

But she didn't live in this world anymore, and nothing was gleaming and gold, and no brown finch trilled, because there was no paradise for a ragged tribe. Only stark reality and the need to survive.

His sketches were just that, sketches, and each sentimentalized his harsh existence beneath muted lines and caring portrayals, renderings that left streaks of longing whenever he contemplated leaving the tribe to find a life for himself. Scents of his childhood, bergamot and roses, tender and hopeful, jumbled with the pointed smell of his loss when his mother had died.

Luca glanced up as a stunning ebony-haired Roma woman approached. She drew a bright green cloak across her shoulders. A plum-striped *diklo*, handkerchief, was tied at her throat. She flipped back her heavy black hair, and large, gold hoop earrings flashed from her ears.

Luca placed the paper on the ground and stood. "Nadya, you're looking well," he said.

"As are you, my friend." She studied him with eagerness, the look she used whenever gazing at a man. "You always look well." Nadya licked her lips and pushed the band of silver bracelets up her arms.

"All these compliments," he mused. "I don't know how to respond."

He expected her to rejoin with an innuendo, for he'd played her flirting game for years.

She remained quiet, a modest concession for all they'd been through. He was silent, also. Perhaps their long-ago attraction and the resulting violence had humbled them both.

Bending slightly, she studied his sketch, purposely allowing an unobstructed view of her loose bodice. He shook his head and smiled. She hadn't changed.

But he had.

As she straightened, Luca wrapped her cloak tighter around her shoulders and secured the laces at the neckline. "'Tis a cold night," he said, an excuse for an explanation.

She granted him an appreciative smile adorned in provocation. "My new husband has vowed to defend me if Marko ever comes near me."

"Aye, congratulations on your marriage. Where is your new husband this evening?"

"He's probably sleeping." She shrugged. "And I

heard that your tribe was recently attacked by the English."

"Trouble-making English men wanting to bring danger and sadness to the Rom," Luca replied. "'Tis always their way."

"The memories of your merciless beating at Marko's hands haunt me still." Nadya took a long breath and fiddled with the sleeves of her cloak. "Luca, I know that if you'd realized that Marko was going to beat me that night after you got away, you would've stayed and tried to protect me. I wanted to give you more food..."

Luca nodded. A pain shot up his leg, a ruthless reminder, although she'd suffered as well. She was a flirt, knowing no other course other than bartering herself for survival. But once, long ago, he'd cared for her. And, in her own way, she'd cared for him.

She shivered. "There's a wind by the sea. Can we speak in your *bender*?"

Once they were inside, Luca lit a candle and set it on a rough table. The flicker of candlelight changed Nadya's slanted eyes to the slit, reflective eyes of a cat.

He poured them both a cup of weak, cold tea. "*Sastimos.*" He raised his cup. "Good health."

"*Sastimos.*"

He leaned against the timbered pole holding up the middle of his tent and observed her. Her honey brown features were striking, although a hardness around her lips and eyes had claimed her former beauty.

"Fabiana and Pulko said you plan to visit the countess's estate again," Nadya said. "Why are you pursuing this woman?"

She asked the question politely. Nevertheless, her voice was too shrill, and he saw the question for what it was—an inquisition, the beginning of a series of interrogations about his life and plans, for which he had no answers because his loyalties to both Patience and his tribe were tearing him apart.

He sipped his tea ever so casually. "Why indeed? The countess saved my life."

Nadya spat into her cup and wiped her mouth with her hand. "Because she saved your life, must you give your life in return and abandon the Rom?"

"I'm not abandoning anyone." His jaw tightened. He tried to keep his tone cool.

"From what I've heard, she's a plain dowager widow. I know you." Nadya's voice lowered. "I know what you like."

"Then surely you don't think you can force me to declare my intentions."

Nadya tossed her cup to the floor. "Let me know when you tire of her." She glanced at his hawking gloves set on his pallet. "May I take these? Since my beating, I cannot stay warm."

"Of course. They were never mine to begin with."

Her long fingernail grazed the fur and traced the embroidered gold initials. "Whose markings are these?"

"Most likely some rich English dandy," Luca replied.

~

Several weeks passed.

Luca lifted his head from the task of skinning the rabbit he'd caught earlier in the day. It was the second time that he'd heard a man's cries for help by the river near the sea. It couldn't be Nanosh's voice, for he rarely left Marko's side, although the voice sounded like his.

An icy breeze, a draconian breath, stormed across Luca's nape. He grabbed his walking stick and hurried toward the shout and the river beyond. The crunchity-crunch of gravel crushed beneath his boots as he reached the river's edge. Violent, cloudy water glutted the embankment.

He spotted Nanosh, a speck of flailing hands and dark hair. Waves pooled around his neck as the current drove him swiftly downstream.

Luca's blood hammered in pulse-stopping panic. He'd never seen Nanosh helpless before. Even when they were children, Nanosh was always the most daring.

"Nanosh! Keep your head up!" Luca shouted.

Water rushed between the rocks, flowed toward the waterfalls, thrusting Nanosh ever farther out of reach. Not daring to look away, Luca darted with the current. He stretched his walking stick over the water. "Here! Reach for this!"

Nanosh thrashed against the raging upsurge and made an attempt to grab the walking stick. Then he disappeared beneath a churning river that didn't care.

An unaccustomed moment of fright swept through Luca. He couldn't swim. And neither could Nanosh. The Rom never had a reason to swim, as they roamed the land, not the sea.

Nanosh thrashed against the raging upsurge and made a frantic attempt to grab the walking stick.

"Dear God," Luca flung his walking stick to the ground. "I know this man is my enemy but I need to help him." Without another thought, he tore off his cloak. Feet braced, arms outstretched, he plunged into the unforgiving depths. Icy water rose to his neck. The waves pushed him downward. He clawed at the soaked hair in his eyes. He had to breathe, had to overcome his fear.

From beneath the muddy water, Nanosh's shouts of panic echoed. He came to the surface, his mouth distorted, his expression torturous. All color drained from his face. Then he disappeared.

Luca no longer saw the cruel adult man with the pot belly. He remembered the skinny Romany boy, fresh-faced and adventurous, playing mischievous tricks on the other boys.

"Where are you?" Luca's cries labored across the river.

The river opened into a pool and the current flowed weaker.

Luca took a deep breath and dove under. Crests of water, smelling of fish, roiled to his chin. Never had he been so powerless to save someone.

He pushed to the surface and saw Pulko extending his arms. "I'll help you."

Nanosh came up beside Luca, his intake of breath guttural. Pulko pulled both Luca and Nanosh to the riverbank. Then he towed Nanosh's heavy, leaden body to dryer land.

Luca braced his arms against the ground and dragged air into his lungs. Half-crawling, he reached Nanosh. Nanosh's head lolled to the side. His black hair clung to his pale face.

"Is he dead?" Pulko asked.

Luca rose to his knees. "Nay." He placed his ear against his mouth. "He's taken in water, but he's breathing."

"He shouldn't have been near our camp," Pulko said.

"As children, we were all friends." Luca placed his hands on Nanosh's ribcage and bore down. Water spurted from Nanosh's mouth. He coughed and sputtered.

"Why are you here, prowling near our tribe?" Pulko shouted at Nanosh.

"Marko wants Luca dead." Nanosh directed his black-eyed glare at Luca. "Did you save me so that you can slice me to pieces?"

"I saved you so that you'd live." Luca glanced at Pulko. "We both did."

"I'll return when Marko commands."

"And if you return and slip into the river again, I'll save you again." Luca came to his feet and grabbed his walking stick. The foul smell of the river clung to the insides of his nose and throat. Coarse silt stuck to the roof of his mouth. His waterlogged clothes chafed against his cold skin.

Luca and Pulko walked away from Nanosh in silence. Luca heard Nanosh's footsteps as he headed into the forest.

After a few moments, Pulko said, "You cannot swim."

"Aye," Luca said.

Unashamed respect shone in Pulko's eyes as he looked up at Luca. "Nevertheless, you dove into the river to save your worst enemy."

"Aye." Luca stared straight ahead at the tattered tents of his tribe. "Because nothing is more important than keeping peace and ensuring the safety of those we love."

Love. Luca shook his head. The thought had just come. Had it sat there idly, all this time, waiting for the right moment to admit how much he cared for Patience?

"I'm returning to Lady Blakwell's estate." He couldn't control the tremor in his voice.

Patience had made him a better man. And he needed to be with her.

CHAPTER TWENTY

*O*liver gave a gruff growl.

Patience jolted up in bed. She rubbed her eyes and squinted into the stark darkness of her bedchamber. Streaks of jagged lightning glistered through the cracks in the window, followed by a thunderclap. Strange weather for late winter, perhaps a hint of spring. With God's grace, Luca was safely with his tribe. Although he was far away, he continued to occupy her thoughts.

She reached to her night table. Even in the dark, she made out the bold lines of the sketch he'd drawn of her. He was naturally talented, his detail painstaking. Several weeks had gone by since his departure, however the hollowness, the empty sadness in her chest by his absence, persisted.

His gift had been heartfelt and genuine. She

hadn't fully realized, nor fully appreciated, his sincerity. Now it was too late to tell him for he was no longer here and she didn't know when he'd return.

A gust of cold air rushed through her room, bringing her musings to the present. With great care, Patience tied the sketch in a blue silk ribbon and placed it in the top drawer of her night table.

She stared at her bedchamber door, securely bolted. The windows were sealed. The chilly gray of an early spring's dawn was hours away, permitting her a few more hours of sleep. Deeply, she inhaled. The scent of lavender soap, soothing and floral, lingered on her skin from her wash.

She tucked her knee-length night dress closer to her body and snuggled beneath thick woolen blankets. Sleep was what she needed to stave off the constant tiredness assailing her. She curved her head into the feather pillow. Just as she drifted off, the tinkling of a pianoforte interrupted her dreams of a dashing, black-eyed Gypsy. She fought off the luring sensation of slumber and opened her eyes.

Somewhere in the house a floorboard groaned, deadened but distinctive. She propped on her elbows, found her breath, and swallowed. No one came in the black of night, although she swore the heavy entry door had creaked open.

Her gaze darted across her bedchamber. Something didn't feel right.

Hackles raised, ears high, Oliver leapt to the

door and emitted one low growl. Patience calmed her quick heartbeat and lurched to her feet. Her head whirled and she sat on the edge of the bed to stop the dizziness. Fumbling in the darkness, she shoved her arms through the sleeves of her morning gown and wrapped a warm cashmere shawl about her shoulders.

She flattened her body close to Oliver and pressed her ear to the door. The familiar voice of her stepson singing off-key coasted through the hallway, along with the eerie finality of a C Minor chord.

"Stay here," she whispered to Oliver. She unfastened the door latch and padded down the wooden stairway. Rounding the corner of the dining room, she searched the shadowed length of the drawing room. A fire burned low in the fireplace. Her stepson, Crispin, occupied the bench in front of the pianoforte, his head lowered over the keys, his wine glass clutched in one hand. The smell of port wine and expensive cologne burdened the air.

She knotted the shawl around her shoulders and waited.

He was here for something. She wasn't sure what, or why, but it had nothing to do with perfecting the coda of a Haydn Sonatina. His loud and wheezy breathing reeked of vengeance, and money, and blackmail.

"Your pianoforte recital in the middle of the

night woke me. Now that you're finished, I'll light more candles so you can see the keys," she said.

Crispin whipped his head up. "Leave them unlit. Beeswax is expensive." He scraped the bench back, stood, and grasped the pianoforte fallboard before weaving his way to the dining room.

His white linen shirt was opened at the neck and exposed a square jaw that reminded her of a lantern. His waistcoat hung undone.

He used his height to his advantage and squinted down at her. "Shall I bid a good evening to the woman who murdered my father?"

Wine reeked from his skin and she debated answering, afraid to edge him on, reluctant to draw back. "Your accusations are untrue, as you certainly know."

"Several months ago, you plotted my father's murder. Were you so desperate to be rid of him that you assumed I'd ignore our English law?" Unblinking, his peculiarly small eyes were unnerving.

He was a strange, unpredictable man, playing the pianoforte softly when he thought no one watched, because men usually didn't play the pianoforte. Then slamming at the keys when he played a passage poorly, therefore making a loud display of that which he'd tried to hide a moment before.

"Digby found my father lying unconscious in this very house, completely alone the night he died. Perhaps you hired a bandit to beat my father senseless, then fled from the crime," Crispin continued.

"All lies," she replied. If he hadn't watched her so closely, she might have surrendered to her fatigue and sank onto a side chair. However, a sign of fragility wasn't a trait she wanted to show a calculating creature like him.

Crispin staggered to a mahogany sideboard and topped off his wine glass. "You were the last person to speak to my father."

"Actually, Digby was the last person," she countered. "On the afternoon of your visit, your father had said he was too busy to see you because of some budgetary work, but I persuaded him to make time for you. The day followed Epiphany, because I remember saying special prayers before I took my dog for a walk."

She didn't add that she'd purposely arranged her walk to avoid her stepson's arrival, as she had no desire to share a meal under his and his father's lecherous scrutiny.

"A convenient excuse as to your whereabouts," Crispin said. "However, no one saw you or your tiny dog anywhere in the village that day."

She waited until he drank another mouthful of wine. "The path I take is often deserted. I prefer the solitude."

"I suspect you met your lover." Crispin quaffed his wine, choked on a mouthful, and spit into his glass. "Is he the mysterious Gypsy the footmen whispered about when they greeted me this evening?"

She crossed her arms. "I have nothing to hide."

He regarded her, his small eyes as frozen as the Thames in January. "Gypsies are backward and primitive, more suited to rat-catching and fortune-telling than actual work. Or did he dance and play his fiddle for you?"

"How can you speak so callously of an entire race of people simply because you don't understand their way of life?" Her blood surged, the breath hot in her throat. Crispin's views were narrow-minded and intolerant, but she didn't want to raise his suspicions by speaking further and perhaps placing Luca in danger.

She shot a glance toward the large glass window. Outdoors, the fields lightened with the emergence of a full moon, brightening the starkness of the room.

"However, at present my interest is finding my father's murderer," Crispin said. "Some servants spoke of my father's roughness with you. Some said they heard muffled screams from your bedchamber when he visited you late in the evening. You wanted him dead, didn't you?"

Her mouth dried. Despite her poorly concealed shudder whenever her husband had touched her, he'd treated her cordially in public. Seldom had they openly quarreled. To the outsider, she seemed an ideal wife, docile, genteel, and all that English society expected.

Of course, she scarcely tolerated the sight of him and her feelings must've shown. And because he knew, he'd used the knowledge to his advantage, taunting her all the more, confident he held all the control. She bore his clammy hands, his smell of vinegar and roiled charcoal when he placed his arms possessively over her shoulders and kissed her with an open mouth.

She lowered her eyes. She was supposed to have loved her husband, not loathe him.

Her inner chastisements were drowned by Crispin's slurred voice. "Heeding your instructions, Digby added ground ginger to father's medicine to ease his discomfort. I believe you disguised a toxic herb in the ginger to finish your cold-hearted deed."

Patience headed for the hallway. "I refuse to listen."

Crispin wound his way around the dining table, his silhouette in the candlelight crisscrossing hers. "Did you make good use of the money I sent last month?"

Although she bore the expense and burden of keeping the ledgers and paying the servants on less than half of what was needed, Crispin was the heir and he controlled the money.

She stared at him, dressed like a dandy with his

gold-buttoned frockcoat, his pointed top hat sitting on the dining table next to his glass of port wine. He always dressed in the latest fashions, trying to show off to anyone who cared to look.

His father, her late husband, had never seemed impressed.

She put a fist over her mouth in her best imitation of a yawn. "We can speak about money in the morning."

She should've departed, and would have, if Crispin hadn't leaned on the dining room table and drummed his fingers in a repetitive, grating rhythm. When he seemed certain he had her attention, he withdrew a stack of paper from his waistcoat and placed them on the table. "If I formally accuse you in court of murdering your husband, a nobleman, and you're found guilty, you'll be charged with petty treason."

"I'm well aware of this."

"The prison you'll be going to will be much worse than debtor's prison."

His cool monotone made her veins drone with an apprehension that filled her ears.

"You cannot withhold one-third of my dower on speculation," she said. "I was a faithful and dutiful wife and your false claims will be scoffed out of court."

"The court won't side with a woman without any family to speak of, and little land to call her own."

"I can plead 'privilege of peerage.'"

"Not for a murder charge." Crispin shook his head, then smiled. "Fortunately for you, I've decided on a satisfactory solution. You'll come and live with me in Mayfair. After all, you're my stepmother."

Her wits went utterly blank. Her legs weakened. "I'll not leave Ipswich and Amelia."

Crispin scrutinized her body at leisure, deliberately insulting. "We'll reside in father's London townhouse. You'll do my bidding and I'll not charge you with murder."

He spoke in vain, for she no longer listened. The drone in her ears vibrated to a howling roar. "Your father drew up a pre-contract with my father," she said. "The terms of my dower rights are clear, as well as the amount agreed upon for my living expenses."

"Money is of no benefit if your future is standing in front of a firing squad." Deep scars blighted Crispin's cheeks as he leered toward her. Her skin pricked and her pulse slowed to a repugnant crawl.

"Never will I live with my late husband's son in the manner you infer," she said.

"You'll consent when you realize that if you don't, you'll lose any remaining wealth, your freedom, and possibly your life."

She felt nauseated. She couldn't swallow. Whirling, she clutched her restless fingers into the creases of her shawl and stormed up the stairwell.

CHAPTER TWENTY-ONE

*L*uca could no longer contain his impatience. He missed Patience more than he could bear and needed to see her. For several long weeks, he'd fished and hunted with Pulko, cod, rabbits, and small game, ensuring the tribe had enough food for the sennights ahead. He'd done enough.

Later that day, when the sun settled low in the sky, Luca grabbed some clean clothes, slid his pouch over his shoulder, and told the tribe of his decision. He was returning to Patience for good.

"We'll starve," Pulko objected. "You'll grow bored and fat and idle and—"

"Pulko, with each passing day I believe that you're a better leader than I am. You're much quicker and have shown yourself to be brave. Besides, I'll be near enough if you need me." Luca grabbed his cloak and slung it over his shoulders.

On foot, the journey would take a couple of days. He bid the tribe an abrupt farewell and headed out of camp.

After hours of traipsing a sandy footpath, thirst and hunger slowed Luca's movements. He hadn't eaten, insistent on saving every bit of food for the tribe.

True, the tribe had provisions, salted and pickled for the days ahead, but food went bad quickly as the weather got warmer. Besides, he planned to feast when he reached Patience's dower house. Amelia was surely simmering a miniature pastry filled with beef marrow, followed by sweet jellies on toast. He grinned. He was beginning to relish English pound cake topped with clotted cream more than a Romany roasted hedgehog dredged in black pepper.

He paused and drank some black tea from a flagon in his pouch.

The past few fortnights had worn on him with tribal tasks and disputes needing prompt, undistracted attention and he'd gotten little sleep. Perhaps he should've waited until morning, but he was anxious to see Patience before another day broke. Besides, he was used to covering ground at dark and blending with the forest.

He let out a moan as pain shot through his leg. Rest, he thought, but he rejected the thought as a waste of precious time. The flat footpath was the longer route to Patience's house. Hiking up the hills was the shorter route, but hills were difficult to navigate with a limp and put undue strain on his bad leg. And he refused to use any wretched tree branch as a walking stick.

Familiar twinges of the muscles burning his calf became a grating agony. He strained on, already feeling the tightening in his thigh.

Tormenting, torturous suffering from a damn gouge refusing to properly and completely heal.

He pulled his orange handkerchief from his head, wiped his brow, then retied the knot around his hair. His limp slowed to faltering footsteps, but each faltering footstep brought him one step closer to Patience.

～

*A*lmost midnight. He should stop. Sleep.

Patience would be the first to tell him thus, worried for him, chiding him for driving himself too far, too long. But he refused to be beaten by any wretched discomfort, for it meant physical pain had won, and his inner drive had lost.

Hour by hour, the clouds grew lower, and denser, and bleaker, marking the hours before dawn. The craggy hills loomed around, behind, ahead.

Luca pictured himself when he was nine and

twenty, when he was fit and able. Running, hiking, climbing. He was only a year older now. Of course he could climb a steep hill. What was simpler than climbing a steep, craggy hill?

He switched his path and determinedly approached the incline.

Think in small steps. Focus.

Weak leg, strong leg, weak leg, strong leg. He paced himself, placing one foot in front of the other, scrambling up the sudden bends, grabbing slender tree trunks to steady himself. If he slowed to a creep, the spasms in his calf were bearable, although that meant a journey of two days would stretch to three. Indeed, three days could stretch to four.

His pouch hung loose from his shoulder as he climbed. The scarf around his hair worked from the knot and sweat pooled down his neck, lingering in a salty line. He shaded his eyes and peered at the peak soaring above.

Surely the peak was unreachable.

The thought, utterly defeating, lowered him to his knees. It hadn't seemed difficult when he'd had Pulko on the journey to help him.

He yanked off his cloak and rubbed the rabbit fur sewn to his cloak sleeve, smoothing the softness against his face. In the past, he'd believed that rabbit fur brought good luck. Now he knew better. The Rom's superstitions were just that. Superstitions.

He peered at the top of the hill and blinked to

clear the shadows. He shook his head, knowing the shadows were phantoms of his own fatigue. Shakily, he stood and stepped hard to avoid a large stone in his path, laying all his weight on his injured leg.

He took a sharp breath. His leg caved. He slipped to the ground and cursed.

Forget the agony. It will pass. He needed to reach Patience because he loved her. Aye, he was bone-deep in love. And she loved him. He knew it, felt it. They needed to be together.

He offered a prayer to her Christian God in his Romany tongue.

Then he pushed himself to his feet and kept walking.

CHAPTER TWENTY-TWO

*L*uca arrived at Patience's dower house just before noon on his third day of travel. He passed a row of primrose on the last curving lane and waved away a swarm of wasps clumped atop a neglected jam pot. Already it was the beginning of May. Soon, yellow wildflowers would carpet the fields, filling the air with the light, lemony fragrance that reminded him of spring.

Keeping himself hidden behind the hedges, his boots scuffed the gravel along a side pathway leading to the back kitchen entrance. He knew the layout of the house so well he could walk it blindfolded.

Oliver danced a greeting at the doorway. The dog flung to his back for a stomach rub, then scampered around Luca. Amelia flattened pastry dough on a wooden table in the kitchen as Luca rapped on the door and entered. Penham stood across from her, slicing green apples and fresh almonds. A pot of vinegar boiled on the stove.

"Leave the dog outside." Amelia wiped a floury hand across her hair, and met Luca's gaze. She gaped. Her eyes bulged. "God alive, Mr. Gypsy, I thought you were the stable man. From the corner of my eye, your clothes resembled little more than rags."

"Thank you," Luca replied dryly. "You're looking well, also."

With a pat on his thigh to Oliver, he let the dog into the field. He closed the door and set his pouch and walking stick on a side table. He wended to Penham's side of the kitchen and was met by the man's condemning scowl. "It took you a long time to return," the man observed.

"Did you and Pulko manage to do any stealing in Colchester?" Amelia clapped her hand over her mouth, seemingly horrified at the audacity of her own question.

Luca's lips twitched. "Stealing isn't an occupation for a Rom so much as a necessity. Aye, Pulko stole chickens and a horse while I hunted."

Amelia's plump fingers went back to shaping the dough into a crust. Penham set the sliced apples in a crock on the side table and grabbed an apple slice.

Amelia's rolling pin flew out to whack his hand, her pastry crust apparently forgotten.

"Those apples are for the tartes, you overgrown servant." Amelia lambasted him with an exasperated look and made an about-face to Luca, granting him a broad smile. "Lady Blakwell has awaited your arrival on tenterhooks when several fortnights passed with no word from you. She fretted you were waylaid."

"I was, by hunting, and fishing, and Rom disputes, and this accursed leg—" Luca snuck a slice of apple, expecting to meet a whack from Amelia's rolling pin, but she radiated her consent.

"I could use more of your special liniment," he said.

Amelia reached into a cupboard and handed him a vial.

"Thank you." Luca took another slice of apple and perused the kitchen. "Where's my beautiful countess?"

"She's in the dining room contemplating a journey," Amelia averred.

"What journey?"

Amelia wrung her hands and gave Luca a pained stare. "Lady Blakwell will soon be journeying to London to live with her stepson, Lord Crispin. He's coerced her into going or he'll charge her formally in court with his father's murder. 'Tis disgraceful. He's five and twenty and has left her with no choice."

Amelia moved about, seeming unable to stay in one place. "'Twill be safer for us all if you leave."

"I'm staying." Luca's voice hardened. He felt a rock taking a firm place in his throat when he tried to swallow. "And don't try to stop me."

"Ssh." With a quick glance over her shoulder and a sound thrust at his chest, Amelia handed Luca his walking stick and sent Luca in reverse. "Penham has chores to finish in the basement, and you need to go outside and hide. 'Tis safer because Crispin's in the drawing room." She banged the door shut.

Luca stood, grasping his walking stick, a Roma man standing in an Englishwoman's garden. Then he eased the door open, slipped into the pantry, and flattened himself against the shelves.

The playing of a Scottish Air on the pianoforte in the drawing room was followed by a gruff male voice. "Who's here, Amelia?"

Luca's eyebrows shot up. Sifting through hazy memories, he recognized the man.

He straightened from the shelves and crouched in the half-open doorway of the pantry, absently petting an orange tabby at his heels. He peered through the doorway and into the drawing room beyond to make certain that the man's face connected to the voice.

Aye, it was the same man, although Luca hadn't known Crispin's name until now. Crispin seated at the pianoforte. He had the same pitted cheeks and lunging nose.

Sickening remembrances surged in Luca's mind. The twelve-year-old Roma girl had been beaten beyond recognition. Crispin had towered over her, guilty, although proclaiming innocence in a high-pitched whine. The stench of her unwashed blood had contaminated the tender green field. The odor of brutality permeated the air.

Luca pushed down the blind fury rising in his chest. He hadn't been able to save her. He'd been too late. Somehow, he quelled the urge to tear into the drawing room and demand justice from the man, the nobleman, who'd deemed himself above the law.

The minutes passed. Fragments of conversation between Amelia and Crispin went by in a drone of faceless voices and a final, crashing pianoforte chord.

"Lord Crispin, perhaps a promenade down the lane will lighten your sour mood?" Amelia asked. "Here's your cloak and top hat," she added gaily. "I'll have your carriage sent round."

When the front entry was secured, Luca bypassed any idle conversation with Amelia and razed a glare toward the front entry. "I know that man and I loathe him."

"There's an air of cruelty about Lord Crispin that chills my brittle bones. He reminds me of his late father, although they never got along." Amelia muttered under her breath, then paused. "Why do you loathe him?"

Luca's jaw tensed, his mind in conflict. Looking back to that terrible day, he felt Crispin's viciousness overtaking the cold spring air, leashed below politeness, contained beneath civility. He wanted to expose Crispin for what he was and wrench off the fur-lined frock cloak shielding the vicious nobleman underneath.

"A long time ago, a young Roma girl bled at Crispin's feet." Luca sighed heavily, spoke quieter. "Behind his silky tongue hides a violent nature."

"What happened?" Amelia asked.

"The girl he murdered was from a neighboring tribe, and word spread quickly, but Crispin spouted drunken denials when her brothers demanded justice because he knew the courts were on his side." Luca wearily rubbed his leg, the ache beginning to rage through his calf. "No one was there to prove otherwise, and it was an English noble's word against a dead Roma girl. Perhaps she'd tried to sell her body—for food or a warm place to sleep. Her tribe was too afraid to avenge her. Had she lived, she was ruined. She was *prastlo,* dishonored. No Roma man would've wanted her."

"This girl was an innocent and the law would've sided with the Gypsies," Amelia said. "I cannot believe your tale."

"Believe it." Luca bent to dab the wetness from

his knee. Infection oozed through his double pair of hose and breeches. Idly, he fingered the spots of blood. "He's the same man who wants Lady Blakwell to live with him in London. Be assured I'll not permit him to take her."

"There's nothing you can do." Amelia fixed her stare on his knee. "My lady has shut herself in the dining room with endless cups of tea and feigned illness until Lord Crispin departs."

Deadly somber, Luca focused on the dining room door. "I'll seek Patience on my own."

How easy it was, he thought grimly, to call the countess by her given name and break English society's damn, strict rules.

Amelia caught his arm. "Don't. You'll get us all killed."

He shook off her hand and grabbed his walking stick. "Keep watch and alert me when Crispin returns."

"I don't answer to you, Mr. Gypsy."

A thread of lively Roma curses came to his lips. He shared them freely with Amelia, then bound across the room. Two steps at a time, his boots resonated like abrupt drum taps on the floor. When he reached the dining room door, he stopped short and let his breathing slow.

He entered without a sound, latched the door closed, and set his pouch on a side chair. The dining room greeting him was not as luxurious as he expected. A pewter pitcher was set on the buffet table, along with a silver tea service, some spoons, sugar and cream. Angled in a wingback chair close to the fireplace, an array of rainbow colored thread lay scattered atop a sewing basket.

Oliver slept near the hooded fireplace. Except for a subtle twitch of his tail, the dog hardly moved. Too late, it occurred to Luca that he should've knocked first. His conscience nagged that Patience wouldn't welcome his interruption. He ordered his conscience to stay silent.

Her back to him, she gazed outdoors at the rain beginning to stream against the paned glass. Lacking the energy she normally displayed, she toyed with the silken curtain sash. Her hands were small and graceful, her movements refined.

Without turning, Patience asked, "Was Crispin shouting in the drawing room because he played the wrong chord at the end of the Sonata again, Amelia?"

Luca willed his legs forward. He willed his hands to reach out and give her shoulders a supportive squeeze. He did neither. What he did made the least bit of sense because it was so contrary to his impetuous nature.

He placed his walking stick on the floor. Then he did nothing. Absolutely nothing. He merely stayed where he was and stared at her like a besotted swain.

She'd shed her confining mob cap. Her hair

shimmered to a rich red-gold in the wavering afternoon sun. She'd secured her mass of curls at the top of her crown with an assortment of pins. A curvy strand tumbled across her cheek and prevented him from seeing her face, only the tilt of her small, turned-up nose. A delicate vision, she seemed too light and airy to be real.

"Amelia?" Patience repeated. "I pray that Crispin will find a tavern in town and never return. He can't force me to live with him in London, can he?" Her posture was rigid.

"Nay, he can't," Luca said.

Patience dropped the sash and swiveled.

Luca's admiring gaze wandered to her shoulders and the exposed, freckled skin of her neckline. His pulse kicked, pounding through his legs, up his stomach and chest, settling at the base of his throat. When he spoke again, his voice grew husky with an uncharted emotion he couldn't name. "You're looking as lovely as ever on this bleak day, *kamadiyo*."

Her eyes rounded. A war of confusion and relief seemed to battle across her expressive face. She laced her hands together and clasped them to her heart.

"Mr. Boldor. I ... I waited so long. I wasn't sure if I'd ever see you again."

"A misunderstanding I wanted to correct as soon as I was able."

She accompanied the nervous edge of her laugh

with a jaunty shake of her head. "You almost made me swoon."

"A brave woman like you never swoons."

"I swooned only once in my life, when I feared you'd fallen to your death."

A smile dawned as he gazed at her exquisite face. "Surely a grand leap out another window might grant me another swoon?" His gaze roamed to her frock. Auburn suited her. Auburn was the color of her hair by firelight and complemented the creaminess of her complexion.

Her hands flew to her neckline as a sheen of color washed her temples. "Why are you here?"

"It seems the question on everyone's tongue this afternoon," he said.

She tilted her head, waiting for an answer he couldn't say aloud.

Because I missed you so very, very much and couldn't stay away a moment longer.

The words had come into his mind without warning. He glanced about the dining room to be certain he hadn't spoken them. He'd never missed anyone in his life. Hell, he'd never cared about anyone enough to miss them. Missing someone spoke of commitment. Certainly, he'd never utter such phrases to a highborn English lady.

He kneaded the taut muscles at the back of his neck. "I came back in case you needed protection from some terrible men. And it seems as though your stepson is one of them."

Tears welled in her eyes. She licked her lips and splayed her hands across her chest. "What am I going to do?" she whispered. Her voice choked with tears. "I can't live with Crispin in London. I can't."

"I can assure you that you won't."

"He's charging me with his father's murder and there's no way to prove my innocence." The color rose in her cheeks. "And if we go to court, he'll win...I know he'll win, the solicitor had said as much when I'd met with him...but I was hoping... And I'll be thrown in prison for a crime I didn't commit if I don't agree to abide by Crispin's demands." Her gaze darted to the doorway. She shivered and rubbed her arms, rocking back and forth.

Luca grabbed her shoulders. "He won't win. I won't let him win. I'll fight anyone who'd ever try to hurt you."

Brave words, although inside, Luca felt helpless. He could no longer demand that she live with him in his tribe, for she'd be hunted by the law. Her life, their lives together, were at the mercy of her vile stepson.

He looked to the floor, uncomfortable, harboring foolish fantasies pointing to a life they were never destined to lead. His chest tightened while he planned, obsessed, about what to do next.

"I can take care of myself." Patience pulled away.

Clearly, she was thinking the same thing he was. Her hand twirled the wisp of hair along her neck and he watched her innocent, modest motions. She was no innocent, he corrected himself. She'd been married several years. Jealousy unexpectedly knocked and Luca clamped his fists together to sheath the eruption of possessiveness at the thought of her living with her stepson.

Nay. That would never happen.

CHAPTER TWENTY-THREE

*L*uca's dark, strong form had come upon Patience with unspoken confidence. Glossy, black hair flowed around his face, his orange scarf tied to one side of his forehead.

He'd come back.

Impulsively, she lifted her fingers to smooth a gleaming lock from his temple. He grabbed her wrists and looped her hands around his nape.

"I'm so grateful and relieved that you've returned. I can't believe you're here, or that you're real," she said.

He switched his weight to his other leg. His face reflected a pain he didn't bother to hide. "Be assured, I'm very real."

She glided her fingertips over the prickle of his beard, then found the corded muscles in his shoulders, kneading the tightness. His body was like him —gruff and tender—a man of startling contrasts. She couldn't stop touching him. So peculiar, for she was a woman who flinched whenever a man tried to pierce her invisible armor by a chance touch of his hand.

"I watched the fields and worried for your safety," she said. "Sometimes I thought I saw you walking along one of the paths, although I was always mistaken. If you were here, you'd keep yourself hidden." She conceded a disparaging smile at her habit of blurting out whatever was on her mind. However, there was little point in trying to hide her joy at seeing him again, her relief at having him near.

Because she was a friend worried about a friend, her reasonable brain prompted. Certainly a strong Gypsy man could take care of himself. However, her heart disagreed with her logic, her happiness too genuine. He had returned. He had returned. He had returned.

Tears formed behind her eyes and worked down her throat.

"I wondered if you ever thought about me all the while you were with your tribe," she added.

He stayed quiet, neither moving nor taking a breath. Apparently, he was impervious to the fact this was the part where he should loudly declare that he'd thought of her as often as she'd thought of him. After all, *he'd* come back to *her*.

He turned his head and pinned his gaze not on her face, nor on her person.

He rested his gaze on the dining room chair. The setting afternoon sun weaved a patchwork of rich orange and pink shades on the silk curtains.

"Be assured I won't leave again, especially since Crispin is here," Luca said, instead of answering her question. "Although he's young, Pulko is managing. However, I'll need to look in on my tribe frequently." Luca's smile wavered, two conflicts playing on his features.

His fingers began a leisurely ascent up her spine.

She studied him for several beats longer than she should have and an ache filled her rash heart. She turned, moved away from him, and looked out the window at the river beyond the fields.

Luca came to stand behind her. This was them together, contented and peaceful. The realization lifted her heart and placed it gently back in her chest.

The last splatter of daylight spilled through the arched glass and she drew the silken curtain sash closed, then turned to him. Only the dwindling embers in the fireplace lit the dining room. She swung toward the mantel to light some candles.

His body blocked hers, although he didn't raise his arms. "I'm happy to be here," he said softly, forcing her to stand with her back against the window frame, facing him. "I made the right decision in returning to you."

Her heart soared a little too perilously. He was hard to resist, especially to a woman who hadn't experienced the headiness of desire in a long time. To bring herself back to earth, she tried to keep in mind who she was, where she was, and that she'd vowed never to trust a man again. How long would he stay this time? Had he really returned for good?

"Why is someone like you so interested in visiting and protecting someone like me? 'Tis because I'm a noblewoman and you want to enjoy the luxuries of English living?"

"You state the reasons that make me want to turn away." Luca grinned, dipped his head, and caught her lips with his. The kiss was over before it began, his warm breath glancing her cheeks. She stayed where she was, rooted to the floor, the cold glass of the windowpane pressing against her back.

He took her hands and tucked them in his grasp. "Do you trust that I'll keep you safe?"

"Aye," she said.

Believing, trusting, safety...For a Gypsy rogue, he was so concerned about honest and just principles, yet he relied on no one, had faith in no one, depended on no one.

The dull sound of a cold rain dashed against the window.

His thumb pad brushed against her palm like

rough-hewn wood. "I'm not your elderly husband. I'll never hurt you." Luca brushed a kiss along her cheekbone, then stared at her and grinned roguishly. "I'm a Romany man with few learned skills, although I've been told that I have a decided skill for kissing, especially for a beautiful woman I've missed very much."

This was precisely how he went about enchanting her.

She stepped away. "My stepson's due to return shortly."

"As a favor to me, Amelia is keeping watch for his return and will notify us with ample warning."

Patience's lips moved in a silent question. Before she could ask why Amelia agreed to such a favor, Luca gave an amused shrug of his shoulders. "I eavesdropped on her entire conversation with your stepson. Your cat and I found a splendid spot in the pantry."

"You seem to be on affable terms with Amelia."

"She's a splendid ally." Luca extended his arm in a gracious gesture and stood to the side. "Of course, if you wish to leave now, you certainly can."

So she was free to leave. Free to rally right past him out of her own dining room and into her own kitchen. She glided around him so they stood a few feet apart.

"I don't know how we'll resolve this situation, although I promise you'll be safe," he added.

It wasn't Luca's promise that kept her hands at her sides. It was his self-assurance keeping her feet firmly planted on the floor.

She shook her head. "You don't understand. My stepson is a madman, a description far too generous if he found us together."

"I'll help you figure out a way to get the best of your stepson."

She blew a strand of hair off her forehead. "Perhaps Gypsy men prefer triple jeopardy, and are attracted to women possessing a cloud of auburn hair and freckles on their face."

"I'm merely a man who returned to the woman who afforded me protection, to now extend my own."

CHAPTER TWENTY-FOUR

*P*atience glanced at the window, noting the darkening shadows. "The servants and my stepson should've returned by now."

"Crispin's in the village, no doubt deep in his cups."

An insistent rap on the dining room door, followed by Amelia's insistent whisper, interrupted them.

"Lady Blakwell, your stepson is walking up the road from the stables. Is Mr. Gypsy there?"

"I'll answer for both of us." Luca reached into his boot and yanked a silver dagger from its sheath.

Patience blinked at his startling transformation. He no longer resembled the man who'd kissed her gently a few scant minutes ago, nor the man who'd suffered a horrific gouge on his leg and closed his eyes to shut out the pain.

He steadied one hand on the side of the chair. In four measured strides he reached the door and pressed his body against it. Slowly, he raised the dagger. "Is anyone with you, Amelia?"

"I'm alone," Amelia answered, "Although there'll be servants milling about soon, especially if the countess doesn't make an appearance in the kitchen."

Luca sheathed the dagger and placed it back into his boot.

"Your stepson should enter the hallway shortly," Amelia said. "I'll deter him. However, he'll become suspicious if I stall too long. And, he mentioned that he'd invited a guest for dinner."

When Amelia's footsteps receded, Luca stayed by the door, grim and silent.

He could've been doing any number of things— retrieving his pouch, buffing his boots, grabbing his tan cloak to depart. He did nothing of the sort. Instead, he occupied himself with simple tasks that normally took seconds—securing his green sash, readjusting his linen shirt, retying the tattered hose around his leg.

She lifted an eyebrow and stared at him. "If Crispin catches you, he'll kill you and ruin my life in the bargain. Depart now, and remain unseen."

Luca trudged to the window. She noted that his

footsteps were heavy and his injured leg dragged. He lifted the curtains and peered at the darkening fields. The little snow left shimmered by the light of an early moon, the window fogging with the heat of his warm breath.

She squeezed her eyes shut, trying to accept what was best for them both. He needed to leave, for his safety as well as her own. He had a tribe to take care of, she had a murder charge to fight while enduring the caresses of her depraved stepson.

She pressed her lips together, reminding herself that a lady must accept whatever life brought her with dignity and grace. With that thought, her spine straightened. Yet her heart shied from the realization, the reality, that a woman and a Gypsy man couldn't fight a London judge and jury.

She gazed at him. She tried to memorize the bump on his nose, his soothing, easy smile.

"Goodbye, Mr. Boldor," she said. "Please be safe."

"I'm not going anywhere."

She glanced at the door. "If you wait much longer, you'll be trapped. You can't tramp past my stepson as he comes into the front hallway."

"'Twould appear that danger lurks in every corner and I'm the only Gypsy knight available."

She shook her head. He spouted cool male bravery, whereas she turned into a stammering fool who tripped over her own tongue.

"My stepson will pull you apart limb by limb if he discovers you here," she said.

"I'm not afraid, Patience."

She blinked. "First you become familiar with my name and now you believe you can fight a murder conviction with no money nor power? What's your grievance with my stepson, anyway? You don't know him like I do."

Luca clenched his fists. "I know him better. He brutally raped and murdered a Roma girl I once knew and left her dead by a raging river."

Patience stiffened and couldn't respond. She only knew that she had to be near Luca because she needed his comforting presence. She stepped to the window beside him. The early evening seemed solemn, the sky growing as sad as his words. She scoured her temples, hard, to take away the images he described.

"Each time I see you, you create more and more havoc in my life," she said.

"Each time I see you, you create more and more meaning in mine." His voice came perfectly soft. He was forever bent on captivating, his magnetism weaving an illusion of happily ever after.

She shook her head. "After all these months, are you now attempting to court me?"

"Is that what you English call it? Then, the answer is 'aye.'" He smiled, all coolness and charisma. "I'll go up to the attic and stay out of sight. You count slowly for two minutes, then go directly into the kitchen to supervise dinner preparations."

He'd reverted to his favorite authoritative tone, the one that made her itch to defy him.

"You cannot command me to count, go, and supervise," she said. "There are more ways of solving problems than assuming you're the new lord of my manor and can dictate all that will happen."

"I'll never be the lord of any English manor." A flicker flashed through his eyes, then his face went expressionless. "I'll meet you in the drawing room at midnight so we can formulate a plan. The servants will be safely asleep by then. In the meantime, I'll listen in on your dinner with Crispin for ideas on how to get you free of his charges. I promise I'll stay hidden."

She flung her hands to her hips. "'Tis too dangerous."

Rapid footsteps sounding from the hallway diverted them. "Lord Crispin is coming," Amelia called through the door.

"Midnight," Luca promised. With the prowess of a sleek panther, he swung the dining room door open, then closed the door behind him.

CHAPTER TWENTY-FIVE

A quarter of an hour, Patience decided, was ample time to dress for dinner, especially when she had no interest in impressing her stepson with her appearance.

Since their confrontation when he'd first arrived and played the pianoforte, she'd managed to avoid Crispin. His flinty stare terrified her. When they'd passed on the path to the stables, or by the kitchen pantry, the hairs on the back of her neck rose and her breath came jerky. In the torchlight, she felt his eyes appraise her as a prized lamb before the slaughter. She'd clutched the swansdown of her woolen pelisse firmly to her neckline, confronted his bravado with a blue-blooded look of disdain, then hastened her steps to get away from him.

After looking in on Cook and the kitchen servants, Patience climbed the stairs and latched her bedchamber door. She bathed at her washbasin and walked to her closet to rummage through her wardrobe. With Amelia's assistance, she chose a short-sleeved black frock trimmed at the waist with white satin ribbons. Amelia snapped a brush through Patience's hair and confined her unmanageable curls to the crown.

After Amelia left the bedchamber, Patience regarded herself in the mirror. Auburn ringlets framed her cheeks, and her youthful face smiled back at her. Marriage had done unspeakable things to her body, but hadn't changed her clear, trusting expression.

She secured a black, sheer mob cap over her head and proceeded to the hallway.

Poised on the top of the stairwell, she pulled on a pair of long white gloves.

Midnight. She was meeting Luca at midnight, here, in her own house. Although she'd spent many hours with him, the thought made her color rise.

As she rounded the last step on the stairwell, she spotted Digby laying out the blue and white tableware and gleaming silver pieces on the dining room table. The clinking of porcelain echoed through the hall. Shiny copper plates filled with nuts and pyramids of sweetmeat set grandly on the side tables.

Her stepson milled by the fireplace. He wore a green cravat at his throat tied with a large bow, and showed off his foppishness in an absurdly tight-fitting waistcoat and matching breeches of the finest blue velvet.

Patience made her way to the kitchen to supervise last-minute preparations. The clashing odors of fennel and mint greeted her. She gagged and caught hold of the doorway as her legs swayed.

"Are you feeling unwell, my lady?" Amelia asked from the kitchen. "Your face is ashen."

With a shaky hand, Patience wiped a line of sweat pooling beneath her mob cap. "The smell of fennel has never agreed with me."

"Since you were a child, mackerel sprinkled with fennel seed has always been one of your favorite dishes," Amelia affirmed.

Patience swallowed the sickness in her throat and held onto the doorway. "I cannot explain my stomach of late. The simplest odor sets my insides roiling, although the nausea will pass."

Amelia picked up a knife and moved to the chopping table.

"What dessert is planned?" Patience asked. "I've noticed that the kitchen pantry is desperately low on spices and sweeteners."

"Ice cream, although it's quite melted," Amelia said with sham repentance.

Before Patience could remark on serving melted ice cream, Amelia bent to Patience's ear and whispered, "Has Mr. Gypsy gone back to his tribe?"

"He's upstairs in the attic, and said that he'll be

staying, although one never knows for certain with him," Patience whispered back. "I'm supposed to see him at midnight."

Amelia's lips widened into the closest beam of endorsement she'd ever displayed. "Wonderful."

"You truly believe 'tis a wonderful idea for a Gypsy to meet me in the drawing room at midnight, with Crispin so near? 'Tis too perilous," Patience whispered.

Amelia grabbed Patience's arm and steered her to a far corner of the room. "Not for him," Amelia whispered. "You won't be in any danger. Mr. Gypsy is the finest, bravest man I've ever met, and he's captivated with you. I approve."

Patience held her gasp. If Amelia had called Luca the most refined man on earth, she wouldn't have been more astonished. Besides chiding Patience to conduct herself as a proper Christian lady, Amelia found fault with every man, declaring the lot of them selfish rascals. Why, Amelia had devoted the greater part of her life, up until Patience married, keeping Patience apart from men. Especially after Patience's adolescent tryst with her smooth-talking cousin.

She sighed. Well, she'd paid dearly for her one night of imprudence with a malicious scar, followed by a resulting scandal and unending humiliation, resulting in the ultimate sacrifice, her marriage to a cruel man.

"You no longer think of Mr. Boldor as a barbarian?" Patience whispered.

"Sometimes, when he has that untamed, faraway look in his eye." With that disheartening comment, Amelia waddled to the stove on the far end of the kitchen to commend Cook for burning the mutton, then laid claim to a stool at the kitchen table.

Patience shook her head, deciding to leave the kitchen preparations to Amelia. She left the kitchen, fastened a cordial smile to her face, and entered the drawing room.

 ～

"*G*ood evening, my lady," Digby said, not because he had any interest in her, merely out of duty. He narrowed his stance, his features void of any interest but politeness. He handed her a cup of green tea which Patience hoped would settle her unending nausea.

Crispin sat on a wingback chair near the fireplace. "Lady Blakwell, how pleasant to have your company at dinner. You haven't joined me for any meals since I arrived."

She shuddered at the eeriness of presiding over a dinner with her stepson.

"I wouldn't have missed our final meal together." She cringed as she spoke.

"'Tis temporary. Soon we'll be together, after

final preparations in London are made." Crispin twisted partly in the wingback chair, then slowly rose to his feet. "Amelia will be missed when you move in with me. She's growing too old to travel."

Instinctively, Patience jerked back as he strode toward her. "Amelia is accustomed to the hard work involved in keeping our estate self-sustaining. I plan to continue to reside in Ipswich with her."

Crispin narrowed his eyes. "Unfortunately, her uncle needs her in Bucklesham."

Patience bit back her response. Crispin knew her attachment to her maid and the obvious unfairness of letting go a servant who'd devoted her life to Patience and her family. Resolutely, she took a sip of tea and allowed the pleasurable sweetness of milk and sugar to ease her throat and quiet her stomach.

"I met someone in the village yesterday," Crispin resumed.

Patience poised her teacup at her lips. "Who?"

"My father's old acquaintance, the Most Honorable Christopher Haringley, Marquess of Wottingham. He favored me by accepting my invitation to dine with us this evening."

Unable to see the marquess, Patience stepped closer to the dining room and placed her cup on an end table. Extending her hand, she smiled at the handsome older man grinning at her.

"Lord Haringley," she said.

Placing his shaking grip on the chair's side arms,

the marquess stood, removed his gloves, and held out his hand. Obligingly, she placed her right hand in his and gave a slight curtsey.

"Lady Blakwell." He brushed his lips over her gloved knuckles. "Such a pleasure to see you again."

"Your presence this evening is a great gift," she answered sincerely.

He was taller than she recalled, with a slim build and alert brown eyes studying her in speculative detail. His white cravat and linen shirt were immaculate beneath a double breasted indigo waistcoat. His hair was graying but showed signs of once being jet-black. Something about him seemed faintly recognizable and definitely disturbing.

"May I extend my belated condolences on the death of your husband, the Earl of Ipswich," the marquess said. "My business has taken me abroad these last few years, and I carved out time when I returned to visit my son, Edmund, in Wiltshire. One never knows what mischief he's been up to. Then I arrived in Ipswich less than a fortnight ago. How fortunate I met up with your stepson in the village."

"How fortunate, indeed," she murmured.

"I mentioned to the marquess that our dinner this evening is more or less a celebration," Crispin said, snapping her awareness back to him. "Do we have cause to celebrate?"

She gave her ringlets a proud toss. "We can certainly celebrate your return to London."

Crispin raised his glass of Ratafia, a sweet cordial, and gestured to the marquess. "My lovely stepmother is considering my proposal to move to London with me. This estate is too large for a widow to manage by herself and I fear for her safety."

"My decisions are slow," she said, wanting to add that he'd left her no choice, but saying nothing. Avoiding Crispin's scowl, she looked at the marquess. His dark eyes lit with warmth and understanding.

"Apparently your stepmother needs more time to come to a decision, Lord Crispin," the marquess said. "Women cannot be pushed into something unless they're convinced 'tis what they want. Otherwise, all the prodding in the world does little good."

Crispin fingered his cravat and glanced at the clock. "Six fifteen. I distinctly recall telling the maid to serve our meal promptly at six."

As if prompted by his statement, the servants marched into the dining room with great ceremony. Two maids in black wearing white ruffled aprons balanced trays filled with hot artichoke soup, pickled vegetables, and baked mackerel. They seemed coolly unconcerned with the burnt mutton they placed in the center of the dining room table.

After she and her guests took their seats around the dining room table, Patience asked for a moment of prayer before they ate. When they finished their prayer, Crispin tasted the soup and his conversing froze. Meanwhile, the marquess stabbed at the seared fat bubbling atop the mutton.

From across the dining room, Patience read Amelia's beam of satisfaction. She'd deliberately prepared the worst meal in Ipswich's history, a mutinous and dangerous attempt to antagonize Crispin.

Half-listening to the conversation swirling around her, Patience felt a smidge of guilt. She should've realized what Amelia had been up to. The marquess was an older man and her guest, and deserved a prompt and decent meal. With a sigh, she fixed her stare on a cobweb in the corner of the ceiling and tried to determine how long it had been there.

~

*D*inner pushed on. Glasses and cups were lowered and lifted. For two hours, food was eaten in a combination of slow motion and a blur. Except for the plink of silver and the charming exploits of the marquess's journeys abroad, the meal consisted of a silent downhill slide of inedible food culminating in dessert.

When the hour neared nine o'clock and the men were about to retire to the drawing room to enjoy their port, Patience turned to the marquess. "You're welcome to stay the night. We have several spare bedchambers available in the other wing of the house, where Lord Crispin stays."

"Your consideration is appreciated, but an old man enjoys his own comfortable surroundings." With a kindly nod he pushed back his chair and stood, thanked them for the meal, then called for his servant to send his carriage round.

After the marquess departed, she bid Crispin a hastened good night.

He watched her. She knew he did, felt his interest boring into her back, as a cat awaiting a wingless wren. And she also knew if she were not extremely vigilant and didn't have Luca by her side, she would never be safe from any man named Blakwell.

CHAPTER TWENTY-SIX

From childhood, Patience had been taught that the stroke of midnight was a time to dread. A bewitching hour. A time for elusive phantoms.

She knew better now. She believed in God.

With an assurance from Amelia that Patience's dog, Oliver, was content to sleep in the kitchen, Patience entered her bedchamber well before midnight.

Then she waited. And waited.

And waited, before slipping quietly down the stairs to sit on the settee in the drawing room.

The first hour went by with no sign of a Gypsy man with soft black eyes. She stared out the window, fidgeted with the sash, and counted the ragged clouds floating across a hazy evening sky. Slowly, the second hour ticked by.

Patience scolded herself for allowing disappointed tears to press against her throat. If anything, she should shout for joy. He gave her emotions a reprieve, for he wasn't coming.

In her own house. In her own drawing room. He wasn't coming.

To her chagrin, the tears reached her eyes. She blinked them away, unpinned her ringlets, then cast her black mob cap on the walnut table near the pianoforte. It mattered naught if he'd fallen asleep and forgotten. She wouldn't be going up to the attic to find him.

The heartless scoundrel.

When the third hour straggled with no sign of him, she resigned herself to the fact that she was, once again, a fool in putting her trust in a man. A fool who thought a man might actually care about her, and not want something in repayment—a dowry, land, or more of herself than she could give. A fool who'd fallen for a charismatic Gypsy's honeyed ways and endless charms and false promises. A fool who'd succumbed to the hope that Luca embodied all a man was supposed to be. Honest. Sincere. Heroic. With an inner sigh of regret, she reminded herself that there was no such man.

Woodenly, she crept up the stairs and prepared for bed. She scrubbed herself with lavender bar soap and donned clean linen night clothes. She yawned, so tired her eyelids leaked.

The logs shifted, the flames sparked and grew dim. She shuffled to the fireplace and warmed her hands. Then she locked her door. Twice. And crept into bed.

~

*S*he always could tell when someone was watching her, even in sleep. She kept her eyes closed, knowing someone stood over her bed. It was not unlikely, nor unusual. Her late husband had entered her bedchamber whenever he pleased.

Caught between dreams and wakefulness, she inhaled, expecting the reek of vinegary herbs. Not a man who smelled of outdoor campfires and warm leather and worn buckskin.

She jolted up.

Lit by twin candles on her night table, Luca's wildly handsome face hovered over her. "Did you sleep well, *kamadiyo?*" His warm breath skimmed over her cheeks.

She gazed into his dark eyes and shoved off the blankets. Scrambling to her feet, she grabbed her shawl hanging by the doorway.

He was all handsomeness, all attraction, all too real.

"How long did you watch me?" she managed to ask, scurrying into the hallway barefoot.

He followed her. The top laces of his linen shirt were loosened, his green sash tied at his waist. "I came as promised."

"You're late."

Something flashed in his eyes. Surprise? Interest? Both quickly masked.

"I'm sorry. You waited up for me?" he asked.

She hesitated. The hint of hopefulness in his tone disarmed her. "I waited in the drawing room as you'd requested."

"My tribe had an urgent matter requiring my attention," he said. "I solved the matter without having to travel far, thanks to Pulko."

His tribe came first and she could ask for nothing more than his steadfast caring for them. Still, she felt rebellious. "You were able to walk to the tribe's encampment and back in one night?"

He gave his typically cool smile. "I told you, I didn't need to travel far."

She directed her gaze to the small hallway window and stared out at the stars, sparkling like diamonds against a black sky. "Crispin's sleeping in the other wing in one of the guest bedchambers. Being with you here is too risky."

"He's *beng*, evil, and you cannot be in this dower house alone with him. I'd contemplated making a *bender* at the edge of your estate and sleeping there until he departed. And then I decided to sleep in the attic as you requested because 'tis closer to you."

She tossed her hands on her hips. "You'd *decided* to sleep in the attic? You overbearing—"

"Gypsy rogue," he finished with a smile.

She allowed herself a moment of frosty silence to stare icily at him while caution clamored in her ears. This was precisely how he went about luring her back into believing he truly cared about her.

"Remember you asked if I wanted to court you?" he asked.

"What an unusual way to go about it—by sneaking into my bedchamber in the middle of the night and scaring me half to death. Shall I add you were also late while my immoral stepson sleeps under my roof?"

He glanced his knuckles over her cheeks. "Trust me. I came back to protect you."

Her respect for him multiplied by his ability to speak openly. He exposed her apprehension for what it was—a nameless panic. The longer she knew him, the more she enjoyed his companionship and the sometimes playful, sometimes serious, sparring they shared. For these simple delights, and the happiness filling her whenever he stepped within ten feet of her, she was willing to believe that she could trust him. He made her chuckle out loud with an impudent remark, his white teeth flashing in his sun-burnished face as he laughed with her. Or, he made her flush with elation when he told her how lovely she looked.

He swept out his hands in an invitation. "Are you ready to go back to sleep? In less than a few hours it will be dawn."

With a shake of her head, she stepped to her bedchamber door. "Truly you're the most impossible man to understand," she said.

"Enigmatic sounds better."

Enigmatic. She added a few words of her own. Mysterious, resourceful, and possessing a wonderful, wry intelligence she never would've anticipated when she'd first met him.

"The truth is, I'm relieved, yet frightened that you're here," she admitted.

He pushed the persistent ringlets from her forehead. "I'll never hurt you."

"I'm not frightened of you," she said. "I'm frightened of myself."

"Sometimes I'm frightened of myself, also." He brushed his lips against her temple. "And know that 'tis a terrible strain on my arms not to keep you in them."

He must've realized his candid confession would soften her limbs to butter. She felt split in two, as if she watched a woman she thought she knew from across the length of the dark hallway. Clutching her shawl closer, she padded across the threshold of her bedchamber and stood close to the doorway.

He kept his gaze on her face and gave her hands a gentle squeeze. "My beautiful countess, I cannot think clearly when we're so close and what I need to say cannot be casually spoken." He spoke low, as if he pondered some serious conversation he'd been having with himself, thoroughly weighed the consequences, and didn't like the outcome. She hoped for the mischievous twinkle to reappear in his eyes, the rough angles of his face to ease, his calm tone to reassure her that all was fine.

He stepped back, keeping a few feet from her. Whatever he had to say was important, and the inkling of apprehension welled in her chest. She tried to quell her uneasiness and turned to glance out the window at the desolate, leafless trees in the distance. The bright yellow moon had started its descent in the last hours before dawn.

"I watched you tonight, wrapped in your fine shawl," Luca began. "And I realized how accustomed you are to elegance. Have you ever slept outdoors in a tent?"

"Nay."

"Have you ever eaten a meal cooked over a campfire?"

"Never."

"I like to sleep under the stars," he said. "I like to watch the waves storming the coast during a thunderstorm, build a campfire in a circle of grass, skin and cook a rabbit I hunted."

"These are the qualities I admire most about you," she said, cautiously trying to gauge his mood. "Your culture, your beliefs, your closeness to nature. You're a man of principle."

"You admire the Romany in me, the best part. But what you're not aware of—" He leaned heavily against the wall, a few steps from her, like a man planning to push through an uncomfortable conversation that he'd initiated.

"What?" she asked.

He walked past her into her bedchamber, led her further into the room, and latched the door behind them. He reached for his waistcoat, which he'd placed on a high wardrobe near the door. His worn cloak followed. He yanked the orange scarf from the seam of his cloak. "Do you know where I was this evening?"

"Tending to your tribe," she ventured.

"Before that. While you enjoyed dinner in the dining room, I assisted Amelia in the kitchen burning the mutton to a crisp when the other servants left the room. Then I hid and listened in on the dinner conversations."

Disconcerted because he was actually talking about food, about burnt mutton and dinner conversations, Patience could only blink.

"I watched your stepson. And I watched your guest, also," Luca said slowly.

"Are you referring to the marquess? He's an elderly, long-time acquaintance and a very kind man."

Luca's eyes sparked, then went flat. So subtle, but she'd seen it.

"He's not kind."

"You know him?" she asked.

She thought Luca flinched, but couldn't be sure.

The tenseness in his body seemed to weigh down the air, making it too heavy to catch her breath. Although he didn't move, she felt him withdrawing, farther and farther away. Soon he'd be only a shadow of a person she once knew, forever out of reach.

"Aye," Luca replied evenly.

"He's generous to his servants. He travels abroad a great deal and recently returned to Ipswich."

A contemptuous snicker pinched Luca's lips. "I know."

"You don't seem to be the type of man to—"

"To grace the same social circles as an English countess, or the esteemed noble peerage?"

"I'm uncomfortable in these circles, as well." There, she'd admitted her lack of confidence, her shrinking into herself whenever she was confronted by a group of wealthy nobility. She knew people whispered and laughed at her scarred face behind their polite, blank facades.

"So how are you acquainted with the marquess?" she persisted.

Luca seemed so uneasy, so defensive, unwilling to allow her into his dark, secretive world.

Two more steps brought him to her bedchamber door. He fumbled with the latch. "He's the part of me I loathe, the proper English part. Lord Christopher Haringley, Marquess of Wottingham, is my despicable father."

CHAPTER TWENTY-SEVEN

"*Y*our father?"

Luca had expected the shock in her voice, the confusion on her face.

But not the suspicion. Not the anger.

Patience pushed past him and shored her back against the bedchamber door. "You never told me you were of noble blood." Her manner accused, shaking with skepticism and disbelief.

"You never asked."

She threw furious daggers with her eyes, sharp as switchblades. "So you decided 'twas best to deceive me? Recuperate in my attic for a sennight, sneak into my bedchamber for an evening—cover me with primrose words—but exclude the fact that you're the son of an English noble?" She shook her head furiously. "You lied by omission. I believed you, tended to you, thought you trustworthy."

"I am."

As he watched her distrustful expression, a wretched feeling hollowed out a place in his stomach. He wanted her confidence and admired her unswerving faith in God, yet Luca had betrayed her by omission. Her God was judgmental. Her God wouldn't be pleased.

"You assumed I was a Roma beggar because of my dark skin. Perhaps you have a misguided sense of what people should look like, what place they should hold in your ideal, pure English world."

She balked, shrinking into the door, as if she didn't believe he was sincere, as if he'd changed into a mythical dragon from a folklore where she didn't belong.

"It doesn't matter to me if you're the lowliest vagrant in England."

He reached out to touch her hand. "I returned to protect you, but also because I missed you very much. You were constantly in my thoughts."

The pink blush on her cheeks rose to her temples. Her shining blue eyes searched his face. "I'm not inexperienced to your attempts to reel me into your net with insincere words."

"Because I'm a Gypsy and therefore beneath a noblewoman like you?" he countered.

"Because you're a scoundrel who preys on my benevolence."

He stiffened. She'd meant to hurt him. And she had. "Alms for the poor?" he drawled bitterly. "You're most charitable, my lady, to help someone less fortunate."

"Can you ever get over this hatred of your father, and by all extension, all English?" she asked.

He blinked. Perhaps he'd been naive in thinking they could figure out a way to be together happily and build a life together. He watched her expression, saw the quiet look of desperation in her eyes. Perhaps she was having the same doubts.

Patience whirled and opened her bedchamber door. "Go."

He gazed at her. She looked extraordinarily gorgeous in that ivory linen nightdress, framed by a sweep of reddish-gold hair, her cheekbones enhanced by a crimson wash of fury.

"I'm no pitiable scoundrel," he said. "And you should know enough about the Roma by now to realize that we don't take lightly to insults."

She stood tall for a small woman, rocking on her tiptoes. "My insults have only begun. Grab your feather quill and scroll for the long list ahead."

The charged silence lasted several minutes before she finally spoke again.

"This has been a difficult and trying few fortnights." Her breath was tight, but her eyes softened.

"I didn't mean my earlier remarks. They came out all wrong and I'm sorry."

He nodded. "Apology accepted."

"You didn't need my charity, although surely you needed food and a warm room when you were suffering so."

He pulled off his orange scarf. It dropped to the floor. "Never, ever pity me."

"I have no reason to pity an English nobleman. 'Tis more likely I'd pity a Gypsy beggar."

"What about a half-breed?" His words slipped out, demanding. Meaningful.

He averted his eyes to escape her answer, for it was better left unsaid.

"Why is your heritage of such importance?" she asked.

He motioned to her bedchamber. "'Tis of utmost importance to a well-bred aristocrat, is it not? Blood lines and good breeding are the main topics of conversation in a proper English drawing room."

She replied without hesitation. "You're fortunate to belong to two races and two cultures. You reap the benefits of each."

"Perhaps I belong to neither." He kept his expression nonchalant, but the troubling reality of his mixed heritage almost broke him as a child, as a young man, as an adult. He was forever obsessed with being the bravest, the strongest, the most agile, all to prove his self-worth.

"Do you prefer an Englishman or a Rom?" he asked.

She bent to pick up his orange scarf and handed it to him. "You're exactly as you should be."

"My Englishness is a millstone around my neck," he said. "The Romanes elders still regard me with suspicion if I do anything they don't approve of."

A torrent of emotions flew across Patience's face before settling into shining eyes and a kind smile. "You took on an oppressive burden caring for an impoverished Gypsy tribe and have never shirked your responsibilities. The elders should be grateful."

Just thinking about the endless hunger and countless deprivations of his tribe filled Luca's chest with commitment and duty. He strode into her bedchamber and to the window, opened it part way, and shoved the silk draperies wide. He gulped a chilly breath. All was serene and silent. Not even a breeze glanced the hedges and hazelnut trees.

"The Rom are good to me," he said softly. "My tribe could've rejected my mother. She'd taken up with a *gadje*, a serious offense for a Roma. They accepted her pregnancy by an Englishman, they accepted me, a half-breed, even after her death."

There was more, but he couldn't speak of it. The twin baby brother who'd died, his mother's sorrow and despair. The long winter days broken only by her muffled crying.

This was his life. Always a struggle. Always such

sadness. He gripped the window frame and closed his eyes, concentrating on the darkness to blot the memories.

Patience came to stand by him and rested her hand on his forearm. "Pray for guidance and listen for a quiet, inner voice."

He shook his head. Pray. He honestly didn't know how.

"When did you last see your father besides this evening?" she asked.

Luca opened his eyes and stared out the window. "I saw him a few times over the years. We've never spoken."

Her hand was on his shoulder. So comforting, so soothing. He'd forgotten how much he'd missed the reassurance of another person's caring touch. He trained his gaze on the twinkling sparkles of light, dewy pastures by moonlight, lit like a far-away fairy kingdom, all make-believe.

"Fabiana told me that my father abandoned my mother and me when I was only two years old," he said.

Patience's hands came firmer on his shoulder. "Surely your father wondered what became of you. You should seek him and talk to him."

"He should seek me. I'm his son. He abandoned me."

There it was, the familiar ache and loneliness pushing out Luca's anger. Every time he thought himself rid of the anger, memories haunted him. He was a child with no parents, no one who truly cared. In thirty years, no one had greeted him in the morning with a warm cup of tea when he awoke, or wished him good night when he retired for the evening to his lonely tent.

"The marquess has been an acquaintance for many years," Patience said. "He's one of the few nobles whom I respect."

"He's a good-for-nothing with a cold heart."

Patience's hands glided across Luca's shoulders in the same way she might soothe a caged tiger. "Now that I look at you, your resemblance to your father is astounding. Your height, the angle of your chin, all remarkably the same. Indeed, your skin is darker, but little else. No one will refute your claim as his heir."

Luca jerked away from her hands. "I have no claim. And if I did, my only claim is that he's a loathsome man and I don't want him as a father. He deserted my mother and me."

"His desertion, for whatever reasons, forced you to become a stronger man."

"If a strong man starves and begs to feed his tribe winter after winter, then I'm very strong indeed."

Patience's huge eyes grew contemplative, the skin beneath smeared with darkened circles. Moonlight came through the window, illuminating the cruel scar on her face, the sprinkle of freckles on her nose and cheeks, making her appear much younger than any image he'd ever harbored of a dowager countess.

"There's much I want to understand about you and your life," she said.

He cupped her face and smoothed the puffiness beneath her eyes. He had no intention of telling her more about himself, because he'd sully her sweetness.

"You should get some sleep," he said.

"Regrettably, I'm more awake now than I was at midnight while I was waiting for you." She cast a sidelong glance at the window. "I can arrange a meeting with your father. To have peace in your life, first you must find it in your heart to forgive."

"How shall I introduce myself at this meeting? We have naught in common. He spends his days practicing his manners, I spend my days practicing survival. Shall I limp into his drawing room as a cripple, dependent on a walking stick?"

"Introduce yourself as the man you are. Valiant, decisive, and daring. You're a leader of a tribe. You're a legend in your own right."

Luca smiled. "People believe I have no weaknesses, although I do have one."

Her face showed a front of humor and disbelief. "You, the legend, admit to a weakness?"

He quirked a brow, then gently kissed her. "Only one, and she soothes my spirit like no one else can."

Patience's hands rested on his shoulders. He breathed in her familiar fragrance, fresh and clean, all lavender and sunshine, despite the dreariness of a cold night.

"Someday I'll bring you a frock the color of the sea, strung with shiny blue beads to match your eyes," he said.

She was purity and unaffected elegance, kind-hearted and glorious, and she'd touched his heart each time she smiled, each time she cared for him.

The low-burning candles on the mantel cast a warm glow on her stunning face. Without warning, she shivered, her eyes tormented. Her expression clouded.

He glanced at the fire in the fireplace, now little more than ashes, and grabbed her hands. "What troubles you, *kamadiyo?*"

"There are memories in this chamber," she said softly. "Hiding under the eaves, summoning to mind cutting insults." Her complexion turned so pale to be almost ethereal, her forehead so tight as to make her thoughts transparent.

Luca squeezed her hands and stared at her. "I'll destroy the memories by slaying them."

The depths of her eyes shimmered a satiny blue before she dropped her gaze to the floor. "Because

of my scar, I'm embarrassed when you look so intently at me."

He pressed a kiss to her cheek, to that very same
pale disfigurement. "I like to look at you."

She kept her eyes lowered. "I'm plain."

"You're beautiful." He glanced at her slight,
dainty hands, and pulled her hands to his. She was so
delicate. Protectiveness for her had taken a firm
place in his chest. "Roma aren't ashamed of scars.
It's part of you and your life."

A crimson blush tinted her freckled white skin.
Life with her took away the pain of seeing his father,
of endless brawls with nameless faces over his mixed
heritage, of long years of loneliness and seeking.

"You'll never abuse me in any way? Not even if
you're terribly angry?" She shook her head. "Both
men that I've been with have hurt me—my late husband and my...smooth-talking cousin."

Lightly, Luca touched the scar on her cheek. "Is
your cousin the man who caused this scar?"

She nodded. "Aye."

He swallowed the prickly lump that had taken
up residence in his throat. and guided her to a side
chair. "*Kamadiyo,* I'll never hurt you." Retrieving
some silk pillows at the foot of the bed, he buoyed
the pillows behind her and sat on the floor at her
feet.

"'Tis almost dawn," he said. "Try to sleep for a
while."

The hours before daybreak went on in a blend of dozing and wakefulness. Lost in thought, he watched her as she slept. She was *wuzho*. Pure and untainted. And, she was the woman he'd been seeking all his life.

CHAPTER TWENTY-EIGHT

*C*rispin departed two days after the dinner with Luca's father. He'd vowed to return within two months. Luca stayed in Patience's attic, knowing that Pulko had grown into a capable leader and could manage the tribe. Every evening, Luca tried to help Patience figure out how to fight charges if Crispin followed through with his threat.

As Luca did each morning, he strode the large expanse of lawn, keeping himself hidden from the servants. Then he found Amelia and Penham sitting together in the kitchen.

He greeted them as he always did, then asked, "Where is Lady Patience?"

"She's somewhere near the stables," Penham replied.

"I'll find her," Luca said.

"Penham will fetch her!" Despite her outburst, Amelia's face waxed deliberately blank when Luca glanced at her. She darted a nervous look at Penham. Without actually acknowledging each other, the two servants seemed to share a private conversation.

"Is there any trouble I should know about that may have happened last evening?" Luca asked carefully.

"Nay!" Both servants shouted in unison.

The lengthening silence was interrupted only by the clank of a rolling pin and the clip of a knife.

"Perhaps I should bathe while I'm waiting for Patience," Luca said.

Amelia rounded on Penham. "Go to the well to fetch buckets of water. then bring a tub to the attic."

"What a bossy woman." Penham cast his knife to the table and trudged out the door.

Amelia set a plate on the table filled with sticky roasted quail, along with a slab of brown bread and a cup of hot tea. Luca bowed his head for a silent prayer, then ate his fill. When he finished, she poured a bowl of creamy custard before him.

While he enjoyed his custard, Amelia grabbed a stool next to him. She pulled off the linen bandages and cleansed his wound, then carped non-stop about the lack of dependable servants and Penham's inability to complete any chore without her detailed instructions.

"Really?" Luca interjected good-naturedly whenever she paused, although it wasn't a question, just a way to feign interest in the conversation.

"Lady Blakwell confided several matters to me last night." The stark change from Amelia's light-hearted chattering to one of quiet gravity was as startling as her normally abrupt change of topics.

"Go on." He tried to respond nonchalantly.

"My lady told me that the Marquess of Wottingham is your father and she wants you and him to meet and resolve your differences."

"He's held no position of value in my life, nor any position at all," Luca pushed back his stool. He forestalled any additional confidences by putting up his hand and striding out the kitchen doorway. He slipped into the kitchen garden, rubbed Oliver's ears, and passed Penham heaving a bucket of water.

"I'll carry it," Luca volunteered to the elderly servant. With a sidewise smile for Amelia and a lengthy, labored breath at the persistent throbbing in his leg, he hoisted the bucket, added a shard of bar soap and several linen cloths, and started up the stairs.

Once in the attic, he grinned to see the tub already partially filled with water. Penham was apparently faster than Luca. A warm afternoon sun streamed through the window. After a trip to the bedchamber below to attend to his needs, he climbed the stairs back to the attic, stripped off his clothes and settled into the bath. He bent his legs to accommodate his long form, washed himself, and scrubbed his hair. When the bath was ended, he dried with a linen towel and pulled clean clothes from his pouch.

As he finished dressing, Patience rushed into the attic and latched the door behind her. She presented a lovely vision. Her color was high, her loose, deep-red hair flying from her shoulders, her luminous blue eyes shining with elation.

He held out his arms and she hurried into them.

Later, he'd remember thinking that her hips seemed ever more rounded then he'd noticed before.

She flung her arms around his shoulders and buried her face in his chest. "You're my Gypsy knight. My perfect dream. Truly, you are a gift from God."

The scent of her satiny, lavender-smelling skin made his blood gallop. Each bend of her delicate limbs, each tender murmur of delight in his ear, was a sound reminder of why he'd returned. He tipped her face and tiny droplets of water remaining on his hands from the bath wet her cheeks.

"How fares your leg today?" she asked.

"Much, much better every day." He was such a cool liar, but he wanted to protect her from worrying about him.

She massaged the clean hair of his scalp and finger combed the wet tendrils from his forehead. Her eyes were perceptive and fun-loving. Her lips were full, a lovely shade of pink.

"Amelia bound my wound in the kitchen and prattled endlessly," he said.

Patience's hands stilled, her demeanor sobered. "You spoke with Amelia...endlessly?"

She bent her head and stared at the bar of soap floating in the tub. He sensed, rather than saw, her mercurial changeover. She kept her eyelids lowered, her fringe of ginger lashes sweeping across her cheekbones. "How long did you converse?" she added.

"Both Amelia and Penham greeted me in the kitchen, as they usually do. Then Penham went to the well and Amelia chattered without a breath while I ate."

"What did Amelia chatter about?" Patience asked.

"As is her way, she complained about Penham and the other servants," Luca replied guardedly. "Why?"

"I wondered if she told you anything else in par-ticular." Patience stepped away to stand by the fire-place. She fingered the neck lacings of her crimson frock. Should he go to her, take her in his arms and demand answers, or should he remain where he was, by the dirty, tepid bathwater, and give her the dis-tance she obviously needed?

"Are you not happy I'm here with you?" he ventured.

She turned from him and faced the fireplace. "Of course. Unbearably happy."

But.

She hadn't uttered the word but her anxiety weighted the very air of the room.

Guardedly, he walked to her. He stood close but not touching, within arm's reach. In case she decided to break away, he could grab her quickly.

"Look at me," he ordered.

She turned slowly. If she was so 'unbearably happy,' the excitement and laughter had long disappeared from her face. Her whole demeanor had shifted, becoming apprehensive and serious. Her naturally radiant complexion was drawn and pale, the freckles fairly jumping from her skin.

This close, he had to touch her. He lightly stroked his knuckles across her smooth cheeks. She froze and briefly closed her eyes.

"I cannot fix what I don't understand." He caught her shoulders, pressed his lips against her hair. "No problem is too great that we can't find a solution together. You know that I'll not allow Crispin to take you to London."

"This isn't about Crispin." She shifted in his arms. "And I fear you'll never accept this one."

He massaged her shoulders, his thumbs kneaded the tight muscles in her back. He took some satisfaction from the fact that she let him hold her.

"Several months ago," he began, "when I was

helpless, I promised I'd protect you because I was indebted to your kindness, remember? Please tell me what's wrong." His hands grazed her sleeves, leaving imprints of his damp fingertips along her shoulders.

She winced and shrank back.

He lifted his hands. "When have you ever been repelled by my touch?"

"'Tis not your touch." Inching forever backward, she eyed him cautiously. She reached the wall, which prevented her from retreating. Frowning, she pressed her palms so hard on either side of herself that her knuckles whitened. "'Tis just that my skin has become more and more sensitive and tender."

Sensitive? Tender? Why?

Suspicion and mistrust screamed through him. The peculiar way Amelia and Penham had behaved. Luca scrambled for suitable reasons for their evasive behaviors, suitable rationales.

"I was gone so often..." He shook his head, thoughts colliding, then strode to her and seized her forearms. "Who is he?"

"How dare you accuse me of behaving as if I were one of your Gypsy strumpets."

Luca's mind shouted, refusing to believe she wanted another man, while his heart fractured into tiny pieces. "You don't lie well, despite your Christian ways."

She leaned against the door. "Take your hands off me."

He loosened his grip. He ached to thrust her traitorous, trembling self away from him as much as he ached to hold her close and feel the exquisite beating of her heart.

She forced him to look at her by brushing her fingers along his tight jaw. And in that moment he knew one thing for certain. She hadn't found another man when he'd returned to his tribe. No woman, however blameworthy, could weave such an expression of indignant fury and confusion, then be so devoted to him since his return.

He slowed his breathing until a breadth of calmness returned and he could see another color besides blood-red anger.

"I'm simply possessive of the woman who has taken away my heart," he admitted.

Her delicate eyebrows snapped together. "Don't blame your outrageous temper on me." She marched to the paned window.

He scraped his hands over his face and blew through his fingers. "I can blame my temper on the fact that I'm a Rom, but in truthfulness, 'tis because I'm hopelessly in love with you."

He didn't know what he'd expected from his admittance because he'd surprised himself for declaring his thoughts aloud.

She swiveled. "And I love you, my Richard the Lionheart."

"Then what's wrong? Everyone seems to know except me."

She stared at the toes of her flat shoes, decorated with a delicate purple bow. "I planned to explain everything later this evening, after I'd finally admitted the truth to myself." She sighed heavily. "Since we first met, you've been concerned that you'd become a cripple, but you should be more concerned about your eyesight, because you're most certainly blind."

She kept her gaze out the paned glass window. Then she splayed her hands protectively over her stomach and gazed out into the deepening dusk.

Luca stood where he was and waited for her to speak.

"Do you know the color of my eyes?" Her voice was low, a rustling whisper with a suspiciously sharp edge.

"Your eyes are blue. As blue as the salty blue sea."

"When you look at me, who do you see?"

"The woman of my dreams," he answered immediately. "The woman I want as my wife."

There was a sharp intake of her breath, followed by a mountain of quiet. Although her back was to him, he knew she'd heard his proposal of marriage. Yet when she turned, her expression was unreadable.

"Do you like children?" she asked.

This was definitely the day for the most unusual questions.

"Aye. The Rom adore children." Luca reached her in three panther-like strides. He cupped his hands around her shoulders. "Why? *Why?*"

She swallowed, seeming to push back tears. After several efforts to speak, she choked, "I'm reassured to hear this."

The scent of sun-dried grass wafted through the window. Tawny pinks and pale orange from the day's end sun filtered through the window and illuminated her fair skin. This near, he admired the sapphire flecks in her eyes despite the clash of emotions they conveyed.

He fumbled for answers. "Is there a child in the village who's ill? Are you ill?"

She gave him a quiet smile. "I didn't mean to worry you."

"Shall I summon Amelia?" he asked.

"Many lady's maids would need to be summoned throughout England for many English ladies because my illness is quite ordinary." She shook her head and sighed. "For some time, I've missed my monthly flux."

"Monthly—"

"I am with child."

Instantly, one question came to mind. How, because the child couldn't be his?

All the air flew from his body. He tried to draw a

clear, full breath, but his lungs wouldn't cooperate. Somewhere from his lost youth, an image came to mind of the child he'd imagined he might be blessed with. He gazed at Patience, visualizing that precious child they'd one day have together—with dark freckled skin, black unruly hair, and eyes the color of sapphires.

"I suspected a while ago, but I waited. When I missed my fourth month, my suspicions were confirmed."

He heard her words, said so softly that they didn't enter the reasoning portion of his brain.

Luca gazed at her, at her body.

Dreadfully calm, he waited. But somewhere in his heart he already knew. God help him, he already knew.

"I've suspected for a while now." She turned. She had the agitated stiffness of a woman conflicted by both joy and sorrow. "I carry my late husband's child."

CHAPTER TWENTY-NINE

*I*t was if she'd struck her fist into his stomach, for the physical suffering was as great as the anguish in his mind. He was breaking into small pieces. Pieces that tore through his insides, accelerating to a tempo and intensity that cut off all rational breath.

He should speak. He didn't react quickly enough. Her words hummed in his brain, her mouth worked in slow motion.

Luca dragged air into his chest and swallowed a deluge of disbelief and lost dreams.

"Your late husband's child. I planned to marry you and all the while you carried your late husband's child. An English child." He shambled to a nearby wooden chair, gripping the wood until his hands were bloodless.

"I feared this might be your reaction," she said. "Knowing the type of man you are—so proud of your customs and loyal to your Gypsy heritage, harboring such ill will toward the English. But I'd hoped you might be happy, at least for me."

He closed his eyes. Frustration and regret didn't allow him to speak.

A better man might've assured her that, indeed, he was quite happy for her. Delighted, in fact. So delighted that he still planned to wed her. So delighted that he'd raise her child as his own, this full-blooded English child who wasn't his.

But he wasn't a better man. He was a half-blood, a destitute man. A man who stole as a way of life, who fought in the dirt with his fists, not atop a prancing black horse. He was a man who'd fibbed and falsified all sorts of tales to the *gadje*, and, aye, laughed at them afterward for their stupidity. But in reality, he'd played a serious game he needed to win every time to survive.

He blew a deep audible breath and opened his eyes. "I'm not an English gentleman, forever polite and chivalrous."

"I know who you are."

"Do you?" He refused to meet her gaze. "Then you know me better than I know myself."

She went to him and touched his chin, forcing him to look at her. "You're kind and tender."

Misery and fury clustered around him like flies

and he swatted at the empty air. "Did you expect a more joyous response to your happy news?"

"Congratulations are in order."

"Congratulations, Lady Blakwell."

"Thank you, Monsieur Boldor." She seemed to chuckle at the ridiculous formality. "Or Monsieur Wottingham?"

"Boldor. I take my mother's surname."

Patience drew a long sigh. "For years, I'd prayed for a child to love, to give me hope when I was alone and afraid, living on this wretched estate."

"The birth of a child is always a reason for celebration," Luca said coolly, carefully. He reached for his boots and cloak, cinched the green sash about his waist.

"Will you not stay—at least until the morrow?" He sensed she wouldn't allow him to leave until he answered, for he recognized the real meaning of her question. All he had to do was change the words.

Will you not stay—permanently, as you promised?

He shrugged into his cloak. "I need time alone."

Her face was as pale as frosted marble, her eyes beseeching. A fortnight ago, a sennight ago, indeed, this very day, she'd called him her perfect dream. Her Gypsy knight. Her gift from God.

But he was a far cry from her dreams, and she could never comprehend his reality.

His Romany life spanned thirty years. His new English experiences, this new English love, this utterly English child, all were a mere speck in the scope of his lifetime.

"Where's the man who wanted to marry me?" she asked quietly. "The Gypsy who vowed to protect me from my unspeakable burdens?"

"He refuses to fight a battle he cannot win."

"Then he's not a true champion if he expects an easy victory. The man I know welcomes a challenge. He's a legend."

Luca wasn't feeling particularly like a legend. He felt numb and tired. He flexed the cramp in his leg and wondered if it was conceivable to feel anything other than pain ever again. Under impossible choices, he was fast becoming a man he neither understood nor respected. He was fast becoming a man like his father, who refused to accept the responsibility of a child.

"I've fought many battles, Lady Blakwell," he said. "A true victor knows his opponent, even when he's outnumbered. But I'm defenseless against a man under a gravestone."

"The man I love is no coward."

"Each time I see the child's English face I'll be reminded of my utter loathing of the English. If the child was between me and you, that would've been wonderful. You're the rare, good English person. But knowing this child is the progeny of a typically cruel one..."

"The child of whom you speak is *my* child, too."

Luca threw his pouch over his shoulder, chancing a glimpse at her as he strode to the door. He knew she'd honed the art of keeping her features unruffled despite her ordeals, except now her face was devoid of any emotion except exposed, raw pain.

~

After all the servants had retired for the evening. Patience found Luca later that night in the drawing room. He stood by a low burning fire in the fireplace, staring into the bluish flames. Only one beeswax candle was lit along the sideboard, offset by the glow thrown by the smoky oil lamps near the entry. Absorbed by the fire, he didn't seem aware that she'd entered.

She sucked in a breath, along with her pride, and went to him.

Lightly, she touched his shoulders. "I feared you'd left without saying goodbye."

He shook her off and raised his hand in a mock salutation. "But here I am, your ever-present servant, owned by you, bound to this dower house. Or rather, owned by the Rom, bound to the tribe." He smiled, seeming to appreciate the irony coloring his words. "I may yet fight so I can find what I've been seeking all my life."

She wanted to rub her fingers along his arm, but

something in his eyes filled her with apprehension. She hesitated, then stiffened her spine.

"Seeking what? Seeking whom?" she asked.

Luca glanced toward her and she saw, for a moment, a hopeful, vulnerable boy in his bloodshot eyes, before life had dealt him inconceivable hardships and poverty.

From behind one of the benches she retrieved a walking stick and held it out to him. "I found this in the attic. Amelia must've made another one for you."

The joke didn't amuse, for his black eyes glittered. "I have no use for it."

She tried again, to initiate a conversation with him, any conversation. "Pulko was here earlier," she began.

"I know. I spoke with him."

She looked down at her hands and swallowed. "I caught him stealing from the pantry. He said your tribe lacked mustard for the cod, and ginger for the port wine he'd swindled from a noble. When I inquired further, he admitted he'd stolen from me for months, and that you knew. I wondered where so much of the food went."

"How did you expect my tribe to eat while I ailed?"

"I didn't mind, but why did you never tell me? If I could, I would've sent more."

His angry silence burned the air in response. She

surveyed the bleak, forbidding outline of his profile and her breath trapped in her chest. Moments like these reminded her of how intimidating he and his mysterious life were. She swallowed bravely. "You didn't want to tell me because of your insufferable pride. You didn't want to admit you needed to depend on someone other than yourself."

"I'll repay any stolen food. I'm not a criminal."

She set the walking stick by the fireplace. Then she stepped nearer to this unfeeling stranger who looked like Luca, talked like Luca, but surely couldn't be the man she loved. His shiny black hair was disheveled. His linen shirt was untucked, his orange scarf and green sash thrown to the floor.

"I want to speak about my baby. Our baby," she said.

"We have no baby." His forehead furrowed, the thought seeming to take every ounce of concentration. "You have a baby."

"There's still the matter of Crispin's threats hanging over us, but I want you to be the father of my baby."

"Unfortunately, that title is already bestowed upon your late husband, Lord Bertram Blakwell."

She dragged air into her tight lungs. "I want you as the true father. I want my baby to know you, learn from you, and love you as I do."

He sank his head to his hands. "You don't want me as a father. I'm the spawn of a malicious man."

Her fingers smoothed the bump on his nose. "Your father is agreeable and well-respected. I've known him for years."

Luca tried to stand, wobbled, and dropped back to the settee. "Once, you asked me once how my nose was broken."

She felt as if she were in a dream and didn't know how to answer. "I assumed you were in a brawl."

"A brawl. A simple brawl. How easily I could defend myself against an equal opponent. Sadly, I harbor a child's hazy memory."

She envisioned him, a sturdy toddler covered in mud, showing off skinned knees and scraped elbows to any tribesman who feigned interest. Shoving up his tattered sleeves and challenging any foe with tiny, upraised fists.

"Did you try to fight the biggest bully in the tribe?" she teased.

"I was pushed."

"Were you pushed by Marko?" she asked.

"I was pushed into the dirt by my esteemed father." Luca shook his head, a seemly attempt to clear the film of sadness on his face. "I remember that my mother had quarreled with him."

Patience went still, a chink of steel heavy in her belly.

Very softly, very gently, she said, "Go on."

"My father said he was leaving. I ran after him,

called out to him. I grabbed his leg as he walked and he pushed me—pushed me so hard I toppled and broke my nose. I still remember how the blood tasted, like sticky metal on my tongue. I remember Fabiana screaming, my mother crying, a brown bird in a birdcage chirping gaily, oblivious to the cruelty."

Holding back tears, Patience said, "You said the memory was hazy."

Luca shook his head. "My father didn't care about my cries. He walked out of my life, out of my mother's life. Fabiana told me they'd quarreled because he didn't want me. I was so dark, so different from him. How could he be proud of a Romanes son?" Luca raised his shoulders in a gesture of indifference. "It matters naught. I no longer care."

"I think," she said softly, "you care a great deal."

"My father resented my mother and me. We'd trapped him in our world and he missed his comfortable English life. My bitterness toward the English will rail against your English child."

"Never. You're a man of principle. You rely on a childhood memory that may not be true."

"Fabiana wouldn't lie. She took me in and raised me after my mother died."

"Fabiana may be harboring her own hatred against the English for her own reasons."

"I won't pull you nor your child into my Romany world."

Patience lifted her hands to feel his face, his hair.

"I want your world. Once we're wed, I want your children."

But he was faster than she, even now his expression clearing. He looked around. "You enjoy your English finery. You refused to live in a Rom tribe. You claim you want my world, although 'tis under your conditions."

"Your opinion of me is low and unwarranted. You know I can't leave while my despicable stepson holds this murder charge over my head."

Luca stood. "Aye."

"You're leaving?" she asked. "I thought you were going to protect me against Crispin."

Luca rubbed his hands across his face and didn't answer.

She waited a few moments, feeling a slow anger simmering inside her. When Luca didn't respond, she grabbed the walking stick, advanced, and slammed the stick into Luca's stomach. Besides an oomph and particularly strong Romanes words, he hardly moved.

She threw the stick to the floor and charged out of the drawing room. At the doorway, she swerved. "Do what you do best, Mr. Boldor. Dash off as soon as things get too difficult. I'll face this obstacle, as I've face every obstacle in my life, on my own."

A storm brewed in his gaze, flashing across his face like a whirlwind.

"You're a coward who can't be trusted to keep his

word," she said. "Wander the whole wretched world like a nomad and take care of your tribe if Pulko needs help, which he doesn't. Just leave me a modest bit of pride and keep away from Ipswich." Her fists tightened. "I had begun to believe that you were a trustworthy man who truly cared, but you're like every other man. I love this baby. I don't need your protection against Crispin nor Marko, nor your meaningless proposals of marriage." Sobs welled and she fought hard to contain them, years and years of sobs, like a torrent with no beginning nor end.

The color leached from Luca's face. His eyes were glazed, a tortured man calling for help, for patience. "*Kamadiyo,* I don't know what to do when a woman cries."

"'Tis easy." She licked at the tears on her upper lip. "Get out!"

"Marko's on his way toward the sea and may be heading toward my tribe. When Pulko came earlier, he said there may be bloodshed. He can't fight Marko's tribe alone."

"Then you must hurry to depart." She swiped at her face, could hardly breathe. "Be sure to take all of your belongings—your clothes, your scarf, your cloak." She felt sick, her fingers tingled with cold. She tried to keep her shoulders straight, her manner dignified.

It would be the last time he saw her, and she didn't want to be remembered as a sniveling, woebegone fool. Furiously, she sniffed and brushed a final tear from her cheeks. Her hands were shaking terribly.

He reached for her. For a wild moment she thought of grabbing his fingers, begging him to stay.

"I'll leave at first light," he said. "I'll come back after—"

She thrust his hands away. Iron replaced her bent spine. "Go back to the Rom. 'Tis where you belong."

CHAPTER THIRTY

*P*atience stood by her bedchamber window while her dog slept by the hooded fireplace. Now and then the dog stretched, yawned, and regarded her with a curious stare.

As she did most days, she stared out the window at the vast, open fields to await the dawn. But this dawn was different. The man she loved was walking out of her life for good.

She shivered, knowing the heat from the fire wouldn't warm her.

She attempted to wrench Luca from her heart, from her mind, by doing what she always did. She swallowed her feelings by burying them at the bottom of her heart where nothing could hurt her. But her stubborn mind insisted on torturing, dredging up his hurtful words.

'Did you expect a more joyous response to your happy news?'

She squeezed her eyes shut to stop the flood of desolation. Self-righteous anger, like a defensive dam, barred her from drowning in self-pity.

Luca. Her trustworthy protector. Her beloved. Just the thought made her broken heart laugh. Her cynical, shattered, broken heart.

She swabbed her eyes with the back of her hand. She had to forget him. With the grace of God, she had to look forward and find a way to defend herself against Crispin's coercion.

But Luca's tenderness flooded her with memories.

'Kamadiyo, you're beautiful.'

She held these memories close, for they calmed the empty place in her heart. Once, he'd been taken with her. She remembered his warm scent of buckskin and exotic spices whenever he stood near.

Her. Skinny, plain, as ordinary as a gray church mouse. They could never be together as Luca and Patience because there was no Patience. That young girl with wide-eyed dreams had become lost a long time ago. For a while with him, she thought she was truly alive, that she'd enjoy a wondrous life, filled with his love.

Luca was a proud, Gypsy man. His Romany beliefs were firmly imbedded in his nature.

She continued to gaze out the window and her

heart did a flip when Luca came into the field, staying low and out of sight. His steps were slow and uneven. A chilly spring wind sent a thin mist of rain through the branches and the trees bent. He glanced at her window and for a moment she thought he'd call out. She stepped away so he wouldn't see her.

She thought to walk downstairs, or take up her sewing. She stayed still, ever patient, her hands on her round stomach, sneaking glances at him through the curtains.

She rendered him free to return to his Gypsy life. No regrets. No trust. No protection. Resentfulness burned, filling Patience's veins with unwanted animosity. She pressed her eyes with her forefingers, refusing to weep. Then she stepped to her wingback chair by the fireplace and sat alone, the landscape of her life.

She dozed. An hour later, she glanced at the window. An unusual flickering of torches on the main road leading to the dower house made her pause. It was too early for the maid-of-all-work to awaken as it was not yet half past five o'clock in the morning. The sound of carriage wheels crunched on the ground.

Patience moved to the window and pressed her face to the glass. Two horses blasting great puffs of steam through their nostrils stopped at the front of the house.

A few moments passed, and the beginning measures of a Haydn Sonatina tinkled on the keys of the pianoforte. More moments, then Crispin's shrill voice sounded from the hall.

Oliver scampered to her bedchamber door and growled. Patience dressed in her morning frock and tied a warm shawl around her shoulders. As soon as she opened the bedchamber door, the dog raced through the hallway and down the stairwell. She rushed after him in time to see Oliver scrabble into the kitchen.

Her stepson, Digby, and Marko stood together in the hallway. She couldn't breathe. She glanced at the stairwell, wondering if she'd make it up the stairs in time to get away from them.

"How lovely you look." Crispin spoke first. "No introductions are in order, as you already have met Marko. He and I came across each other in London."

She looked anything but lovely after a night of weeping. She caught a glimpse of herself in the window's reflection. Her nose was red, her face pale as death, the lines of sadness etched below her mouth.

So this was how it must be. Men who were once strangers, banding together against her. If she had any doubt they were up to evil, all she need do was gaze at their grim faces and the hard glint in their stares.

Crispin removed his top hat and tucked it under his arm. "'Tis rumored you consorted again with a

Gypsy man." He waved an accusing finger. "Scandal will never do if you expect to win your case against me in court."

Marko mopped his sweaty face with a dirty handkerchief. His thick fingers were scarred, the tiny yellow flares from his eyes ferocious. "Luca will come with me."

"He's not here," she said.

Marko stepped closer. The memory of his cruelty immobilized her.

"He was here," she clarified, "but he left."

Foolishly, she threw a fleeting glimpse toward the door and Marko's suspicious scowl followed her. She averted her gaze to the kitchen and saw movement. Most likely Oliver cowered behind the cupboards with the maid-of-all-work.

"Where are my other servants?" she demanded of Crispin, to keep the men talking and occupied until she thought of a way to escape.

"I sent Penham and Amelia on a fool's errand to the village for supplies," Crispin said.

"Why do you want to hurt me with these false murder accusations?" she asked.

Crispin pushed back his shoulders, looking the foolish fop from his gold-buckled shoes to his yellow satin cravat. "I want to protect my inheritance. I plotted my father's killing and paid Italian bandits a handsome sum to do the deed. My father hoarded his riches. Old men like him live forever."

"Why did you blame me for his death?"

"You were a convenient suspect. When I was in London, I often played the pianoforte and thought of my father constantly ridiculing me. He said men didn't play the pianoforte, only women. Nonetheless, I was the real man in the end because I had the last say."

"Your father ridiculed everyone," she said.

Crispin smiled. "Then I heard from a former scullery maid several months ago, that the servants suspected you might be pregnant because you'd complained about feeling nauseated. I knew the child was my late father's. I've waited a long time for my inheritance and no stepbrother or sister will jeopardize it. I know what your father had written in the marriage contract and that a certain amount of money would be set aside for any children. This, I assure you, won't happen. You'll travel to London with me when Marko is finished with you."

"Try it." Luca stood in the kitchen doorway, looking like fury himself. "Any of you."

Patience whirled as Digby lunged for her. She dodged him, lost her footing, and collided with the balustrade near the stairwell. Digby clamped his hands around her shoulders and her muscles shook with the effort of trying to hold still. If he jerked her forward, she'd fall face-first to the floor and she might lose her baby if she was injured.

Two pulses of aggression and violence, Marko

and Crispin, intercepted Luca midway in his flight to reach her. Marko caught Luca's ankles.

Luca reeled. Crispin kicked him to the floor, leaned over Luca, and held down his arms.

Marko seized the walking stick by the fireplace. He took aim and swung at Luca's kneecap. The hall exploded with the sickening snap of solid wood smashing into bone and muscle.

"Needing this to walk, aye? Becoming a simpering cripple, like a *gadje*?" Marko shouted, punching again and again at Luca's leg.

Patience's heartbeat maddened, her limbs trembling uncontrollably in Digby's grip. She heard herself screaming Luca's name, tracking the horrible scene as if it were performed in slow motion.

Luca moaned, his body jerked. The dagger fell from his hand and skidded across the floor. His left leg twisted helplessly. His buckskin breeches grew red, then black with blood.

Oliver charged into the hall. Crispin's grip loosened on her as he tripped over the dog. With a heroic leap and a bar of pointed canine teeth, the dog bit into Marko's swinging arm. Oliver held his bite, tiny in contrast, attached to the mammoth Gypsy.

For a stunned second, Marko cursed savagely. He dropped the walking stick and wrenched the offending dog from his arm. "What vile, evil spirit is this?" He flung the dog to the floor. Whimpering,

Oliver's tiny pink tongue protruded from his mouth and his eyes lost their sheen. Blood coursed from the side of his small, shaggy body.

Patience lurched free from Digby. She tore across the hallway to her dog and took Oliver in her arms.

Luca rolled, then drove his fists into Marko's husky chest. Marko's legs buckled. A table crashed and shattered while splinters flew through the air. A vicious strike from Crispin sent Luca sprawling.

Patience's high-pitched cries stuck in her throat. She made a move to stand and met Digby's enraged eyes and unforgiving grip. "You're becoming more and more of an inconvenience, Lady Blakwell."

"As are you." Brandishing a gun, Pulko strode into the room and pointed it at Digby.

The muscles in Digby's veiny neck stood out and his jaw slackened. He vanished into the shadows of the hallway.

Patience huddled her dog to her chest. "Pulko, thank God—." She wanted to say more, but dizziness spun around her.

The constable of a neighboring town, short and thin with a ripple of blonde whiskers, trotted into the room behind Luca's father.

"Put that gun down, you filthy troublemaker!" the constable shouted at Pulko.

With noticeable reluctance, Pulko lowered the gun.

Luca's father assisted Patience to a side chair in the dining room. Then he turned to Luca, then Marko, then Pulko. "Who are all these troublemaker Gypsies? Constable, arrest them all."

Luca winced, his right eye bloody and closed. He drew a long-suffering breath. "Father."

CHAPTER THIRTY-ONE

*L*uca's father had been overcome at Luca's address. He'd promptly sent the constable away and admonished Crispin and Digby when the facts emerged. Pulko had returned to Colchester and his tribe by the sea.

A sennight later, Patience perched on a settee in the drawing room with Oliver snuggled in the crook of her arm. A low fire kindled in the grate, enough to take the chilliness out of the air. Bowls of strawberries and clotted cream were set on the dining room table.

Luca occupied the wingback chair near the fireplace. As always, his clothes were a cacophony of colors and styles. She'd mended his linen shirt. His buckskin breeches, slit to the knees, had been laundered several times, the bloodstains a somber reminder of the brutal struggle that had occurred. He'd tied the orange scarf around his throat instead of his hair, giving him a dashing, debonair appearance.

He tendered her with a bemused look. "Sometimes I think you give your dog more notice than me."

"Oliver was injured only a few short days ago."

"As was I," Luca reminded.

"Amelia fretted over your wounds and reapplied her liniment every day."

These were as good excuses as any, because she couldn't bring herself to be too near him. Her emotions were precariously close to the surface.

"My leg healed nicely. 'Twould have been more to my liking, though, if Amelia had tended to Oliver and you had tended to me."

Patience scraped her chair farther from him. "Oliver is my devoted companion and fought off Marko. Oliver is a hero."

Luca raised dark eyebrows. "You can sit nearer, my lady. Unlike your dog, I don't bite."

"Amelia said you requested a roasted hedgehog for dinner, but she decided on roasted pheasant, instead." Inwardly, Patience congratulated herself on changing the direction of the conversation so smoothly.

"We can enjoy roasted hedgehog together next time."

Next time? Surely he jested. There'd be no next time.

He'd told her that he was leaving at first light. Pulko had sent word that Nanosh had visited their tribe. There'd been no fighting, no bloodshed, no attacks. Perhaps peace was met with peace, as God intended.

Luca hadn't explained where he was going, but she assumed he planned to return to his tribe, although Pulko was clearly now the leader.

Luca hadn't mentioned Patience's unborn child. He hadn't mentioned his marriage proposal, although he'd cried off that a sennight ago. Nothing had changed, although she kept her reflections to herself.

She glanced out the window. The afternoon shadows lengthened and the stone arches of the field walls were spangled in streaks of firelight. A groundskeeper was lighting the evening torches earlier than usual in anticipation of their honored guest.

"Are you certain you're ready for your father to dine with us?" she asked.

"I've been ready since I was a babe."

"Good, because he's arrived and we should greet him at the portico." She stood, kissed Oliver's moist black nose, and bundled the dog on a quilt by the fire. To her surprise, the dog shook off the quilt and trotted to the kitchen.

As Patience walked past Luca, he caught her hand. "If my father wants to speak to me, he knows where I am."

At his touch, an uninvited quiver heated her body. She tossed her long ringlets over her shoulder and wrenched her hand free. "Your father helped Pulko find the constable and saved us all," she reminded.

"Soon, I'll need a tally sheet to keep track of all the heroes."

"Because of your father and Pulko, Crispin and Marko will remain in prison a long time. Surely he's worth the effort of a welcome as a sign of respect."

"Perhaps if I could walk on two strong legs, I might reconsider, but I'd be forced to limp in order to greet him properly."

"So limp. It makes no difference."

He met her gaze. "My entire life I resented him, although part of me wanted to prove I'd grown into a man he was proud to call his own."

"And you have."

Luca shook his head. "I'm a cripple forced to take shelter and aid from a woman."

Before Patience could fire a rejoinder, Penham, in his loftiest manner, ushered 'Lord Haringley, Marquess of Wottingham,' into the hallway.

Patience scurried up to greet Luca's father. They reached the drawing room and the marquess removed his top hat and overcoat and handed them to

Penham. With noticeable reluctance, Luca grabbed his walking stick and stood.

"Well," Patience said to both men brightly, "I'm certain both father and son wish to speak in private. I'll be outdoors, as my dog is well enough for a walk."

"I like you near me when there are obstacles to confront," Luca murmured.

"You'll need to confront them on your own," she replied.

She walked to the hallway, shrugged on her muslin pelisse, and glanced back. He must've given his features strict orders not to reveal any emotion because his face was bland and she couldn't read his thoughts.

～

*L*uca's gaze settled on the tall, angular man standing across from him. His father wore a squared off blue waistcoat trimmed in sable fur, a silky white cravat around his neck, and sable breeches tucked into black leather boots with tassels. His brown eyes lit with affection.

As Luca stared, the indigo blue coloring of his father's waistcoat became too vibrant, and the drawing room walls seemed to push forward and block the hasty retreat he'd planned if their conversation grew too uncomfortable.

He scratched the stubble on his chin. This reunion with his father—he should've never allowed Patience to talk him into it. Unenthusiastically, he accepted his father's handshake, noting they were the exact same height.

His father kept hold of Luca's hand. "When I realized 'twas you, so horribly beaten by Marko and Crispin, I could hardly breathe. I lost you once. To lose you again would be too much for an old man to accept."

Luca stiffened in surprise, but allowed his father to maintain his grasp. Before his father had entered the hall, he'd decided to feign an obligatory civility, if for no other reason than to appease Patience. His heart still harbored bitterness for this elderly man to allow any new feelings to get in the way of his old ones.

"When did you ever lose me?" Luca asked.

"Fabiana sent word about a year after your mother's death. She said you'd perished while you wandered through the forest and your body was never found." He opened his mouth, closed it. "I was beside myself with grief. First I lost your mother, then I lost my young son."

Luca dropped his hand and stepped back to study his father. "Why would you believe Fabiana?"

"She was your mother's dearest friend." He retrieved a linen handkerchief from his waistcoat and unabashedly wiped at his eyes. "I've lived so many years without you and—"

Luca permitted his father to guide him to the wingback chair. His father settled opposite. An unobtrusive Penham set two cups of tea beside them and quit the room.

"Why did you leave our tribe?" Luca let his question, the question that plagued his entire life, hang between them.

"Your mother ordered me out of the Gypsy camp. She knew I was torn between my English ways and her Gypsy ones. 'Tis my greatest regret, my fatal flaw as a man, not standing beside the woman I loved. My family didn't accept her but I should've fought harder. They threatened to cut off my inheritance. Fool that I was, I bowed to their prejudices, vowing I'd return to her someday. Sadly, I never had the chance."

Aware his jaw hardened as he grimly cast off his father's excuses, Luca charged, "You didn't have the decency to marry my mother."

"On the contrary. Of course I married her. Fabiana was in attendance."

Luca grabbed and squeezed the handle of the delicate teacup. He took an acrid sip of bitter black tea and swallowed all the wasted years of his life.

"We had a small Gypsy ceremony and I jumped over a broomstick. A *pliashka*, your mother called it," his father said. "My parents said the ceremony wasn't legal, although it was. Now that I've found you, my son, I want to bestow you with your own estate. My other son, Edmund, is your twin brother. He manages my estate in Wiltshire."

Luca sucked down a mouthful of air, trying to get his thoughts to connect. "Fabiana said my twin brother died at birth." He'd believed Fabiana was a trusted friend. How could she have cheated him out of knowing his father and brother?

"Edmund was frail compared to you," his father said. "After your mother and I quarreled that last time, we agreed we could no longer live together. She allowed me to raise Edmund, and I consented as long as I could still see you. A few months afterward, I was told your mother was dead, and that you'd died shortly afterward. I mourned for a long time." He paused, pulled the handkerchief from his waistcoat. "Forgive me. I weep like a child."

Luca said quietly, "I admire you more for weeping, not less."

His father nodded, slow, thoughtful. "Eventually, I remarried, and the woman is English. We've raised your brother, Edmund, as our English son, as my first-born legitimate heir."

"My twin brother is Lord Edmund Haringley of Wiltshire." Luca sank back into the wingback chair, focused on the fireplace, and ironically shook his head. "If he's missing a pair of black hawking gloves with gold initials, tell him I gave them to a friend who needed them more."

"I pray someday you can meet him," his father said. "I should warn you, though, that your brother is quite a hellion if provoked." He sighed. "And he's been a disappointment as I don't approve of his abrasive behavior nor his habits."

Luca took a tentative breath. He strove to find his expressionless mask to place over his face, but it couldn't be found. All this time, he'd had a father, a brother, and a real home.

He turned to his father and saw the sadness and regret in the specks of familiar amber, so much like his own. He shuddered, feeling his body wanting to bolt, refusing this final confrontation. But he needed to breach his bitter walls, because by denying his English heritage, he'd denied a part of himself and he wanted to bring the ill will toward his father to an end. He needed to swallow his monstrous pride.

"Do you recall the last time you saw me?" Luca asked. "I was a toddler. I ran to you and grabbed your leg. I didn't want to let you go."

"When I was with your mother, living as a Gypsy in the tribe, I existed outside reality. There were neither rules nor requirements beyond the daily chore of living. I liked that."

"But not enough to give up a wealthy English life."

"Not enough." Sorrow tapped the earlier joy

from his father's face, leaving him as ashen as Patience's white linen. The weariness of carrying his guilt, a heavy iron chain, seemed tight around his neck.

"This isn't the reply I wanted to hear," Luca said.

"I was hot-tempered in those days, as was your mother. We'd agreed that your twin brother, Edmund, would come with me. That last day, he waited for me in my coach with a servant."

"I fell when you pushed me away," Luca said. "My nose was broken."

His father closed his eyes, as if he'd tried to shut out those final images.

"I never knew you were hurt. The Gypsy elders and Fabiana were shouting, cursing—"

Luca wavered, grabbed for his walking stick. "You left us. You left me lying on the ground." He raised his voice at his father, he heard it, but couldn't stop. In a moment, he'd scream his misery.

He breathed deeply. Nay. A Roma man never screamed.

His father stood and steadied Luca. "Before I came here, I visited your tribe. Fabiana's prejudices against the English are still strong. Fortunately, Pulko seems more open-minded and very mature. In their favor, I believe any strong opinions against the English stem more from their love for you rather than any hatred toward English society."

A nerve pulsated in Luca's temple. Consumed

with wrath for Fabiana's deceit, he was hardly aware of his father's next words.

"Luca, will you have patience for an old man, who thought he'd lost his son? I'm seeking your forgiveness for deserting you."

Luca paused to be sure his voice wouldn't break when he spoke. He swallowed. "Aye. And please forgive me for my preconceived opinions without knowing all the facts. My opinions were unfair and biased."

And he'd been wrong in so many ways. He'd been obsessed with confronting his father for his wrongdoings. And he'd found him, neither saint nor monster, simply a man trying to do his best.

⌒

*H*ours later, Luca and his father had scarcely touched their tea. Judging by the shadows, afternoon was well past. He'd nodded at his father's stories, stories of his life, stories of all that Luca had missed. But in truth, he'd hardly listened.

With the next lull in the conversation, Luca grabbed his walking stick and cloak. He excused himself, assuring his father that he'd return with Patience in time for the evening meal. He went through the entryway, past the road, and into the fields. It was an early spring evening, and a cool breeze nipped the air.

He pulled on his cloak and pushed his pace, his steps as brisk as his limp allowed.

She wasn't in the stables, nor the gardens, nor any of the outlying fields.

"Patience," he called.

Had she worn a cloak? He couldn't remember. Surely she was cold and shivering after staying outdoors the entire afternoon.

He neared the crofter's cottage. "Patience?"

He didn't see her at first. A whipple tree, dark greenish-brown branches twisted in the shape of a cross, had hidden her from view.

She was clad in a blue velvet frock, a paisley shawl wrapped around her shoulders. The heady perfume of fresh dirt and green plants filled the air. A crop of pink wildflowers with dotted yellow centers peeked from the earth.

She knelt beside two stone urns, spade in hand, arranging a row of cream and purple flowers. A watering pot sat beside her. Despite the roundness of her body, she looked so small.

His heart cried out at the sight of her. The gray of early evening painted her profile in a pensive hue.

And she was humming.

Humming, after everything she'd endured. That same sweet cadence that had reached him in his darkest nightmares, singing those same cheerful songs of fair maidens and faraway kingdoms.

She'd stood by him with undying courage and faith, all the while her pregnancy took a toll on her body and explained her fatigue. Not once had he tended to her, nor asked if she'd wanted to rest her feet. Not once had he even so much as pulled up a chair for her.

He limped briskly to her. "You sang those songs to me when I was ill."

She kept digging into the moist, fresh earth, tucking fragile seedlings in straight rows, not turning to acknowledge his presence.

"These violets are beautiful," she said. "The flowers bloom splendidly in the spring."

"The flowers can wait."

She placed the spade on the ground and brushed the dirt from her frock. "Stop that."

"I'm sorry if I sound curt. I'm trying to catch my breath after the long walk. I hurried because I need to speak to you."

She turned. "I feel your eyes on me every time you look at me."

She was right, of course. He couldn't keep his gaze off her.

"How was your visit with your father?" She was tending to the flowers again.

Like a marionette, Luca's feet were tied to an imaginary pole, mere inches from her.

"He's a good man. Finally, I found the answers I've sought all my life." Luca knelt beside her. "I have a twin brother, Edmund. He's been raised as an English gentleman."

"How wonderful that you'll never be alone."

"And my father bestowed me with an estate and wealth beyond my wildest imaginings," Luca said.

Those busy hands, packing the soil around each fragile bud. How much attention did wildflowers need? She watered the soil around the flowers and hesitated, holding the watering pot in the air. "I assume you're leaving for your tribe at dawn."

"Nay."

She pressed her lips together and bent to place another flower in the dirt.

Luca lifted her face and gazed at her. She was crying. Tears gathered beneath her eyes and streamed down her cheeks, a silent, shuddering river. And she hadn't wanted him to see.

He was the man who'd broken her heart, and she hadn't wanted him to see.

He gathered her to his chest. She didn't struggle. He held her close, trying to take in her sadness. "I came to ask your forgiveness." He threaded his fingers through the ringlets of her gleaming hair. "When you needed me most, I abandoned you. Yet when I needed you, you were always with me. While my hours were darkest I heard your voice and your prayers pulling me back to the surface."

She sniffed and looked away.

"You bore the brunt of my bitterness and prejudices." He tipped her head and brushed the tears from her face. Tenderly, he kissed her. "Don't cry, *kamadiyo*, for I become weak-kneed and defenseless. I love you. I love your child. When a man finds a treasure, he'll not relinquish her for the world. I was wrong. Say you'll marry me."

She hardly moved, although she nodded. He felt her heart pounding against her ribs.

"I love you, too," she whispered.

"We can have a proper English wedding or a Romany wedding, a *pliashka*. Are you willing to jump over a broomstick for me?"

Her lips trembled. "Aye."

"We'll wed by the sea and make our home an English home."

"What about your tribe?"

"They're managing very well under Pulko's capable hands. He's proven that he's a proficient and skilled leader. 'Twas my pride that didn't want to admit the truth earlier.

He and Patience sat together in the darkening countryside. After a long while, Luca stood. "'Tis a long walk back to the house and my sore leg dreads the thought."

Instantly, she surged to her feet. "Are you in pain?"

He looked toward the crofter's cottage. "We can

rest there for a while. 'Tis private without a maid pounding on the door or a vigilant, shaggy dog set‑tled as a guardian by the entry. My father might wait awhile in the dining room before taking his meal, but eventually he'll realize we were detained."

~

*H*ours later, Patience and Luca sat together on a blanket in the crofter's cottage. A tidy fire burned in the grate. A soothing, fine rain drizzled on the windows.

She dozed, cradled in his wool cloak, his cravat as a pillow.

"I love you," he murmured.

She opened her sparkling blue eyes and stared up at him. "Are you never tired?"

He laughed. "When do you wish to marry, *kamadiyo?*"

"Perhaps in a few months."

"Next week," Luca said decisively. "We can settle here in Ipswich."

"This dower house holds too many bad memo‑ries. We can move to Whitehaven, where my cousin, Faith, and her sister and brother live."

"Or, we can move out of England altogether and settle in Wales," Luca said. "My good friend, Valentina, lives there with her husband."

"When will you see your tribe if we move that far away?"

"The Romany can live anywhere. When you marry a former Roma lord, you also inherit the entire tribe. Be assured Pulko will guide the tribe to Wales so that they can camp near us on occasion."

Patience's eyes clouded. "You truly don't mind relinquishing your leadership? You're a legend."

"A legend is a fable based on a tidbit of fact, *kamadiyo*."

"Now that you mention it, you never told me the meaning of the word."

He chuckled and placed a kiss on each of her cheeks. "Someday, I will tell you, sweetheart."

A NOTE FROM THE AUTHOR

Dear Reader,

Seeking Patience is the third book in my Inspirational Regency romance "Seeking" series, and one of my favorite books to write.

I hope you enjoyed it. Please help other people find this book and write a review.

This book is also available on Audiobook and ebook.

Josie Riviera

HONEY CAKE RECIPE

Easy and delicious, with ingredients you may have on hand:

Ingredients:
- 1 cup white sugar
- 1 cup honey
- 1/2 cup vegetable oil
- 4 eggs
- 2 teaspoons orange zest
- 1 cup orange juice
- 2 1/2 cups all-purpose flour
- 3 tsp baking powder
- 1/2 teaspoon baking soda
- pinch of salt
- 1 teaspoon ground cinnamon

Directions:

1. Preheat oven to 350. Grease and flour a 9x13 inch pan.

2. Sift together flour, baking powder, baking soda, salt and cinnamon.

3. In large bowl, combine sugar, honey, oil, eggs and orange zest. Beat in the flour mixture alternately with the orange juice, mixing just until incorporated. Pour batter into prepared pan.

4. Bake in preheated oven for 50 minutes, then cool and enjoy!

ACKNOWLEDGMENTS

An appreciative thank you to my patient husband, Dave, and our three wonderful children.

ABOUT THE AUTHOR

USA TODAY bestselling author, Josie Riviera, writes Historical, Inspirational, and Sweet Romances. She lives in the Charlotte, NC, area with her wonderfully supportive husband. They share their home with an adorable shih tzu, who constantly needs grooming, and live in an old house forever needing renovations.

To receive my Newsletter and your free sweet romance novella ebook as a thank you gift, sign up HERE.

Join my Read and Review VIP Facebook group for exclusive giveaways and ARCs.

josieriviera.com/
josieriviera@aol.com

EXCERPT FROM A CHRISTMAS TO CHERISH, CHAPTER ONE

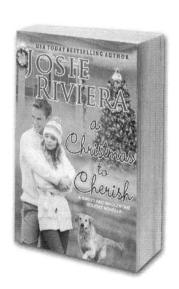

Emmanuelle Sumter surveyed the picturesque town

of Cherish, South Carolina, brightly lit in crimson and green holiday decor. The town looked as if it had emerged from a Christmas card. Glittering frost framed bare tree branches, and local artists were setting up their canvases for an art walk. The coldness in the air was soundless and serene, comforting in its own way.

She exited the Cherish Central train station, zippered her cobalt-blue puffer coat to her chin, and stepped onto the curb.

Who believed an actual, breathing town could resemble a holiday snow globe?

Evidently, her friend Dorothy did, considering her enthusiasm whenever she described her idyllic South Carolina town.

Emmanuelle stood on the curb and shoved her hands in her pockets. A cold December gust slapped her cheeks, sharp streams of frigid air. She swept a wisp of hair from her cheek and searched for Nicholas, Dorothy's older brother. He was supposed to pick her up. People were shouting greetings, kissing, cooing over babies. A teeming mass of humanity.

But no Nicholas.

A taxi's horn spiked. Emmanuelle jumped, an involuntary nervous reaction.

Take a deep breath. Relax. Dorothy had assured her Cherish was a safe haven, a harbor in a storm.

Repeating her mantra, Emmanuelle hailed the

black-bearded taxi driver parked at the curb. She still didn't see any sign of Nicholas, so she'd take the cab.

She handed the driver her suitcase, then slid into the backseat and gave the address of Dorothy's music store, Musically Yours.

They passed charming shops decorated in glittering lights, and a sign advertising a historic home tour. A few minutes later, the driver pointed at the Musically Yours lighted outdoor sign and idled at the corner of Myrtle and Magnolia Streets.

"The store's two hoots and a holler away, ma'am." He hoisted her suitcase from the trunk and set it on the sidewalk. "We've reached your destination."

Destination. Was this where her journey ended after a year filled with pain and abuse? Did hope and encouragement wait for her in this little town?

A new life. With perseverance, she could start fresh.

"Thanks." She climbed from the taxi, paid the driver and grabbed her suitcase.

Daylight faded as dusk crept in, and she tipped her head to take in Evergreen Street. Family-owned businesses had switched on their storefront lights, transforming the town into a fairy-tale sparkle of miniature white lights. The tantalizing scent of honey roasted almonds wafted through the air. Boughs of fragrant holly tied with red velvet bows hung cheerily from tall solitary lampposts. Bright-faced children skipped by, lifting their faces skyward to catch a sprinkling of snow. Their conscientious parents followed close behind.

"Emmanuelle! You arrived right on time!" Dorothy flung open the door of the music store and pressed a welcoming kiss to Emmanuelle's cheek. Dorothy's brown hair was swept up in a French braid, her creamy complexion glowing with an enthusiasm Emmanuelle didn't recall from their days working as struggling musicians in New York.

Dorothy had lived there before moving back to Cherish, her hometown, and marrying her high school crush, Ryan Edwards. He had been an opera star in the making and had given up his touring career to settle in Cherish. They were newlyweds. They were in love.

Love. The beginning was always so alluring. It was the end Emmanuelle feared.

Dorothy regarded the departing taxi. "Apparently Nicholas didn't pick you up?"

"I didn't see him so I took a cab."

Emmanuelle turned from Dorothy and admired Musically Yours' frosty window display, bedecked in an infinite array of treble clef signs. A pine wreath, embellished in antique ornaments—tiny pianos, violins, and harps—adorned the front door.

"It's wonderful," she said. "You've worked so hard to set this up."

"Thanks. Ryan and I are still learning the business, and we're inspired by anything musical."

Emmanuelle smiled, but then shivered. "It's colder here than I expected. At least the blizzard that threatened to shut down New York never came."

"The storm hit after you left," Dorothy replied. "You escaped the worst of it."

Did she? She couldn't answer at first, finally whispering, "Hopefully."

Dorothy raised a delicate eyebrow, but Emmanuelle didn't elaborate. Sure, she'd escaped the snowstorm. An escape from George, her ex, was yet to be determined.

Please God, be with me now in my dark season, when I'm so out of place. The world around me is glowing with the promise of Christmas and I feel dark and empty inside.

She leaned forward to admire two animated polar bears sitting amidst the treble clef signs in the shop's window. Beneath a starry sky, the bears tapped drums to the tune of "Jingle Bells."

"Very clever." She couldn't help a grin. "Thanks for the invite to Cherish."

"We're thrilled you agreed to join us for Christmas." Dorothy grabbed her hands for a reassuring squeeze. She was so pleasant and gracious, Emmanuelle thought. So jovial.

On the other hand, Emmanuelle felt the opposite. All she had become in twenty-five years—a dependable, straightforward woman as well as an esteemed harpist—she'd lost in six months to George.

She'd once been like Dorothy, resilient, independent and a woman of God.

Her ex had taken it all away.

Deep in her coat pocket, her fingers worried an angel ornament she'd purchased at the New York airport. For her, the ornament symbolized the sacred Christmas season, its optimism, dreams, and promise.

She hadn't taken it out of her pocket yet.

"You've been difficult to reach these past few months." Dorothy studiously appraised Emmanuelle. "You hardly ever answered your phone."

"I've been busy with concert engagements." Emmanuelle forced her features to remain blank. "You know, musician stuff." It was a lie, and with the lie came heaviness, a wide band of disapproval. Where had her sense of decency gone?

She tightened her paisley scarf around her neck. Although the violent purple and yellow bruises had faded, she still felt self-conscious.

Dorothy guided her into the music store. "My brother will blame his forgetfulness on his new job, or that gigantic puppy he bought at the animal shelter. You'd think he'd know better at thirty years old."

"He's a good guy," Emmanuelle said. "Nicholas and I Skyped every night for months when you were in rehab."

"Thanks to you both, I'm better." Dorothy smiled. "And most important, thanks to God."

Once, Emmanuelle would have readily agreed. God was her salvation, her refuge. Now she didn't know how to answer because her faith had wavered.

Truly I tell you, if you have faith as small as a mustard seed, you can say to this mountain, "Move from here to there," and it will move. The verse from Matthew 17-20 came to her mind, a reminder of her strength. All she had to do was reach for it, if she was brave enough.

Inside the store, Dorothy ran a finger along one of the shelves, grinning when she was assured it was dust free. "Ryan and I purchased a cottage-style bungalow four blocks from here and there's an extra bedroom."

"This is your first Christmas as a married couple." Emmanuelle set her suitcase out of the way of a passing customer. "Please celebrate the holiday without me in the middle."

"I insist you stay with us."

"For an entire month?" Emmanuelle shook her head. "Insist all you want. I booked a room at the Cherish Hills Inn. You raved about the inn's accommodations being top-quality when you returned to Cherish for your brother's wedding last year."

"The wedding that didn't happen." Ruefully, Dorothy sighed. "Nicholas is still healing from the embarrassment and heartbreak."

The ending stages of love. Dreams shattered.

Without warning, the front door burst open. Instinctively, Emmanuelle held up a hand, shielding herself from view.

A heavy-set woman, her hair helmeted in a tight gray bun, ambled inside. She called out a jovial hello to Dorothy.

"Be with you in a minute, Mrs. McManus." Dorothy gave a flap of her hands, and then turned back to Emmanuelle. "Sorry. What were we discussing?"

Emmanuelle blew out a breath. This uneasiness, this fear of being followed, had to stop.

Still shaken, she kept her focus on a Mozart statue topped with a red plush Santa hat sitting on the counter.

"We were discussing the wedding that didn't happen," she replied. "Whenever Nicholas and I talked when you were in rehab, he always reminded me we should place our trust in God."

"Sadly, people change, beliefs change." Worry replaced Dorothy's earlier smile. "Hard knocks can shake the faith of the most devout. I pray he'll go to church again because he's faltered since the breakup."

Suggesting Emmanuelle put her suitcase behind the front counter, Dorothy led her past a display table. As Dorothy paused to rearrange two pairs of oboe earrings so they lined up side by side, she said,

"God had other plans for him and for me. I believe things work out for the best."

Emmanuelle frowned and nodded, aborting both actions.

For Dorothy, perhaps. For Ryan. For anyone in this idyllic snow globe town. But not for me. And apparently not for Nicholas.

Her cell phone buzzed. She retrieved it from her tote bag and scanned the screen. *Unknown caller*. Her heart stopped. A telemarketer? A wrong number?

"Who is it?"

Looking up, she saw Dorothy was studying her with keen interest.

"No one." Fumbling, Emmanuelle tucked the phone back into her faux leather tote. "You're right. People change for many reasons." And she'd changed most of all. She'd been a competent, successful woman. Now a chill crept up her spine when a door opened into a harmless music store.

"Are you okay?" Dorothy asked.

"I'm fine, just tired from traveling." Emmanuelle's eyes welled with tears, and she averted her gaze. She'd applied makeup, the first time in months, attempting to conceal her sleep deprivation. The endless worrying and crying had taken a toll.

"We're organizing a concert in the town square the weekend before Christmas," Dorothy was saying. "I meant to ask you to bring your harp—"

"My harp weighs nearly eighty pounds." She picked up a pair of piano earrings and fingered the tiny keyboard. "It's in New York."

Broken. She wouldn't reveal how George had destroyed her harp in one of his lightning-fast rages. The memory caused a block of ice to form in her stomach, a block that she knew would be slow to thaw. She hated the thought of her beloved instrument, splintered into pieces, lying on a New York curb under a pile of snow.

Better the harp than you splintered into pieces.

But his shouted insults and rough slaps had been her fault. She'd provoked him.

No, no, no. Her inner voice took on a sharp edge. That was the old Emmanuelle talking. The new Emmanuelle knew she wasn't a dishtowel to be thrown around on a whim. In hindsight, she should have known George was abusive. The warning signs were there.

She blew out a breath. She'd resolved to find peace and comfort in this holiday ... in this town ... somewhere ... and find her footing again.

"Enough about me." She set down the earrings and dismissed herself with a flutter of her fingers. "Where's Ryan?"

"He's rehearsing in nearby Stanley Valley today and will arrive this evening. He'll be singing 'O Holy Night' for a Christmas Cantata service. He gives so freely of his talent." Dorothy's smile was as radiant as a Merry Christmas bouquet. "He's featured throughout the Carolinas in many guest appearances. Plus, the Atlanta opera house asked him to perform the role of Zoroastro in Handel's opera, *Orlando*. I'm incredibly proud of him."

"You should be." Dorothy's smile was contagious, and Emmanuelle managed a warm grin. "He's famous and extremely talented."

"And you? Any upcoming concerts?"

"None." She answered in a firm tone that she expected would discourage her friend from probing. Judging by the way Dorothy's eyebrows drew together, she'd succeeded.

Fortunately, an acoustic guitar arrangement of "Lo, How a Rose Is Blooming" piped in the background, the ideal holiday music to smooth a lull in the conversation.

"I'm sure you're keen to check in." Dorothy broke the silence. "I'll deal with these last few customers, close the store, and give you a lift. Unless you'd rather walk the three blocks to the inn?"

"No, no. I'll wait for you."

She'd never walk alone again. Not in New York, not in Cherish. Not anywhere, because she'd never feel safe again.

Dorothy gestured toward the front of the store. "If you care to browse, the Christmas music section is on your left. There's a lovely harp arrangement of *The Nutcracker*."

"Thanks. Your store is a music-lover's dream."

Intrigued, Emmanuelle stepped past a buyer laden with music bookmarks and made her way to the sheet music. She thumbed through endless arrangements of Christmas solos, wondering what madness had brought her to this town. She didn't belong here among all this gaiety. Her sadness was a burden refusing to go away.

Disheartened, she stared, trancelike, at the display window. A whimsical model train circled the polar bears, and the sight was enchanting.

Beyond, past the cheery town, past the exuberant children and the enormous Christmas tree illuminating the town square, a darkened sky had followed dusk.

*** End of Excerpt *A Christmas To Cherish* by Josie Riviera ***

Read the rest of Emmanuelle's story.

Pick up your copy of A Christmas To Cherish.

Free on KU!

ALSO BY JOSIE RIVIERA

Made in the USA
Middletown, DE
12 April 2020